Brenna Lyons

THE LAST OF FION'S DAUGHTERS

Kegin Histories

Fireborn Publishing Copyright Statement

PUBLISHER

DEDICATION

My husband, who told me to always write my dreams.

Elizabeth Burton, for the second edit on Schente Night and Fion's Daughter. As always, it is a delight working with you!

Beth, Lisa, Dawn, and Kiersten, my proofers who always scream for MORE! Especially Lisa, who is always "willing" to test drive my ideas.

Fae and Beth, who gave me the idea of a garden witch.

Bridgette, who demanded to get to know Ro Ti better.

Fion, for introducing me to her special children.

The cosmos at large, for the ideas that sometimes it's the person standing next to you that you've always wanted to find and that prayers aren't always answered in the way we think they will be.

Welcome to the ancient world of Kegin. The era before Unification was a bloodthirsty time in Keen history. But, at the turning point, there existed four women with the power to tear nations apart and bring them back together. Each of them believed she was the "last of Fion's Daughters on the face of Kegin."

Happy reading!
Brenna

GLOSSARY OF KEEN TERMS USED IN THE BOOK

NOTE: Keen is a lyrical language, and minor changes in pitch and inflection denote a slightly different word in the language. See Keen calendar, following this section.

Abinatine- the sacred dagger of one of Fion's Priestesses: used in her healing, to take the life of a worthy opponent, and when she takes a mate

Ag- according to, by

Auguren- a disinfectant used in the paste with Felgren to sterilize skin and equipment

Braek- barbarian

Burgel- a small blue flower that blooms late in winter/early in spring as the last of the snow recedes

Chel- feet

Chidan- beloved

Choc- a soft, brown color

Cimmeg- a heavy spice like cinnamon and vanilla mixed that strengthens the blood and aids in healing

Cuvia- a female sire-cousin, one of Fion's children born of the same sire and different mothers

Cuvie- a male sire-cousin

Diten- tradition

Dolgen- a yellow/orange scrubby plant which yields a powerful aphrodisiac; sucre sweet, it can be ingested in a tea; for the most powerful and immediate potency, it is mixed in oil and applied to genitalia

E- at

Eir- an evergreen tree that gives a thick sugary sap

which is edible and used for bottling fruits

Emi bead- a soft (consistency of amber) clear emerald green stone usually shaped into beads and used for decoration

Felgren- a choc plant with antibiotic properties; can be ingested in a tea, used in a paste with Auguren to sterilize skin and equipment, and burned to create acidic fumes to ward off dangerous animals and enemies

Fion- Keen queen of the gods; Goddess of love, balance, and mercy

*Fion's Children/Daughters-*The matriarchal priestess race wiped out by the Lengar in Ti 10-452

Garigol- a powerful sedative and muscle relaxant derived from the leaves of the tree of the same name; causes confusion and lethargy followed by sleep in higher doses; Jaglin crave it and will attack to steal stores of it, so it is stored in air-tight containers

Geela- a cliff-diving, carrion eating bird with gray and black feathers

Gelgrin- a confection made of Eir sap, lizor berries, implin, and cream

Gola- a plant that resembles mistletoe; its pink berries produce a poison that induces miscarriage and kills if left untreated; used to treat mother's sickness, it is treated with Triclum; a pernicious bush

Han- safely

Hi- prince, Your/His Highness

Hir- princess, Your/Her Highness

Hottel- a horse-like creature (mare pony-size and war-buck Clydesdale size)

Hypocil- a metal pen-shaped device that injects medications through the dermis without an open site or risk of infection

Implin- a Kegin fruit akin to a Bosc pear; the core is a strong stimulant; the main ingredient in lover's repast

Iri- golden flowers that grow on vines as thick as a man's wrist; makes a soothing topical drug for use on rashes, minor burns and abrasions

Jaglin- large jaguar-like cats with thick black fur, dotted with gray spots as cubs

Ken- knelt

Kit- breeding cattle, which are used for food

Kittle- a small, furry domestic animal like a cross between a kitten and a rabbit

Lamor- a fish that tastes like salmon but has blue-tinged meat

Len- God of the underworld, vows broken, trickery, and havoc

Lengar- the people to the North who sought to rule the world before unification

Li: Lord, nobleman

Lio- little

Lizor- a fragrant purple flower whose berries make a calming tea, the stems make a powerful sedative to relax the mind and body, lizor is also used in forming a healing circle

Lover's Repast- the traditional cake of new lovers and new mother's; Cimmeg and Implin cakes with warmed sucre sap served on the side

Ma- my

Mag- Keen king of the gods; God of justice, law, and vows unbroken

Magden- the race ruled by Ro Ti in the days before unification

Nuglin- a noose-like hunting tool with a locking device, designed for capturing large carnivores like jaglin

Olum- a drug like an opiate that relaxes muscles,

relieves pain, and suppresses the drive to vomit

Palaz: a high Lengar mansion with stone columns and colored glass windows set into arches

Peak Chol- a legendary flower that grows in the crag above the Surian Basin in the late autumn every seven years

Pris- called

Sa-safe

Satil- a stiff, thick material used to make farthingale-type skirts for presentation of heirs, also used for paintings due to its long life

Schaen- a male harem that, in ancient times, was kept for the use of royal females; named for the Schen.

Schen- the insatiable sex drive of a pregnant Keen woman

Schente- a harem of sterilized women kept for the use of royal or noble men

Silin- a silk-like fabric that most women's clothing and royal bedding are made from

Stride- a measure of distance; the distance the average war-buck can travel at a loping stride (half-speed) in the space of five minutes

Sucre- a thick sugar syrup from Eir trees

Ti- conqueror, king who takes his land by force

Tie- take

Trial Moon- an ancient custom by which a Keen man may demand a contract by a woman he has had sex with if certain conditions are met

Triclum- the drug used to treat gola poison

Trin- throne

Tu- there

Veltian- a Lengar device used at the taking of a mate and in sex games. It consists of a wedge-shaped center cushion with cushioned metal arms extending out from it. There are a series of clips to hold the mating bands in place for various sexual positions.

Veltina- the first consort of Len

Walla- a deep green wild herb that will act as a contraceptive when taken in a tea or used as a paste

Wariken- a large gray or deep choc furred beast which runs wild in packs in mountain areas; can be trained as a hunting beast or companion though always a bit wild

Zura- a gray bush; used in protection oils for blessing and healing circles; makes a tonic when mixed with Garigol that eases painful breathing

Zuragol- the main ingredient in Triclum; treats poisons

KEEN CALENDAR

A year on Kegin is roughly equivalent to an Earth year. Days are twenty Earth hours long, but the year is separated into twelve months, consisting of thirty-seven days each. A week on Kegin consists of eight of their days. I formatted the calendar as if the Keen year started in January like an Earth year. In reality, the Keen year begins in Endl. The end of winter and beginning of spring is a time of rebirth, and so it is the start of the Keen New Year.

Pri- January
Ite- February
Endl- March
Wos- April
Zor- May
Fim- June
Jad- July
Caj- August
Wend- September
Abrin- October
Veril- November
Iric- December

SECTION ⊕NE
Mother Deliya
Fion's Daughter

*"Every story has a beginning, every age a dawn.
Unification begins here."*

Mother Deliya

PROLOGUE

Wos 10th, Ti 10-449
The Mother's Tower at Rintal, Fion's Children's Lands

"You have my instructions," Mother Leiana of Fion's Children said formally, stoically.

She was The Source, the latest in the line of Most Chosen. Tears were beneath her. The fury she wished to vent at the hopeless situation she'd been dealt was beneath her. Selfish wishes were beneath her. Only the future mattered now. That future stood before her, a boy. *Dear Mother, let me have chosen well.*

Loric bowed deeply. "With my life, Mother Leiana," he promised.

At sixteen, Loric had already enjoyed the pleasures of training under the priestesses for more than a year. Syron had delivered a son of him only a week earlier, and Jolia carried a child of his loins, conceived on her challenge night. He had also managed to force Juvia to failure at challenge, the first male to do that in more than a decade. He was the perfect choice to send along.

Loric was close to Deliya's age, and he was not a relation of either herself or Deliya's father, Celdin, for at least four generations back. He would be able to train Deliya well and challenge her, if things went poorly in the villages.

Leiana suppressed a shiver. Things would go badly. Lengar troops under the command of that son of Len, Jurin, and his son, Jurel, prepared to attack Rintal even now. Leiana crumpled the missive in her hand distractedly.

She'd begged Sol Ti for Magden aid in repelling the

1

Lengar and had been refused. Kor Hi, the heir apparent, and his son Ro Hi had delivered the aging leader's answer personally. Kor, in confidence, had expressed his regrets and shame at his father's stubborn refusal to ally with Leiana to crush the Lengar threat. He promised his aid when he ascended to his rightful place—the only vow he could make.

Sol was dying, but he would not die in time to save the village of Rintal. He might not die in time to save Fion's Children, and so Leiana was forced to this mad scheme. She would send her true heir, her precious daughter Deliya, into hiding, in hopes that she might rebuild their people in the aftermath of Leiana's defeat. She did not doubt that she would be defeated—if not this night then some other.

"Mother Leiana?" Loric asked uncertainly.

She nodded. "Prepare, Loric. You leave within the hour."

He looked up at her, his eyes wild. Then he bolted down the two stories of stairs from her chamber and out of the tower.

The structure was nearly silent in his wake. The sanctuary on the first level had been abandoned when the protective oils and healing balms had been mixed, the circle scattered and the sacred fire fed. The study rooms on the floor just above were similarly empty. This was no time for study. This was the time to anoint loved ones and enjoy one final embrace as she had with Celdin. Above her was only the observatory. There was no need to use that; Jurin had doused his fires to hide his movements more than an hour earlier, and Leiana didn't need the interpretations of the stars to foresee the end of this night.

Loric shouted orders for preparations; she heard it clearly through the silin drapes over the open window slits.

Yes. Loric was perfect, and he was very fertile. Perhaps her daughter would find him beautiful when she matured; he was a comely boy that turned many of the young priestess's heads—and a few older ones'.

It was early for thoughts like that. To a girl Deliya's age, he would still seem a playmate. That was one of the reasons Leiana chose him; he was one of her daughter's playmates—when she indulged in play. Perhaps she was already working her way through fledgling feelings of attraction. No, that was too much to hope for.

Still, Leiana realized the danger in this plan. There was the slim possibility that he would die without producing heirs by Deliya, yet she could not send two men with her daughter. If she were correct and both men survived until her daughter's eighteenth year, they would likely kill each other—or Deliya—in pursuit of the last remaining priestess, as men often will. No. It was safer to send only one.

If the Mother were kind, Loric and Deliya would be the last hope for their race. If She showed not that tender mercy, Deliya had a much different path in store, a path that Vela would fight with the last breath in her body.

As if her thoughts summoned the old woman, Vela cleared her throat, reminding Leiana that she was wasting valuable time when Deliya should be away. Leiana didn't have to look at her to know that her face was set in the grim line that announced her displeasure, her hands held stiffly at her sides, her back straight as it had been when she was The Source, despite the years that had withered her body to a frail shadow of what she once was.

"I know, Grandmother. It is hard to send your heir away, the daughter you carried and suckled, taught and protected."

"She will be safe with us and far from harm. I have chosen a place deep in Magden lands, the range of the Garesh Mountains, where they dare not live. You know the valley I mean."

Leiana nodded. The name of the place would never be spoken aloud. "I do. Continue her training. If that Len-be-damned Magden king dies soon, Deliya may yet lead our people."

"You do not hold out hope of that," Vela breathed.

Leiana pulled back the drape and observed her daughter by the light of one of the bonfires set around Fion's circle. At nearly thirteen years, Deliya matched her mother in height, and she would grow more. She was beautiful. Leiana smiled at that. It was a foolish bit of mother's pride. If asked, she could not have said what made Deliya's looks so remarkable, what Leiana found so endearing but that it was *her* child she watched.

Deliya was one of Fion's Daughters, snow white hair braided down her back, the Mother's green eyes, bold, responsible, sure—She strapped on her Vambrace, looking serious and focused. It was right that Deliya would be The Source, but had Leiana bought her only a generation of reprieve?

"No. I do not believe Deliya will have a people to lead when she reaches the spring celebration of her eighteenth year," Leiana admitted.

"We should take more," Vela urged, careful not to instruct Fion's Source openly. "Even a few more couples—"

Leiana smiled a wry smile and moved her attention to Jolia and the two dozen who traveled with her. "Who, Vela? No priestess will accept the dishonor of fleeing the battle. No priestess will send her heirs off without her. Deliya only goes, because she has not faced her challenge and is mine to order away. It is all I can do to send Jolia and the others who carry or have nursing young to Gidlore. I may demand that much of them but no more."

Vela bowed her head in acceptance of the truth.

"Deliya will be tall like her father—and you. Will you give her your armor, when she is a woman?" Leiana requested.

"You know I will. I am old, Leiana. I was old when I passed the honor to your mother. All those years without a true heir; I feared I would have only sons." Vela brushed her hand through Leiana's hair. "I was overjoyed that Turila conceived you less than a year after her challenge."

"And died less than a year after mine," Leiana reminded her sadly.

"Long enough to pass on the leadership in an appropriate manner. She died in the knowledge that you had conceived an heir and committed to share your life with Celdin."

"I will not live to see my daughter meet her challenge. I will not pass my blade into her hand that night, but she will be Fion's Source." Leiana pulled the abinatine from her belt, stroking her fingers over the dagger that proclaimed her place, willing her hand not to shake. "When the time is right, give Deliya my blade."

Vela gasped. "You cannot lead the battle without this."

"They are Lengar soldiers, Grandmother. There is not a soul among them worth the honor of dying by my abinatine."

"Jurel—"

"Is a beast," she spat. "No better than the foulest geela. Take this before that beast takes it as spoils and wears it on his filthy Lengar belt. I will make it as hard for him as I can, but unless Sol dies—"

Vela nodded and took the blade, kissing the symbol of Fion reverently and tucking it into her pack.

"Go now. Leave me. I need to center myself before I take leave of my child."

Leiana continued watching Deliya for a long moment after Vela left her, releasing the drape at last with a sigh. It was a foolhardy move, sending her daughter away with this ragged trio, but what other choice had she?

She went to her worktable at the North Point of the room, emptied now of the crocks and flasks that had been stashed for her flight from the battle in kittle holes along the deep forest trail to Gidlore. Only the oil lamp, a few writing supplies and empty vessels and the Great Book graced the engraved Aster Wood surface now. It was too uncluttered—too barren for her tastes.

She opened the Great Book at the marker. Her tears fell on the page. "Lead my daughter well, Mother Fion," Leiana pleaded. She read the passage again, hopelessness making her nearly ill. "Vela will never see this possibility for Deliya. She will train my daughter in the old traditions, not prepare her for the world that waits to devour her."

To Vela, the passage was a sign of weakness, not one of hope. It was one of the few philosophical differences between Leiana and her grandmother, but what other priestess would agree to accompany her daughter? "None," she reminded herself.

She ripped the page from the book, circled her intended message and penned a missive to Deliya in the margin. She folded it carefully and inserted it into an empty wide-mouthed flask, sealing it with the wax of a deep green used only for the highest matters of state.

Leiana wiped her tears and held her head high, walking into the fire-lit darkness. It was well past middle-night, the darkest time before the dawn, the safest time for the small band to travel. She passed the Great Book to Jolia with a nod that sent the young priestess on her way with the others in her care.

Deliya looked up from her hottel pack, as Leiana approached. "All is ready, Mother." She would make a fine leader, if Fion were gracious enough to grant her a people to lead.

Leiana forced a smile to her face, feeling as if the strain of it would make her composure crack. "I would expect no less from my true heir," she said proudly.

Deliya blushed. It was not their way to give idle praise. "Only because I was trained so well."

Leiana placed the flask in her hand. "There are hard days ahead, Deliya. There will be times you believe you will not be able to go on. When you feel you cannot live another day without my guidance, you must open this flask. You should not do so until you feel you have nothing left—until you have no hope."

Deliya swallowed hard. "Will it come to that?"

"It will."

Her daughter raised her chin and held the flask to her heart. "When there is no hope," she promised.

Leiana kissed her cheek, holding back sobs. "Then put on your helm, young warrior. Your battle will come in time."

Deliya stored the flask in her pack and swung onto her war-buck, pulling her helm over her bound hair.

Celdin wrapped his arms around Leiana, and the scent of their farewell teased her senses. "I could not leave without touching you again," he breathed into her ear.

Leiana swallowed another sob. She would lose her daughter and her mate this night. "My heart cannot take the grief," she apologized.

"One kiss and I take my leave," he begged. "Do not make me leave you without that much."

She resisted the urge to point out that she'd already gifted him with much more than a simple kiss. Leiana wanted that kiss too much, and sending away her mate was nearly as difficult as sending away her daughter. She turned into his arms, kissing him passionately. She wound her hands in his tunic as if she would hold him forever.

But her daughter needed him more. *And, he will be safe with Deliya. How would you go on, if you saw him fall beside you in battle? A priestess will give her life for her family.*

Leiana eased her grip and backed away, touching his face, probably for the last time. She looked from Celdin to Vela and finally to Deliya. *This is my family, and I die before my time that they might live to die a natural death.*

She looked back to Celdin again, smiling weakly. "I entrust my daughter into your care," she informed him. Placing a child in her grandmother's, while the mother lived—or in her father's care, ever—was an odd thing to do, unnatural. Children were of their mothers, hers alone until they faced their challenge, but Leiana had to put her duty to their people first.

Celdin kissed her forehead. "I have always loved her, Leiana. I will protect Deliya until she takes her place."

"I know you will. Go, before I disgrace myself with tears."

He mounted his hottel without a backward glance. Leiana wished she could spare a buck for him, but the priestesses would need them in battle. If Celdin were to stay and fight, he'd ride a buck in battle as her mate. *And that would make him Jurel's target, here in battle or while traveling. A male of our race on buck could only be my mate.* Still, she winced that she had to send him off on a mare.

"Go now," she ordered hoarsely. "Be far from here before the sun begins its journey."

Deliya bowed her head and urged her war-buck to a run, the three mares at point.

"Guard them well," Leiana prayed. She blinked back tears, stiffening her spine before she turned to the older priestesses who would command groups in battle. "They will attack with the dawn to use the sun against us. We have three hours to plan."

She resisted the urge to take one last look into the darkness closing around her family. *Losing my mate is just as hard as losing my child,* she admitted. Then she squatted to the map in the center of the circle and laid out their plan of defense.

CHAPTER ⊕NE

Jad 37th, Ti 10-459
Ten Years Later
Deep in the Garesh Mountains, Magden Republic

"I did not realize anyone lived in this region," Donic commented in confusion. Ro's advisor-general lowered his oculars and shaded his eyes against the mid-day glare. "Do you think they are refugees from the Lengar outposts over the mountains?"

Ro Ti shook his head. "Unlikely." He scanned his own oculars over the farm nestled deep in the valley. "Refugees would travel much further from their former masters." He lowered his hand, considering the unexpected discovery their scouts had reported, smoke in an area believed unpopulated. "No, they are not Lengar. This land has been farmed for at least a decade, by my guess. The Lengar were nowhere near here then."

Donic nodded; he didn't need to ask where the Lengar were a decade ago. They had been busy slaughtering Fion's priestesses, their mates and children.

Ro needed no reminder of the hopeless feeling of being unable to honor his vow to protect those who needed him. It still haunted him. It had been senseless and selfish; if his grandfather had helped Fion's Children early in the wars, they would have ended long ago. Now the Lengar had entrenched themselves in the highly-defensible lands once held by Fion's Children, exploiting the very topography that allowed Mother Leiana to hold off Jurel as long as she had. He sighed. And, if he didn't act quickly, Jurel would extend his borders further into Magden land by taking this lush valley, slaughtering these farmers as his show of force.

"What do you wish to do?" Donic asked.

Ro stored the oculars in the case at his hip, shifting the hand-sized pouch further back on his belt to avoid hitting his Cuisses on it in battle. "Lengar troops will descend on this valley in force within the hour. If even a quarter are amassed so far, we cannot afford to wait them out. We must get the inhabitants to safety."

"These people likely have no love for you, Majesty. Worse, the Lengar will not hesitate to attack if they spy you in the open."

"I swore a vow. The same vow my father swore and his father before him." *Unlike Sol Ti, I keep my vows.* "Those people are innocents. Love for me or no, they need my help and protection. The Lengar will slaughter them for no crime but residing within my borders. I cannot allow that."

"Let someone else go. Let me," Donic requested, nearly begged of him. "Without you—"

Ro silenced his most trusted general with a severe look. "I will go myself. My people will know my dedication to them."

Donic bowed. "As you wish, my King." His jaw was clenched, as it always was when he called Ro "my king." Raised as an older servant-brother in Kor's household, responsible for the safety of the young royals, trained at battle alongside Ro, always at his back in love or war— it troubled Donic deeply that his king was no longer a child to be swept away from danger.

Ro settled his helm on his head and slapped the visor down.

Donic was right in many ways. These farmers

would likely not thank him for his help. Still, Ro Ti would not cower in the wood while others chanced a battle. He could not appear weak.

He set out, smiling behind the visor as Donic waved up a squad of men to protect him and took his usual position at Ro's back. Donic lived to see the end to hostilities—perhaps the unification of the races into a Keen Republic, and his younger sister's husband was not a strong enough tactician and soldier to take Ro's place in the war to achieve it.

Donic also lived to see Ro produce heirs to lead the fight after Ro went to the soul's reward. He sobered at that. His life was not fit for a woman. It would be cruel to subject her to his constant absences as he fought back Lengar's incursions into Magden. Still, whether he wanted to commit to a contract or not, a king had a duty to produce heirs—if he ever found the time to court a woman.

Ro pulled his war-buck to a stop a few footfalls from the door to the small house, looking around the deserted space warily. There was no sign of people, no smoke or movement, though a tunic and trousers hung on a drying rack, waving lightly in the breeze.

Donic drew up beside him, his buck's prancing echoing the general's tension. "It is a trap," he decided. "We should withdraw." Donic saw traps in every encounter.

A shiver of awareness raced up Ro's spine. "No. They are in hiding. They watch us even now."

"To attack."

"I do not believe so. They wish to be left in peace. It is a shame that I cannot oblige them."

He dismounted and strode toward the house,

waving for Donic to stay put and tucking his helm under his arm. If these people feared him, approaching in numbers would only make them more fearful. "We wish you no harm," he called out. "You are in danger here."

No answer.

He pushed the door open, sure that he would find the inhabitants within rather than hiding in one of the outbuildings. It was small—little more than a shack—but solidly built. It appeared deserted, but Ro's instincts belied that. They were here. He stepped inside and searched for any possible hiding place with his typical scrutiny.

The blade nestled to his throat silently and without warning, announcing the willingness of the owner to kill him if he posed a threat. The warrior had planned his move perfectly. The soldiers outside knew nothing of the threat to their king; and to protect this unknown adversary, Ro would keep it that way as long as the threat remained simply a threat.

He smiled at the gall of his adversary. "I mean you no harm," he repeated.

"Then leave my home."

The voice that whispered to him was strong and determined but young, lacking a mature man's deep rumbling. Ro sobered. Was a boy the ablest warrior these people had? It was likely. The house could not be home to more than three, and that would be crowded.

"I cannot. Warriors descend on this valley. There will be a battle before the sun sinks from its zenith. You cannot stay here."

"Why should I believe you? Perhaps I should send you to your lying Lord in his Underworld."

Ro frowned, confusion overriding his fury at being assumed one of those Len-be-damned—"You do not recognize my armor or weapons?" he asked. How isolated were these children that they could not identify the trappings of their king? The crimson armor and the seals on the hilts of his dagger and sword clearly announced who Ro was. Had they no elders to instruct them? "You fear me, because you believe I am one of Jurel's troops?"

"I fear no one," the boy growled. "Who—" The blade shifted against Ro's throat, and there was a slight rustling of movement behind him. "If you are not, who are you to invade my home this way?"

Ro started to turn, and the blade pressed deeper in response. He stilled, cursing under his breath. "You do not know the Magden?"

"I know them," his captor spat. "Spineless coward. Leave this place. Your kind is not welcome here."

"Spineless?" Ro ground out fiercely, ignoring the bite of the blade. "What madness have you been taught?"

"Perhaps Magden soldiers prefer to forget the less admirable and glorious tomes in their history, but others do not. Where were the Magden when the Lengar attacked Fion's Children? When Fion's High Priestess stooped to beg for Magden aid? Have you forgotten, Magden? You were hiding in your stone forts."

The boy is not Magden—or he has been taught to hate his own race. That realization made his head spin.

Ro felt his face heat as the rest of the message filtered in. His grandfather's decision had been shameful; his father's bid to rectify the situation too late.

"Are you Lengar?" he demanded quietly. If these people fled Jurel's cruelty, Ro would show them mercy and shelter them from their own, but that would be difficult. The Magden soldiers outside would not support this move.

It is a sacred trust, he reminded himself. These people are innocents, even if they escaped the enemy, especially if they fled the enemy. He sent up a prayer that they were Magden who had disassociated themselves from their race in anger at Sol Ti's decision not to aid Fion's Children. That would make protecting them easier—at least as far as dealing with his men was concerned.

The boy growled in displeasure. "Animals. You dare compare me to those animals? I would cut my heart from my body had I been born to those butchers. Tell me, Magden, when did you fight? When the Lengar turned their weapons on you? At least the Lengar are not cowards, whatever else they will be damned for."

Ro grasped the wrist that held the blade, roaring out his fury as he turned on the boy-man. His helm skittered across the floor, unheeded as he stared down at his foe.

His opponent was armored, a strange sort of armor unlike any that he had seen before—or had he? No. Not exactly, but he had seen something similar—perhaps when he was a child. He examined it quickly.

It was made of metal mesh covered in thick hottel-hide leather scales, the tan leather painted in blocks of choc and green for forest battle. It was light but strong, allowing the wearer speed and agility; but it was not designed for heavy battle, as if the wearer expected to either reach glory quickly or die in battle at the same pace. The helm was ornately etched and painted like the armor, with a full-face visor of at least two layers of the mesh set in a metal grid work. It was a stunning design.

Though young and not heavily muscled, the boy stood as high as Ro's cheek. He was fast but not skilled as a fighter, as if he'd had little practice. His intended blow, launched in the split second that Ro paused to make his assessment, never landed.

Ro ducked the jab aimed at his head and back-fisted the boy solidly into the stone wall. The youngster sank to the floor with a grunt of pain and the rustle of metal mesh. His hand slid from the dagger, and Ro snatched the hilt as he fell, mindful that the blade might be poisoned. It seemed unlikely, but a good soldier never took foolish chances.

Donic shot through the doorway with a battle cry, his sword drawn. He took in Ro standing over the downed boy, his expression a mixture of concern and anger.

Ro squatted and dragged the helm from his opponent's head then dropped to his knees in shock, the helm clattering across the stones.

Golden hair—*hastily piled into the helm as we approached, no doubt*—tumbled in long waves around pink, sun-touched cheeks. Leaf green eyes, wide in fear, narrowed as the truth crashed over Ro. Lush, full lips of deep red thinned to a line above a narrow chin marred by a deep scar.

The woman lunged at him, taking advantage of his shock to grasp at her dagger, still clutched in his now-numb fingers.

Donic struck her straight-arm, forcing her back to

the wall. His blade settled at her throat. "Be still, witch," he growled.

"Do not harm her, Donic," Ro whispered.

She was one of Fion's Children—one of the high priestess' class, if he was recalling the ornamentation and design of her armor correctly. He had last seen that armor at the fall of Gidlore. How long ago that was! Had it really been seven years? The inhabitants of this house were, it seemed, the last of an extinct race, and this was their young protector. It was her sacred duty to see to their safety above all else.

The woman raised her chin in challenge. "An intelligent move for a Magden," she commented coldly.

Donic pressed his blade to her chin, forcing her to look to him. "Show respect, woman."

She didn't flinch. "If you injure me, geela, my mother will show you no mercy."

Ro motioned Donic to silence, his heart pounding. She didn't know the fate of her people; that much was clear.

"Who is your mother, Priestess?" he asked formally.

"She is Mother Leiana, fool. Surely, you recognize my armor and seal as her own."

Ro glanced at the dagger in his hand, touching the seal of Fion with shaking fingers. Leiana had been the last High Priestess of Fion's Children. For all that her people were a pure church state, this woman had been akin to a princess. Now she was a queen—a queen without a people to lead and without knowledge of either situation.

A soldier rushed in the door, bowing clumsily. "The enemy approaches," he panted.

Ro nodded. "Where are the others, Princess?"

* * * *

Deliya met the dark choc eyes of the great redheaded oaf. "I am not one of your useless, pampered princesses. I am a priestess of Fion's Children and daughter of the high priestess, Mother Leiana, the Mother's Source and Keeper of the Word."

His face darkened, and a muscle twitched in his jaw. "Where are the others?" he repeated more slowly, as if she were a dimwitted child and not a warrior.

She hesitated. Perhaps, it was better not to tell him. If the Magden believed she had others waiting to help her, he might not mistreat her. Still, Mother Fion frowned on untruths. "Where you will never touch them," she whispered. *I did not lie, Mother Fion. He cannot harm those in your arms.*

"We have no time for games, Priestess. The Lengar approach. They will slaughter you and all you protect."

"Am I to trust a Magden? Your kind has never come to the aid of Fion's Children in the past."

"That was a mistake in my grandfather's day," he growled. "Kor Ti tried to set it right."

"Not that I have seen," she spat. If the Magden were truly aiding her mother's troops, surely Leiana would have sent for her by now.

"Majesty," the soldier pleaded.

"In a moment," he thundered, seemingly furious at either the young soldier or herself.

Deliya swallowed painfully against the blade at her throat. So, this beast was king of the Magden. He was too young to be Kor; the king must have had a very short reign for his son to succeed so soon. Perhaps, that was why they chose to fight. Perhaps, Jurin and Jurel killed Kor and spurred them to action.

The red one sighed, closing his eyes and reining in his emotions. He motioned the man at her throat away. *Donic*, she reminded herself. *His name is Donic.* She breathed a sigh of relief. The Magden would leave her to her own devices, as Magden had always left Fion's Children.

The king grasped Deliya's helm and handed it to her then pulled her to her feet, face to face with him. "Burn it," he ordered his man, his eyes locked on hers. "Burn the crops and buildings. Burn anything that will burn."

She gripped his arm. "No," she gasped. "You cannot do this."

"Where are the others?" he asked calmly.

"There are none. My guards...The others are all dead—more than a year," Deliya admitted, grimacing that she had given the Magden that victory.

"Then why should I not burn this place?"

It is my home, her mind argued fiercely. But, it wasn't even that. It was a bit of Magden land that she had stolen and made her own; and the Lengar would destroy it when they came, if he spoke the truth. "My seed and herbs. Please. Your people do not cultivate the healing plants. I cannot leave them."

His eyes softened and filled with emotion. "We will take as much as we can. You have my vow. Where are these things?"

Deliya pushed from his hands and rushed to the storeroom, pointing to the twenty sacks of seed then loaded her dried herbs and oils in two large packs. She did it quickly, without the usual care she showed for the task. There would be time to order them properly later. When she turned back, she was surprised to see they had taken all.

The red one lifted the packs from her shoulders. "Is there anything else?"

She shook her head, acutely aware of his proximity. It had been a long time since someone had stood so close to her, at least four years. "No. Nothing of value," she managed.

He pulled her toward the door, his step purposeful.

The Lengar troops must be close. Deliya turned her face to the wind then broke from him and took the torch from one of his soldiers, lighting fire to the field behind her home. She nodded her thanks and handed the torch back.

"The wind will take it east," their king bellowed. "Light the last field as we ride."

"No," Deliya ordered. "Leave it."

The soldier with the torch looked to her in surprise then to the king.

"Why?" he demanded. "The Lengar troops—"

Deliya laughed heartily. "It is called gola berry. It tastes sweet, but it is a vicious poison, a poison the Lengar will not be able to treat."

A young soldier cursed solidly, dropping a handful of the dark pink berries.

She shook her head in exasperation. "How many did you eat?" *Foolish child.*

"S—six, I believe," he stammered.

"I will brew a tea for you when we are safe. It will not taste as sweet as the berries did, but it will save your life."

He knelt to one knee and kissed her hand. "Thank

you, Priestess."

The king lifted Deliya to his war-buck, setting her astride the forward hump with a fierce look at his men. He mounted behind her and took up the reins, urging the buck to a loping run.

"My animals," she reminded him, annoyed that he treated her like a child before his troops.

"They are tethered to mounts in the rear of the column. You will have your buck when we stop."

"Why are you treating me like a helpless child?" she demanded quietly.

"My men will not dare approach you after this. I assume that would be your choice."

"It would," she admitted.

He paused at the top of the hill, allowing Deliya one last look at the only home she'd had for the last ten years. She blinked back tears, her eyes on the field of gola berry. Her mother would know Deliya lived by that sign. Leiana would never stop looking for her.

Donic pulled up beside them. "The fires have blocked the Lengar, Ro," he stated in obvious amusement.

Deliya squinted through the smoke to the troops milling across the valley. The fires had reached the Felgren. She calculated the number of Lengar that would become ill from the acidic fumes, nodding her approval.

The king wrapped an arm around her waist.

"Ro," she breathed. His name was Ro Ti.

"Yes," he assured her. "What name may I call you, Priestess?"

"Deliya."

CHAPTER TWO

"I never thought anyone would grow a poison," the miserable young soldier complained.

Deliya sighed, panning her eyes over the three men in her healing circle. They had bent to her traditions, stripping off their shirts and armor, their boots and weapons. She turned back to the tea she was preparing, reminding herself that men would forever be men.

Ro shook his head, his red locks pulled back in a leather tie at his neck. "Will he live?" he asked in a tense voice.

He knelt stiffly beside the poisoned soldier, his back straight, his face strained. He kept a respectful distance from her fire, choosing a spot at the edge of the sacred space so as not to disturb her work. She sighed at that. After four years, she had people willing to enter her circle again, and still she felt alone within its boundaries.

Deliya nodded, noting that he showed as much concern for his men as her mother would. It was an unexpected pleasure as was his willingness to accept her conditions of healing.

"He will live to be a wiser man—I hope." You could never tell with men. They did the most unexpected things.

She glanced at Ro's chest then away again, reminding herself that he was nothing more than a male—though a striking specimen. She'd learned he was muscular, pressed to his chest for the two hours they had traveled before the toxin completely incapacitated the soldier. Deliya had wanted to stop sooner, but Ro had refused when he learned that the boy couldn't be moved immediately after her healing and he'd assured himself that the additional wait would do him no lasting harm.

He'd silenced a complaint from Donic about the space she required for her circle, though she heard the sour man grumble about the wasted time to observe her practice. In truth, the most time-consuming part of drawing her circle had been finding the many herbs in her packs. Ro's man within had even lit her fire while she closed them in.

A soldier passed by, veering away at her look of warning when he ventured too close to the boundaries she'd set. Donic kept most too busy to stand and stare. For that, Deliya was grateful. Still, it was unnerving to look up and see them ogling from a distance.

She scowled at the young soldier. "Never assume any plant appealing in taste or appearance is safe. Even watching the animals may not save you. Kittle nibble gola berries as part of their defensive mechanism. They do not actually swallow the fruit but spread it in their fur to poison predators. You might survive one or two gola berries, though you would be at the gates of the soul's reward for weeks for your trouble. Never even sample an unknown plant," she lectured.

The soldier nodded, groaning as he turned his sweat-soaked face to vomit.

Deliya stirred the tea again. "Not long now," she soothed him. "Hold on." She added a spoon of olum into the mixture and watched it dissolve. In truth, the tea was ready, but it was the way of her people to allow a patient who had made such a disastrous error a few moments to regret the mistake so as not to repeat it.

She poured the tea into a mug and turned to the young man. Deliya nodded to the soldier behind him. "Lift him."

He complied without question, as his king had ordered.

She spooned in the first mouthful, and the boy swallowed. Deliya smiled in encouragement and started to fill his mouth again. The soldier brought the tea back up. She furrowed her brow. That was unexpected. The olum should have stifled that response in the dosage she gave him. She tried again, with the same results.

Deliya leaned across his stained chest and pulled his eyelid back. She checked his pulse in disbelief then stood, throwing the mug into the fire in fury. She paced the diameter of the healing circle, cursing fluently and lifting her arms in supplication to the Mother.

"Mother Fion, save me from Magden fools," she pleaded hopelessly. Men were more undisciplined than children and Magden men the worst she had ever met.

"What is it?" Ro asked.

"He cannot drink the tea."

"Can you do nothing?"

Deliya motioned at the wilderness around them. "With no equipment? No. I can do nothing. The fool couldn't do this where I had supplies, of course."

"What equipment do you require? Perhaps, I can provide it," he suggested hopefully.

"A hypocil and a metal cup or ladle."

Ro nodded. "Donic," he roared.

Deliya turned toward the man rushing at them, motioning frantically for him to stop. Donic skidded to a halt, sending a fine spray of soil into the circle but ending his charge a hand length outside her consecrated ground.

She let out a shuddering breath and pressed a hand to her stomach. "Do not," she whispered. "Do not ever cross the boundaries of a healing circle. I would have to re-consecrate before I continued."

Donic scowled at her. "Your herbs will cease to function if I do?" he scoffed.

Deliya straightened her spine. "No," she admitted. "They will not, but it would be an affront to the Goddess whose knowledge cures this man and who blesses him. Can you show no appreciation or respect for Fion's mercy and kindness?" she challenged.

Donic opened his mouth, no doubt to make another ignorant remark.

"He will," Ro warned his general. He rose from his place on the ground, his muscles taut as he stepped up beside her. He glared around the camp at the soldiers who'd stopped to stare at the unfolding encounter. "They all will."

Donic sneered at Deliya then bowed his head to Ro. "As you wish, my King."

Ro waved him away, a clear dismissal of his general. "Collect a hypocil from Bron and a ladle from the cook. Novin cannot drink the tea."

"She waited too long," Donic accused. "If Novin dies this way, his father will—"

Deliya stepped to the edge of the circle, coming eye to eye with the general. "It would not have been 'too long,' if he had told me the truth," she snapped. "He did not eat six berries. His physical condition indicates that it was at least double that. What sort of fool lies to the healer who would save him?

"Now, every moment you waste lets the poison gain

power. If you truly wish me to save this man, go while there is time. Or—stand here and argue while he dies. It is your choice."

"Go," Ro ordered.

Donic stalked away, his hands fisted so tight his knuckles stood out white against his sun-darkened skin in the dimming light. Deliya watched him go then returned to the fire to stir the tea. She rubbed the tension from her neck and stood to stretch her back.

She startled as hands closed on her shoulders. She turned to Ro as he pulled them away, his bare chest too close for her peace of mind. The urge to touch him was insistent, and she fisted her hand in response. What would his skin feel like beneath her fingertips? Beneath her lips? The tang of his musk on her tongue? It had been too long—

No! She backed off a step then planted her feet, reminding herself that a priestess backs down from no challenge.

He looked stricken. "I apologize," he grumbled. "I only meant to ease your discomfort."

She shifted, trying to put her reaction into words. Ro's touch caused her unease. Not because she feared him, Deliya was quick to assure herself. He gave her no reason to fear him. He would regret it, if he did.

No. It was something else. The man, himself, unnerved her—the proprietary way he had with her, the way he had cradled her to his body on his war-buck, the way his touch made her want to lean into him for comfort.

Deliya had been without aid of any kind for more than a year and without aid in her circle for almost four. No man had comforted her save her father since

Loric died; that had been a season before Vela had, leaving her in Celdin's sole company.

She shivered at the memory of the night Loric died. He had rubbed at her shoulders much as Ro had just done. That was the cause of her present upset—and nothing more.

The sheer size and fighting skill of the man had nothing to do with it. She was out of practice; she'd not had a decent bout since Vela fell ill, and before that— What could one expect of a priestess whose training was completed by an old woman and two dishonored men?

"I am unaccustomed to being touched," she admitted.

Ro grimaced. "Have I offended your Goddess?" he asked urgently. "Tell me how to appease her, and I will."

Deliya looked at him in stunned fascination. "You would do that?"

"If your Fion shows mercy on the son of my cousin and spares his foolish hide, I will learn to honor her. You have my vow."

She searched his face for signs of deception, but Ro seemed sincere. "Then learn this—there was no offense to ask forgiveness for. It is not against the Mother's word for a priestess to be shown comfort while she performs a healing. It is common."

"You never wished to be shown comfort?" he asked in confusion.

"I have been alone for a long time," she reminded him patiently.

"A year," he noted sadly.

"Longer," she whispered. "My father refused to enter my healing circles." In the years after Loric's death,

Celdin had refused to touch her at all, unless it was unavoidable.

Ro's eyes widened. "Why?"

"He believed himself unclean, beyond redemption. Celdin thought the Mother would not bless my work if he stood on my consecrated ground."

He crossed his arms over his chest, peering down at her as if examining a strange phenomenon. "Why would he believe that?"

It was on the tip of her tongue to offer an excuse not to tell him, but that would be its own sort of lie. Her patient vomited again, reminding Deliya that sullying her healing circle would be unwise.

"He killed one of my other guards. Vela, my mentor, was forced to purify me after the act. Loric...The man's blood stained my skin. That his death was unavoidable made no difference to Celdin. He had killed another of Fion's Children in front of two priestesses and without our consent to kill."

"Would you have given consent?"

"If I did not respect his decision, I would have banished him from my home," she answered honestly.

Ro nodded, something resembling admiration in his dark eyes. "Would you permit me to ease your pain?" he asked formally.

"Yes. I would appreciate it."

* * * *

Ro watched Deliya from across the clearing, unable to shift his eyes from her for longer than a few moments at a time. She gauged Novin's pulse, her fingertips pressed to his throat, then hung her head wearily. She had worked tirelessly, giving the young man six injections of the antidote in as many hours before destroying her healing circle and deigning to eat a bit of food.

She weaved on her feet as she stood; Ro took to his own, striding to her. The soldier who was tending her fire reached to steady her, but Ro warned him off with one of his most menacing looks. Deliya was not theirs to touch any more than any other woman of his household was. He only tolerated them staring at her so directly because of the novelty of having one of Fion's Children in the flesh walking among them like a pale apparition.

Deliya shivered as he closed his hands on her shoulders and pulled her back into the shelter of his chest, but she didn't stiffen as she had earlier. He savored the feel of her in his arms for a moment, reinforcing the show he made for his men. None of them would dare touch her as long as they believed he had an interest.

He sobered at the realization that he did have an interest in the stunning beauty with the cunning of a warrior and the bearing of a queen.

"Come," he whispered. "You should sleep. You have worked long and hard tonight."

Deliya yawned widely. "Novin will not be able to ride for at least five days. Your men will have to build a litter to be borne between two hottel. My two choc mares are sedate enough and accustomed to working a plow in tandem. You are welcome to use them."

Ro nodded, kneading her shoulders. "In the morning," he assured her. He brushed his lips over her neck, healing her while he fed his power off of the arousal her scent raised in him. She smelled of herbs and sweat—and female. Ro hadn't had schente in nearly two weeks; he wouldn't risk them so near the fighting, but he wouldn't blame this fascination on lack of competition or under-indulged urges. Deliya would demand his full attention, whether he had schente or not.

"He should drink more of the tea while we travel," she continued in a voice that wavered slightly. "Every few hours."

"It will be done."

"I have prepared the tea," Deliya informed him.

Ro kissed her neck, his healing forgotten.

"A mug full," she rushed on. "It may be administered cold. We need not stop to build a fire."

A stab of jealousy settled in Ro's gut. Had she attention for nothing but the damned foolish boy she treated? He turned her toward his pavilion.

Deliya didn't meet his eyes. She crossed her arms over nipples that stood out as mountain peaks beneath her man's tunic. "Food. Only broth and juice for two days. Then Novin may have bread and vegetables. No meat until he can ride steadily—perhaps six days. If he—"

Ro turned her to face him, and she stopped speaking. She licked her lips and took a deep breath. He smiled, breathing in her scent. Yes. She was aroused.

"Ro?" she asked, her voice low.

He glanced at yet another soldier who stopped to stare openly at them, and the whelp turned away. This was not the time and place for this. "You saved Novin, and you saved me my cousin's displeasure. I am in your debt. I thank you."

Deliya turned and hurried toward the pavilion, smoothing her pale braid. "A ridiculous thought," she snapped at him without seeking his eyes. "His father would be angered to have Novin die of a poison when he sent him off to die in battle." She made a sound of disgust.

Ro matched her pace. "Actually, Andrel did not send him. Novin is an adult and decided to come, despite the fact that he is his father's only heir."

"Your cousin—He has no other children?"

"No other sons," he explained. "Only two daughters."

"Magden." The word left her lips as a curse, and she made the same sound of disgust.

Ro ignored her. "Andrel charged me with keeping his heir alive. So, I keep Novin at my side to keep him safe."

"Safe?" she asked in disbelief.

He shrugged. "Safer than he would be anywhere else," Ro admitted. "Tell me. What would you have?"

Deliya furrowed her brow over troubled green eyes. "Have?"

"I am in your debt," he reminded her.

She stepped around Donic and settled next to the fire at Ro's pavilion, reaching for her armor. "I do not understand." Deliya didn't look at him as she strapped on her chasses.

"Why are you doing that?" Ro asked.

"It is the way of my people to never leave ourselves unarmed when the enemy is near." She looked toward Novin then back to her work. "Unless we are performing acts of Fion's mercy," she qualified. "Then we trust that the Mother will protect us."

"Or you die," Donic growled.

Ro sent him a quelling look and knelt beside her, stilling her hands with his own. Deliya's fingers trembled beneath his.

"Let me protect you," he offered.

Deliya pulled her hand from his grasp and moved to the next fastener. "It is not our way," she whispered.

Donic made a rude gesture that Ro pretended not to see. Her refusal hurt him much more than he wanted to admit. Donic's behavior was a minor irritation by comparison.

"What does it mean to have a Magden man in your debt?" she asked, returning to their original conversation.

"A Magden *king*," he emphasized. "It means you may ask anything within my power to grant you, and I will comply."

Deliya looked up, her eyes full of hope. "Deliver me to my mother."

Ro's heart stuttered. He should have realized she'd ask for that. "That is not within my power," he choked out.

"Why not?" She swallowed hard, and pain filled her eyes. "Rintal fell," she whispered. "When she sent me away...My people have not come for me, because they think I was at Rintal when it fell." Deliya started on the next fastener furiously. "You must take me to Gidlore. My people would have retreated there."

They had. It had been the site of her mother's last stand. Ro took a deep breath to steady his nerves and reached for her hands, intent on breaking the truth to her gently.

Deliya hurried on, creating her fantasy of the glorious fight of her people. "Gidlore is closer to here. I should have asked you to take me there to begin with. It is less of an imposition," she rattled on.

Ro clasped her hands, pulling them from her armor gently. Deliya looked up into his eyes, wary, perhaps even knowing yet denying what he had to tell her.

Donic snorted. "Gidlore fell seven years ago," he informed her coldly.

Ro cringed at that. Donic had never been a man to pad a blow, but this was tactless—even for him. He sighed, trying to find the words to ease her pain.

"They say your mother was the last to fall," the general continued, laughing harshly. "If you live, the stories are wrong."

"He lies," she said weakly. Her eyes pleaded with Ro to tell her it was not true, that Donic was playing a cruel prank on her.

"I am sorry," Ro offered, realizing that he should say more.

Tears pooled in her eyes, and she straightened her spine, removing her hands from his. Deliya swallowed and blinked back the tears, looking every inch her regal heritage.

"Liars," she breathed.

Ro looked at her in surprise, barely keeping his balance as she punched him across the cheek. She grasped the rest of her armor and bolted toward the thicker trees. Ro struggled to his feet with a curse, pushing the open-mouthed Donic out of his way as he gave chase. She would go to the stand where their war-buck were tethered. Deliya had too much honor to steal a beast. She would take her own or none, and the distraction of trying to find him would slow her down.

Ro sprinted to the row of mounts, cursing Donic the entire way. His advisor had never trusted Fion's priestesses, believing they harbored ill will for Sol's refusal of aid and would attack at the first opportunity when the Lengar were vanquished. It was likely a relief of sorts for Donic when Gidlore fell.

Worse, the older priestesses' disdain for men of power and grudging acceptance of Ro as an equal always made the general distinctly nervous—or perhaps it offended him. Despite Deliya's easy manner in comparison, it seemed the mistrust had not faded. Of course, she had held a blade to Ro's throat at their first meeting, and that was not the way to win Donic over. Shattering her dreams likely gave him a sense of satisfaction, as if he had bested her in battle.

Ro was still at a full run when he grasped her around the waist and knocked her blade from her hand. She let loose another punch with a frustrated grunt. He ducked it easily. It took several long moments and several more ducked punches before he had her trapped between his body and a thick tree trunk.

"Stop this, Deliya," he ordered in a low voice. "You cannot run off into the night."

"I am a priestess of Fion," she insisted, "and I am safer with jaglin than with lying Magden."

Ro tightened his grip slightly, as she attacked again. "I am a Magden king," he assured her, willing his voice not to shake. "My vow is worth more than my life."

"Then it is still worthless," she spat. "When you make an enemy of Fion's Daughters, your life is worthless."

"You are the last of Fion's Daughters, and for that, I

am sorry. If Mag granted me the power to turn back time, I would do so and defend your people with all of my armies. I cannot undo what is."

"You owe me a debt."

"I do," he agreed.

"Take me to Gidlore. Prove to me that my people are no more."

"I cannot. Gidlore is behind Lengar lines. I would do it, if I could."

"Convenient," Deliya decided. "A useful excuse to keep me here. Whatever you hope to gain by holding me, you will not win. My mother...My people will leave me to Fion's protection. They do not bargain. Not even for me."

Ro shook his head. "I wish there was someone left to bargain with, but your Goddess is the only one left for me to beg from, not that I would know what to ask her for."

"We shall see," she promised.

"Meaning?" he asked suspiciously.

"If I am not your prisoner, I am free to take my herbs and war-buck, my armor and weapons and part company with you here—in the morning, if it disturbs you to have me leave in the night."

An icy finger ran down Ro's spine. "To Gidlore in Lengar lands?" he guessed.

"To Gidlore and whatever fate the Merciful Mother has set for me."

Ro shook his head. He'd seen more than enough of Fion's mercy. Their Goddess hadn't saved Deliya's people from their fate. *Her chosen? What good is She? Not good enough for Leiana, and not good enough for Deliya!*

"No," he stated emphatically. "I will make you a bargain."

"Fion's priestesses—"

"Do not," Ro ordered. "If I can prove to you that Gidlore is cut off from us by Lengar troops on the two sides we travel, will you concede that it is lost?"

Deliya didn't respond. Her breathing hitched in the darkness. Was she trying to hold back a sob?

"Promise me you will not run from me," he asked. "Promise me that you will not travel to Gidlore alone as you threatened, and you will keep all that is yours, including your weapons."

"And, if I refuse to make that vow?" she replied calmly.

The image came into his mind abruptly. "I will shackle you to my side all day and tie you to my bed at night," he vowed. Oh, but his body liked that idea.

"You have left me little choice in the matter," she noted wryly.

"Your word, Deliya."

"I give it. I will not run from you."

Ro nodded and backed away, settling her to the ground and grasping her elbow lightly. "Good. Then we will retrieve your blade and go back."

"Where," she began.

"My bed."

Deliya planted her feet with a gasp.

Ro sighed. "I will not lay an unwelcome hand on your person," he promised. Would that he were welcome—

CHAPTER THREE

Abrin 25th, Ti 10-455
Deliya's Farm in the Garesh Mountains

"Calm yourself," Vela ordered.

Deliya rubbed her eyes and looked at the darkness outside the window in confusion then squinted at the light filtering under the door to her room. Why in the Mother's sacred name were her companions about at this time of night?

"What can I possibly tell her?" Loric demanded.

"I said calm, boy." Vela's voice went dangerously cold, a tone Deliya had only heard once before.

Loric's voice dropped to a whisper.

Deliya pushed up from her bed, smiling that he was back, despite whatever mischief had landed him on Vela's bad side. He had been gone for nearly a month. Deliya had missed his company—and his training.

"Calm," Vela ordered in a fierce whisper. "Nothing has changed."

Deliya furrowed her brow. Loric had always been excitable, as young men often were, but Vela rarely had to order him to do anything more than once. Three times was unheard of.

She headed to the door, straightening her knee-length tunic over her chest.

Loric paced the main room of the farmhouse, his white-blonde hair wind blown and his clothing torn and stained. "Deliya is an adult now," he growled.

Celdin rubbed his temples, leaning back against the hearth-surround. Her father's tunic was rumpled and his hair mussed from sleep; he'd no doubt come directly from the men's beds above the stable. "You knew this was a possibility," he stated. "You knew there was a chance of failure."

"I wanted to—" Loric went silent as he turned and saw Deliya in the doorway.

"What difference does it make that I am an adult?" she asked, a niggling of unease settling in her stomach.

Vela continued her sewing, leaning close to the oil lamp on the table as if it were commonplace for her to be mending work clothing before sun-up—and as if Loric weren't acting like he'd seen Lengar in her shed. "Loric wanted to surprise you with a gift that he could not get. He is upset."

"What gift could possibly upset you that much?" she asked Loric.

He blushed, looking to Vela then Celdin miserably.

Vela shook her head, clucking her displeasure. "The silly boy heard me talking about the Peak Chol flowers. He hoped this would be the year they would appear."

Deliya hid her smile behind her hand as Loric's face darkened. The Peak Chol were a children's tale, a legendary flower that was said to only bloom late in the fall every seven years at the crag above the Surian basin. Priestesses had sent young trainees scouring the crag for centuries, based on that story. Deliya had looked for it herself every birthday from her tenth to her twelfth.

Loric sighed at her amusement. "I promised you a wonderful gift. I failed you."

Deliya strode to him, kissing his cheek. "You gave me a wonderful gift. You came back." She kissed him again, lingering over his lips. "I missed you," she whispered.

"You did?" he asked, his voice hopeful.

"I did."

"Enough to consider training with me later today?" he suggested, nipping her ear.

"Enough to consider training with you now," she assured him. Deliya didn't have to stroke him to know that Loric was prepared for her with that little enticement. "After all, the spring festival is less than half a year away, and I will have to face the challenge."

The room went unnaturally still. Loric's breathing was harsh in her ear. He nipped at her again. "Promise me that I can challenge you," he pleaded.

A thrill shot through Deliya. Loric didn't dare ask her to choose to promise with him, but his possessiveness was hard to miss. If he challenged her and she promised with him, Loric would be the only man to touch her sexually in her lifetime. Most priestesses had many lovers from their training to the challenge and to the production of children—unless they took a true mate just after challenge as she planned to do.

She feigned consideration. "It would not really be a challenge," she suggested. "Perhaps, I should choose another."

Loric moved back half an arm's length. His look of disbelief melted into staunch determination. He'd taken the bait she'd laid out for him; men were so easy to anticipate. She crossed her arms over her chest and raised an eyebrow at him.

"Now," he agreed, guiding Deliya to her room. "If you make a single sound this night, the challenge is mine."

"Did I promise that?" she asked in an innocent

voice.

Celdin chuckled at their play.

Loric leaned close to her ear. "I did," he growled in a low voice.

Deliya blushed at that. What if Celdin had heard it? Or Vela? "You think to order one of Fion's priestesses?" she demanded. She had been asking Loric that since he'd begun her training almost two years earlier. It was bad enough that he'd made her wait until she was sixteen to start her training; then he became so—insufferably male.

"Never," he laughed.

But, he did. Loric had dared to dictate their sexual relationship throughout her training. The lessons required a certain amount of instruction on Loric's part but not as much as he engaged in.

And yet, you do not stop him.

Deliya shivered as her body prepared for him, her sheath wet with her juices and her breasts coming to little points that begged for his tongue. She loved that Loric was so sexually dominant, though Mother Leiana would surely disapprove of her allowing Loric's antics to continue.

He swung the door shut and stripped off Deliya's tunic, tossing it over his shoulder. He leaned to kiss at the tips of her breasts. "You did miss me," he crooned. "I smell how much you want me."

"Will you make me wait until daybreak?" she huffed.

"I should. Saying you would let another man challenge you."

"Let?" That was going too far. "I choose who I take to my bed, Loric. You would do well to remember that."

41

He pulled off his tunic and dropped it to the floor then unfastened his trousers and pushed them off over his bare feet. He led her to the bed and settled her on it, on her knees, facing away from him.

He didn't touch her, only his breath teasing the skin of her shoulder. Deliya leaned back, swallowing a groan as the hard lines of his chest pressed against her. He shifted, playing his muscles over her. His cock teased at her buttocks with promise of pleasures yet to come, his hips circling against her. Still, his hands did not stray to her body.

"Lay forward," he instructed. "Up on your knees but with your arms folded under your head."

Deliya hesitated then complied. She closed her eyes, as Loric's lips traced down her spine. He kissed at the bundle of nerves at her lower back. He didn't need to speak the words; she shivered in the unspoken prospect of having heirs by him, of his healing her as she eased them forth into her mother's hands.

Loric shouldered her thighs wider and tasted her depths. Deliya bit her lip and let her mind wander.

Would she conceive the night of her challenge, as Jolia had? She secretly hoped she would. It was the ultimate blessing of the Mother to conceive at challenge—only slightly less a blessing to conceive on the promise night.

While it was illegal to use herbs on either partner to increase the chances of conception that night, many priestesses promised their counterparts any pleasures they wished to come to their beds after the challenge and take them multiple times in hopes of a child. She scowled. Loric had taken Jolia three times.

But, how long should she make Loric wait before

taking him as her mate? If she waited too long, he might agree to warm other beds. He was single-minded now, but would that change when they returned home and there were dozens of young priestesses offering him their bodies? If he were not promised to Deliya, would he accept those offers? If he did, she could not protest it.

She shifted against Loric's tongue, and his stroking became more insistent. He knew her body so well he could hold off her climax or make her shatter to his whim.

No, there was an appropriate length of time to wait; but if Deliya conceived, she could take Loric to mate immediately, claiming a love-schen. She would conceive. She would not chance less. She would invite Loric to her bed as often as she could and not appear fixated, perhaps even sneak off with him to secluded places in the fields or forest at other stolen moments. She would have her heir and have it quickly.

As if sensing her wandering mind, Loric sucked at her hood hard then thrust his tongue into her again. Deliya shuddered as she ground her teeth against the pleasure he gave her. She forced her mind back to her task. She would choose no other man to challenge her unless Loric refused her, but she would not give him the satisfaction of being granted the privilege easily.

His mouth worked her furiously: sucking, nibbling, stroking and kissing. The sensations were maddening. He darted back and forth, inside and out, from the sensitive spot forward of her hood to the globes of her buttocks and between.

Deliya fisted her fingernails into her hands, pressing her forehead hard to the bed, stiffening her back as her climax loomed closer. She sucked in her breath, relaxing her body into the crest, allowing herself to ride the waves of pleasure.

Loric groaned into her body, pushing her control to its limits. Just as Deliya felt sure she would triumph, he did the unexpected. His hands, hands that hadn't played with her up to that point, seemed to be everywhere at once. The fingers of one breached her body and teased at her inner pleasure spot, while the others pinched her nipple hard.

Deliya cried out in pain and surprise as her body exploded with sensation, her inner muscles pulling at his questing fingers. She turned on the bed, aiming a slap for his cheek. Loric caught her wrist and fell with her to the mattress.

"How dare you!" she fumed, pushing at his chest.

"The challenge is mine," he informed her.

"It is not," she decided. "You cheated. You know full well that you will not be permitted to do that during the challenge."

"No. I will not, but I will be permitted to do things that will shatter your composure even more effectively than that."

Deliya felt her face heat at the truth of it. There were things more pleasurable and more painful allowed in the challenge. *Expected in it.* She cursed herself for her failure.

"You allowed yourself to be complacent. Because I had not used my hands, you forgot the possibility existed. You cannot ever allow yourself to make that mistake again.

"You are the true heir of Mother Leiana. Your line has ruled for twenty-eight generations. Never a priestess among them who failed in challenge, even the second daughters. Never a priestess dishonored. Never a priestess who failed to produce a true heir. I will not hesitate to challenge you. I will do my best to see you fail, so none may doubt that you are truly ordained by Fion for your place; and if the Mother is pleased, you will conceive a daughter of me at that challenge."

She pressed her body to his, the idea of carrying his daughter, stated so plainly, nearly her undoing. Loric paused in his tirade, his breathing hitching. He kissed her passionately, his need fast overriding the lecturing he seemed to love so much.

Deliya stroked his length, smiling as he shivered in restraint. "I would trust no one but you to challenge me," she whispered.

Loric didn't thank her. He closed his eyes, grasping her shoulders. "You challenge my resolve," he gasped.

Training had to be maddening for Loric. He lived for the challenge, for the day that he might give her heirs. There were no other priestesses for him to sate his drive with, no one with whom he need not show restraint. There were rules—pleasures they could not give each other until after the challenge, pleasures that Loric had enjoyed until he became her guard.

She sobered. "Will I still inspire you when you are surrounded by other priestesses who want your seed to fill their wombs with heirs?"

His eyes flew open. Loric looked at her miserably, touching her cheek. "Never," he promised.

"Loric?" Something was not right. Deliya thought back over the conversation in the main room. She'd been led astray from things that bothered her, again and again. If she didn't know her companions' dedication, she might have believed they were lying to her.

"I want the child you will carry," he admitted, his eyes darting to the closed door.

Something was desperately wrong. Loric should not have said that. Until that moment, Deliya would have sworn he would not have presumed so much. The punishment Vela would serve him for it was not worth daring to utter such a bold statement—if Deliya were to tell her mentor what went on in this room.

She stroked his length more purposefully, using the drops of his readiness pooled on the tip as a lubricant to tease the head. "How many times will you take me on my challenge night, Loric? How many of the restricted pleasures will you teach me?"

He groaned.

"At the sanctuary on the night of the spring festival," she whispered, laying a kiss on his chest.

Loric grimaced, and Deliya changed her approach to stave off his release.

"The firelight dancing on the green stone. You calling out my triumph for my mother to come witness, while you give me an heir to deliver into her hands."

He shot her a look part pure ecstasy and part true dismay.

Deliya brushed the tips of her breasts over the wall of his chest, feeling her way to the truth he was hiding from her. "Tell me how it will be. Tell me the truth of it." It was dishonest to use his pleasure to prod him to truthfulness, but he should not have lied to her.

"Deliya..." he begged.

She pushed him more roughly, driving his need to release. "Will you challenge me?" she asked.

"Yes," he gasped. He kissed her, his body taut. "It was Mother Leiana's wish that I would."

"Will you take me to the sanctuary at Rintal?"

He met her eyes. "Only if your mother calls for you first."

"You went to Rintal when you left? Your gift was going to be to deliver me home?"

"Yes," he admitted.

"My mother would miss my challenge?" She was heartsick at the thought of having her challenge without Leiana present. It was the dream of every young priestess to take her place as an adult with her mother's praise of her accomplishment ringing in her ears. It was tradition, and Fion's Children, her chosen ones, prided themselves on their rich traditions.

She furrowed her brow. How would she become Fion's Source if her mother wasn't present to bestow the honor on her challenge night? Surely, Leiana didn't intend to let Vela do so. If she did intend it, Vela would have her mother's abinatine somewhere in her belongings. Deliya shuddered at the idea of Leiana leading the battle without her most sacred seal of office in her possession.

"It is not her wish," he assured her. "Vela..." He looked to the door nervously, no doubt envisioning what Vela would do to him for going against her orders.

Deliya kissed him, offering what comfort she could for the position she had placed him in. Soon, she would be legally an adult, and Vela would be her lesser. A few more precious months until she ascended to her position as Fion's Source and leader of their people. Until then, they would have to keep this discussion between themselves.

She played the head of his cock in the lubricant preparing her, dipping the head a breath-stealing fraction of a finger inside and letting her outer lips close around him then pulling him free again and continuing her stroking. Loric broke off the kiss, watching Deliya's teasing with wide eyes. She gave him another taste of her and retreated again, as his hands tightened on her shoulders, leaving bruises he would have to heal before he left her bed.

"What you say is between us," she promised. "I will not tell Vela what is said. Why will I not return home now that I near my challenge?"

"Too dangerous," he whispered, nipping at her jawline as Deliya teased him toward release.

"Dangerous?" she managed in a fierce whisper. "I am a priestess of Fion."

"The survival of our people hangs in a fragile balance. It is too dangerous to have all the highest family in one place. Your mother asks this boon of you. She asks you not to force a time of trial now, not while the Lengar are so close."

Deliya nodded thoughtfully. If the whole line were lost, the priestesses would be leaderless without the trial to find Fion's new most-chosen. And, the trial would leave all their best unable to fight until long after the decision was made—until the gola and Auguren cleared their systems fully. "What does my mother wish of me?"

"Produce a true heir."

"But, I would not return home for—"

Loric kissed her to still her words. "Shhh. I know. You will not take your place for more than a year past the time you should, but the line will be assured."

"My mother chooses my mate for me?" Deliya asked, indignant.

"Never. You could refuse me," he said, though he choked on the words. "Your duty is simply to produce an heir." He looked ill at the prospect that she might choose another to mate with.

"And when I have produced my true heir?" she breathed.

"You know your future." Loric cried out as he climaxed, his seed washing, wave after wave, over her sex.

Deliya licked her lips as he swelled in her hand and applied the pressure he needed to truly enjoy the encounter. "Then my heir will be of your loins," she promised, pouring the words into his lips.

Loric rolled over Deliya, his mouth urgent on hers. She stroked his cock in their mixed fluids, a promise of the mating to come.

"You will never regret this," he vowed.

CHAPTER FOUR

Deliya stifled a sob with her hand, wiping the shameful tears onto her tunic.

Ro touched her hair from his side of the pallet. "I am sorry, Deliya. I would take back every word Donic spoke as a lie if I could—if it would save you your tears."

"Tears?" she asked in an unwavering voice. "A priestess of Fion does not weep in front of her adversaries, not even as she dies."

"I do not have to be your adversary," he suggested. "That is why you wear your armor to bed, isn't it? The enemy you speak of is not the Lengar. It is the Magden."

"Only a fool would trust the Magden in my place."

He sighed. "I cannot change the truth. I can only wait and hope you see it soon."

"You lie," she stated confidently. *Loric saw my mother only four years ago. He promised on Fion's name that I would take my place when I had produced an heir. Loric could not have lied in the Mother's name.*

Ro removed his hand. "A Magden king does not lie," he growled.

"Neither do Fion's Children."

* * * *

Deliya stirred the tea in the pot, bringing a large quantity of dried lizor berry and lizor stems to a rolling boil. For two days, she'd tried to find a way to escape Ro, but the man was relentless. As if he expected her to break her word, she was all but tied to him day and night.

She slept under his arm every night. When she tried to leave the pavilion on the ruse of checking on Novin, he or Donic accompanied her to the young man's side. She was ordered to ride between him and his general—for her own protection, of course. She was not even permitted to relieve herself without him standing guard on the other side of the bush.

This was her only hope. She added more of the lizor stem then some of her precious store of sucre sap to cut the bitter edge the stems would give the tea. She strained out the stems and left the deep purple liquid to reduce.

She didn't look up as Donic and Ro returned to the fire, discussing the next campaign. The Magden were like that, every moment immersed in talk of ways to kill and die.

Without asking, Deliya filled a steaming mug for each and offered them to the men. They stopped talking and stared at the mugs warily.

"Trying to poison us, Priestess?" Donic drawled.

Ro had convinced his general more than a day earlier to consider his life's worth if he called Deliya "witch" again. While Deliya was not a bloodthirsty individual by nature, the secret wish to see Donic run through for insulting her again was hard to banish. As far as she could tell, the man was a hateful beast who trusted no one; and while she could appreciate the latter in present company, the former was unforgivable.

She had expected this response. "Choose one," she offered. "Go on. You saw me fill them from the same pot. Choose one for me to drink down, and then I will refill it for you."

"Ro's," Donic decided. "Then I know he will be safe."

Ro's smile widened. "She does not like you very much, Donic. Perhaps you would be better served worrying about yourself," he teased.

Deliya heaved an affected sigh. "Very well. I will drink them both and refill them." She'd actually taken enough of the stimulant, Implin core, to counter four cups of the tea. She drained the mugs and filled them again, hoping Donic would only demand this of her once. She could ingest more implin core to keep herself awake, but a higher dose would mean excessive delays to relieve herself while she traveled.

Ro took his cheerfully and sipped at it. His smile widened. "Wonderful. Lizor berry." He sipped again. "And sucre."

"Just a bit," she replied, genuinely happy that he liked the tea. *Better the chance he will drink deeply of it.*

Donic stared into his cup suspiciously, casting nervous glances at Ro. Deliya strode into the pavilion and stretched out on the pallet. Perhaps if she didn't hover, he would drink. If he didn't, this could never work. It wasn't enough for Ro to sleep.

"Try it, Donic," Ro urged.

"Are you insane? She is a...She knows sweet-tasting poisons."

"She also drank it first."

"Perhaps, she already took the antidote."

Deliya laughed heartily, earning her a dirty look from Donic. "There is no such thing as an antidote I can take before a poison," she assured him. "What would it fight?"

The general grunted. "Perhaps. I have only your word on that."

52

Deliya shrugged, playing as if his insult meant nothing to her. "As you wish. I am sure Ro will not let the tea go to waste."

Ro tipped his empty mug. "You are a fool to miss something so good." He refilled it.

Deliya smiled. Ro would need at least two mugs of the tea to affect him as she wished. Three would be better. Ro took another sip, and Donic did the same. Her plan would work. She closed her eyes, willing her body to rest. Voices drifted in and out of her consciousness, causing her to wonder if she'd made the tea stronger than she had intended to.

She came fully awake as Ro settled next to her on the pallet, sucking in her breath, as he loomed over her, his eyes glittering in the firelight. He kissed her chin then her lips, brushing his mouth over hers.

"Take off your armor," he requested.

"It is not our way," she reminded him. *You are my enemy.*

Ro fumbled with the straps to her Cuirass. "I cannot make love to you with your armor on."

Deliya tried to escape his grasp. The tea was a strong sedative. It relaxed the mind and body, but this was not what she had in mind when she set out to relax him.

His body covered hers, and she considered screaming. She dismissed the idea. Screaming would ruin any chance of escape and alert Ro's men that their king had been drugged.

"Please, let me make love to you," he breathed into her ear.

She shook her head, praying he was rational enough to heed her refusal. That was the one thing she could not willingly give him, even for the promise of escape. Fion's priestesses did not mate with outsiders. They mated with males of their own kind.

His lips pressed to hers again. This was something she could give him. It was something she wanted to give him, and Deliya couldn't deny that. She parted her lips tentatively, admitting his tongue.

Ro was relentless. His mouth plundered hers: nipping and sucking, his tongue pushing deep inside her. It was like nothing she'd ever felt before, like nothing Loric had taught her. Compared to Ro, Loric had been a foolish boy. Or perhaps, this was what Loric would have been had he not been restrained with her.

"I want you," he whispered.

It is the lizor stems. He wants a female, not you specifically. "Tomorrow, Ro."

He kissed her brow, smiling, then rolled to his side and nestled her to his chest. "Tomorrow," he slurred. "Sleep well, Deliya."

She held her breath. Did Ro truly know who she was and want her? Perhaps, but what difference did it make?

None. In four hours, at the height of their sleep, she would be gone.

* * * *

Ro woke as the first rays of sunlight stole into his pavilion. He smiled, rolling the shoulder that had been so tense the night before. He'd had a wonderful night's sleep and even more fantastic dreams.

One thing was no dream. Deliya had been the stuff of fantasies incarnate. She hadn't permitted him to make love to her, but she had been passionate; and that kiss gave the promise of everything he'd hoped for since he'd first set eyes on her.

Tomorrow, Ro. She'd promised him...

He turned to wrap his arms around her, and his smile disappeared. Deliya was gone. He sat up, searching for clues to her whereabouts. Her packs were gone—and her weapons.

Ro cursed fluently as he pulled on his armor. He glanced at Donic then decided not to wake him. There was only one place Deliya would go, and Donic would shackle him before he'd let Ro follow her to Gidlore.

He strode across the camp, nodding to his men as he went. He should have seen this coming. They were only a two-hour ride from the cliffs overlooking Gidlore. He mounted his war-buck, frustrated as much with himself for falling for her trick as he was at her for doing it.

Deliya had given her word, and his father had taught Ro that Fion's Children were bound by their word by law—a sacred trust with their goddess. Before Deliya answered to her Goddess, Ro would make sure she answered to him for this breech of trust.

* * * *

The Village of Gidlore

Deliya lay at the edge of the cliff, ignoring the curious stares of the geela who nested there. Her heart in her throat, she raised the oculars to her face, training them on the valley below.

There were fields laid out, but the pattern was

wrong. There were no pink gola berries to ward off pests, no bright patches of yellow-orange Dolgen and eye-green Walla, no lines of gray Zura bush and choc Felgren. They were ordinary crops that the Lengar or Magden might grow.

She stifled a sob as she turned the oculars to the village. Fion's circle had been desecrated, the precious green stone smashed and scattered. The Mother's tower lay in ruins, overgrown with iri vines. That was all the proof she needed that her people were dead. None of them would have let this sacrilege happen while they drew breath.

She scanned the homes, seemingly innocent homes with children playing in the yards and women hanging wash on wooden racks fashioned by Fion's Children's hands. Deliya curled away from the edge, letting her tears fall. *Hanging wash...*

The women were hanging the uniforms of the Lengar butchers who had killed her people to dry on the racks built by their victims, living in the homes stolen from them...It was all too much.

Sobs wracked her body. She begged the Mother for answers, but there were none. Why would Fion save her only to see this? Any move she made to avenge her people would see her dead as well.

No, she reminded herself. *Vengeance is not one of Fion's virtues. Fion is love, life and laughter—crushed beneath the heel of the vow-breaking disease of the Lengar!*

Then what did Fion want of her?

A hand covered her mouth, and strong arms crushed her to an armored chest, before she had a chance to retaliate. Deliya tried to drag her feet against the pulling hands.

"Stop," Ro whispered. "You are raising dust."

Deliya relaxed, letting him pull her back to the stand of trees where she'd tethered her war-buck. He settled her to the ground then grasped her arm and pulled a loop of rope with a slip knot snug against her wrist. She panicked, trying to yank her arms away, but Ro was the stronger. All her struggles were for naught. Before she quite knew what was happening, he lay atop her with one hand clamped over her mouth and her wrists trapped in the other.

"Be still," he growled.

Deliya nodded. Ro uncovered her mouth and went back to binding her hands.

"What are you doing?" she asked calmly.

"Enacting your penalty."

"Penalty? I do not understand," she moaned. Why did the Magden culture have to be so confusing?

"You vowed not to do this. I told you what I would do if you broke your oath."

"I will not run from you, Ro," she promised miserably. "It seems I have nowhere to run."

"We will discuss the length of your penalty when I have calmed down, but Mag's law demands justice when vows are broken."

"This is not justice," she hissed. "This is—" Deliya bit her lip as Ro shot her a hard look. "Vengeance," she whispered.

Oh, Mother Fion, guide me. I do not know what You intend. He is vengeance. Ro is Mag's justice personified.

* * * *

Ro looked at the ropes in dismay. It *was* vengeance. He was doing this, because Deliya had fled his bed. Not for a broken vow, but because that vow had been to stay by his side.

He touched her tear-swollen cheeks tenderly. What had he expected of her? Her guards had either lied to her or not known the truth. *'Fion's Children do not lie.'* The former was likely. They told Deliya her mother was alive. They laid out plans that would never come to pass, they wove a web of safe lies—perhaps to make her days happy, and they took the truth to the pyre with them.

Three days ago, Donic had crushed those beliefs, the hopes that had sustained her when she was left alone to wait for a summons that would never come. How could Ro have believed she would not question? That a woman like Deliya would follow blindly the path he set? Would he have in her place?

He kissed her cheeks. "I am sorry." He started to untie her hands.

Deliya shook her head. "No. I broke my vow. You must do as your law demands."

"No one but the two of us knew of this penalty," he reasoned. "No one will know if I show leniency. Mercy is a gift from your Mother Fion, is it not?"

"You are not one of Fion's Children," she reminded him. "Mag demands strict adherence to vows. To be honest, Fion does not look kindly on lying either. Please, do as you must."

He nodded.

Deliya raised her bound hands to touch his lips. "Do not frown, Ro."

Her fingertips shook against his face, and her eyes

were wide and pleading. He dropped his head to taste her mouth again. Her responses were slow and sweet, deep and painfully pure.

"We should not," she whispered.

"Not here," he agreed.

Ro untethered Deliya's mount and tied it to his own then swung her up into his lap, thanking Mag that his armor kept her from rubbing the aching bulge of his erection directly.

* * * *

Deliya looked at the small cave in dismay, the crevice that led into it so tiny that Ro had to crawl inside. "We really cannot reach your men today?"

He shook his head. "Donic will have moved them on. If I do not rejoin the group in three days, they will search for me." He untied her wrists and draped the rope over his thigh.

"Will Donic be very angry?"

He grinned. "Furious. He treats me like a child at times, but that is the least of my worries."

Deliya didn't have to ask what his true worries were. They had made Magden territory without incident, but they were still two very important targets traveling unprotected not far from the Lengar border.

She gasped, as Ro started removing her Cuirass. "What are you doing?"

"I promised you could keep these things if you kept your vow."

"But..." she protested, a lump in her throat.

"You will wear them while we ride and get them back permanently when your penalty is over."

59

Deliya nodded. "A fair proposition," she decided. She reminded herself that she was in no position to argue. Ro had come to collect her from her foolhardy rush into enemy hands at great risk to himself, and she had broken a vow to him. The Mother had placed her in Ro's keeping—for now.

He grunted, undoing the fasteners, gently peeling away layers of leather and mail. He reached her weapons toward the growing pile.

"No," she protested, reaching for her abinatine.

He pulled the ceremonial dagger to his hip, shooting her a warning look. "Weapons were part of the vow," he reminded her.

"It is not a weapon," she whispered, staring at the seal that marked her long-lost lineage. "Please, Ro. You cannot keep it from me." She was reduced to begging, as her mother had begged for Sol's help.

Ro raised an eyebrow in disbelief. "I have had the displeasure of very nearly tasting this blade twice. I think it is safe to say that it is a weapon."

"It is a ceremonial blade called an abinatine. It is sacred, consecrated. It is only used to kill in very specific circumstances. Had I..." She took a shuddering breath at how wrong she would have been to kill Ro. "Your men would have found only my sword."

"What are you saying? Why would I have tasted this blade?"

"In my home, I knew only that you were important and bold. You were a most worthy adversary. When I ran—I would have shown you dishonor if I hadn't..."

She shook her head. He wouldn't understand. Deliya stared at her empty hands.

Ro placed the abinatine in them. "Never raise it

against me again, or I will take it as a weapon," he warned her.

She nodded, pushing the sheath into the back of her trousers. "Thank you, Ro."

She couldn't look at him. The offering itself was too much to expect. If she didn't look at him, she could imagine that he had a scowl on his face, a look of warning.

He removed his armor much more quickly than he had hers. Ro cupped her chin and tilted it up, so she faced him. His eyes seemed full of pain.

"I must do this," he assured her.

Deliya nodded as the loop of rope circled her wrist again. He bound her hands then tied the loose end to one of his own wrists. He lay back on the quilt he'd spread on the floor, pulling her with him.

His free hand settled on her waist. "Do you always dress this way?" he asked. "Like a man?"

"How should one dress to raise crops and fight?" she countered testily. "It is appropriate to the life I lead."

He stroked his thumb up and down her stomach through the tunic, sending delicious curls of pleasure through her body. Would every touch affect her this way? Her nipples stood out, hard and aching for the handling she remembered so well.

Ro brushed his lips over her jaw, the stubble that announced the haste with which he had given chase making trails as hot as his breath. "Was that all life was for you? You had no occasion to wear anything else?"

"What else could there be?" she asked breathlessly. A traitorous wish for him to tell her what else there was beat at her conscience.

He drew her tight to his body, growling as his erection pressed to her mound. Deliya closed her eyes, as his musk washed over her senses. She'd forgotten how good this felt—or perhaps Ro felt better than Loric had.

No. Ro is the wrong man. He is Magden. Loric was one of Fion's Children, the one who should have been her mate. Her mother had chosen him with that eventuality in mind.

But Loric had not been a stable man. She moaned at the memory.

Ro turned over her until his stiff cock nestled tight into the cradle of her thighs. How could a Magden feel so right? He was larger than Loric had been in both body and his attributes for mating. Deliya hadn't forgotten that much.

He rocked that length against her, and she arched up to him. Her body was on fire, and the hand that closed on her breast scattered her senses. She gasped at the ache deep inside her, an ache that she knew instinctively Ro could soothe.

Oh, Mother Fion. Why did Loric never make me feel like this?

Ro drew her hands above her head, wrapping his around them. Her protest, weak as it was, dissolved in a moan of delight as his mouth closed on her breast. His tongue batted back and forth over the sensitive tip, making the ache in her throb in time with his movements.

His mouth left her breast, and the cold air made her harden further. The rough fabric stroked the crest with each breath. Should she beg him to take that tip back into the heat of his mouth? To take away the last

62

vestiges of her thinking mind?

She might have done that had that mouth not closed on hers, hard and insistent, the short whiskers on his face rasping her cheek and chin. His scent wrapped around her; and Deliya drank it in, potent, drugging. She met him as she had the previous night, body to body, mouth to mouth, frantic for sensations she could barely remember yet craved as if she had felt them only moments ago.

Ro rained kisses over her face. "Silin," he breathed as he nipped at her ear. "This was what the gods gave us silin for. A beautiful gown of green silin to match your eyes."

Deliya remembered her silin robes, sky blue with a green overmantle for ceremonies. Unbidden and unwelcome, the last time she wore her robes came to mind—*Vela cutting the blood-soaked and ruined silin from her body and tossing the tattered scraps into the fire to begin the purification ritual.*

"No," she whispered, pulling at his grip on her hands.

Ro eased back and looked at her in surprise. "Deliya?"

She fought him harder, visions of a stunned Loric as his life was taken dancing in her mind. Deliya battled back her panic. She was a priestess of Fion. She should not panic, but she had panicked—that night and now.

She swallowed a scream. Screams brought death, loss, blood. Loric died, because she'd lost her composure and screamed. Had she simply fought him—reasoned more strenuously with him, he would have lived. He would have lived in dishonor, but he would be alive.

"No. Release me. You cannot..." She slowed her breathing. She was hyperventilating, letting the panic win.

"You are frightened. Why?" Ro asked in confusion.

"Release me. Please." She pulled at his hold again.

"What have I done?"

"Nothing," she lied. "I cannot...We cannot..." Deliya took a shuddering breath and blinked back tears.

Ro released her bound hands and slid off of her, touching her face gently. "You are trembling. Please, tell me my offense."

She shook her head. "I cannot do this. I am sorry, Ro." It was unkind to excite a man and not pay him return for his arousal, but Deliya felt unequal to the task of caring for Ro. Sleep pulled at her weary mind and body.

He pulled her to his chest, rubbing her back in calming circles. "I am not Lengar, Deliya. If you are unwilling, I will not continue."

She turned her face further into his chest, fighting down the discord in her mind. The Lengar had never been the greatest threat to her.

Chapter Five

Pri 28th, Ti 10-455
Deliya's Farm in the Garesh Mountains

Loric kneaded her shoulders as she stirred the fire. The light from the small flames and the two lamps danced off the stone walls of her sanctuary. It wasn't a proper sanctuary. It was a cramped space in the shed behind her home, not even large enough for a proper set of shelves; she had to store her wares in the house and carry out her packs when the time came to close her circle. It was simple and largely unadorned. There was none of the precious green stone inlaid in the floor, though Celdin had painstakingly carved the ancient runes in the common stone and even fashioned a work table not unlike her mother's as a gift marking her eighteenth year.

Deliya reached for the brush she would use to scatter her circle, but Loric caught her hand.

"Not yet." He kissed the back of her neck above the cowl she'd lowered at the end of her work.

It had taken hours, but the herbal for Vela had been completed. If the Mother were kind, her mentor might live to see one more spring despite the failing of her ancient lungs.

"The Mother's blessing is not required for that," she teased.

"It could not hurt to beg for Her help," he teased in return.

Deliya shivered. Only Loric would say something so irreverent.

He kissed her again, plucking her nipples through

the silin of her robes. "Please, Deliya."

She turned, placing her hand over his pounding heart. His chest was bare for the ceremony, strong but slim. She'd once thought of Loric as a brother but not since he'd begun her training in the love arts. Since the first time he drove her to a climax that left her shivering, she'd seen him as nothing but a very talented and loving male.

"What shall you teach me today?" she asked.

Loric chuckled. "Kiss me," he instructed.

She feigned an indignant look. "You seek to order a priestess of Fion?" she demanded in a fierce whisper.

He captured her mouth and lifted her against the ridge of his cock straining against his trousers then lowered her to the floor, caressing her body through the silin while his mouth plundered hers. She pulled away, nipping at the well of musk at his throat playfully. It was a rare night when he was this close to the edges of control, and it was her duty to calm the fervor a bit.

"This is not a proper lesson," she informed him, winding her hands in his shoulder-length hair, the white locks pale even against her winter pallor. "You have done nothing new."

"So impatient," he chided her. He pulled her hands above her head and held them in the grip of one of his.

Deliya looked at him in confusion and concern. "What is this?"

"When you take your challenge," he hinted.

She nodded, still confused. What did this have to do with her challenge?

"Learn the beauty of not touching."

Her heart raced. She nodded her encouragement.

Loric lowered his head, kissing her as he dragged

her robes to a point high on her chest. He moved lower, suckling her breasts.

It was maddening. She wasn't sure how anyone survived the challenge, let alone why some of the men agreed to this torture more than once in their lives. She moved beneath him, needing what she couldn't have.

"Loric," she pleaded.

"Silence," he whispered.

"I am allowed to speak," she reminded him indignantly. Even in challenge, she would be allowed to speak.

She bit back a scream of pleasure as his fingers breached her. That would not be a part of the challenge, she reminded herself.

No. The challenge will be worse. Loric was testing her resolve.

Deliya met his eyes, defying his test, as he stroked her inside and out, coaxing her toward a climax. Just as her internal muscles started the first flutterings of her coming release, he withdrew. She glared at him, swallowing the cry of frustration he had no doubt hoped to wring from her.

Loric chuckled, licking her essence from his fingertips, his eyes bright and playful. He moved his attention from her face to her core, licking his lips slowly.

She shivered in anticipation then smiled smugly. "And how will you hold me?" she inquired.

He raised an eyebrow at the insinuation that he could not then pulled the cord from his silin pants with a look of pure triumph. He bound her hands then wound the cord around the leg of her Aster wood worktable. Heavy as soft stone, it would not be moved by less than two strong men. The table had been constructed inside her sanctuary rather than carried in whole. He knotted the cord to finish the job.

His hand rested between her thighs, stroking slowly. Deliya tipped her hips to his touch, craving release.

"Soon," he promised.

He stroked both hands down her body, using the silin trapped beneath her to tease and excite her further. When he thrust his tongue into her, she shattered, grinding her teeth to hold back the sweet sounds of her climax.

Hearing her wouldn't disturb Vela and Celdin; they would know what was going on. Loric had to inform them of Deliya's agreement before training began, after all. But, this *was* training, and Deliya was practiced enough to meet the challenge. Loveplay was time to vent her pleasure, but Loric had made it clear that he was training her in earnest this time. That meant silence in pleasure and pain.

He settled back on his heels, pumping his length. Deliya had watched while he handled his own release many times. As much as she liked driving his body as he drove hers, she couldn't deny that she liked to watch him pleasure himself as well.

He closed his eyes, his muscles tensing. "Would you like to learn something new?" he offered.

"Yes," she pleaded. "Will you teach me to pleasure you?"

Females weren't typically trained to take a male orally to climax. It was too intimate and led to uncontrolled drive in an unchallenged female. That was a pleasure for after the challenge, but he had introduced her to other pleasures—not restricted pleasures but ones that were frowned upon during training, claiming his wish that she succeed whatever he might do to fail her.

If Vela knew he did it, she gave no sign of it. Perhaps all priestesses learned them in seeming secret, but Deliya wouldn't risk losing so precious a gift or advantage by revealing the fact to Vela in trust that it was true.

He shivered at her offer. "No. Not this time."

She nodded. "What then?"

Loric took a flask down from her table and returned it almost as quickly, hiding the colors and size that would tell her its contents. He rubbed the oil over his length, grimacing as he did so, then laid his body over hers, his cock brushing her core.

She stiffened, her breathing strangled as his meaning became clear—as the smell of the Dolgen oil assaulted her. "No," she pleaded, scanning the intact circle. If Loric took her here, now, she'd be tied to him. "You cannot do this. My training has pushed you too far."

He captured her lips. "You are my mate," he assured her. "I would never harm you." He kissed her again. "You are ready to meet Fion's challenge."

Deliya couldn't breathe. This wasn't the challenge. He wouldn't dare! If he did this—if he proceeded without the proper ritual, he'd be an outcast. He'd bring down Fion's displeasure on himself. He'd never be able to mate with one of their own, not Deliya or any other priestess, not even with a dishonored woman.

She shook her head, stumbling over her plea to him. He was insane. She could help him, but not if he persisted. If he took her this way, against the traditions, she could not save him.

Loric smiled. "Do not fear. You know what you can do to save us both. Take the challenge."

"Take the—" She gasped. He wanted her to accept him willingly, to agree to be his mate, and to do so this way.

"You are my mate," he whispered. "I have waited so long for you. If you turn me away, there is no hope for me."

"Let us do this the proper way—at the proper time," she reasoned, praying he would not force her to this choice.

"If you want me, it is time." His eyes pleaded with her: to accept him, to love him, to defile the ceremony for him.

"Untie me and let me do this as we always have," she bargained. "Now, but according to custom. Please." She could save him if that was their course. There would be repercussions, but her mother had decreed that Deliya was to produce a true heir, and she would not be returning to the sanctuary for her challenge. Loric had confided that to her only days earlier.

Loric paused, abruptly uncertain. Deliya forced one breath then another. He understood. She knew he did. Loric would stop before he crossed the line and completed this bastardized version of the challenge and promise combined.

As it was, the fact that he used Dolgen oil for her challenge would be difficult to explain away, but if they completed the promise after the challenge—If Deliya cut his hands free of the bonds and sealed him to her while Vela stood witness outside her circle, it would be done, and her former mentor wouldn't dare balk her will openly. There was no other course open to them now. The Dolgen oil would steal the last of his tenuous sanity if he were not permitted to release himself properly.

He trained his eyes on her, sad eyes, then touched her cheek gently. "It does not matter now. If you love me, you must accept me. If you do not, I am already dead. We are all dead."

The waiting has driven him mad. "You need help, Loric. Let me help you." She opened her mouth to call for Vela.

Loric's hand muffled the sound. She went still as her abinatine touched her throat. Tears filled her eyes. How could he do this to her? She had loved him her whole life, and he would do this to her?

He pulled his hand away slowly, wiping a tear with the pad of this thumb. "Do not cry, Deliya. I—We have a duty to produce an heir. It is a sacred trust, and we must do our duty. I have always loved you."

"Then do not do this," she begged of him, willing her lip not to tremble.

Again he hesitated. The blade left her throat. Loric forced one of her fists open and pierced her thumb then his own. "I am bound to you in this life and the next, the father of your heirs, the seed to your soil. You are the missing half of my heart."

Deliya shook in stunned dismay, as he pressed his hand to hers and mixed their blood. She'd dreamed of making the promise with him many times, but not this way.

"Let me do this the right way," she insisted. "Please, Loric. Let me appease Fion for us both."

"No. You will leave me."

"I will not. You have my vow."

"We are bound, blood to blood and heart to heart. I vow to walk with you in this life and meet you in the soul's reward. I will not allow you to come to harm while I can prevent it." Loric planted his hands on the floor above her shoulders. "I will not touch you for the challenge," he promised.

He moved his hand next to her cheek, the blade lying on her shoulder, perhaps in warning.

"Loric," she demanded. "Do not do this. As your priestess—"

He kissed her gently. "I have no choice. It is our last hope."

Deliya shook her head in denial. She would not have thought Loric was capable of this. He would defile her circle, defile her. If she allowed this without a fight, she would be as guilty as he. If she fought, she would die by her own blade.

I am a priestess of Fion. I am no coward. "I will not submit," she informed him, her voice a choked whisper. *Do not make me do this to you. Do not make me testify to your dishonor.*

"If you have any love for me, you must." He seated his cock inside her entrance, meeting her eyes with a mad look of decision. "I will anoint you after your challenge," he assured her.

Deliya screamed, a full-throated sound of terror that seemed to go on long after her lungs started to ache in protest. Loric startled; his expression changed to confusion then realization. Deliya gasped as he pushed away, her blade slicing deep into her chin.

In the abrupt silence, Loric looked at her stained blade in dismay. He used the edge of her green overmantle to staunch the flow of blood coursing down her throat. She shied from his touch.

He winced. "I never meant..." he stammered. "The Merciful Mother help me, I—" He looked up as Celdin burst through the door, paling as his situation became clear to him.

Her father's eyes panned over Deliya: bound, bleeding, her cheeks tear-stained, and her legs spread wide around Loric. He barely breathed as he took in Loric: holding Deliya's blade, the length and his hands stained with her blood, and his pants half off.

Vela pushed in behind Celdin. Deliya met her mentor's eyes and sobbed in relief. Vela would set everything right. Loric hadn't gone too far.

Deliya never learned if it was her sob that broke Celdin's control. One moment, he was frozen in shock with his sword in hand. The next, he pounded across the stone toward them, sword swinging in a deadly arc.

"No," Vela screamed. "Do not kill him."

But, her order came too late. Deliya screamed again as Loric fell over her. She screamed in fear, but she also screamed in frustration that she hadn't kept her head long enough to save his life.

Loric smiled weakly and touched her cheek with fingers coated in blood. Whether it was his blood or hers was immaterial. Fresh tears escaped Deliya's eyes. She shook her head. He couldn't die.

Celdin dragged him off of her, and Deliya shook with sobs at the sight of him. Bile rose in her throat. There was no way to save Loric. The blow had laid the muscles of his chest open, baring two ribs, one clearly splintered. Already, he had surrendered consciousness to blood loss. He would be dead in minutes. She looked after them, as Celdin dragged her dying lover from her sanctuary.

Vela cut the cord that tethered Deliya to the table and tipped her chin up to check the gash. She sighed in relief. She grasped Deliya's hand then examined the cut on her thumb. "Did he complete the ceremony?" she asked urgently.

"No. I could not let...The law," she forced out through chattering teeth.

Vela's expression grew grimmer. She nodded. "Be still now," she soothed. "I will make it right."

Deliya shivered from shock and the chill air washing through the open door over the blood-soaked robes plastered to her body. Vela nodded again and started to cut them away, tossing ruined fabric into the flames in the pit.

Celdin returned, edging toward her. "It is over."

Deliya's breathing hitched. "No," she pleaded.

"Get out," Vela snapped at him.

He looked at her in surprise. "Deliya..." he began.

"You have sullied her with innocent blood. You have crossed onto consecrated ground and killed within its boundaries." Vela met his eyes. "You have taken the one who should have been Deliya's mate from her."

Celdin paled. He looked toward the door, seeming to stagger with the realization that Loric was dead. He reached for Deliya, a stricken look on his face. "The Mother's plan," he breathed.

Vela slapped his hand away. "Out," she ordered. "Do not sully her further. You have done more than enough damage."

She threw her herbal into the fire bitterly, the last of the Zura in the dried stores. It would be summer before Deliya would be able to brew the medicinal that made her existence tolerable again. But, Vela was proud. She believed Deliya's healing tainted by the death in the circle. She would not drink the herbal now, even if she knew Len waited in the shadows to steal her soul.

Celdin bowed his head and turned away, looking tortured. Vela's refusal of her herbal was not lost on him. Nor was the implication. If the priestess did not survive the spring, she would blame him. He started toward the door, his step slow and shoulders hunched in defeat.

Deliya reached for him. "Celdin," she whispered. She tried to pull the Len-be-damned bonds from her hands, wincing as the cord cut into her wrists. "Father," she cried out desperately. She hadn't wanted him to hold her since her temple training began when she was ten. She needed a father's comfort now.

He paused, looking back at her hopefully.

"Go," Vela shouted in fury.

"No," Deliya pleaded. "Stay with me."

Celdin dropped his gaze. "I am sorry, Priestess. Vela must tend to you now."

She stopped fighting the bonds. He was walking away from her. He had called her "Priestess," not "Deliya" or "Daughter."

"I will make things right," Vela assured her, cutting away the last of her clothing and moving on to the silin tie that bound her wrists.

Celdin shut the door without looking back at them. Vela wasted no time, taking down the brush and scattering the broken circle in readiness to make one anew.

"No," Deliya whispered. *Nothing will be the same.*

Chapter Six

Ro snapped awake as Deliya yanked at her bonds, wrenching his arm in the process. His irritation melted into concern, as she sobbed.

"Celdin," she whispered. "Father, no. Stay with me."

He winced, imagining what it must have been like for her when her father died. Celdin had been the last of her protectors. She'd tilled his ashes in the newly thawed soil with her own two hands. The pain in her eyes when she spoke of his lingering illness had been heartbreaking, and he wondered how a healer like Deliya would come to terms with not being able to save not one but two of her protectors with her vast skill in healing. The last, at least, wasn't her concern or responsibility. She had said that Celdin killed the guard, and that he was justified in doing so.

Ro pulled her against him in an effort to comfort her. She wasn't alone anymore. She needn't be alone ever again.

Deliya screamed, pulling at her bindings more forcefully. Ro startled, clasping her hands in the darkness to keep her from injuring herself. The result was disconcerting.

She threw her head back and forth, her thick hair tangling in his as she fought his grip. "Do not do this," she sobbed. "Loric, please..."

Ro searched his memory frantically. Loric was the one her father had killed.

"The proper way," she mumbled. "The proper time. Do not do this."

He ran his free hand in soothing circles over her back. "Deliya," he called softly, trying to break her from her dream.

Her voice went cold and sharp as a blade. "I will not submit."

Ro shuddered with a sudden chill. His mind worked over everything she'd said in the last few days. Celdin had broken with their traditions, crossed into her circle and killed within. Killed with cause.

'I will not submit.'

The truth seared him. Fion's Children did not abandon their traditions lightly. If her father did so, he did it because Loric's crime had been of the worst sort.

Oh, Leiana. Even sending your daughter away didn't save her the indignities you hoped to.

A vision of a young male of her race...

"No," he breathed, pushing the image away before it could fully form. He tightened his grip on her reflexively, as if he could protect her from that long-ago trauma.

Deliya screamed, an ear-splitting shriek, panicked, terrified, pulling frantically at her bound hands and intent on escape. She thrashed against him, her movements more purposeful as she woke. She fought his hold, twisting and arching her body violently.

"Deliya," he commanded. "Stop this. I will not harm you."

"Untie me," she pleaded. "Please, release me. I cannot..." She crumpled, sobbing.

He fumbled at the knots, desperate to free her. When the ropes slid off her hands, she scrambled away. Ro followed, afraid she would injure herself. She stumbled out of the cave, landing on her hands and knees, sucking in the icy mountain air, her entire body trembling. He touched her with caution, afraid she would bolt again.

"I am sorry," she breathed. "I gave my word."

"Your word?"

"The ropes. I gave my word," she explained miserably.

Ro eased her onto his lap, tangling his fingers in her half-undone braid and pressing her cheek to his chest. "Your penalty is ended," he assured her. *Had I known, I never would have bound her.*

She nodded.

"How old—" He took a calming breath. "It is not my place to ask," he decided bitterly.

"I was eighteen," she whispered.

Ro grimaced. She hadn't even been an adult when he—

"Loric was twenty-two. He was...He should have been..."

"Your mate?" he guessed.

"Yes. I think he realized it was wrong before he died. He was sane for a moment, lucid. When he traveled to Rintal on my birthday, he must have learned the truth. He must have known that my mother...that everyone else was dead. I was all he had left, myself and the children we would have had." Deliya stroked at her scar distractedly.

"He did that?" Ro growled. "He put a blade to your throat?"

She didn't answer him. Instead, she buried her face in his neck, shivering from her memories—or in the frigid air; Ro couldn't be sure which.

"Would you allow me to take you inside?" he asked. "You are shivering, and there are quilts."

She nodded.

Ro eased them both inside the cave and wrapped the quilts around their intertwined bodies. There were so many questions he wanted to ask, but Deliya wasn't in any condition to answer them. He shook himself mentally. Did he have any right to question her, even when she was?

* * * *

Ro came up off the empty quilts in a panic, scrambling out into the clearing, his heart pounding. He took a calming breath, thanking Mag that Deliya hadn't run from him again. She knelt beneath a tree, a body length from the stream.

She looked up from a small wooden bowl with a paste of her ground herbs in it, blushing. "I made a curative for your wrist." She stared into the bowl, stirring the tan mixture. "Would you allow me to use it?"

He looked at the wrist he'd taken the rope from in confusion. It was lightly bruised. She was worried about that? He knelt beside her and offered his arm, reluctant to offend her by refusing her healing, though he hardly felt it necessary to treat something so minor.

Deliya didn't meet his eyes. She smoothed the cool paste onto his wrist, her touch hesitant, as if she were afraid to lay hands on him. When his skin was coated, she set the bowl aside and pushed her tunic sleeves up her arms to treat herself.

Ro winced at the deep bruises marring her pale skin and cradled her wrist up to his lips. Deliya looked at him in shock, as he started healing her. She shook her head, yanking her arm away and clutching it to her

80

chest.

"Let me heal you," he insisted.

She shook her head, trembling. "You should not—"

"Your Goddess holds some grudge against the healing magic?" he asked, knowing She did not. It was only her priestess's stubborn independence that made her unwilling to accept his aid.

Deliya opened her mouth as if to speak then blanched and shook her head.

"Men have been given the ability to safeguard their women and children," he offered logically, ignoring the obvious counter-argument that it was the opposite in her culture.

"Men have been given the ability so as to ease children from a woman. It is a sacred trust and nothing more."

"If that was the only reason, it would not close gashes and help knit broken bones," he argued.

"A woman can—"

"A birth correctly handled includes none of that."

Deliya flushed. "You are right. It should not, but there are rare occurrences when the babe will not pass without tearing or breaking bones. A few children must be surgically taken."

Ro shivered at that. "Still, it would be an affront to the gods to ignore all but one of the benefits of their gifts."

She closed her eyes. "You may heal me," she whispered.

He brought her wrist to his mouth, healing the bruises slowly, savoring her skin under his lips. Deliya watched him, barely breathing. When he finished, he laid a kiss in her palm.

Deliya let go a shaky breath. "Thank you."

Her voice wavered, and she grimaced. Ro tried to meet her eyes, but she looked away.

"I know why you cannot trust me," he assured her. "But I am not like Loric. I will not force you."

Her eyes met his as if in challenge. "It has nothing to do with that," she denied. "Loric presumed too much in his madness. He used my training to try to trick me, to fill his sense of loss."

"Because he knew you were the last two capable of producing more of your race?"

Deliya stood and ambled to the stream, crouching to rinse her bowl in the running water.

Ro followed, watching the tension in her jaw uneasily. "Deliya?"

"Do Magden men ever create life with someone other than a true mate?" she asked.

"Occasionally."

"What happens?"

"Happens?" he asked, confused. "What typically happens when a child is created?"

"Does the child belong to him? Heirs belong to their fathers in Magden law, do they not?"

"Only if the couple contract," he explained. "Unless...Well, there are some cases where the man can demand a contract, but only if certain conditions are met. It is quite complex."

"And, if there is no contract? If they are not true mates?"

He furrowed his brow. "He has no hold over her or her child. If there is no contract, the child is hers alone by law."

"Do you think they miss those children? Mourn for

them if they are lost?" she asked sadly.

"The men who fathered them?"

She turned to look up at him and nodded, a strained smile on her face.

"I imagine many of them do. Some men are simply shortsighted in not demanding their rights immediately. If the mother of his child refuses him later, there is no recourse for him."

"I thought that might be so," she decided miserably.

"Deliya?"

"Loric had fathered two children by other priestesses before we fled."

"He wanted to replace the children he lost?" It sounded like something that could drive a man to madness.

"By our laws, they were never truly his children. He could watch them grow and take pride in how strong and bold they were, but they were not his to claim."

"Because there was no contract," he decided.

"Because he was male. My mother sent me with my father. It was unheard of, Ro. We always know who sired us, but Celdin was my lesser from the day I started my training. I loved him, but I owed him nothing more than the courtesy shown the mate of Mother Leiana. Had they not been true mates, I would not have owed him that much.

"Still, he loved me, despite the fact that he could never claim me openly as his. Perhaps Loric loved his children as well. It was not unusual to see males playing with children when the work was done. It would take a fool not to see that they played most often with those they sired. Perhaps...Oh, what does it matter? He wanted to know his child grew in my womb; that much was clear."

Ro considered her culture uneasily. "He was not your equal. What of me?"

She blushed. "You are not one of Fion's Children. You are a Magden king. I suppose...you are my equal."

"But, Fion's priestesses do not choose an equal as a mate," he reasoned, unable to keep the bitterness from his tone.

Deliya stood, her expression wary. "Fion's Priestess takes none but another of Fion's Children as mate."

"That would seem a little difficult, Priestess." Her rejection stung.

"Loric was right," she whispered. "I killed us all."

Before Ro could form a response to that, she'd returned to the cave, most likely to don her armor. He groaned. Surely, she didn't think that she was responsible for Loric's attack on her? That was a discussion for a time when she wasn't already on the defensive.

* * * *

Donic was highly displeased when they reached camp; only Ro's warning glare kept his general's comments corked. Deliya pulled away when the man tried to disarm her, shooting Ro an uneasy look.

He nodded. "Leave it, Donic. The priestess will not be armored for sleep any longer, but she is retaining full rights otherwise."

"Ro..." she began.

He scowled at her. "It is within my rights to strip you of your arms and has been since the first time you raised a weapon against me."

She opened her mouth, probably to protest again that her abinatine was not a weapon. He silenced her with a hard look, and she nodded her acceptance.

Donic laughed harshly. "Will she retain her poisons?" he demanded.

"I never poisoned you," Deliya argued. "You undoubtedly woke feeling relaxed and refreshed."

"And, if the Lengar had attacked while we slept?" he asked pointedly.

She paled. "You are correct, of course, and you have my apologies for it. I had not considered that possibility in a group as large as this and in Magden lands."

"Ro," he growled. "You cannot chance—"

Ro shook his head. "The priestess will not be cooking for us again. She will have no opportunity to use her herbs to drug us."

Deliya grasped her packs and stormed into the camp.

"No further than my pavilion," he ordered.

She shot him a look of pure fury.

Donic watched her go, suspicion etched on his face. "That one will kill you if she has the chance," he growled.

Ro smiled. "No. That one will be my greatest challenge."

"Challenge? Ro, bedding that female would be like bedding a jaglin in heat."

"I do not question that it would, but I doubt she means to let that happen."

"Then what?"

"Peace first. Once we have established that, I will pursue any opening she gives me."

* * * *

Deliya stared at Ro across the fire. She moved her eyes to the pallet they would soon share. He insisted that it was the only way to protect her from his men. She wondered who would protect her from herself.

Ro stood, crossing to her and offering his hand.

She stared at it for a moment. "I think I will sit up a while longer," she decided.

"We have a long ride."

She met his eyes in challenge. "You think to order one of Fion's priestesses?" she countered, praying that the threat worked better on Ro than it typically had on Loric. "You think I am a babe who needs a keeper?"

"I think I will tie you to my bed, if you balk me much more."

Donic laughed heartily but, surprisingly, made no comment.

Deliya swallowed hard, her body and mind playing traitor. Visions of Ro lying over her again assaulted her, his cock cradled in the apex of her sex and her arms held down in his larger hand. She took a sharp breath as her body responded—and drew in more of his scent. *That is not helping matters.*

Ro nodded and crooked his fingers, demanding her hand. "Now."

She surrendered and followed him into his pavilion, pulling free and removing her armor before he could offer to help. She was certain she wouldn't survive that.

He had removed his armor after they ate; she went still when the sound of his boots hitting dirt was followed by the slide of material. A traitorous supposition of just how much of his clothing he intended to remove assaulted her. She didn't look. It would be better not to see him further unclothed than she already had. She heard the pallet shift and shivered, knowing that he waited patiently for her to join him. She muttered a silent prayer that he wasn't as the gods formed him when she joined him on the pallet.

Her hands trembled as she removed the last of her armor, leaving the simple woven tunic and trousers beneath. She longed for the days when she slept in a long tunic—or unclothed, but she would not encourage Ro, even if it meant discomfort as she slept. For a moment, she stood with her back to him, feeling his gaze like a caress, her body already in a riot for him though he hadn't touched her.

Oh, Mother Fion! Has my training been that remiss?

Deliya turned, her mouth going dry at the sight of him. With nothing in the pavilion but a roll of clothing, stacks of armor and weapons, and the pallet, there was little choice of where her gaze would settle; but once it had, there was no looking away.

Ro was stretched out with the quilts pooled at his hips, his tunic off and his hair unbound. The muscles of his abdomen were outlined in the moonlight and firelight streaming past the flap. She took a moment to memorize the sight.

"Come to bed, Deliya," he ordered. His expression was fierce and unwavering.

She nodded, sinking to the pallet beside him. Though the quilts were always aired before evening came, they still held the pungent but enticing perfume of their mixed musk. In addition, his fire was banked with Eir wood as usual; the sweet, soothing smoke lulled them to sleep more effectively than any sleeping potion but Garigol or Lizor stem would.

He shifted; she tensed, expecting a sexual advance she would have a difficult time convincing herself not to accept.

He chuckled, as if he knew her mind. "I gave my word, Deliya. You have nothing to fear from me."

"I do not fear you," she denied, asking Fion's forgiveness for the untruth.

"Liar. You said Fion does not care for lies any more than Mag does. Should I take a penalty?"

"You unnerve me," she asserted. "It is not the same thing."

"I apologize."

"As well you should."

"Why did you not return home when Celdin died?"

Deliya shifted nervously. "I was ordered not to. The chance of being taken alone—"

"You did not think your mother would want to know?"

"If she did not want me to chance returning to choose another..." She sighed. "But, that was a lie as well," she noted wryly.

"Tell me about your guards," he requested.

"Why?" she asked suspiciously.

"You mention them so often. Tell me about them. I want to know them. Perhaps if I see how much they cared for you, I might appreciate how they could lie to you to keep you from the pain of the truth."

"Vela was my mentor, the oldest female of my line. She trained me as a priestess and continued my training as a warrior after we left my mother."

"She was your grandmother?"

"My grandmother's mother. The Mother before Leiana and Turila."

Ro nodded, turning toward her to meet her gaze fully. "Go on."

"She was a strict teacher, a hard taskmistress, but she trained me well. As well as one so old could train a headstrong, proud young priestess. I owe her many prayers of thanks, more than I can count.

"Celdin always smiled, except in battle. He was always ready with a joke or story to pass the time." *Until he killed Loric.* "He trained me for battle when Vela became too old to swing a sword. He trained me to run a farm. He was a strong man."

"And protective?" Ro suggested.

"Yes. That is why my mother entrusted me to his care. If she had not believed in his commitment, Leiana would never have trusted him with my safety.

"Leiana knew when she sent Celdin away that she would likely never see him again, but she sent him. I pretended not to notice her anguish. I still wonder whether she sent him away because he was the most dedicated guard for me or to save his life, so that she would not see him fall in battle. A priestess will give her life for her family, as Leiana did."

Ro leaned up on his elbow, looking down at her. "Tell me about Loric."

Her stomach clenched. "Why?"

His eyes narrowed, a clear warning that he would not be denied. "I wish to know."

"He was...Loric was four years my senior. When my mother sent us away, he was like the older brother Fion never granted me. He played at being a guard. He acted the part of a man, though he was a half-trained boy."

Ro nodded. "Go on. What did he train you in?"

Deliya took a calming breath, looking toward the pavilion flap and the flames beyond. Donic had retreated to the flap of his own pavilion and sat, sharpening his sword. That was good. She had no intentions of discussing Loric with the general within earshot.

"The love arts," she admitted.

"And?"

"He was a most diligent teacher. Loric feared Vela; she terrified him. When he asked to train me...Loric waited a full year past the usual time out of fear of informing Vela that he would be coming to my bed. I imagine he was desperate for a woman's touch by then. He hadn't taken another in almost four years, and knowing that he could touch me if I accepted him...Loric knew me better than anyone."

Ro turned her face back to him. "And, he used what he knew against you."

She didn't deny it. She'd lied once that night. Once was more than enough.

"What 'proper time' were you waiting for?"

Deliya grimaced. "We...There is a tradition. I would have been legally an adult at the spring celebration. Loric did not want to wait. I had reached the anniversary of my birth. He wanted to become my true mate."

"But, you had already—"

She shook her head. "Never with the possibility of conceiving a child together. A woman may not until she is legally an adult."

"Did you love him?"

"Yes. I did." She said it simply and without

hesitation.

Ro uttered a harsh curse and dropped to his back. "He knew you did."

Deliya found it hard to breathe. "I should not have let it go on," she managed hoarsely.

"Loving him?" Ro asked in surprise.

"His—attitude. Loric did not act like he should have. He was too familiar, too flippant, too aggressive and dominant."

"You disliked that?" he asked in a tone that said he knew better.

Deliya turned away. Ro did know better, and that reminder hurt.

He wrapped an arm around her waist and pressed his chest to her back. She waited for a comment that would light the pyre under her carefully constructed lies. Ro didn't offer any comments. He didn't touch her sexually.

"Thank you," she whispered.

"You could not have known that Loric had changed. Sleep well, Deliya."

She closed her eyes, certain she could not sleep, but Ro's arms soothed her into peaceful dreams.

CHAPTER SEVEN

Caj 12ᵗʰ, Ti 10-459

Deliya smiled, as Novin approached the small clearing she'd found to take her rest in. They'd been riding since a little after sunrise and—even at less than a loping pace—had covered nearly forty stride. They would rest for a few hours as they did every day when the sun was at its zenith then set off again at a more leisurely pace.

It was a beautiful spot, full of flowering and fruit-bearing trees and sweet herbs grown wild. She couldn't have chosen a better place to relax if she'd tried.

Novin bowed from the edge of the trees. "May I enter?" he asked reverently.

Of all Ro's men, he showed the most respect for her beliefs. He kept his eyes downcast until invited to meet her gaze and didn't gape as many did. Though few soldiers dared approach her directly, Novin was the only one who stopped at a safe distance and asked if she had consecrated ground to be wary of before approaching.

She chuckled. "You may. I have drawn no circle."

He ambled to her, his tan armor gleaming in the midday sun. He handed her meat and fruit set on a thick slab of sweet bread.

She nodded her thanks. Ro had sent him out to make sure she ate—and more. Deliya sighed, as he sank to the grass next to her.

"He sent you to guard me," she noted in exasperation.

"Ro?" Novin asked, feigning innocence.

92

Deliya glared at him, rolling her eyes as he blushed. She took a bite of the meat and closed her eyes in pleasure. Ro's cook was a wonder. She swore the man could make Gelgrin from Eir bark and lizor stems.

Novin sighed. "It is not that he does not trust you, Priestess."

"I know. Ro believes I am one of your helpless women," she grumbled.

"He worries about you."

"Ro is possessive," she stated calmly. "He has no right to be."

"Would Ro make such a horrible husband?" Novin asked with honest curiosity. "I can tell you truthfully and on Mag's name that he has never shown as much interest in a woman as he has in you."

Deliya's heart stuttered at that. Len had tortured her nightly since Ro's first kiss. Her sanity would not handle the weight of his unwavering attention. "He is not one of Fion's Children, Novin. Interested or not, Ro is not a mate my vows allow me to take."

Novin winced. "He will not be happy to hear that."

"He has heard it. He chooses not to listen. I cannot remedy that." She took another bite of the huge portion of meat, praying that he would not pursue the topic.

She froze at the sound of a growl from behind them; she didn't need the scent that would soon carry to them to recognize a jaglin. *The Mother answers prayers in her own way,* she reminded herself.

Deliya grasped Novin's wrist as he reached for his sword. "Be still. There is no need for your weapon."

He shot her a look of pure fear, and she patted his hand in reassurance. She reached into the pouch at her hip, removing several bags of herbs slowly, herbs every priestess carried for moments like this. She opened the small bag of lizor and poured it over the remaining meat, massaging it in with her fingertips.

Novin stiffened at a closer, rumbling growl. The jaglin was stalking them, confirming Deliya's suspicions. She added olum to the meat hurriedly. There was little time left.

"I must..." Novin whispered.

"Be still," she breathed. "Do not provoke the beast."

Deliya tossed the meat over her shoulder, listening for the sounds of the jaglin eating. She breathed a sigh of relief as the great cat devoured the offering. As she supposed, the beast was desperate enough to eat it, herbs and all.

She turned to her hands and knees slowly, returning the last of the olum to her pouch and removing the Garigol sprigs. Novin grasped her arm, shaking his head adamantly.

"It is not enough," she informed him. "I have done this before." *Once.* There was no use in frightening him. The jaglin needed her help. Deliya smiled. "Trust me."

Novin pulled his hand away, grimacing as if he were in pain. "Ro will kill me for this," he grumbled.

She scowled. "Ro has no right."

She crawled toward the jaglin. It was a young female with nursing young. She was injured, no doubt. A jaglin would not consider people as prey unless it came upon a child unguarded or was unable to hunt and starving. Deliya hoped she could save the mother, or the babes would die with the adult.

She advanced slowly, keeping her head up and shoulders tensed. She didn't blink, locking her eyes on the beast's. The jaglin would recognize this as the stance of a high-ranked female. Hopefully, the olum and lizor would confuse her enough that she would accept a person imitating the motions.

The jaglin shook her head, dazed by the olum and lizor entering her bloodstream via her tongue. It was time. Deliya opened the airtight container of Garigol, and the jaglin's head came up again. She scented the air and bared her sharp teeth.

Deliya tossed the container to the beast. The jaglin attacked the Garigol, drawn by the fragrance as they always were. The herb worked as an anesthetic on all forms of life, but only a jaglin would eat it into unconsciousness.

Novin drew his sword, rising to his knees with a look somewhere between fear and fury on his face. Deliya motioned him back. The jaglin was reacting as expected.

The vixen weaved on her feet then slumped to the ground. Deliya moved to her side, searching for the injury.

"Let me," Novin spoke from behind her.

Deliya looked up at his raised sword in dismay. "No," she gasped.

"It is a dangerous animal, Priestess, but its pelt would make you a fine—"

"No. She has young, and jaglin serve a purpose, Novin. They hunt animals who threaten crops." She went back to looking for an injury.

"What are you doing?"

"Healing her...if I can. She has young," she explained. "If I lose her, we will lose her entire litter. At this time of year, they cannot yet be capable of surviving without her."

"You went to all this trouble to heal a jaglin?"

"Of course." Deliya smiled as she found the thorn in the female's rear hip. It was a large one from a Garigol tree. "And still you insist on ingesting it," she teased the great beast.

The thorn was buried deep in the hip muscle, rendering the vixen unable to crouch or run without driving it further into the joint.

"There," she crooned. She grasped the thorn and eased it free.

The jaglin roared, swiping at her armored chest. Deliya ducked the blow, shaking off Novin, when he grasped her shoulder and raised the damned sword again.

"Kneel," she ordered in a low voice. "Sword down. She fears you."

"Fears *me*," Novin growled dangerously. "A jaglin fears me." Still, he dropped to his knees and lowered the sword.

Deliya ignored his complaints, examining the jaglin's wound gingerly. There was no sign of infection and no pronounced swelling. That was good. She would heal quickly and be hunting again within days.

The jaglin made a rumbling sound of happiness and nuzzled Deliya's face in thanks. Her tongue rasped over Deliya's cheek, and she wrapped her forelegs around Deliya's torso. Deliya laughed in delight.

* * * *

Ro sprinted from the fireside at the sound of the jaglin's roar. He muttered harsh curses as he raced into the trees in the direction Deliya and Novin had taken.

Men crashed along behind him, loyal men willing to take on a jaglin with only a sword in hand, if their king's life depended on it. If Deliya were in danger, his life would depend on it.

He came to an abrupt halt as he breached the edge of the clearing. Deliya sat, trapped in the jaglin's grasp, the beast face to face with her.

He looked at Novin. The young man knelt behind Deliya, his eyes wild, motioning frantically beneath the jaglin's field of vision for him to kneel and be still. Ro did so, motioning for his men to do likewise, as they emerged from the trees.

Donic leaned close, his breathing rough. "What is this?" he asked.

"It...The beast is playing with her like a tamed wariken, cleaning her face."

"More like a kittle," Donic noted in a stunned voice.

As if proving him correct, the jaglin rubbed its huge head around both sides of Deliya's face. She laughed a light, lilting laugh and wrapped her arms around the beast's neck. A murmur started among Ro's men, and he stilled it with a sharp look.

The jaglin lay back, pulling Deliya atop it. She smiled, scrubbing her hands in the thick, black fur and crooning as if to a babe. Ro tensed as the creature rolled away to crouch over her. He tightened his jaw in fury as Deliya laughed harder, encouraging the beast. Visions of her beneath him—smiling and laughing, her color high and her hands stroking his body as she stroked the jaglin's fur—made him ache in wanting her.

The jaglin looked in Ro's direction and its demeanor changed. The beast's muscles tensed; and it roared, pushing Deliya hard to the grass. Deliya looked up, paling as she took in the line of soldiers. She turned to Novin, shaking lightly and speaking low. He grimaced and motioned the men back.

Donic snorted. "She cannot be serious," he protested.

"Pull back, Donic. You and the rest. Stay low. We do not want to startle the beast while it has her."

"You have gone insane."

"Now," Ro growled.

Donic obeyed, retreating deep into the trees with the other men. The jaglin watched them warily then met Ro's eyes in challenge. He knelt, still and stiff, his eyes locked on the beast's.

Deliya stroked the fur under the jaglin's chin, speaking words he couldn't hear. The beast moved cautiously, placing itself between her and its perceived enemies, teeth bared and muscles taut.

Ro held his breath, as Deliya eased onto her knees. She wrapped her hands in the beast's shoulder fur and tugged. The jaglin turned with her; and Deliya patted its haunch, sending it off into the trees.

Novin let out an explosive breath and collapsed to his back, rubbing a shaking hand over his sweat-soaked face. "Dear Mag," he groaned. "I thought you were as good as dead."

Ro vaulted to his feet and stormed to Deliya, dragging her to her feet and running his fingers over the claw marks in her leather plate. "And whose fault would that have been, Novin?" he asked pointedly.

Deliya tried to pull from his grasp. "Were it not for the interference of you and your men—" she shouted.

Ro dropped his face to hers, stilling as she gasped in surprise, his lips a few finger widths from his goal.

She shook her head, her eyes wide.

No. He couldn't do that to her. No matter how much he wanted to stake a claim she couldn't deny, she wasn't a Magden woman and would not appreciate such a spectacle in front of his men, even if she would respond favorably in the heat of the moment. He nuzzled her cheek, smelling the jaglin's scent on her.

"You want to stop my heart in fear," he whispered, too low for even Novin to hear.

"No," she denied.

He nuzzled her face again, hardening as her rising musk mixed with the smell of the jaglin, announcing her arousal clearly. "Do not frighten me like that again," he ordered.

Deliya shook her head. "You have...You have my word."

Ro smiled at her expression of heavy-lidded passion. She had never been one for hiding her emotions well.

"If you do, there will be a penalty."

Her eyes snapped wide open. "No. No penalties," she breathed.

Ro nodded, releasing her. "Then you will not tame jaglin again—or anything else dangerous."

"I..." Her face darkened; she turned, striding for the woods with her back straight and chin up.

Ro glared at Novin as the young man chuckled. He laid back on the grass with his arms crossed under his head. As always, he bounced back from every threat as if he had never been endangered.

"You are not free of my wrath yet," Ro warned him. "It is one thing to be foolhardy with yourself, as you seem to love to do. It is another to be foolhardy with one you are charged with protecting."

Novin sobered. "She is amazing, Ro, but I fear you hope for what is not to be."

"What do you mean?"

"The Priestess walks closely with her goddess."

"She is a woman with a woman's hungers." And a Keen woman's hungers far outweighed those of the men. In a highly sexual people, that was saying a lot. "I see it and smell it on her every time she is in my arms."

Novin sighed harshly. "She has taken vows to her goddess. If the Priestess must choose between her goddess and you, I would not wager highly on your success, Ro. Fion's priestesses are trained to obey and to serve. Is there room for more in her life?"

Ro nodded, though with a cold spike in his stomach at that thought. If Deliya had truly taken vows, there was no hope. Her goddess was all that was left of her culture. Deliya would not release that without a fight to the death, and he could not steal her last ties to her heritage from her.

CHAPTER EIGHT

Caj 20th, Ti 10-459
The Stronghold at Aiten, Magden Republic

Deliya looked at the great gates of Ro's home fearfully, pulling her buck to a stop.

Ro grasped her bridle and tugged her forward gently. "The gates and walls are there for your safety," he reminded her.

She nodded sheepishly and urged her mount forward, a subtle hint for Ro to release her. Thankfully, he did.

They dismounted at the doors, and Ro ordered men to care for their bucks and her mares, tethered behind Novin's mount. She climbed the wide stone stairs with Ro a step behind her. Her cheeks grew hot as servants and guards stopped their headlong rush to tend to their king—or speak to him—and stared at her in wide-mouthed wonder. Ro touched the base of her spine as she straightened.

"What is it?" he asked.

"I am an oddity," she noted in what she hoped was a bland voice.

"You are a pleasant surprise," he assured her.

"I am nothing of the sort."

Ro motioned to a dark-haired woman little more than Deliya's age who bowed deeply to her. "Deliya, this is Laril. She will serve you."

"I require no servants," Deliya informed him, stifling the urge to remind Ro that she was not one of his pampered Magden women. "A place to bathe will be sufficient."

He nodded. "Laril, show Mother Deliya to the room on the third level and arrange for those things that a woman needs."

Deliya opened her mouth to protest the title he assigned her then shut it. She could not argue that it belonged to her, though it held little meaning now. What use was a mother with no children to look after?

"Thank you, Ro."

He touched her cheek fondly, stroking the backs of his fingers along the curve of her jaw. "We will discuss our plans at evening meal," he promised.

"As you wish."

She followed Laril the two levels up a stone staircase and down a richly appointed corridor. She ground her teeth at the unease the opulence aroused in her; Fion's priestesses were unaccustomed to such useless frills. Homes were functional. Even temples were not as ornate as Ro's home. The green stone of the sanctuary and the circle were beautiful, but they served a purpose. Their beauty was a testament to the Mother, as was the tower's strength.

Laril preceded her into a huge room and disappeared through a second doorway. Deliya stopped, all but gaping at the immense bed in dismay. The entire room was decorated in rich fabrics of red and gold, thick carpets and furniture as would befit a Magden king. She prayed fervently that her room did not adjoin Ro's—that she would not be required to share his bed any longer. The previous two nights in his arms had nearly stolen her sanity.

She ambled to the bed, touching the footboard and pushing away the image of Ro laying in it, waiting for her to join him. "Whose room is this?" Deliya called to

Laril. "It is not Ro's, of course," she joked weakly.

The woman reappeared, a frown of confusion on her pretty face. "This is your room, Mother Deliya. His Majesty's room is just down the hall."

"My..." Deliya faltered, grasping the footboard as she weaved. This room alone was as large as the home she had left, and there were three doors leading off of it not counting the one that led to the corridor. "A mistake..."

Laril ran to her, steadying her and guiding her to sit on the bed. "Do you require a woman healer?" she asked urgently, but with a puzzling note of excitement that Deliya couldn't interpret.

She paused in her inspection of the furnishings and decoration. "A woman healer? Why would I..." She gasped as Laril's knowing smile sank in. "No," she assured the servant. "I need nothing of the sort." Her cheeks heated at the thought. The servants believed she was warming Ro's—

She groaned. She *was* warming it, but she wasn't warming Ro.

Laril sighed. "A pity. I had hoped his Majesty had chosen a woman, at last."

"Is that what this room is? A place for Ro's women?" Deliya asked, aghast.

Laril smiled and shook her head. "This room was— is intended for his heir, if his Majesty ever graces the house with one."

"I imagine—" Deliya cursed herself for her weakness in caring about Ro's personal life and set to work on her armor as if it were true that she did not care, acting unaffected as she continued. "I imagine Ro has many women in his bed."

Laril laughed heartily. "Schente," she informed Deliya, as if that word explained everything. "His Majesty has never looked kindly on a whole woman before. Until you," she added in a singsong voice as she returned to the other room and started water running.

Deliya paused with one leg unarmored and headed to the bath, unfastening her Cuirass as she walked. "Schente?" she asked.

Laril trailed her fingers in the water to check the temperature and reached to the shelf over the tub. "Implin or Lizor?" she asked.

"Pardon?"

"Your cleansing oil?"

"Oh. Lizor, if you please."

Laril added the oil to the water as Deliya dropped her breastplate to the floor and knelt to uncover her other leg.

"What is a schente?" she asked, reminding Laril of the unanswered question.

The serving woman paused, seeming confused again. "A schente. A sterile female who serves a man sexually for a short period of time."

Deliya furrowed her brow, working on the fastener at her wrist. "Born sterile?" Surely, there weren't many women like that.

"Of course not. Their ovum sacs are taken in the terms of contract."

Deliya sat down abruptly, earning her a look of concern from Laril. "Why?" she asked hopelessly. Why would anyone mar a perfect body that way?

"It is not a bad life," Laril assured her, sitting on the edge of the tub and stirring the water to mix in the cleansing oil. "Women who do not want children and who would rather have a guaranteed life in service than life in a marriage they do not wish—or no husband at all..." She shrugged. "We can still experience sexual bliss."

"Simple climax, yes, but few women feel the second pleasure once their sacs are taken." The rest of Laril's statement filtered in. "You are a schente?" she asked in disbelief. Good Goddess! Why would a woman of such physical appeal and strength choose such a life? Had she no hope of children? Were Magden men blind to what fine heirs such a woman would raise?

"Former schente," Laril qualified. "My sexual service is ended, though I would gladly go back into service for the thrill of..." She blushed deeply and turned her face to the tub, reaching to turn off the flow of water. "I serve as a hostess to his Majesty's guests now. I enjoy my work."

Deliya waved her armored arm hopelessly as she fought to find the words to express her outrage. "Why?" she demanded.

Laril looked up in confusion. "Ro is a kind master, and I enjoy the people I meet. Having you here—"

"No. Why?" she asked again.

"Why what?"

"Why sacrifice the ovum sacs when you could use Walla tea? If the woman changes her mind later, there is no undoing the surgery."

"There is a failure rate with Walla. Is there not?"

"A small percentage," Deliya confirmed. "Perhaps one in several thousand."

"That is why. What king would risk having heirs on a servant?"

Deliya pushed to her feet and stormed to the door,

Laril close at her heels.

"Mother Deliya?" she pleaded. "Have I angered you?"

"Never you, Laril," she promised. *But, Ro! If a priestess can survive nothing but loveplay for three years, surely a Magden king can do likewise.*

The guard at Ro's door looked up in surprise as Deliya marched toward him, moving to intercept her. She struck him soundly across the face and pushed past him into Ro's rooms, as Laril gasped in awe.

* * * *

Ro snapped his head up at the grunt and thump from the hall. Deliya barged in, red faced, with Laril and his guard at her heels. Everyone spoke at once.

"How dare you!"

"Majesty, should I remove—"

"Majesty, I do not know what I said wrong."

"Deliya? What is it?" he asked calmly.

"Schente," Deliya shouted at him, her fists planted on her hips.

"The priestess," the guard's voice rose to be heard over her.

"It seemed innocent enough—"

"Damn you to Len's dungeon's you—"

"Quiet!" Ro roared.

The room fell silent save for Deliya's outraged panting.

"Better," he decided. "Laril, go about your duties. Prill, get that bruise cared for."

Deliya winced.

Ro nodded, as the door shut behind them. "Now,

what is the cause of this?"

"How dare you mutilate and use those women," she stated in controlled fury. Her knuckles were white and her muscles strung tight.

"What women?" he asked, confused.

"The schente, you great red oaf."

Ro rubbed his fingertips over the tension in his forehead. "It has been well over a week since you have called me that," he noted. "I do not mutilate schente."

"No. Of course not. You have your butchers do it for you."

"It is a simple medical procedure that the women choose to have. It has always been this way."

She glared at him.

"The women seek out service. I do not go looking for them."

"But, you benefit from their choice, and despite what they profess, it must be a hard one for them."

"No more than you benefited from your men," he snapped. "You used them as surely as I have used my schente."

"The men always had a choice. No man was required to accept a priestess' offer of sex. If he did not wish it, it did not happen."

"And if the schente did not wish this life, they would not have contracted to it. I admit that I benefit from it. Why can you not admit the same?"

"Because it is not the same." Deliya started pacing. "Our men were not sterilized for our use."

"It would have been kinder had they been."

"In what way?"

"The children they fathered were never theirs. You benefited from that. If the men wanted sex, they forfeited rights to the fruits of the joining."

"A child is not the necessary outcome. There are other ways, Ro—ways you know of and do not use."

"The ways you used with Loric?" He shouldn't make this personal, and he knew it; but her constant refusals beat at him. She refused to admit there were faults in her system, and she refused him as a man. That didn't stop his body from reacting fiercely to her proximity, which made the sting of her refusal even worse.

She stopped pacing. "You would do well to learn other ways to sate yourself," she exploded. "Yes. There are many ways to prevent pregnancy that do no lasting injury. You use none of them."

"And when these methods fail?"

"Not all of them fail."

"For instance?"

Deliya met his eyes steadily then panned her gaze to his half-erect cock. Ro stirred, and she watched him rise further through the trousers he still wore. Had she taken a few more moments to seek him out, there would have been no clothing to strain against.

"For instance?" he asked again, annoyed that she affected him this way without even trying.

She shook her head and looked back to his face, shifting nervously. She backed off a step. "I can instruct your women."

Ro sighed. "What is it that you want of me?"

"Stop this barbaric custom. There are other ways."

"Yes. There are," he conceded, a plan taking form.

Her eyes narrowed. Deliya was perceptive as always. "What ways?" she managed.

Ro closed the distance between them, not touching her but standing intimately close. "If a man has a woman he loves, what use has he of schente?" he whispered.

Deliya turned a deep red not unlike windburn, stammering out an incoherent response. Surely, his interest wasn't such a surprise to her.

She shook her head.

"You see injustice, but you dare not end it," he noted wryly.

"My traditions..." she explained.

"You have your traditions and the Magden have theirs. It is not an easy thing to change a tradition, even if there is a better way."

"No. It is not," she agreed sadly.

Ro ran his fingertips up her arm slowly. "Can you ask me to change Magden traditions when yours are completely inflexible?"

"No. I cannot." Her voice was a ragged whisper.

He hardened further, as her scent intensified. "Can traditions change?" he asked.

"Perhaps they can—bend."

Ro nodded, wondering how far she was willing to bend. As if answering his unasked question, Deliya rose to touch her mouth to his. Her tongue sought entrance that he granted, meeting her with all the hunger he'd buried while they traveled. Her fingers went to work on his trousers; and he kissed her more urgently, saying prayers of thanks for her willingness. He went still, meeting her eyes, as Deliya massaged him expertly. Ro tensed, his climax building.

"Deliya..." he warned.

She kissed him, a hard, fierce kiss that stole his sanity. Her hand movement became more insistent.

Ro pulled back. "Deliya." It was a plea, a prayer.

He reached for her tunic, but she brushed his hand away. He tried to draw her to the bed, but she resisted.

"Shhh. Be still," she whispered, nipping at his lower lip.

"I cannot—"

"Relax. Let it wash over you."

"Let...what...wash..." he gasped, his mind mired in the task of staving off his release.

Deliya cupped his sac in her free hand, stroking his hardening body while he tightened his grip on her shoulders. She met his mouth passionately and pinched a spot beneath his sac. Ro froze, his eyes wide in shock, as Deliya's hand left his sac and braced his head to hers.

Then the moment of his release was on him, and his seed pumped out in a draining rush. Ro roared into her mouth, and she shuddered at the sound she muted. Her fist closed hard on the head of his cock as he engorged. He attacked her mouth, fevered by the sensation of that stimulation. Deliya held him until he subsided.

She met his eyes and nodded, stepping away. Ro reached for her, but she evaded him.

"I do not understand," he managed. He had to give her ease. It was selfish to accept such pleasure without sating her needs in return.

Deliya smiled weakly. "You had use of me, Ro. I would wager that you have not climaxed so hard or fast in quite some time."

He groaned at the truth of it. "Come to my bed," he pleaded, knowing she had no intention of it.

She ignored his plea. "You reached your pleasure with no risk of pregnancy." She started to turn then paused. "Ro?"

"Yes?" he asked, suddenly drained.

"Never insinuate that I have given less than I have taken of a man, no matter what else we engaged in." She left before he could form an answer.

Ro strode to the bath and spun the handle, muttering curses. It wasn't enough for Deliya to please him so selflessly. He wanted to feel her moving against him, to feel and hear her climax—things she had no intention of giving him.

He peeled off his clothing and sank into the bath to wash away the proof of his failure.

Chapter Nine

Deliya shut the door and ambled across the room, feeling miserable, glad that Laril had gone to attend to other duties. The scent of Ro's climax taunted her. Walking away from him had been nearly impossible; every cell in her body had screamed at her to go back to him. She cursed her weakness. There was more to the gift than sex.

She groaned, heading for the tub Laril had drawn for her and peeling off her remaining armor and clothing. She stared at the drying slick of Ro's seed on her hand, her mouth watering to taste him; but her battered nerves would not stand that.

If she tasted the musk, she'd go to him; and the tradition would be broken. Ro was not a man to place himself completely in her hands, and a proper challenge was one tradition that Deliya would not forego. She would not for Loric, and she would not for Ro.

Still, if he were willing...

She groaned, visions of her riding his body to both their pleasure making her already wet center throb for him. She leaned back against the wall, dipping the fingers coated in Ro's fluids in the well of her own. She massaged her hard nipples as she often had since Loric's death; but it was no longer Loric's face behind her closed eyelids.

Her fingers became Ro's, touching her, his mouth tasting her. Deliya arched her back, offering herself to him. The fingers inside her were his cock, thrusting madly toward a shattering release; and her body pulsed in time with those thrusts.

She swallowed her cry of release as she would have in reality. Her body spasmed around her fingers, her knees shaking. She gulped in the air, trying to ground herself; and sank into the still-hot Lizor-scented bath wearily.

She had to leave this place before she lost herself and her traditions to Ro. While she might use him to meet several of her needs, she could never take him as true mate and bind her soul to him. Now she had only to convince her soul of that.

* * * *

Ro smiled as Deliya strode into the dining hall. She held her head high; but her spine was stiff, as if she were discomfited somehow. The silin dress she wore would have reached the knees of any other woman within the walls, but it was almost a hand-length shorter on Deliya, a fact that brought his groin to attention again.

The room quieted as she crossed to the place set for her, and she blushed. Ro sighed. The reaction of his people was not helping to put her at ease. She had been correct. She was an oddity in this new world, and her guards had not prepared her for it.

She nodded to him and took the cup of implin wine. She wasted no time. "What are my options?" she asked.

Ro met her eyes, and her blush deepened. He didn't need to remind her of her first option, but it seemed that coming to his bed was not to her liking.

"You will stay here until planting season comes again."

She swallowed a mouthful of the wine, staring at a

spot somewhere above her plate of food. She cleared her throat yet spoke in a sure voice. "Here?"

"Yes. It is the safest place for you."

Deliya looked up, her expression one of challenge.

Ro motioned for peace. The last thing he needed was another reminder of her Len-be-damned status. "You have no army. Shortly, you will not even have Jurel's ignorance of your existence to protect you. By now, one of the men we blocked with the fire has reported seeing you. Your armor is—difficult to miss."

"Why would Jurel care? I am one lone survivor."

He scrubbed at his face, wondering how much he should tell her. "Your mother killed Jurin. She balked Jurel at every turn. It would please him to take the last victory your mother stole from him."

Deliya's eyes misted with unshed tears. "How could you know this?"

"When my troops reached Gidlore, there were a few priestesses still clinging to life. They did not survive long. Only long enough to curse us for failing them." *Even as we tried in vain to save them.*

"My mother?" she asked weakly.

"I placed her body on the pyre myself." Visions of the past stole Ro's appetite. He pushed his plate away and drank deeply from his cup. "We lost Gidlore to Jurel a few months later."

He had freed Leiana's body from the green stone floor of the sanctuary where it was tied down, wrapping his cloak around her naked form. He tried not to see what had been done to her, what he had been too late to stop.

Like many of the priestesses, Leiana had borne the Lengar brutality in an unholy silence captured enemy

114

soldiers whispered of in horror before their executions, even years later. Many of them talked about Leiana. She had stolen Jurel's confidence, if only momentarily. Leiana had endured his body without a sound then took his blade in the same silence. It had unnerved the Lengar leader.

"She was the last to fall," Ro whispered, "but she fell nobly."

"Ro?" Deliya asked.

He took another drink of the golden vintage. "Yes?"

"What happens when planting season comes again?"

"I will give you workers and soldiers, fields—a safe place to rebuild what was stolen from you."

"Is that possible?" she asked sadly.

Ro sighed. "As much as I can give you, I will."

Deliya studied him hopefully. "I have your vow on that?" she asked.

"Of course."

Her smile was stunning. She sipped her wine and reached for her plate. Ro watched her in wonder, trying desperately to understand what he'd done so right. He would give anything to see that smile again.

* * * *

Deliya mixed the herbs carefully, smiling to herself. It would take several weeks for the teas to do their work; but when they did, Ro would live to his vow to give her what she had lost.

The soldiers and workers were a generous offer. The land and home were beyond anything she dared pray for, but there was one thing Deliya lacked—an heir.

When the time was right, Ro would provide her with one. If her herbs worked as they should, the child would be female, a true heir.

She sobered, remembering his opinion of her traditions. She would be using him, as he had accused her of doing; but he had given his word to return what was taken from her.

"What is a mother without a people to look after?" she whispered brokenly.

Chapter Ten

Caj 28th, Ti 10-459

"What campaign is this?" Donic asked, spying the papers scattered across Ro's desk. He picked up an order for troop transfer, whistling at the numbers. "Ten dozen from Lind. Six dozen from Caran. So, this is what you have been up to this last week. I smell a battle." He smiled a feral grin.

"Yes. You do," Ro admitted. He tried to concentrate on the map in front of him, knowing there was a closer battle than the one Donic anticipated, the one about to take place in this office.

"Who are the unlucky Lengar?"

"The ones residing at Gidlore."

Donic's smile disappeared. "She's bewitched you," he exploded. "Our plans—"

"Have changed," he interrupted in a warning tone. "I do not deny that I am doing this for Deliya." He raised a hand to halt Donic's outburst before it could begin. "She has not requested this."

"Ro..." Donic pushed a hand through his unruly mop of black curls. "What do you hope to gain?"

Ro stared at the map, trying desperately to put his wishes into words his advisor would respect.

"If this is about Mother Leiana—"

"No," Ro assured him, fairly certain that it wasn't. "Deliya only knows that her mother fell in battle. That is all she needs to know. Am I understood?"

It couldn't hurt to warn Donic in advance this time. What Ro saw in the sanctuary was not widely known; it was unlikely that anyone else would tell her. Deliya had suffered enough, and if she decided to avenge her mother...

He shuddered at the thought of placing Deliya's body on the pyre.

"You want her," Donic growled. "Not as a mistress. You want heirs by her."

Ro didn't deny it. Donic wasn't blind.

"Her traditions do not allow that," he replied simply.

"What do you intend?"

"To return what is lost to her and keep it for her this time."

Donic dropped into a chair, looking stunned. "You love her. You must to go to these lengths for her."

"All the better reason to see her to her land quickly," Ro snapped, annoyed at the truth of it.

"Does she know?"

"Does it matter? Her traditions are all she has left. Should I force the issue and steal that from her?"

"Then there is a chance..." Donic began hopefully.

"No. There is not."

Donic's jaw tightened.

"This is not your concern, Donic. If I keep my distance until she leaves, I will see this through." *If I touch her again, I cannot promise my control.*

* * * *

Wend 8th, Ti 10-459

Deliya watched the troops amassing outside the wall. Their timing was bad, she decided miserably. The herbs should be effective now, but Ro would be leaving for a battle.

She worried her lower lip between her teeth. Perhaps the troops were not leaving until the morning. A night might be enough. If Ro's lust for her was strong enough and the herbs did their job, she could have her heir by morning.

She went to the corridor, smoothing her dress over her thighs self-consciously. She had chosen this dress carefully, one of the shorter ones she'd worn before Ro's clothier had made ones to suit her height.

She cursed her lack of experience with men. Loric had pursued her; there had been no need to invite more. Her teasing had been a personal matter between them. Deliya had only her observations of the household servants to learn from. Leiana and Vela had never taught her to invite a man's attention. Fion's Children did not play at games like that. A woman offered, and a man answered with his choice. It was all very civilized.

But Ro was Magden. According to Deliya's observations, the Magden played seduction games that were foreign to her. She sighed. It seemed games would be necessary.

Three weeks ago, she would have offered herself without games, but something had changed in those three weeks. Ro avoided her, brushing off her touch. He didn't call her by name. Rather, he used her titles as if they were something loathsome.

Deliya grimaced. She'd alienated him with her refusal. His interest had cooled. Deliya hoped it was still possible to reignite it.

She smiled, striding across the room with a sway in her hips much like the one Laril used when she sought a man to warm her bed. Ro noticed her, his gaze sliding over her then moving back to the general beside him. The general's eyes lingered longer, an appreciative smile curving his lips. Deliya ignored him, concentrating on Ro. She didn't want this strange general. Though his rank would indicate strong stock, she would not chance her heir to an unknown quantity.

She pushed away the thought that it was more than that. Ro was attentive, and his touch scattered her senses. Such a man was worthy to challenge her. He must, however, challenge her properly, or she could not proceed to the production of an heir.

"Ro," she called softly. "I must speak with you."

"This is not a good time." He glanced at the general and followed the other man's line of sight to her. He scowled. "You should go," he ordered coldly. "My men ride into battle this afternoon. They do not need distractions—Priestess."

The general paled and looked away.

Deliya's stomach sank. This afternoon? There was no time to accomplish her task before he left. "Will you be away long?" she asked, attempting to mask her upset.

Ro met her eyes at last, his look unreadable.

Donic appeared from behind her, grasping her elbow gently and turning her toward the door she'd entered by. "This way, Priestess," he growled in a voice that brooked no argument.

Deliya glanced back to Ro in confusion, but he was deep in conversation with the general. She sighed, letting Donic lead her back to her room.

He released her, standing in the doorway. "I suggest you stay here until Ro is gone."

"Why?" she challenged.

"You are a distraction." He turned to leave.

"Surely one general with a moment of inattention will not undermine—"

He turned on her, furious. "Not the generals," he snapped, "though that is dangerous enough. Ro needs his mind clear for the battle to come." He ran his eyes down her body with a sneer. "Whatever your game, it is unwelcome. I will not permit Ro to die in battle because of it."

He left, slamming the door behind him. Deliya stared after him for a long moment, sinking to the bed.

"Unwelcome," she whispered. Then there was no chance of attaining what she wished.

There are ways, her mind argued. *Dolgen...*

Deliya's breath hitched. Did she dare go that far? And how would she arrange it?

Chapter Eleven

Wend 24th, Ti 10-459

Deliya halted, her smile fading at the sight of the bloody bandage on Ro's upper arm. She tore down the stairs, intent on rendering any aid she could.

Donic met her halfway, blocking her bodily. "Away," he whispered fiercely. "A Magden king does not show weakness."

"I am a healer," she protested.

He turned her and half-dragged her up the stairs and toward her room. "One of the surgeons will attend to him after the men are attended to."

"After—"

"The men come first," he snapped. "It is our way."

"But I can help."

"No. You can do nothing helpful," he spat. He opened the door to her room and waved her inside.

She hesitated.

"I will force you inside and post a guard," he warned.

Deliya stepped into the room. "How have I offended you so grievously, Donic?" she asked hopelessly.

"You upset years of battle plans and caused a battle the likes of which I have never seen before. I hope never to again."

"I what? What madness is this?"

Donic glared at her. "Congratulations, Priestess. Ro has returned Gidlore to you."

Deliya had to concentrate to force her lungs to function and her heart to beat.

"Now, will you remain here or must I post a guard

to make you keep your distance?"

"I will stay," she managed in a strangled voice. The door closed, while she stood frozen in shock.

She couldn't move, couldn't seem to order her unruly thoughts. Ro had never mentioned his intention to restore her own lands to her. He kept it well hidden, as if he was afraid he would fail and didn't want to raise her hopes.

She moved to the small table next to her bed and started to load her pack slowly, listening with a nervous fluttering in her stomach to the sound of footsteps in the corridor as Ro entered his rooms and sent Donic away. She owed it to Ro to tend his wound. He had been injured while retaking Gidlore for her.

She sighed. She would heal him. She would use a mug of the tea—and no more unless he requested it. If Ro didn't want her, Deliya would concede defeat. She owed him that much for the kindness he'd shown her.

She peeked into the hall, breathing a sigh of relief that there was no guard on Ro's door. She hoisted her pack and balanced a tray of other supplies on her hand, supplies she had arranged with a very different purpose in mind. Teas were teas; with the added supplies loaded in her pack and the mugs and hot water on the tray, she could make every tea required to tend to him properly.

* * * *

Ro looked up in surprise as Deliya entered his room without knocking. "Priestess?" he asked uncertainly, reminding himself to keep the distance between them he'd created.

The sight of her on the stairs had nearly broken him, as had the sight of her before he left. If it weren't for Donic, he might have forsaken his vow not to pursue her. Deliya enflamed him. She seemed unaware of how she affected him. For his sanity, it had to remain that way.

She bowed her head slightly. "I would offer my services as a healer, Ro."

His heart stuttered at the idea of Deliya laying hands on him again. It would not be wise. "I require no healing," he replied brusquely.

Deliya stiffened. Her eyes narrowed. "You have suffered infection from a similar injury. I have heard your servants speak of it."

Ro darkened, wondering which of his servants would be the target of his ire for this interference. "At a battle site," he admitted. His habit of letting his men seek treatment first had not always been a wise one.

She strode to the bed, placing a tray on the table beside him and setting a pack next to his hip. She handed him a steaming mug. "Drink this."

Ro stared into the pink liquid dubiously. Donic would lock him in shackles for even considering drinking a concoction that could be a sweet-tasting poison.

Deliya plucked the mug from his fingers and drank deeply. She settled it back in his hand. "I will not ask you to accept any treatment I will not prove the safety of. I will explain everything I do. The tea is lizor berry with olum. Not lizor stem as I gave you the last time, but the simple berry. It will relax your muscles and relieve pain. It is bittersweet." She sat on the edge of the mattress and removed several jars from her pack.

Ro drank deeply from the mug. It was bittersweet, as she said it would be, as lizor and olum should be. He scanned her breasts, straining against the silin bodice of her gown, then gulped down the rest of the tea, reminding himself that Deliya had taken vows that did not include accepting his advances.

She took the mug from his hand with a nod, crushing sweet-smelling dried herbs between her fingertips into a second mug with just enough hot water from the pot on the tray to make a paste. She set the mixture aside and added two more powders to the first mug, dissolving them in water and mixing it well. Again, she gave him the mug.

Ro stared at the orange liquid. "What does this do?"

Deliya took the mug from him and drank a mouthful before handing it back. "Prevents infection and speeds healing," she informed him. This one is sucre sap sweet."

He smiled as he drank it. "It's very good." His body felt warm and relaxed.

She looked up, her green eyes glittering and her color high. "The more you drink, the better. Would you like more?"

Ro nodded. "Will you share it with me?" Donic would not be as incensed if he made sure she shared every mug with him.

Her blush deepened. "If you wish it."

"I do." The sweet smell of her body seemed to surround him. *It must be the drugs,* he reasoned. Deliya could not be so aroused.

She nodded and made him another mug, drinking a mouthful of it before she handed it to him. She picked up the mug full of paste. "This must be rubbed into the wound. I could cut myself to prove its safety, but it cannot be eaten."

"Do not do something so ridiculous," he slurred. He looked at her through a pleasant haze.

"As you wish." Deliya painted the warm herbs over the cut with her fingertips, rubbing lightly over the stitches Donic had placed in Ro's hide himself. "The paste aids in healing and reduces pain and inflammation," she explained.

Ro nodded, suddenly and acutely aware of his lengthening cock. He stared at her pert breasts, his mouth watering. Dear Mag, but he wanted to bury his face in those breasts.

Deliya leaned away to take a clean bandage from the bedside table, and Ro drank down the rest of the sweet tea. He held the mug out to her with an unsteady hand.

She met his eyes uncertainly. "More?"

"The more, the better." He watched her movements as she made more of the tea. *It prevents infection. I must do that, because if she comes to my bed again to treat me, I cannot promise to keep to my vow.*

Deliya held his eyes as she drank several mouthfuls from the mug and placed it in his hand. Ro hardened further, as she wrapped the bandage, gulping down the medicine. He was going to need several schente to stay sane after this.

He sucked in his breath, as Deliya massaged his arm. "What are you doing?"

"Increasing blood flow past the injury. It will make the herbs more effective and speed healing." She moved her hands to his chest, stroking in delicious circles through the red curls.

His male nipples hardened; he bit back a moan in response. His cock ached, a maddening burning and throbbing. Deliya pressed her breasts to him, kneading the muscles of his shoulders. Her scent was a heady mix of the herbs and her musk that made the throbbing worse.

Ro kissed her throat. "Deliya," he breathed, wanting to hold her.

She moaned, though her hands didn't pause in their diligent service. "Yes, Ro."

It wasn't a question. It should have been a question, shouldn't it? His mind was muddled. "No." He kissed her again, nuzzling the rising scent at her pulse point. "You should go."

If she didn't, he would do something dishonorable.

"Why?"

"I want you," he admitted, nipping at the site he'd kissed.

"I know. Would you—"

"You do?" he asked in a bleary sort of understanding.

She nodded, leaning back to meet his eyes. "Would you do something for me?"

"Anything," he groaned.

"Let me show you the way of my people," she whispered, "the first time."

"Yes. What is your way?" *First time? I will thank Mag and Fion both for more than once.*

She met his mouth urgently. Ro pulled her astride him, pushing the dress up to her hips. He wanted her: hard, fast and often.

She pulled his hand to her core. "Feel how much I want you," she whispered. "All of you, Ro."

"Now," he growled, stroking at her hood. Her honey coated his fingers, inviting more.

Deliya bit her lip, rocking against his hand. "My way—this time."

"Teach me," he pleaded. *Quickly.*

She stripped off her dress, and Ro cupped a breast up, sucking the deep red tip slowly into his mouth.

Deliya moved against him restlessly. "No. You may not use your hands."

Ro sat back, looking at her in confusion. "What? What madness is this?"

"The first mating between a man and woman is always thus. Will you give me this?"

"Only the first?" he asked.

Deliya nodded, looking uncertain. "Only the first," she promised.

Ro sighed, his insistent body driving him near mad for her. "What must I do?"

She showed him a pair of silin cords. Ro shook his head. Deliya started to push away, seemingly crushed by his refusal of her tradition.

He grasped her arms lightly, desperate to have her. "Why do you do this? Explain the tradition to me."

"The priestess chooses a man. Out of respect for her position, he gives himself over completely to her the first time they mate. He may do anything he wishes during the mating, but he may not use his hands to touch her."

"He puts himself at her mercy," Ro challenged.

"You think I have so little honor?" Deliya wasn't angered by that. She seemed hurt.

"Fion would be displeased if you—"

A look of horror settled on her face. "Used the

promise of ecstasy to kill? I would lose the soul's reward. I would—"

Ro drew her mouth to his, stealing her words in a kiss that left them both panting. "I trust you. Teach me."

Deliya nodded. Her hands shook as she bound his wrists to the posts of the bed. To Ro's surprise, the ropes were very loose. He could freely move, even raise his torso from the bed, but he could not quite embrace Deliya's body.

He licked his lips as she unfastened his lounging pants and slid them down his legs. She straddled him again, rubbing her core against his cock.

Ro wondered at the force of his arousal. "Take me," he begged. "Please, take me."

She lay over him, tasting his nipples much as he had tasted hers. It was an exquisite torture, making him want her, yet denying him the relief of her heat. She slid up his body, pausing long enough to offer her breasts then moving on. Ro tasted her as she passed, drunk on the feel of her skin beneath his lips, nipping and suckling at all of her, whatever piece of her ventured near his questing mouth.

She straddled his face. Ro didn't need to ask what she wanted. He circled her hood with his tongue then sucked it hard.

"Yes, Ro. Taste me. Teach me."

He slid his tongue down her seam, licking inside her; he slid deeper, her musk acting as the potent aphrodisiac it was. He sucked her, licked her, massaged her inner pleasure spot.

Deliya arched her back, driving him deeper. "Now, Ro. Please." Her inner muscles contracted against his tongue.

Ro sucked at her core, drinking in her lubricant as it wept from her. The throbbing in his groin was insistent. "I need you," he gasped, barely holding back his need to release.

She moved down his body, stroking his length and guiding it to her entrance. "Slowly," she requested.

He cried out, as she sank around him. Staying still while she took him into her tight body a finger-width at a time was more frustrating than not having her at all. Deliya was hot, and her sheath gripped him hard.

Sweat coated his body, and every muscle tensed. *It has been a long time for her. Loric died four years ago. She needs this, and I gave myself up to her.* He groaned in the agony of holding back. *Mag, give me strength! This may kill me.*

Deliya's face was a study in intense concentration. She met his eyes, as he...

Realization came suddenly.

"No," he breathed. *Her first time. Dear Mag, it isn't just her first time with me but her first time with a man.* "Not like this."

"It is our way." Deliya pushed down fully against him, swallowing a scream of pain as her barrier tore.

Ro roared in disbelief, pulling at the silin cords. "No," he pleaded as his body started to release. *Not this way. Please, not this way.*

But his body wasn't listening to rational arguments. Knowing he was her first stole his self-control. Ro surged up into her as he erupted. If he didn't do that much, he might injure her when he swelled. He cursed himself as his cock locked into her stim band.

Deliya's eyes opened wide. She ground her teeth,

holding back whatever sound sought to escape her, looking pained. She curled onto his chest, shivering, a single, silent sob wracking her form.

Ro brushed his lips over her hair. "Please, let me hold you."

She nodded, fumbling the ropes off.

He wrapped her in his arms, angry with her for not telling him, disgruntled with himself for not making the experience better for her, for taking his pleasure so selfishly and finding delight in her barrier when she had felt only pain. Most of all, he felt disbelief that he wanted her again—desperately. His body ached for her, a maddening need to have her.

"You should have told me," he whispered. "One of your men would have known."

She nodded.

"I am sorry."

"Do not be," she assured him.

"You did not enjoy it," he replied miserably, feeling his failure acutely.

Deliya raised her head and shot him a look of confusion. "Are you insane?"

Ro stroked her cheek, trying to make sense of what she was saying.

She kissed his chest. "The first time, a priestess must take both pleasure and pain in silence," she explained. She ran her fingers through his curls, following with her face as if drinking in his scent again.

He lessened in her and released her band, though his cock was still stiff and pleading for more of her. "The first time?" he asked for qualification. "You are free to voice your pleasure after that?"

Deliya nodded solemnly. "I met the Mother's

challenge and passed."

Ro turned her beneath him and surged into her. Deliya let out a whimper of pleasure, grasping his arms, her nails digging into him as she rolled her hips in invitation.

"Now you meet mine," he assured her. "A Magden woman does not hold in her pleasure."

He drew her legs around his hips. Deliya's breathing was quick. She touched his face as he started stroking deep inside her and closed her eyes as he drove her on.

"Come for me, Deliya," he whispered.

Her hands moved to his shoulders, seeking a better anchor; and her short nails dug deep into his skin as she sought her pleasure. "Ro," she pleaded, her legs tightening.

Ro pushed up slightly to lay his hand over her woman's curls. He played his thumb over her hood, watching her intently. Deliya's face contorted, announcing the sweet agony of her joy. She screamed harshly as her body contracted around him. He couldn't hold off his release; her body had barely unknotted from her climax when he sent her into another by stimulating her egg.

In the aftermath, Ro held Deliya close, his heart pounding in his chest. She had given herself to him freely. Deliya was his. He would never let her go.

CHAPTER TWELVE

Wend 25th, Ti 10-459

Deliya eased from the bed, casting a smile at Ro. Her plan had worked well. If Fion were kind, their night would result in a child. A girl would be best, but even a male child was capable of learning the secrets of her race.

She shrugged into the silin dress and gathered up her herbs. Using her knowledge to win a child from Ro rode the edges of propriety, but there was precedent for enticing her body to produce a viable heir with a man who was willing to share her bed for a single night.

A priestess could take a man to warm her bed simply for the production of a child if it were deemed that true mating would be a mockery of the Mother's gift. Since children were of the mother's house, paternity was immaterial in anything but ensuring that children borne of the mating didn't mate with other progeny of the same sire. It was immaterial if she took a true mate later, since the fact that she had children with other men was not his concern. Securing strong heirs to Fion's service was always what was most important.

So, her aim had been sound; but using an aphrodisiac to accomplish it had been underhanded. Deliya sobered as she shouldered her pack. Ro would wake soon, confused by his mad urges to mate with her. He would be angry and might demand she leave his house.

She bit back a sob and strode to the door, her head high. If Ro cast her out for her treachery, she would go calmly. She deserved no better. Deliya made her plans in resignation. She would bathe and eat heartily. It might be the last time for quite a while that such luxuries would be readily available to her.

* * * *

Ro reached for Deliya, ready to sate his insistent body again. Three times during the night had barely whetted his appetite for her. He opened his eyes, staring at the empty bed in confusion and dismay.

"Deliya?" He pushed unsteadily to his feet, making a thorough sweep of his rooms. He pulled on his robe and marched to the door. Uneducated or not, she should have known better than to leave his bed this way. Down the hall, he opened her door without knocking, nodding to the guard who had come on duty sometime during the night to protect them while they slept.

Deliya's eyes widened in shock, and she stood, turning her back on a tray of food. She shifted nervously. "Good day, Ro."

"You left my bed," he noted in annoyance.

Her brow furrowed. "Of course."

Of course?

He crossed the room in two long strides and pulled her to his chest, seeking her mouth urgently. Deliya moaned as her lips parted beneath his.

She leaned back, breaking off the kiss, her breathing ragged, dragging a shaky hand through her mussed hair. "Oh, no," she whispered miserably. "What have I done?"

Ro stood, frozen in amazement with his hands on

her shoulders, as Deliya felt the pulse at his throat then checked the dilation of his eyes. The confusion etched on her face couldn't compare to his.

"Your pupils are not dilated," she mused. "Your pulse is slow and steady. I haven't given you too much."

"Deliya?" he half-asked, half-demanded. "What do you mean?"

She didn't seem to hear his question. She bit her lip and checked his pulse again. Ro suppressed the urge to tell her that he was well aware it was speeding in apprehension.

Deliya wrenched from his hands and started to pace. "What have I missed? The effect should have faded."

"Deliya," Ro barked, making her jump in response. "What effect? What are you talking about?"

She winced. "You still want," she faltered. "You should not want...Donic said...I do not understand," she pleaded.

"Still want what? And what has Donic to do with this?"

"Me. You should not want me," she answered, distracted. "What have I done wrong?"

"I have wanted you since I dragged the helm off your head in that shack you called home. Why should that change?"

She scowled, then laughed nervously. "Thank the Mother, then. It is simply your male drive."

"Male drive?" Ro had a male drive, a fierce need to possess her again—once he had settled this madness.

"The urge to mate," she explained patiently.

"And why would that change?" he prodded.

"Because...I thought..." Deliya met his eyes and

flushed. She swallowed slowly, raising her chin in challenge.

Ro crossed his arms over his chest, prepared for what he assumed would be a very interesting discussion. "You drugged me?" he asked. "A witches' brew to increase my...drive?"

"I did," she admitted. "I will understand if you wish me to leave."

"Leave? Why would I ask you to leave?"

"I...You accept that I used my herbs on you in such a way?" She was so delightfully naïve.

"You thought I would not want you in my bed unless you did this?"

"Donic said..." She nodded slowly.

Ro pushed back a spike of fury. Donic had caused this. He forced himself to more constructive paths. She really thought he didn't want her? Was she blind? But of course, Deliya had known no men but her father and that Len-be-damned guard since she had been sexually an adult. A strange man's interest was alien to her.

Ro pulled her back against his chest, smothering her gasp of surprise with his mouth. She met him tentatively then pulled him closer, her responses fevered. He guided her toward the bed, groaning as her nipples beaded through her silin robe, brushing his chest through his own.

"You wasted your herbs," he growled. "You are mine, Deliya."

"Yours?" she managed in a thick voice. Her musk was heavy, potent. She ran her fingers over the scratches she'd left on his shoulder the night before. "A priestess of Fion belongs to no man."

Ro pressed her to the hard line of his aching cock,

laying his claim in her rising arousal. Deliya's eyes dilated and her breathing hitched. Her fingers shook against his skin.

"You came to me," he informed her. "You gave yourself to me. You will accept my claim."

Her eyes widened, and she shook her head. She pushed from his embrace, resuming her pacing, her movements quick and jerky.

Ro watched her warily. "You will contract with me, Deliya."

She stopped, going pale. "I never said that. It was never—"

"What did you want from me, Deliya? Why come to my bed if you did not want to be there permanently?"

Deliya didn't respond. She took a step back, casting her eyes about as if searching for escape.

"What did you want?" Ro demanded in the low, dangerous voice he usually reserved for soldiers in need of correction.

"A—a child."

He stared at her in shocked disbelief. She had used him as nothing more than a stud for breeding?

She backed away from him, straightening her spine despite the look of pure fear on her face. "You gave your vow. Fion's Children—" she began in a calming voice.

"I am not one of Fion's Children," he thundered. "You are dealing with a Magden king. You are on Magden land and ruled by Magden law. By Magden law, I call you to a trial moon."

She shot a look of pleading skyward then met his eyes again, visibly reining in her frustration. "Trial moon? And what in the Mother's name is a trial moon?"

"Trial moon. For one month's time, you will share

my bed. You may have the child you wish." He managed a tight smile. "In fact, I hope you do carry my child."

"You do?" she stammered, backing off another step.

He took a stride toward her, his body announcing his excitement at that idea. "I most certainly do."

"Wh—" Deliya cleared her throat, her eyes fastening on the length of him tenting his robe. "Why?"

"By the law of trial moon, if you carry my child by the end of the month, you will contract with me."

"And if I do not carry your child at that time?" she breathed.

"You will," he promised.

"You cannot force this on me. Your own laws say that."

Ro took another stride toward her, closing the distance between them, even though Deliya backed to the wall to escape him. "I will not force you to me, though I may encourage you."

Deliya swallowed with some difficulty, his point made clear by her body's response. Enticing her would be simple enough.

He strode to her cabinet and collected her packs of herbs.

"Ro?" She tried to keep the panic from her voice, though her hands fisted at her sides.

He offered her a hungry smile. "I will not force you. Neither will you use your knowledge to prevent or to end a pregnancy. I am sure you know ways to do both." He took her belongings to the door and handed them to the guard with orders to deliver them to his rooms. He ambled back across the room, considering her carefully.

"If I give my vow..." she whispered, looking at the closed door, her expression one of longing such as he hadn't seen since she believed he would take her abinatine from her. He wondered if her possessions had always been so precious to her or if having so little made that which she held more dear.

"As you gave your vow not to run from me on the trail?" he noted.

She blushed, dropping her gaze. "I had to know, Ro. You know I did."

"Would you need to escape my contract as strongly?"

Deliya shook her head, tears escaping down her cheek. She seemed to have forgotten her rule about weeping in front of an adversary—or perhaps she no longer viewed him as an adversary. He doubted that highly.

"I am sure you've done nothing to prevent a child so far. You wanted one. It would not serve your purpose to do anything that would prevent it."

She laughed harshly. "No. You might say that I am too cautious for something like that." She grimaced.

Something was not right. "What is it?"

"It is none of your concern," she replied crisply, stiffening her posture as if in military review.

Ro took her gently by the shoulders, resisting the urge to make a show of his strength. "If it concerns our child, it is," he assured her.

"I took steps to encourage my body to conceive. I thought I would only have the night."

"How long does it last? This 'encouragement' that you used?" His voice was rough with self-restraint. Knowing she was even more fertile than the typical Keen woman gave his hunger for her a sharper edge.

"A few days," she admitted.

"For the next few days, you will be more receptive?"

She nodded, looking discomfited by the notion now that it would benefit Ro that she was.

"How much more?" Ro nuzzled at her cheek then nipped her jawline.

Deliya gasped.

"How much more?" he repeated.

"Double," she whispered.

"Hmm." His cock was pulsing insistently in response to their mixed musk. "That means our odds are one in eight now?" he asked.

"Six." Deliya dipped her head to the curls above his robe, drinking in his scent.

"It is very powerful, is it not?" Ro growled. "The call of a fertile male body? A man who wants to spread those pale thighs and make the ache go away?"

Deliya rubbed her cheek in his chest hair, her body heating, her scent signaling her need for more.

"You do ache, do you not, Deliya? You are not accustomed to these sensations. Let me still the ache."

"One in four," she groaned.

"Not so much less than six," he reasoned. He skated his fingertips over her hipbone, massaging the sensitive spot at the join of her thigh and buttocks.

"You do not own me," she pleaded. "You cannot own me."

He untied his robe and let it slide apart, uncovering his body to her. Deliya circled his length with an unsteady hand, her green eyes glazed in need.

Ro stroked his fingers over the damp head, collecting a bit of his essence. She watched his fingers as he raised them to her face. He passed them under her nose, and her nostrils flared in response.

"I am ready for you, Deliya," he said, echoing her teasing of the previous night. "You see how much I want you. You smell it."

She shivered. "I—I took other steps," she stuttered.

"What steps?" he whispered, his mouth watering as she licked the offered moisture from his fingers. He was winning. Deliya's defenses were falling to him in minute increments.

"The child..." She rolled her tongue over his fingertips again, her eyes closing in pleasure. "Any child you give me in the near future would likely be female, a Daughter of Fion and not an heir to your battles. You want—"

"Good. I would like a daughter," he told her honestly. *The sons will come later.* "You could teach her your healing arts. She will have the blessings of both Fion and Mag." *All our children could, but saying that will scare her away.*

"You would allow that?" she asked, her eyes hopeful.

"Unite the Children of Fion and the Magden with me. We could have a strong people who worship Fion's gifts and goodness along with Mag's might. We could bring peace and prosperity to Kegin. Join with me."

Deliya stroked his length. "A priestess of Fion has never taken an outsider as true mate."

"Your Mother Fion's approval would convince you?"

She shot him a pained look. "Producing a child proves nothing. A child can be produced between souls who loathe the sight of one another."

"No. Your schen. Let your schen decide."

"In what way?"

"Spend the trial moon with me. I will give you my

141

child. If your schen drives you to me within three weeks of conceiving, you will know that your Mother commands this. Agreed?"

"And if it does not?"

"The laws of trial moon say that you still may choose to contract with me. By demanding the trial, I state my intent to convince you, my wish to contract. I am bound by your choice and our agreement."

"If I refuse you, I will leave to ease your pain."

Pure panic coursed through him at the thought. *And take my child and yourself from me? I cannot allow that. I have to convince her.* Ro's eyes met hers. If he didn't agree, Deliya would not let him share her bed. That much was a given. He nodded stiffly. *I will convince her, but only a love-schen will be enough to drive her to me. Please, Fion. I do not know the proper way to honor you, but I ask for Deliya's love. Nothing more than that.*

Deliya nipped at his chest. "Agreed," she breathed against his skin.

Yes. He shrugged out of his robe and went to work on hers. When she stood naked before him, Deliya shot him a skittish look, as if the night before had never occurred, as if she were a maiden.

Ro wrapped her in his arms. "What is it?"

"I do not know your customs, Ro. How does a trial moon...Am I akin to a vanquished foe or one of your schente or..." She blushed. Her hands shook, though she obviously tried to still them.

He drew her chin up and captured her mouth slowly, drawing out her passion as the sun enticed the lizors to bloom. "You are my love," he whispered.

Deliya sank to the bed, pulling Ro with her. She

pressed the golden curls of her mound to him, as if desperate to be his again.

"Slowly," he rasped. He had never been a man who favored slow, gentle coupling. He took a woman deep and fast to screaming release. But, Deliya wasn't any other woman. He had never wanted a woman to love him before. He'd never wanted a child before. His child would not be rushed.

He suckled at her breast tenderly, imagining his son doing the same. *No. Not a son. Deliya will give me a daughter first, a tall beauty, a warrior woman with her mother's spirit who will learn the secrets of Fion's Children.*

Deliya pushed against him, pleading for completion. He pulled her tight to his body, on fire for her.

"Give me a daughter," he invited. *Give me yourself.*

She cried out as he slid deep inside her. He took her in slow, insistent strokes. Yes, Deliya would tell their daughter about this, about the pleasure a man could give a woman he loved if he took her with patience. Her reactions said as much.

Deliya clutched at his shoulders, winding her legs around his hips. "You want that," she murmured. "You really want a daughter."

"Yes. I do." *Desperately. Our child together. One that I will hold. You will not leave me.*

She came quickly at that, screaming his name at her pinnacle. That was where Ro's patience ended. He followed her over, shivering as she released an egg for him.

Just her love so she will stay. Mother Fion, please grant me that one gift.

CHAPTER THIRTEEN

Abrin 10th, Ti 10-459

Ro nuzzled his face into her breasts, drinking in their mixed scent. He would kill or die to spend every day in Deliya's bed like this.

Her hand traced his shoulder, and she opened her eyes. After almost three weeks of waking next to him, she still studied him curiously, as if the sight of him beside her was new and unexpected.

"What is troubling you?" she asked.

"You know me so well." *And not at all, if you believe I will ever give you up.*

He couldn't tell her how desperate he was for her to greet his presence in her bed with a smile instead of studied indifference.

"Ro?"

His mind snapped to another issue they needed to discuss. "The doctors would like to have your antidote for gola poisoning," he blurted out.

She stilled then put distance between them, a wary look on her face. Ro wrapped his hands around her waist, shaking his head.

"Why?" she asked.

"A distillation may be able to do in one injection what you did in six. You know that it is medically sound."

"Gola is not a plant that grows wild, Ro. What is your plan?"

"We will plant it in fields near the border as if it is one of our crops. Our people will know the danger."

"But the Lengar will not—at first," she reasoned.

"Gola is not an easy plant to eradicate. If you do this, it will continue to grow within your borders. It will spread if left unchecked."

Ro nodded.

"The children—"

"Will have the antidote, and they will be taught not to eat the berries, as your people were taught not to eat them. Please, Deliya. The damage we can do to them by using their own raiding parties would be immeasurable."

"It will take years to make a decent bush grow from seed."

"We have already transplanted the ones left in your fields—adult plants already producing."

She seemed at a loss for words. "It is not Fion's way to entrust the sacred knowledge to doctors."

"To outsiders," he challenged.

Deliya looked away, her color high.

Ro turned her face back to him. "You still do not trust me," he accused.

"Of course I do."

"Prove it."

"The antidote?" Her eyes darted about, as if she were trapped.

"No. Not the antidote. You had no problem poisoning the Lengar at your home. In time, you will see the beauty of this plan. It is precisely what you did."

She nodded. "You are correct in that. I will...I will share the antidote with your doctors."

"Good. Now prove you trust me."

"Prove I...Prove it?" she stammered.

"Yes."

Deliya swallowed hard and met his eyes. "I trust

you."

"We shall see."

* * * *

Deliya took a calming breath, unsure of what Ro had in mind. *Remember your training. Meet the challenge. Ro will not harm you.*

"This iri blossom is truly beautiful," Ro interrupted her thoughts.

She tensed. "Must you talk about that now?"

He chuckled. "So tense," he teased.

"I trust you," she insisted. *He wants to unnerve me, as Loric often did.*

Ro ignored her comment. "But, it is beautiful. The bud of an iri blossom is not gold, but pale and soft, much like your skin."

"Ro," she warned. *Why does he insist on talking about something so ridiculous when I am focused?* Deliya knew very well what an immature iri blossom looked like, though she wondered where in his home was warm enough to produce a fully immature blossom this late in the season. She concentrated on the healing properties of iri to calm her pounding heart.

He stroked the petals over her lips. "So soft," he whispered.

Deliya shivered, her body heating. "There are better things you could be doing," she snapped.

"Yes." His voice came from just beside her ear. "Yes. There are."

The flower retreated then feathered over her distended nipples. Deliya arched, pulling against the jaglin fur restraints that bound her wrists and ankles to the bed. She closed her eyes, though the blindfold was secure.

The blossom touched her hood then retreated again, and she groaned. She waited, tensed and prepared for his touch, her breathing harsh. Nothing happened. Where was he? What was Ro planning for her next?

"Talk to me," she gasped, needing to fix his location.

She bowed up again as the flower trailed lazily along her inner thigh from her knee to the moisture gathering on her sex. It disappeared; and she sobbed, craving the matching trail up the opposite leg.

It didn't come. Deliya shook, painfully aroused by his teasing. Her nipples strained into the chill air. Her sex felt hot and heavy. Nothing Loric taught her had prepared Deliya for this. She couldn't touch herself. She couldn't even press her thighs together to relieve the ache building in her. She was helpless, waiting for Ro to ease or to torture her further.

The flower returned, brushing over her lips. Her body reacted fiercely to the scent of their mixed musk on the petals. Ro was prepared for her, and he had painted his essence on the flower to tell her. Deliya licked at the petals, groaning when it disappeared after the barest taste of him.

"Please, talk to me," she begged. She felt as if she were lost in a pool of water, floating without direction.

Ro remained silent. Not even his breathing gave away his location—though her hearing was muted by the thick blindfold.

The flower traced slow circles around her breasts, rising to tease a nipple, darting across to trace the other. On and on, Ro followed that path until Deliya thought she might go mad. The stroking seemed to cover her entire body simultaneously, touching all of her and firing every individual nerve at once. She fisted her hands in the fur and raised her hips, shamelessly begging for more. The flower disappeared again.

Deliya hardly had time to draw a breath before it was back. The blossom traced the trail up her opposite thigh then over her sex. She jerked against the restraints, groaning at the feel of the iri blossom following her seam and praying that Ro wouldn't remove it again.

He didn't. Deliya rubbed against the soft touch of the petals, needing more. She threw her head back and forth, feeling her climax looming over her. It was so close. It would take so little—

Deliya cried out, as Ro's mouth closed on her breast. She collapsed to the mattress, the quickening of her orgasm overpowering her conscious mind. His fingers breached her body, thrusting into her while he pressed the flower hard to her hood. Her breathing hitched. She screamed, pinpoints of light dancing in the darkness behind the blindfold.

Ro whipped the blindfold off, settling his cock deep within her spasming body. Deliya met his eyes, stuttering out incoherent pleas. He went motionless, buried to the hilt, watching her face as her body begged for final completion.

"For you," he whispered, his face twisting in exquisite pleasure as he joined her.

They shouted out together as Ro's seed flooded her body, hot and potent. His cock swelled, and Deliya waited for the shocks that signaled the release of her stimulated egg.

The sensation didn't come.

She gazed on his face through the fog of her tears. It wasn't right. Fion could not ask that this be her last moment with Ro, this perfect pinnacle he'd brought her to. She would never know his body again, though her body screamed for it already.

* * * *

The warm lassitude in Ro's muscles disappeared as he saw the first tear fall. He touched Deliya's cheek in confusion. "What is it?"

She shook her head, swallowing a sob.

There was nothing in all his experience that had made Ro feel this helpless, lying locked inside her while Deliya cried and he had no idea why. A sick certainty assaulted him, and his blood ran cold.

"Oh gods. You...If you did not want what I was doing, you had only to ask. I would never have knowingly—"

"It is not that."

"Then what?"

"I did not release an egg."

His heart sank. Deliya had conceived, and she wasn't yet convinced. If she were, she would not be crying.

"Let me love you," he pleaded.

She sobbed, shaking her head.

With that refusal, he understood what true helplessness was. "Then I have three weeks to convince you."

Deliya stiffened. She looked at her bound hands fearfully. "Convince?" she squeaked. "That was not our deal."

"I will do nothing," he promised. "Do you trust me?"

She nodded. "Then what did you mean?"

Ro covered her lips with his fingertips then unbound her hands. "When you turn to me, I will be in your bed waiting for you."

Her eyes widened in understanding. "But, you cannot," she gasped.

"If you have no drive to be mine, it will be no different than when you shared my pallet on the trail home," he reasoned.

Deliya swallowed hard, and Ro bit back a smile. His greatest hope was that she wanted him. Her schen would do the rest, if she did. If only that weren't her greatest fear.

CHAPTER FOURTEEN

Abrin 24th, Ti 10-459

Deliya sank into the heat of the bath, letting the water battle the chill of her pregnancy signs. She sighed, moving her hands over her body then stilling them. Even out of his sight, Deliya felt phantoms of Ro's hands on her.

He had agreed to give her privacy for bathing, but it hardly seemed to matter. She still pictured him intruding on her bath, his hands exploring her body, his mouth following, sliding into the wide tub...

She fisted her hands at her sides. This need went beyond distracting to maddening. Worse, there was still more than a week to go. Deliya looked at her body through water tinted pink with the cleansing oil she loved so much. Her hands shook, and her nipples beaded as if waiting for Ro's touch. The time until she left his home would be pure torture.

She clenched her teeth, smiling grimly. She could survive this. One favor Loric had done her was training her well. Her deal with Ro never stipulated that she couldn't find her own pleasure, only that she couldn't turn to him for it without becoming his queen. And Fion's priestesses could take their pleasure in silence.

She closed her eyes, her nerves humming in anticipation. She sank her fingers into her body, biting her lip as her skin heated, rivaling the temperature of the water. Ro filled her mind, his mouth teasing at nipples that hardened further in the eddies swirling and stroking past them. His hands caressed her, driving her higher. It had been too long since she'd felt his body in hers.

"Deliya?"

She froze, opening her eyes to the sight of Ro in the doorway. She swallowed hard, taking in his look of hunger as he stared at her. His entire body was rigid, and his cock had risen to the occasion. For one timeless moment, he was the embodiment of her fantasies. He would stride to her, take her in her bath as she dreamed.

Dear Mother, what am I thinking?

Deliya followed his line of sight to her hands; and she moved them hurriedly, pushing against the far wall of the tub with her knees drawn up to shield her body from his inspection. He strode toward her, and Deliya scrambled from the water, pulling a robe around her. The silin lay against her wet body like a second skin.

Ro stopped, running his eyes over her as if she were a plate of Gelgrin. "Deliya," he growled.

His scent taunted her senses; and Deliya fought the urge to step to him, to bury her face in the fragrant curls on his chest and make her madness complete. "You promised," she whispered.

He nodded. "The meal has arrived. You have been in here for quite a while."

She eased past him, gasping at the lungful of his musk she inhaled. She rushed to her cabinet, pulling out a dress with trembling fingers.

Ro's hands closed on her shoulders, kneading her muscles. "You cannot deny what you need forever," he breathed into her neck.

Perhaps not even long enough to escape him, she thought bitterly. "This is not an appropriate test," she snapped.

152

"In what way?" he asked in the calm voice that he adopted when she yelled at him. He knew that voice infuriated her, but he used it regardless, as if she were a child in need of scolding.

"You are always near me and always aroused. Your scent is driving me mad."

"It does not have to."

Deliya turned on him, pushing him back. "What sort of test is this?" she demanded. "You make me crazy and offer yourself."

"What would you have me do?" he asked, a smile pulling at the corners of his mouth.

She bit back her fury, desperate to make herself clear on this matter. "I have no options but you and madness," she exploded, realizing she could not remain calm in the face of his mocking smile.

His smirk disappeared. Ro crossed his arms over his chest. "You want schaen?" he asked, his voice cold.

Deliya furrowed her brow. "What is a schaen?" Sometimes, it seemed they didn't even share a common language.

"A sterile male to satisfy a woman's urges," he snapped, as if she should have known the term. His shoulder muscles bunched and his eyes were as cold as his voice.

She stood frozen in disbelief; the concept shocked her on many levels. She wished she could honestly claim it was the idea of stealing a male's fertility that bothered her most about the practice. It didn't.

She felt ill, nauseated by the idea of taking another man. Worse, a fire burned deep in her gut at the idea of Ro's willingness to give her to another man so easily. Loric would never have sent her to another if he could convince her otherwise.

She ground her teeth in anger and smacked Ro's cheek hard. "I would never!"

He grasped her hand before she could strike him a second time. "Why not? You want release. You simply do not want me. Why not schaen?" His eyes flashed dangerously.

Because, it wouldn't be you.

Deliya shook her head to dislodge that idea. "A *sterile* male," she spat.

He pulled her to his body, his muscles tense and his breathing ragged. "Who is it that you want, Deliya?"

You. She shook her head hopelessly.

"You want another man? You want to invite another man to your bed as you could in your precious villages?"

"You would allow that?" she stammered, forcing back tears. How could he allow that if he cared for her? Were Magden men who wished to take a mate so different than Fion's Children?

"You are denying any right I have to prevent it," he challenged.

Deliya felt her face heat. "I want nothing," she attested. "I want no one. Not you and not one of your men—or your schaen."

His eyes narrowed. "Why did you not choose him to give you a child to begin with?"

She recoiled in surprise. Did he truly doubt her word that there was no other man? "I told you—"

Ro's mouth covered hers, devouring her, making her head swim. Deliya stumbled against his chest. His mouth softened. He tasted her slowly; and she groaned, pressing closer to him. He released her arm, running his hand to the small of her back as he left her mouth, nibbling along her jawline.

Deliya closed her eyes and laid her head back with a sigh. She groaned his name, her whole body weak and pliant. She molded to him as he lifted her to fit him. He eased her to the bed and lay beside her. Deliya stared into his face, knowing he would make love to her, knowing she would let him.

He leaned over her, his breath a warm breeze over her sensitized lips. "Is it me that you want?" he asked.

Deliya fisted her hand in his tunic, stunned to silence. She couldn't force the words past her lips. Didn't he know what she wanted by now?

Ro pried her hand open, shaking his head. "When you can say it." He pushed off the bed and walked away.

She stared after him in disbelief, burying her face in the pillow as the door closed behind him. She sobbed, rubbing her aching temples. She had to leave before this game drove her insane, before she forgot her duty and let her body rule her mind.

* * * *

Deliya paused in the shadows, watching Ro's guards move further away. She ran for the stable, slipping jaglin-soft into the low building. She berated herself again. Was it really worth leaving this way? Unarmed and unarmored without her seeds and herbs? She didn't even have trousers to wear, and winter would be upon her all too soon. Would she really flee into the night in one of Ro's silin gowns with her abinatine as her only means of defense?

She sighed. She had argued this with herself a dozen times. She wouldn't survive another week with Ro without begging him to ease her schen. Having him beside her was driving her mad.

Why can you not simply take this as a sign from the Mother?

Because, I am weak, and I will not use the excuse that this is the Mother's will to hide from that fact. If any of her people had intermarried in the past, Deliya could accept that this was Fion's will, but they had not and it was not.

There had never been a need to intermarry until now, her traitorous heart protested.

She pushed that thought away. How would she explain herself to Mother Fion and Mother Leiana at her death if she did such a thing? She had to leave. If she left, there would be nothing to explain.

Deliya found her war-buck in the dim light sifting through the half-doors of the stall backs, open to let in the mild autumn air. She stroked his face, reaching for a bridle.

She stilled, the bridle fisted in her hand, sensing that she was not alone. She sucked in her breath, as a hand closed on her wrist and dragged her to a chest so familiar that she eased into it in relief.

"Ro," she whispered, drinking in his scent. Her nerves buzzed in awareness of him.

He took the bridle from her hand. "You broke our agreement," he growled. "Again."

Deliya nodded. "I know. I can offer no explanation..." In truth, she couldn't remember why she ran—not while she was in Ro's arms.

"Because there is no excuse." Ro drew her further

into the stable then tugged on her wrist, urging her to her knees beside a feed cube.

She watched him in the near darkness, her mind muddled. She sucked in her breath as he released his erect length from his trousers. Was this her penalty? To be at his use? Her blood heated at the prospect.

Deliya stroked her free hand over his cock then took it in her mouth. Ro's hand fisted in her hair and stopped her. She teased at him with her tongue, moaning as his flavor swirled inside her mouth, the slight release of his readiness taunting her with the musk she would taste at his climax.

"What are you doing?" he panted.

She didn't answer. His grip lessened, and she took him deeper. He trembled, his scent intensifying. Deliya worked his length; she'd always wanted to do this but had never dreamed it would be this good.

"Mag alive," he groaned. His arm tightened again, and he backed from her, removing his cock from her mouth. "No. Not this way."

Deliya sank to the floor, her wrist still in Ro's grasp. She licked her lips, the flutter in her stomach turning into a crawling in her skin that his touch would still.

Ro knelt in front of her, his lips nearly brushing hers. "You broke our agreement," he repeated.

"Yes. I did."

He caressed her breast, plucking at her nipple lightly. "Why did you run?"

She groaned, arching into his touch. It would be so easy not to fight her schen, to give in and live to their agreement, to tell him that she ran because he had won.

"Why, Deliya?"

She shook her head; it would be too easy.

Ro pulled her up to her knees and met her lips gently. He nipped at her chin then her lower lip, drawing it into his mouth. Deliya opened to him, no longer caring that she was surrendering. He released her mouth and turned her, draping her over the feed block and pressing her hands to the far edge beneath one of his.

She shuddered as he lifted the back of her skirt. He was taking a penalty. Would he take her hard and fast? She bit back a groan at the realization that she didn't care how he took her, as long as he did it soon. She spread her legs in silent invitation.

His fingers sank deep in her, stroking her slowly. "You want me," he breathed.

Deliya didn't deny it. She laid her cheek on his arm, delighting in the brush of his coarse hair and cool skin over her heated face.

Ro's hand retreated and he eased inside her. Deliya strained back against him. He rocked inside her in long, leisurely strokes that stole her sanity. She had been prepared for him to be rushed, not tender. He threaded his fingers through hers and eased his free hand around her hip, cradling her to his body.

"So hot," he murmured. "Your schen makes you like fire in my hands."

She rolled her cheek on his arm, feeling the end coming for her. She screamed harshly as her climax washed over her, an icy shock to her overheated body. Ro groaned, and his hands tightened on her as her body milked at his. She pushed back hard on him, craving completion.

"You want me locked inside you." He didn't ask. He

didn't have to.

Deliya nodded, gasping as he released her hands.

He moved away, cursing fluently as his seed shot onto the feed block and her inner thigh. He pressed her hard against the block, hands fisted in her dress until she thought he might tear it in two.

Her eyes flew open in surprise and dismay. She turned her head, searching out the faint outlines of his face in the darkness. She stroked the taut muscles of his neck, shaking her head as tears spilled down her cheek.

"You should not," she stammered.

Ro was playing a dangerous game. It was instinct for the male to complete in the stim band—or at least with pressure applied to the head at climax. A male couldn't pull out like that too many times or he would drive himself mad.

His hands eased. He pulled away from her, straightened her dress, his fingers lingering on her hip. He stood and strode a few arms'-lengths away, fastening his trousers.

"Ro?" she called after him, as stunned by his sudden physical withdrawal as she had been by his sexual withdrawal.

He put his hand down to pull her to her feet. He guided her back across the courtyard and into his home without a word. He didn't pause as he led her back to her room, waving Donic off when the general tried to speak to him. Deliya turned her face from the sour look Donic shot her. She couldn't argue that she deserved his ire this time.

Ro closed the door, releasing her elbow and crossing his arms over his chest. "You had something to ask me?" he inquired coldly.

Deliya backed off a step; this was a new and disconcerting side of Ro. "You should not do that. The danger—"

"You wanted me to take you to completion?" he interrupted her.

She felt her face heat. "I admitted that."

He closed the distance, stopping mere finger-widths from her. Deliya breathed in his scent, the faint taste of him still echoing within her.

"Say it now," Ro ordered. "Say it without tricks, and sign the contract."

Deliya bit her lip, fighting back the urge to do as he demanded. It would be easy. *Too easy.* She was better trained than this.

Ro nodded. "I could have taken you to completion in the stable and claimed your submission as proof of your need. I did not do that."

"Why?" she asked weakly. "Why did you give up your victory?"

His hands closed on her shoulders. "I do not seek a tactical engagement with you. When you come to me, it will not be because I used my knowledge of your weaknesses to crumble your defenses. It will be because you have abandoned them and come to me willingly."

Deliya nodded. "And my penalty? Was the stable..."

"No. The stable was—an affirmation. I will not try its like again." He released her and backed off a stride. "Despite your willingness, I had no right to take advantage that way."

"My penalty?" she asked again.

Ro stroked her cheek, smiling sadly. "Your penalty

is an extra week to convince you to agree to the contract."

Deliya bit back her protest. She had broken her word; and by Magden law, Ro would be expected to exact a penalty. What penalty had she expected? She had been prepared for a harsh lesson, but she had to admit that Ro's kindness would be more difficult to ignore.

"It is an appropriate penalty."

"I am glad you agree," he noted wryly.

Deliya forced a smile to her reluctant lips. "Who would I lodge a formal grievance with, if I chose to?"

Ro laughed harshly at that.

"As I thought. Then I suppose complaining is a waste of my time."

"It is."

"Will you be coming to bed now?" she asked.

Ro's smile disappeared. "Not tonight. After the stable, I think it best if I sleep in my own bed."

"Are you concerned about my self-control or your own?" she snapped, irritated at the sense of loss she felt.

Ro threaded his hands in her hair, cupping her face up, sweeping his lips across hers and stepping away as her body responded. Her eyes wandered to his groin, watching the rising proof of his own lack of control.

"Both," he growled. "Sleep well, Deliya." He strode to the door and yanked it open then paused, taking a calming breath. "Do not try to escape me again. There will be guards at the door and below your window. If you break your vow, there will be a new penalty for you."

"What will you do?" Deliya asked nervously.

"You will not leave me," he whispered. "Ever. If you run from me again, you will contract with me."

Deliya sank to the bed in resignation. Ro left without looking back. She laid her head on the pillows, cursing her body as she inhaled his scent on her bedding. Tomorrow he would be back, a living, breathing temptation. There was no escape. She couldn't even brew a tea to entice herself to sleep.

Chapter Fifteen

Abrin 30th, Ti 10-459

Deliya looked up from her writing as Ro strode into her room then gaped in amazement. He was armored and armed. His jaw was tight with fury and his step heavy as he went about collecting his belongings. She watched him, annoyed at the sense of loss she felt at the thought of him leaving her room.

"Ro? What has happened?"

"Jurel's troops have broken through our lines. I cannot ask my men to fight him alone."

Deliya sighed in relief that she cursed herself for feeling. "How long will you be gone?"

He shrugged, as if it were of no consequence how long he lingered in battle. "Two weeks, perhaps. Longer if needs be."

She fisted her pen, her mind reeling. What did this mean with regard to their agreement?

As if reading her thoughts, he sighed. "I vowed to win you within the four weeks or release you," he managed in a tight voice. "I will live to my vow. If there were any way to avoid this battle, I would. I would convince you, no matter the cost, if I could risk my people in good conscience, but I cannot."

"You are asking me to leave?" Deliya whispered. She should be happy; she had what she wanted, but the thought of never seeing him again made her heart ache.

Ro turned to her. "Never, but I cannot live with you and not touch you. I cannot even for an heir from you. If you will not contract, my men will take you to a home farther within Magden lands where you will be safe. You will have land to grow your crops and men to protect you, to farm your land for you. You can rebuild your people as you wished.

"The choice is yours. I fail by leaving you. I know that. If you choose to stay, I would thank your Goddess Fion for showing me mercy. I do not anticipate that I will be doing that. Will I?"

Deliya stared at him in open-mouthed wonder. He was walking away and giving her the freedom she'd asked for, and she couldn't find the heart to thank him for that gift.

Ro turned to the door, pain in his eyes.

She jumped up, spilling ink over the page of the Great Book she'd been transcribing from memory. Her eyes passed over it without concern for the hours she'd just rendered useless. She ran to him, touching his arm.

"Wait," she pleaded.

He looked at her in surprise, the hope burning in his eyes melting into a wary reserve. "Yes?"

She hesitated, looking to her hand, torn. Deliya opened her mouth to speak then shut it again; she couldn't promise him his contract, but she couldn't let him leave this way either.

"Deliya, I have no time for games," he warned.

"Let me anoint you," she burst out. "Let me ask Fion to protect you in battle."

"What?" he demanded, his fury returned.

Deliya's cheeks burned; she couldn't lie to him—not about this. "A priestess does this before one she cares for goes into battle," she whispered, praying for his understanding.

Ro looked down at her, his eyes flashing with some

strong emotion. "There is only one blessing I want from you. If you cannot give it freely, I do not wish any at all."

Deliya sucked in her breath in shock, turning from him. She blinked back tears, reminding herself sternly that he didn't understand what asking for his protection meant to her, and she could not tell him without giving him what he wanted most.

"I thought not," he growled.

She cringed, as the door slammed behind him and the sound of his footsteps faded down the hall. She went to the window overlooking the courtyard on shaking legs to watch Ro mount his war-buck. He didn't look at her window. He seemed to make a point of not looking.

Deliya turned to the door as it opened again, smoothing the front of her robe.

A guard entered and placed her packs on the bed. He kept his eyes focused on the floor near his feet as most of Ro's men did. "His Majesty ordered me to return these to you."

"Thank you." She managed an unwavering voice somehow, though she wasn't certain how.

"Do you require anything else of me, Priestess?"

I require Ro. She shook her head. This young man could not give her what she needed most. No one could.

He turned away.

"Yes," she decided. "Where is this battle?"

"Why would you need to know that?" he asked warily.

"Do you not pray for those who have gone to battle?"

"Of course."

Deliya waited, drumming her fingers on her thigh to punctuate her demand for an answer.

The guard sighed. "Jurel broke through at Gidlore."

"Thank you. Please leave me."

She swallowed a sour wave of bile. Ro was going to defend the land he had won for her at the same time he granted her freedom. Deliya rubbed at her forehead, the thought making her head ache; it was impossible to understand Ro.

She forced herself to think logically. He had taken the land from Jurel and had to defend it from the Lengar now. It was not connected to his pursuit of her in any way.

Still, the knowledge further scrambled her already muddled thoughts and feelings. What Ro was doing was a noble thing. Could she be any less noble? What would it cost her to give him the remaining ten days when he returned?

"My sanity," she decided miserably, "and his." It would be unkind to build up his hopes by staying only to fight her hardest to leave when the time was up. If he touched her again, she might surrender to his demand. Was she prepared to concede defeat? To set aside the ways of her people and take him as her mate?

"No. I cannot." Every facet of her training told Deliya that she could never compromise on that point. Her duty was simple; she couldn't muddy the crystal clarity of it with emotion. She was trained not to.

She sank to the bed between her packs, tears coursing down her face. Training or not, giving up Ro hurt. She pulled the closer pack open, irritated with herself. There was nothing left for her but to ask the guards to take her away as Ro offered. What was the sense in crying about that?

"None," she chided herself, her voice holding the same bitter edge Vela's often had when doing the same.

She would check her packs, take those few things that were hers and leave. She stood and wiped the tears away impatiently, arranging her crocks and flasks on the bed in the time-honored pattern that would tell her at a glance if she were missing any of her wares. She focused her attention on the task, blocking the troubling jumble of thoughts from her mind.

"Lizor berry," she whispered. She set it in its proper place in the center of the pattern. "Gola berry." *To the left of lizor berry.* "Walla." *To the right and above lizor berry.* "Olum." *Below Walla and to the right of lizor berry.*

Crock after crock and flask after flask, she lined up the tools of her healing, until the oils and herbs, roots and distillations formed a calming pattern. She laid her abinatine at the lower edge to complete the ceremony and bowed her head reverently, pausing in confusion at the lump she saw in one of her packs. She glanced at the design and assured herself that nothing was missing.

She pulled the object out, smiling weakly as she recognized the flask sealed with green wax. Deliya remembered it well; for the first three years of her exile, she had looked at it constantly. She'd alternately worried about what bad times were coming and considered opening it when her loneliness was crushing.

She had only considered opening it for a moment when Loric and Vela died, but Celdin had been another matter. Deliya sobbed at the memory. She had sat staring at the flask for hours after she tilled his ashes into the soil, solitude closing in around her. If only she'd known how complete that solitude was, she would have opened it then.

As it was, she'd forced herself to tour her land, convinced herself that she had not lost hope. Most of the planting had been accomplished; she had food and traps, work animals and knowledge. Her mother would send for her soon and end the torture of waiting for true adulthood while battles raged on without her.

Deliya sobbed, curling onto her bed with her sacred stores. She took a shuddering breath. "What do I have now, Mother?"

She stopped crying, the answer as clear in her mind as if her mother had spoken it aloud. "Nothing." She had nothing but herself and her child. There would be no crops this year. She had no family, no friends, no home. She owned nothing but the medicinals around her, armor that would not fit in a few short months, a single change of clothing that would likewise become useless, a war-buck and two mares, and the bags of seed she wouldn't be capable of planting without Ro's workmen when it would need to be done.

Everything around her—Every comfort belonged to Ro.

Deliya stared at the room through her tears. It was strange how hollow her devotion to duty felt. If she lived according to the traditions, she would be a Mother without a people to lead, a woman without a mate and without hope of giving her child something better than she had. She would be sentencing her child to the same choice she now faced.

But they could both have everything wonderful in

life if she simply accepted Ro as her mate.

She lay her hand over her womb. Taking Ro as her mate wouldn't stop her from imparting her culture to her child. Ro had given his vow that their child would have both worlds. And if she turned her back on the traditions, their child could marry anyone he or she wished without this anguish. Keeping the traditions meant that she had no hope of providing a happy life for her child.

"No hope," Deliya breathed. "Oh Mother! If there was ever a time that I needed your guidance, this is it."

She sat up, using her abinatine to break the seal on the flask, her hands shaking. She pulled out the cork, tipping it over her palm. It was empty.

Deliya bit back a harsh laugh. "Was that what you wanted to tell me?" she demanded. "That I had no one to depend on but myself?" She flung the flask at the wall, curling on the bed and closing her eyes as the pottery shattered.

The door flew open.

"Priestess?" the guard asked.

"Leave me," she sniffed.

He crossed the room but not toward her. "I will get a servant to clean this," he informed her.

"I will do it."

"You will cut yourself. His Majesty would have my head, if I allowed that." The guard sifted through the shards then crossed to the bed. A sheet of paper fluttered to the quilt next to her cheek. He turned away. "I will bring a servant," he repeated with a note of warning in his tone.

Deliya opened her eyes as the door closed, squinting at the paper. She sat up abruptly, looking at the shattered flask in understanding. She spread the note that had been stuck stubbornly inside flat on the bed and began to read.

"Merciful Mother," she breathed. It was a page torn from the Great Book. A paragraph was circled in ink much newer than that of the book itself, and a missive in her mother's hand graced the wide margin.

Deliya trailed her finger over her mother's words, reading them aloud, though she heard Mother Leiana's voice in her memory. "My dearest daughter, my heir—" She wiped away fresh tears at that.

I fear I may leave nothing but this advice for you, and for that I must ask your forgiveness. If you read this, I can only assume that you are alone in the world. Remember your earliest training at my hand. Remember my love for you, a mother's love for her child. Most of all, remember that Fion leads by example.

She scanned the passage her mother had circled, grimacing at the faded words and tear-stained page. She closed her eyes, calling the words from memory and translating them from the ancient tongue.

"Mag left his throne and took Fion safely home. He knelt at Fion's feet and called her beloved. Fion took the king of gods according to tradition." Deliya recited it again, her mind whirling. "Fion leads by example," she whispered excitedly. Fion took Mag as mate. She was Fion's daughter and Ro was one of Mag's sons.

Had her mother foreseen that she would have no mate unless she took a Magden man? Had Leiana known her daughter would reach this desperate moment where she felt she had to choose between duty and hope?

Deliya ran to her cabinet and pulled on the trouskit, tunic and boots Ro had provided her with for riding. She vaulted down the stairs and sprinted to the stable. One of the guards tried to wave her down as she rode across the courtyard, but Deliya kneed her buck to a full run and made the opening before the soldiers could slam the gate shut.

She didn't pause, working her mount hard as she headed after Ro on the trail to Gidlore. She didn't question her need to go to him now. She couldn't allow him to go into battle believing that he would never see her again. Such a thing could distract him in battle.

But she had to hurry. He had more than an hour's lead on her.

* * * *

Ro pulled his war-buck to a halt at the shouts behind him.

"What in Len's unholy underworld is that about?" Donic groused.

"Len, indeed," Ro growled, as the flash of white gold hair appeared, streaking through the meadow alongside the column of men. He urged his buck to a run on an intercept course.

Deliya pulled up short as he blocked her path. He grasped her reins, furious with her. Her mount was sweat-coated and tired from a long, hard run; and her breathing was no better. Worse, her abinatine was not on her belt. Nor was her sword.

Ro met her eyes, his tirade sticking in his throat. He touched her tear-stained cheek. Her hair was wind whipped and her eyes swollen.

"Ro, I have to speak with you—" she began urgently.

Common sense intruded. He scanned the forest on their unprotected side warily. The Lengar were near. She could not stay here.

"Are you insane? Riding out like this?" he thundered, gesturing to indicate her unarmed and unarmored state. "Did you ride like that the whole way?"

Deliya's brow wrinkled in confusion. "Like what?"

"Unguarded. Unarmored. Your pace alone would have seen you killed had you been thrown."

She grimaced. "Ro—"

"There is no excuse for this. You will return home immediately."

"After I speak to you," she insisted.

"When I return. We had time to discuss whatever you wished before I left." *More than enough time, and you did not say anything of importance then.*

"A few moments," she pleaded.

"Not here and not now. Novin!" he bellowed.

"Ro!"

He ignored her, handing her reins off to Novin. "Take the priestess back home. Take four men with you for her safety. Mind that she travels at a leisurely pace this time. If she escapes again, you will face me, your father be damned."

Novin grinned widely. "As you wish, Ro."

Deliya watched their exchange in open-mouthed amazement. "Ro, this is important," she protested.

Ro grasped her head between his hands, half-dragging her into his lap as he brought her mouth to his, taking the kiss he should have taken before he left. Her hand splayed over his chest, and her skin burned hot even through his gloved hands, her mouth urgent. He set her back on her buck, shifting uncomfortably.

"There is only one important thing now." He tipped his chin to her flat stomach. "Go home, Deliya."

She hesitated, sighing in resignation. "Be safe," she whispered.

As Novin led her mount away, Ro took heart in the fact that she glanced back at him several times. She seemed uncertain, moreso than he had ever seen her.

Novin motioned to four of the men, and they fell into formation around Deliya. Ro sighed in relief at the ones he chose; he would miss those five good men in battle, but it was more important that Deliya have them. They closed around her, and she rode straight and proud in their midst, her hands on her thighs battle-style.

Ro sighed again. He rode back up the column, cursing his erection soundly.

"What was that?" Donic asked.

It was no secret he thought Ro's arrangement with Deliya was foolhardy, but he had learned to keep his mouth shut about it. It was unlikely anyone but Donic had any clue that Deliya carried his child, and Ro wanted to keep it that way until he won his bride. To everyone else within the walls of his house, she was simply a mistress, though an important one.

He scowled, regretting already that he hadn't let Deliya say what she had come to say. It might really have taken only a moment. "I have no idea," he admitted.

"She rode out here for no reason?"

"She had a reason, but this was not the time or place to discuss it." He winced, remembering her tears. It would be weeks before he would know...if Deliya didn't escape again before then.

He pushed back his annoyance. When he did see her again, she would learn how much this stunt had unnerved him. If he was forced to hunt her down for that confrontation, she would need the protection of her goddess when he found her.

CHAPTER SIXTEEN

Veril 18th, Ti 10-459

Deliya watched Ro mount the front stairs from her window, turning back to the bed as he passed from her field of vision. She pressed her hands to her stomach nervously. He was sure to be furious at her for following him toward the battle. At the moment she looked at her bed a little more than three weeks earlier and saw her abinatine still nestled below the assorted crocks and flasks, she had realized just how foolish she had been.

Would he confront her immediately or tend to his needs first? Deliya paced the floor. There was no reason she couldn't go to him. Perhaps if she offered her apologies before he came to her—

She turned toward the door as it opened.

Ro met her eyes, closing the door behind him and leaning against it, his jaw tight in barely leashed fury. He must have shed his armor as he walked to have come to her so quickly.

"I suppose you have an explanation for your actions," he prodded her.

She went to the table that held her herbs, pulled out the page from the Great Book with shaking hands, and turned. She gasped as she came face to face with Ro; he'd moved swiftly and silently. *He must be deadly in battle,* she mused.

Ro cleared his throat, and she offered him the page. He took it from her hand and read it, his face in the same hard, inflexible expression.

"And this means what?" he demanded.

"Have you heard the story before?"

He shrugged. "Perhaps. When I was young. It never seemed—"

"Important?"

Ro motioned to the paper. "Is it?"

Deliya nodded. "You see the missive?" she asked, pointing.

"Your mother sent you to me," he noted. "She wanted the Magden to ally with Fion's children as Fion and Mag allied when Len attacked the soul's reward and was banished to his dungeons." He pushed the page back at her.

She shook her head as she took it. "No. You are misinterpreting the text," she explained.

Ro looked at her dubiously. "How so?"

Deliya took a calming breath. She traced the faded words with a fingertip. "*Mag Ti le ti trin. Tie Fion han so.* Mag left his throne. He took Fion safely home."

He nodded. "They allied."

"No!" She calmed herself and began again. "You see the faded bit?"

Ro raised an eyebrow in warning.

"As part of a priestess's early training, she is required to memorize every word of the Great Book."

"And?"

"I didn't feel it was important. I memorized the words, but I never internalized them. I could not see when they would ever be of use."

"What would?" Ro asked impatiently.

"*Mag ken e Fion chel Pris Chidan. Fion tie Ti ag diten,*" she quoted from memory. She held her breath and waited for his response.

He pulled the page from her hands and ambled across the room, staring at the faint words she'd quoted. How clear was it? Would he believe her if he couldn't see the words clearly?

Deliya inched after him, stopping at the foot of the bed as he whipped around to face her.

"Why was this so important that you endangered yourself and our child to come after me?"

"I..." She pressed a hand to the squirming in her stomach and leaned against the footboard of the bed, her heart sinking. It meant nothing to him and probably would not even when she explained it.

He strode to her, taking her gently by her upper arms. "What did you ride out to tell me?"

"That I would sign your contract."

"That is all?"

She shrugged, his grip making the motion awkward.

Ro pushed away from her. "Because the gods were wed, you decided to sign a contract with me," he spat. He pushed a hand through his hair, muttering curses as he turned from her. He turned back, starting to speak then stopping again with a growl of frustration.

How dare he!

Deliya looked around for the closest object at hand. Ro ducked in surprise, and the crock of lizor berry powder sailed over his head and shattered against the wall. He looked at the mess then back at her, his fury fading into hopeless confusion.

Her fury wasn't appeased at all. Deliya tried to still her shaking hands as she snatched up the crock of olum. "Say it again, and I will not miss," she promised.

She tried to calm herself. Fury was unbecoming. It was beneath one of Fion's priestesses. It had taken the extinction of their race to enrage Vela. *I should make an effort to make my mentor proud of how well I internalized her teachings.*

To Len's Dungeons with that! She threw the second crock with a grunt of pure frustration and reached for a third.

Ro caught the olum, tossing it on the bed as he stepped to her and captured her hands, staying the flight of the crock of Walla that would have come next. His expression was abruptly unsure. "Why are you doing this?" he asked.

"Are all Magden males this stupid?" she inquired coldly. "If so, I can't see how your race survives."

He pried the crock from her fingers and set it on the table she had snatched it from. Deliya balled up her fists, barely corking the urge to strike him hard across his insulting mouth.

"Do not try it," he warned. "Now. I will take a wild leap of faith and suppose that you are angry with me, because you love me."

She crossed her arms under her breasts and stared at a point over his shoulder, doing her best to ignore him. Ro turned her face back to his gently; she met his eyes in challenge, unwilling to seem the sulking child by not doing so.

"You have never told me that you do, so it is not unexpected that I would have to suppose such a thing."

"Any fool with eyes and a heart—" she stormed.

"Would see what?"

"What difference does it make?"

"It makes a difference," he assured her. "Why did you ride after me?" Ro waited a moment for her answer then dropped his lips to hers.

Deliya's body seemed intent on answering for her.

Her blood heated, and visions of their encounter in the stable filled her mind. Deliya lost herself in their rising passion, her anger at his dismissal quickly forgotten.

Ro unwound her hands from his tunic, pressing them to the edge of the footboard beside her thighs and covering them with his. "This was why you came after me," he whispered. "Wasn't it?"

"Ro, please." She nipped at his chin.

"What did the text mean to you?"

"That the reasons I gave myself for pushing you away were ridiculous," she admitted. "Fion Herself took Mag as mate. How could one of Her daughters be seen as a traitor for loving one of Mag's sons?"

"Loving?" He pressed his body to hers, his erect length seeking her core. "And you denied that love despite the fact that you serve the Goddess of Love?"

Deliya groaned at the truth of that. "I could not let you think for another moment that I had no love for you. I could not let you go into battle believing that I would have disappeared with our child before you returned."

Ro chuckled. "I gave orders that you were to remain here until I returned," he informed her.

"It did not work," she reminded him.

"You came after me to put my mind at ease?"

"To convince you that I love you. I would have knelt at your feet to prove it."

"A priestess of Fion kneels to no man," he quoted her.

"I knelt before you in the stable," she whispered. "I would kneel before you now," she offered, tipping her mound to him.

Ro shivered, his breathing ragged. "I am a Magden

king," he reminded her. "I kneel to no man."

"I know. I do not ask you to kneel to me." The idea of kneeling before Ro, of pleasuring him as a sign of her sincerity, made her body throb.

He shook his head and sank to his knees. "I kneel to no man," he repeated. "I kneel to you. I would have knelt to you at any time for the promise of your love."

"You do not have to do this."

"Mag knelt at Fion's feet and called her beloved." Ro pulled her robe open in a single movement, and his lips closed on her hood.

Deliya jerked, stunned by his unexpected move. He lifted her onto the footboard, spreading her legs wider. His tongue caressed her, and Deliya gripped the board tighter.

"Beloved," he breathed into her. *"Ma Chidan."* He stroked his tongue over her slowly, as if he were bathing her.

"I love you," Deliya whispered.

He buried his tongue deep inside her at that, his groan a delicious counterpoint to the first whispers of her climax. Ro was relentless. His tongue tasted and taunted, darted and danced until Deliya threw her head back and vented a formless howl of release.

Ro stood, nipping at her trembling lips. "We will do this your way," he informed her. "Tell me how that is. Is it like the first time? Must I place myself in your hands?"

"My ceremony?" she asked.

"Am I unworthy—"

Deliya covered his lips with her hand, shaking her head. "Never think that."

Ro nodded, kissing her fingertips. "What needs

done? Am I placing myself in your hands?"

"No. That is only necessary for the challenge." Her head spun at the implications. Ro wanted her ceremony.

"Would you like," he began.

"No. Not this time," she answered, distracted.

"Deliya?"

She met his eyes. "Yes?"

"Quickly." He guided her hand to his cock. It jumped at her touch.

Deliya slid to her feet and turned to the bed, grasping the footboard and heaving it toward her a half a hand.

Ro covered her hands with his, removing them gently. He kissed the shell of her ear. "Tell me what you need," he instructed.

"Pull the bed from the wall."

"How far?"

"An arm's length."

He kissed her throat. "Do whatever else needs done."

Deliya left the circle of his arms reluctantly, smiling as he moved the bed in one smooth motion. She pulled a long, green silin dress from the cabinet and discarded her robe in favor of the garment. She stilled as she turned to face Ro.

* * * *

Ro fisted his hand in his tunic, every muscle bunching as he stared at Deliya, unable even to let the material fall to the floor. His eyes traveled the length of her left leg, bared in the slit of the presentation dress.

Her pale breasts peeked into the upper slit, making him ache to peel the dress back and frame them in the dark silin.

He locked down on his self-control. He had never asked her to wear that dress. He'd never told her what the significance of it was. Deliya could not know the restraint it took not to fall on her at the sight of her in it.

She met his eyes, questioning his tension silently. He wondered at her choice. It could not be coincidence that she chose that dress. Could she not simply let him honor Fion for the gift of her love without trying to appease his Magden sensibilities?

"I said we would consummate our contract your way," he growled.

Deliya backed off a step in confusion. "I do not understand."

"The dress."

"I require a long, silin gown," she whispered. "Traditionally, I would wear my robes and overmantle, but in the absence of them, this will suffice."

Ro swallowed with some difficulty. It would more than suffice.

"This dress has some meaning to you," she guessed. "If it is inappropriate to wear it—"

"It is more appropriate than you can comprehend at this moment," he assured her, raking his hungry eyes over her body again.

She blushed then sauntered to him. "And will you show me what the dress means to a Magden king?" she offered in a voice low and sultry in invitation.

Ro locked down on his muscles, gulping in air, the urge do so all but undoing his resolve to properly thank her Goddess. "Next time," he replied solemnly. "You will wear this for me again."

Deliya nodded, her nipples calling him, beaded against the silin. "You have my vow."

"Your ceremony," he reminded her.

She turned to the table beside the foot of the bed and took up her bowl, anointing it with a sweet-smelling oil and saying a blessing much like the one she had used when she made the healing circle for Novin. Deliya picked up the bowl and kissed the side, leaving a sheen of the oil on her lips that made Ro want to lick it off.

"Should I completely disrobe?" he asked, unsure of what was required for her ceremony. Her healing circle had very specific rules. When he was within the boundaries, he had been required to remove only his shirt, armor, boots and weapons.

Deliya smiled. "It is much easier if you do," she teased.

Ro pulled off his boots and trousers, glad for that favor. He smiled as Deliya bent to her work, an idea taking hold. He stood behind her, tracing his hands over her hips.

She paused in adding a gray powder to the bowl, pressing back against him, her skin heating beneath his fingers. "Ro, if you want me to finish quickly..." she pleaded.

He trailed his hands up her stomach to cup her breasts. "You were trained to face the challenge," he reminded her.

She dropped the powder into the bowl and planted her hands on the tabletop. "Women in the challenge are not pregnant, Ro," she snapped.

He chuckled. "My touch disturbs you?"

Deliya turned on him, pushing at his chest with a burning, trembling hand. "Ro Ti, you face a woman in her schen—a love-schen, who has not had use of the man she loves for more than three weeks. I gave my vow not to raise my blade against you, but I am a trained warrior, and if you tease me much more..." She let the threat hang between them.

He removed his hands, smiling in victory. "As you wish, my love," he conceded.

She nodded and returned to her work. Ro turned around her and leaned back on the footboard, watching her. She added ingredients, mixing them with the point of her blade. She muttered to herself, glancing at his body in undisguised longing. Ro bit back a laugh at that.

Deliya furrowed her brow, touching each crock she'd used in turn. She snatched up the one from the bed and set it back in an empty place on the table with a hearty thunk. She scanned the bed and table again. She bit her lip and rubbed at her forehead.

Ro pushed off the bed and planted his lips on her forehead, healing her. "You should have told me," he whispered, rubbing the knots from her shoulders.

"It is not..." Deliya growled in frustration.

Ro moved to the next knot along her spine. "Is it not?" he challenged.

She groaned and shifted to guide him to another tense spot. "Of course, I feel the signs," she reasoned.

"Not while you carry my child," he grumbled. "I will heal you as often as you require."

"I meant, that is not causing my concern."

"What is?"

"My lizor berry powder. I had it minutes ago when I was checking my stores. What have I done with it?"

Ro grimaced. "What does this powder look like?" he asked, hoping he was wrong.

"Deep red."

"In a purple crock with a red lid?"

Deliya smiled. "Yes. Where did I put it?"

Ro sighed and turned her toward the shattered crock. "I believe you were aiming for me."

She covered her mouth with her hand, looking pained, then strode to the mess and squatted next to it, pulling bits of pottery out with her fingertips.

"Deliya, you will cut yourself," he pleaded. "We can get lizor powder from the kitchen."

"It will not be pure."

"We can wait to do this."

Deliya scooped up a handful of the powder and returned to the table. "Lizor blooms in summer, Ro. I assume you want to consummate before our child is born?" she asked as she mixed the powder into the bowl.

"I certainly hope so," he growled.

She nodded as she said another quiet prayer. "I will close the circle in a few moments," she told him.

"How long will we be inside the circle?" Ro asked, suddenly aware of the myriad of problems this could cause.

Deliya smiled widely. "Quite a while, I imagine. You are rather virile, as I recall."

"Do not close the circle yet," he ordered, striding to the door.

"Ro, you are nude," she gasped.

He laughed loud and long. "I am a Magden king," he

stated, looking at her and pausing again at the sight of her in the presentation gown. "You should go in the other room for a moment," he suggested.

She placed her fists on her hips, darkening. "You may walk about unclothed, but I must hide away while I am clothed?" she demanded.

"No, but it is too much to expect that my men would be able to resist looking at you in that dress. They barely avoid my blade on a daily basis as it is, and I have no wish to kill them for presuming too much."

Deliya turned and fled, shooting him a look of disbelief as she closed the door to the bath.

Ro ordered the man outside the room to send for food, hesitated, then added Lover's Repast to his orders. He closed them in again and knocked on the bath door. "Deliya?"

She opened the door, looking uncertain. "You were joking. Were you not?" she whispered.

"About?"

"You would really kill a man for looking at me?"

"No," he admitted. "I would not kill a man who dared to look, though I would be within my rights to." He cupped her cheek. "If he touched you, it would be another matter."

She dropped her gaze. "Others have died for presuming that much."

And will again, if it comes to that. Ro kissed her, groaning as she pressed to his body. "They had better hurry with the food," he grumbled. "I will not survive this erection forever."

Deliya smiled a secretive smile. "We shall see."

* * * *

Ro stretched out on the bed, watching as Deliya sprinkled the last handful of the light purple powder to close the circle. She bent her head and asked Fion's blessing then turned to him.

"You have to stand for the first bit," she told him.

He nodded and stood beside the bed, furrowing his brow as she returned with her abinatine and a flask.

She grinned as she set the flask and sheath on the bed and held the blade between them. "This is your last chance to back out, Ro."

"Are you mad? Why would I want to do that?"

Her smile disappeared. "A priestess may take men to her bed to produce heirs or to sate her needs with protection to prevent that eventuality, but only once does she pledge her heart. A priestess who loses her love before adequate heirs are born will take men to produce heirs, but she never performs this ceremony a second time. She never chooses another true mate." Deliya cleared her throat. "Neither does a male."

"You mate for life?" he asked in surprise.

Deliya nodded. "If you do not wish that, we can use your ceremony." Her eyes showed pain at that thought.

"Perform the ceremony. I will be bound by it," he promised.

She sighed in relief. Ro resisted the urge to pull her close. Had she really worried that he'd shy at the idea of mating for life? It was a relief knowing she wouldn't be looking to dissolve their contract for a penalty. Would that Magden women believed the same.

Deliya met his eyes. "A priestess of Fion does not choose a mate lightly," she intoned. "I ask you now, Ro Ti of the Magden, son of Kor Ti, if you will be bound to me alone in this life and the next, father of my heirs, seed to my soil, the missing half of my heart."

"I will."

She nodded. Deliya used the tip of her blade to pierce the pad of her left thumb then took his right. She drew his blood quickly and with little pain.

She positioned his hand with the palm toward hers and pressed them together. "We are bound, blood to blood and heart to heart. I vow to walk with you in this life and meet you in the soul's reward. I will not ever, by action or inaction, allow you to come to harm while I live to prevent it." She motioned to him.

Ro nodded in understanding. "I am blood of your blood and heart of your heart. We are one. I will be only for you in this life and the next. I will never allow you to come to harm."

She removed her hand slowly and sheathed the abinatine, placing it at the foot of the bed. Deliya picked up the flask and uncorked it, pouring a bit of the oil into her hand. Ro tensed as she smoothed it down his length from the head to base. She cupped his sac, oiling all of him, stroking him over and over.

He grasped her shoulders, his knees shaking. "Deliya, I cannot," he gasped. If he didn't make it inside her soon, he'd disgrace himself.

"You will feel it soon," she promised.

"Feel—" He roared out his release, as the heat and throbbing hit him full force. The sensation was vaguely familiar, and he realized that whatever Deliya had given him to fire his lust the night she wanted to conceive had been administered again in a much stronger dose.

Deliya eased him to the bed, smiling as he groaned. "It is a common response," she soothed him.

Ro ground his teeth as the throbbing intensified again. His erection lessened but did not completely subside. He pulled her over him, desperate to bury himself in her. She mounted him smoothly, easing the madness and intensifying the throbbing simultaneously. Her eyes closed as she took him fully and went still.

"No!" Ro commanded.

He wrapped his hands around her hips, lifting her and pulling her tight to him again. Deliya took up the pace he set: fevered, rough, a possession and nothing less, but who possessed whom remained to be seen. Ro gave himself over fully to the concept that Deliya might own him, body and soul.

Her body pulsed around his, and Ro thrust deep, filling her with his seed and locking into her depths, the throbbing sated. Deliya lay over him, panting in the aftermath of their passion.

Ro laid kisses across her forehead, his rational mind reminding him only then that she carried his child. "Have I hurt you?" he asked, his heart pounding in terror.

Deliya chuckled against his chest, and the feeling radiating over his length made him ache for her again.

"No," she assured him. "You would never hurt me."

He gasped as the throbbing became more insistent. "Gods, but I might before this is through. How long does this last?"

She shrugged. "It varies. A few hours, at least."

He groaned as his control started to slip again. "If you tire, you must promise to tie me down. When I...I cannot swear to my self-control in these circumstances."

Deliya laughed heartily. "I have my schen to sate," she reminded him.

Ro nuzzled her lips. "How do women who are not pregnant handle this?" He started stroking inside her, unable to be still when he needed to feed the fire for her.

"Mmm." She smiled. "Typically, the male applies the Dolgen oil to the female, as well. I understand it is an experience not to be missed."

"Understand?" he breathed, nipping at her nipple lightly and taking the peak in his mouth.

Deliya's skin heated again, her schen in full sway. "Many couples conceive the night of their promise."

"You have never experienced it?" Ro moved to the other nipple, licking it slowly before he captured it in his mouth.

She shook her head. "When would I?"

"Loric...I am sorry. You said he wanted to perform this ceremony." Ro shook his head, frustrated by his lack of understanding.

"He could not use the Dolgen oil on me until I had met Fion's challenge. Loric was mad and desperate, but he did not dare risk causing me to cry out during the challenge. He planned to anoint me once I had...But, that is not important."

"Let me anoint you."

"It is not necessary. I have my schen."

"Will it harm you or our child?"

"No. Dolgen is perfectly safe."

Ro smiled and rolled her beneath him, snatching the flask of oil as he slid free of her body. The need to be inside her again was immediate and humbling. He ground his teeth in restraint.

Deliya shook her head. "It is a waste of the oil, Ro. There is no force more powerful than a love-schen."

"Has your training taught you that? Have you been instructed that the oil will have no effect while you carry?"

"No," she admitted. "I doubt anyone has ever tried it."

Ro uncorked the flask. "I think it is time that someone did." He coated his fingers and stroked her hood, playing his fingers ever lower. "Inside?" he asked.

"Yes," she pleaded.

He watched her face as he painted the oil over her. Deliya trembled, her eyes dilating. She bowed up to meet his fingers with a strangled cry.

"It does work," he breathed. "Tell me what you want." He had to take her soon. The throbbing was stealing his sanity.

"Take me as you did in the stable."

CHAPTER SEVENTEEN

Veril 35th, Ti 10-459

Deliya smiled at Ro from the stairs. He waved her down, obviously excited to introduce her to the guests he'd sent Novin to summon her to meet, then turned back to the small lounge off the foyer, laughing at something.

She went to him, taking his hand as she faced the group in the room. Her smile disappeared as all conversation stopped. The woman and two men stared at her in open-mouthed shock.

Ro wrapped an arm around her waist, ignoring their reactions. "This is my bride," he announced happily, bringing her hand to his lips and kissing it tenderly. "May I introduce Mother Deliya, daughter of the former Mother Leiana of Fion's Children."

The woman leapt to her feet. The man beside her steadied her as the weight of her pregnant belly nearly sent her toppling forward. She was a tiny woman, only as tall as Deliya's chest. Her striking shade of red hair marked her as a relative of Ro's, though she didn't look like him otherwise.

The men, of course, were dark-haired. The one steadying the woman was not much older than Deliya was, slim and nearly as tall as Ro. The other was much older, strands of gray showing in his beard and close-cropped hair. This one favored Ro just a bit—his build and a bit in the face.

For a moment, no one moved.

"Welcome," Deliya said.

As if her voice had spurred them into action,

everyone spoke at once.

The woman gasped. "When you said you had a surprise, Ro..."

"How in the world—"

"I thought..."

Ro laughed heartily. "Deliya, this is my younger sister Muria, her husband Benel, and my cousin, Novin's father Andrel."

She bowed her head to each of them in turn, smiling at Andrel. "Novin is a fine man," she complimented him. "He is a worthy heir."

Ro chuckled. "It is a high honor for one of Fion's priestesses to declare a male child as a worthy heir," he noted.

Deliya felt her face go crimson. "I meant no disrespect," she apologized.

Andrel shook his head. "I am honored that you think my son praiseworthy, Priestess."

"I do," she assured him. "Why, the jag..."

Ro shook his head in warning. Apparently, there were many topics that would make the Magden nervous.

An uncomfortable moment of silence ensued. Deliya looked at Ro uncertainly.

Muria waddled forward, offering her hand. "You are most welcome, Priestess."

Deliya nodded, studying Muria's pregnancy intently. "You are very far along," she noted. "Your woman healer approved your travel from Caran?" *And so quickly? Even if Ro's messengers passed his missive hand to hand in an unbroken chain, his family's speed in reaching Aiten must have courted Len's humor.*

Muria turned a shade of crimson that rivaled her

hair.

Benel howled in laughter. "Of course not. The woman healer is livid with her, but try convincing a woman to mind when she learns her brother has finally taken a bride."

Deliya raised an eyebrow. "Not that I disagree with the woman healer, but why should Muria *mind* you?" she challenged.

Benel's smile disappeared.

"She is a grown woman who knows her mind. All Magden women would do better to do likewise."

He blanched. "I meant no offense, Priestess...Majesty..." He looked to Ro, seemingly lost.

Ro offered no help, allowing her to make her own reply.

Deliya executed a curt nod. "Priestess or Mother Deliya would suit me best, Benel."

He bowed his head. "Mother Deliya."

She wound her arm through Muria's and turned her toward the corridor. "Ro has a lovely churning bath, Muria. Would you care to join me in a warm soak and Lover's Repast to hold us until evening meal?"

Muria laughed heartily. "I would like nothing better."

* * * *

Ro bit back a blast of laughter, as his bride and sister made their way up the stairs. Benel and Andrel stared after them, frozen in something between stunned dismay and shock.

"Not exactly a biddable female," Andrel noted diplomatically.

Ro did laugh at that. "If she were, I doubt I would have noticed her."

"Can she be trusted?" he asked with even greater caution. "After we failed her people..."

Ro sobered. "With my life. And with your son's. She saved Novin within moments of meeting him."

"Why did no one tell me this?" Andrel demanded, red-faced.

"Because Novin was unlikely to admit that he'd ingested poison berries to you."

"Poison?" Andrel heaved a sigh. "She saved my son?"

"While she still believed us her enemies. She worked through most of a night without rest or food to undo the damage. Novin was near death for days after. Deliya saw to his care personally and tirelessly."

His cousin dropped into the chair he'd vacated heavily and rubbed a hand over his face. "Then I am in her debt."

A niggling thought ate at Ro. "As am I, and I have not managed to fulfill what she asked of me yet."

Benel looked away from the stairs in surprise. "*You* cannot fulfill what she asked?"

Ro shook his head miserably.

"What did she ask of you?"

"To return her to her people—to the life that she lost," he admitted.

"What will you do?"

"The only thing I can. I will allow her to retain her culture and return her people's lands as our seat of power. That is the best I can do for her."

* * * *

"How did you meet Ro?" Muria asked, lowering herself into the warm tub with a sigh of relief.

Deliya felt her cheeks heat. "I met him in battle. In any case, I felt it was battle."

She waited nervously, sure that Muria would protest Deliya raising a blade to her brother. For a long moment, the smaller woman stared at her, shocked to silence. Then she started laughing, great whooping laughs, tears gathering in her dark eyes.

"Tell me you bested him."

"Sometimes. At others, Ro was the victor. I tricked him more than once."

"Good. No wonder he loves you."

Deliya smiled.

"I imagine you had no wealth of love for the Magden," Muria noted sadly.

Deliya sobered, sinking deeper into the churning water as she considered that. "The Magden are not what I was taught, but I know that my mother had a great respect for your father. She told me once that you should judge a man by his actions. She asserted that even a Lengar king could be a good man in the right circumstances."

Muria snorted in a most unladylike way. "I will believe that when I see it."

Deliya chuckled. "I told her the same thing—much more respectfully, of course."

Muria played her hand in the water, staring at it rather than meeting Deliya's eyes. "It must be very difficult, losing everyone you care for."

"It is, but the Mother provides. When I learned I had lost all, She sent me Ro and gave me his love."

Deliya cast her eyes over the swell of Muria's belly. "Your babe will be very large. Has your woman healer discussed the birth with you?"

Muria shot her an apprehensive look. "Discussed? What is there to discuss?"

"You are—tiny. Too large a babe poses a danger to you both."

"Yes. The healer said the same."

"Then why has she done nothing to prevent it?" Deliya inquired.

"What do you mean?"

"There are herbs that will prepare your body for birth and others that will entice the babe to deliver before it is too large for safety."

"That must be dangerous to the child," she protested.

"Not if it is handled well. A time can be chosen that is best for mother and child."

Muria seemed stunned; the look quickly became one of deep respect. "It seems you have knowledge and training that our woman healers do not. Have you considered training them?"

Deliya considered that. Why had she never realized it before? Perhaps because she thought the Magden woman healers wouldn't accept the Mother's teachings along with her practical knowledge? It was her duty to teach, to make life better where she could, to protect women and children...to protect anyone under her care. She was the Magden queen now. Didn't that mean that the Magden people were under her care?

And if the woman healers will not learn the Mother's way? She bit her lip at that, weighing her options. She could not force them to accept her traditions, but she could impart the knowledge to ease the burden of many Magden women. That, in itself, was the embodiment of her duty.

"Yes. I could do that."

"They would not be your people but—"

"Oh, but they would," Deliya decided excitedly. "The Mother always provides. Perhaps this is the future for Fion's priestesses that She envisioned all along, the knowledge and duty passed mother to daughter as it always has been." She smiled, plans taking shape in her mind.

* * * *

Ro folded Deliya into his arms as the women came to the table. She practically glowed in happiness.

"What is it?" he asked, hoping that this meant Deliya had found a sister of the heart in Muria.

"Muria has given me the most wondrous idea," she told him breathlessly.

He grimaced. "My sister's ideas have caused many grief," he warned.

Muria shot him a dirty look, daring him to tell his bride the many bad ideas she had devised and he or others had followed when they were young and impulsive.

"This one is inspired, Mother led," Deliya assured him.

Servants began to lay out the food.

"Sit down and tell us about it." *Hopefully, it is a better idea than the one about chasing geela away from the young kittle,* he prayed silently. Ro still bore the scar he earned saving his sister from that fiasco.

Deliya kissed his cheek and took her place, picking a lizor berry off her plate and biting it with a look of rapture. "Your woman healers have learned the beginnings of what I would teach a young priestess. Why not complete their training? Oh, Ro. Do you see it? The woman healers can train each other, pass the knowledge mother to daughter as Fion's priestesses always have." Her eyes glittered with excitement.

Ro smiled at Muria in appreciation. Deliya had found something better than a sister of the heart; Muria had shown her that she could lead a people other than her own, something he had been hard pressed to impart to her. "My sister has outdone herself."

"Your sister is not eight years of age any longer," Muria snapped, "and no one forced you to help me."

"Very true," he conceded. "Well, this makes my surprise all the more appropriate."

"Surprise?" Muria squealed, sounding like the eight-year-old girl she denied being. "I love surprises. Tell us."

Ro waved over a servant with the box that held the larger of his gifts. He presented it to Deliya.

Her eyes widened. "It has been many years since someone has given me a gift."

"Open it," Muria urged her.

Deliya gasped as she uncovered the contents of the box. She touched the silin with shaking fingers.

Ro smoothed her hair, praying he hadn't upset her when he hoped to please her. "I saw your mother's robes and overmantle when she received my father before the fall of Rintal. If anything is amiss, the clothier will make it right. She will make you as many as you wish—one for every day of the week if you would

199

be most comfortable in them or you wish to teach your priestesses in them. You have only to ask."

A single tear spilled down her cheek. "Thank you, Ro. It is beautiful."

He pulled the hair clips from his jacket pocket, showing them to Deliya then placing them in her hair. "I took the liberty of having a jeweler recreate your seal."

She wound her hands around his neck and into the fall of his unbound hair, leaning in to seek his mouth. "Shall I wear your gown later in thanks?" she murmured in his ear.

Ro groaned as his cock responded with customary ferocity. "Only if you wish to learn what a Magden bride can expect from her husband."

"I think I would enjoy that," she teased, massaging the bundle of nerves at the nape of his neck and sending heat curling through his body.

"I trust you would."

Benel roared in laughter. "I believe Ro's next announcement will be that he has produced an heir," he prophesized. "Would anyone care to lay odds on how long that will be?"

"Two weeks," Muria decided, chewing a slice of cheese.

Ro smiled, running his hand over Deliya's womb. "My wager would be that I announce it tonight."

The room went silent; even the servants stopped their work to stare at them in astonishment. Deliya blushed, casting a sidelong glance at Muria and nodding her affirmation.

Muria clapped her hands in glee. "Wonderful," she cheered. "Our children will be like brothers."

"Or sisters," Deliya reminded her.

Benel furrowed his brow. "You do not hope to give Ro an heir?" he asked in confusion.

Ro shot him a hard look. "Ro hopes for a beautiful daughter. Perhaps my bride will grant me a son one day, but my daughter will be born for better things."

Deliya turned his face back to hers. "You will have as many sons as Fion grants us," she promised.

CHAPTER EIGHTEEN

Veril 36th, Ti 10-459

Deliya looked up sharply at the pounding on the door. No one dared disturb them once their room was shut tight; it could only be an emergency.

Ro stormed to the door, yanking it open and catching Benel as he half-ran, half-fell into the room. "What is it?" he asked.

Benel looked to Deliya, his expression frantic. "Mother Deliya, we need you," he begged.

Deliya ran for her packs, pulling her robe and overmantle from the cabinet. It was likely that she would need them. "The babe?" she asked, knowing in her heart that it was. She had watched Muria's wan complexion with apprehension all day, worried at her insistence on traveling the next morning. It was better that the babe came tonight rather than on the road to Caran.

Ro took the packs from her shoulders, motioning her toward the door.

"Yes," Benel confirmed. "The woman healer says we must choose between the babe and Muria." He faltered, as Deliya turned to him in dismay. "Muria says you can help. She begs for you. Can you—"

"Assuredly." She jogged from the room with the men at her heels. She chewed at her lip, knowing that Benel would balk at what might have to be done to save his bride. "Bring me a kettle of boiling water," she ordered him, as they reached the stairs. "I will have to make teas to aid me in the procedure."

Benel froze, paling. "But, Muria—"

"Benel," Ro barked. "Go now. Muria needs you."

Deliya thanked Mother Fion silently for his intercession. "You can best serve this way for now. Muria will need you in the days to come."

Benel growled a harsh curse, but he ran for the kitchen. She turned from the stairs, rushing down the hall to the opposite wing; getting a boiling pot would not take Benel nearly long enough if invasive procedures were called for.

Ro wrapped his hand around her hip. "If this goes badly, he will hold it against us both."

"If it goes badly, I will at least have tried to save them both. It is unlikely that I will lose even one of them and nearly impossible that I will lose both."

He nodded, pushing open the door to Muria's room without warning.

Deliya pulled her packs from his shoulders, pushing past Ro and dropping them on the table at the foot of the wide bed that also held the woman healer's supplies. She opened the crock of Auguren and Felgren paste she kept for emergencies like this then scrubbed it into her hands with a clean cloth.

"What have you found, woman healer?" she asked as she moved her eyes over their patient.

Muria lay panting and bathed in sweat. The young princess grimaced, pleading silently for help. Deliya stepped to her side and pulled the quilts back.

"The babe is too large to pass," the woman healer reported. "We must either break many of the princess's bones or most of the babe's to force him to pass. One of them will not survive what we must do."

Deliya snorted in disgust, settling on the bed between Muria's feet. She eased her hand into the laboring woman to check on the babe.

"Majesty, the risk of infection," the healer protested.

"Quiet," she growled. "I have used a paste to prevent that." Deliya closed her eyes and let her hand tell her all she needed to know. "The shoulders are too wide," she confirmed, "and the head is nearly so."

Muria sobbed. "Please, Deliya..."

Deliya opened her eyes and withdrew her hand, meeting her heart sister's hopeful gaze. "I can save you both, but there is a price."

"Anything."

"I can take the babe surgically."

"The surgeon is too far," the healer informed her. "They will both be dead by the time he arrives to care for them."

Deliya shot her a stern look. "Fion's priestesses do not depend on Magden surgeons to do their work. I am capable of doing this without him. I learned the technique when I was a novice."

The healer paled. "At what cost?"

Deliya met Muria's eyes again. This would be hard for her to hear. It was always a difficult decision for a mother to make. "If I do this, you will have no more children. The cut is the same as the one that ends fertility, and while I could repair that damage, it is better that I not. The incision will weaken your womb. Another child would surely kill you. The choice is yours, Muria. I can save you both, if I act quickly."

Muria looked toward Ro. He kept his face studiously neutral.

"Benel?" she gasped.

"The choice is *yours*," Deliya repeated. "You can let me do this, or you can die for your child. Either way,

Benel will only have one child of you. If the woman healer kills the babe...I am sorry. I cannot take part in that. It is not Fion's way."

"If the babe is female," she panted.

"She will not fight wars," Deliya interrupted. "I would train her as a priestess, if you both wished it."

Muria looked to Ro again then back to Deliya. "Do it."

Deliya nodded. "Healer, collect the kettle from Benel and find some errand for him while you come back to assist me. Ro...You will have to keep him away until we are through."

The healer paled but nodded. She slipped into the corridor.

Ro clasped her shoulders. "Is this the only way?" he whispered.

Deliya leaned her cheek to the back of his hand, sighing. "I wish it were not, but it is."

"Then don your robes, while I move the bed. You will need a healing circle."

She looked at her husband, tears misting her eyes. Ro was so respectful of her beliefs, it seemed almost too much gift from the Mother.

Deliya took his hand and stood. "Yes. Yes, I will." She rushed to mix the herbs she would need.

* * * *

It took two mugs of lizor stem and olum tea to send Muria into deep sleep. Deliya took a calming breath. "Coat your hands in that mixture—and your blade," she instructed the healer as she rubbed a new coating on her own and her abinatine. She said prayers to Fion

205

under her breath then bared Muria's abdomen and used the mixture over the site she would use. "We must work quickly; she is growing weak. When I free the babe, you must sever the cord and clean her mouth of blood and fluids immediately."

"Yes, Mother Deliya."

Deliya held her breath and made the first incision, trying to ignore the muted voices from the corridor. Benel's errand had not taken as long as she had hoped. She made the second incision, cringing at the scream of pure fury from the corridor.

"Lord Benel," the healer gasped at the sound of a crash outside the door.

"No!" Benel thundered. There were more sounds of a struggle. "You cannot allow her to do this."

Deliya grasped the babe and eased it back from the gates of the womb—slowly, so as not to damage either mother or child.

The healer said a prayer to Mag in a stunned voice.

"Ro will handle him. Our duty is to Muria and her child," Deliya snapped.

"Yes, Mother Deliya."

"It is the only way," she heard Ro reply at a lull in the struggle. His voice was calm and soothing. "If you do not wish to lose Muria or your child, there is no other choice."

"No! Ro, you cannot allow this."

The sounds of their struggle receded. No doubt Ro was dragging Benel away from the room as gently as he could.

Deliya breathed a sigh of relief as the child slid free. "Take the babe quickly," she ordered.

The healer reached around her and took the blood-streaked infant. Deliya noted grimly that it was male. At one time, she would have grieved for the young mother with only a son and no prospect of another child. But Muria and Benel were Magden; this was good news for them. Benel would likely accept his wife's sterility only because he had a son by her—if he accepted it at all. Had the child been female, he would have cursed them all for what she was doing.

Deliya stitched the incisions inside and out, taking special care to seal the egg tubes as she worked. She waved the healer over and helped the woman change the bloodied linens.

Muria was dressed in a nursing gown by the time she woke. She moved sluggishly, groaning at the pain.

Deliya forced herself not to wince. "The incisions are more than the healing magic can repair," she apologized. "You will have to remain here for a full month. The healer has gone to collect healing foods; you will only have Lover's Repast, broth and healing teas for two days. Then you will have meat, cheese and fruits to build your milk."

"My babe?" Muria whispered.

Deliya pointed to the cradle she'd had delivered from the royal nursery. "Your son is well, Muria. He will wake soon for a meal."

Tears spilled down the young mother's cheeks.

Deliya wiped them away with a smile. "Benel will be allowed in once you have eaten. You will have to name your son soon."

Muria shook her head and grasped Deliya's hand. "I would have been proud to gift you with a young priestess. What would *you* have me name him?"

Celdin's face swam in her mind, but Deliya shook

away the image of a dead race. "Give him a strong Magden name, Muria. Raise him to be a good man as befits his mother."

* * * *

Ro looked up when Deliya cleared her throat. He intercepted Benel as the younger man hurtled toward her with murder in his eyes. Keeping Benel cornered in the lounge for the last two hours had been nerve wracking, but Ro had managed not to involve guards—so far.

"Tell me," Benel growled.

"They are both well," Deliya assured him. "Muria wishes to see you." She turned away and headed for the stairs, speaking quickly, as she always did after a difficult healing. "Muria will be unable to travel for a month, and her mother's fast will be doubled, but she will still feel completion."

Ro tightened his grip on Benel and added a look of warning. No matter how shattering this moment was for him, Ro would not allow him to harm Deliya. An extra month without Muria in his bed was little cost for both of their lives. At least, she would still feel the release of eggs, unlike schente. Ro thanked Mag that Deliya had been able to save that for them—then thanked Fion for the knowledge she'd used to do it.

"There will be teas to help her heal and control her pain," she continued, oblivious to the threat Benel posed—or perhaps trusting Ro to make sure she was not harmed. "Muria will be incapable of moving about for a week and then only with your help."

Benel growled a harsh curse.

Deliya shot him a hard look. "Your bride and child both live. You should thank Fion for your blessings, Benel. It took a lot of courage for Muria to choose to live for you. She could have chosen to leave you just as easily—or to take your child from you." She quickened her step and pushed through the door into Muria's rooms ahead of them.

Benel panned his eyes over his bride and swallowed hard, stumbling to the bed and sinking gingerly to her side. He laid a kiss on her pale cheek and ran his fingers through the babe's black curls, examining the steady motion of sucking as the child ate its first meal.

"You are well?" he choked out.

Muria nodded and touched his cheek. Benel kissed her palm, meeting her eyes.

Ro nodded in understanding. *He is afraid to ask.* "What is your child's name, Muria?" he asked, preparing himself to stop Benel should he turn on either of the women.

She smiled at her husband. "This is your son. I named him Benir."

Benel sobbed. He kissed her mouth tenderly. "Thank you," he whispered. "Thank you for doing this for me."

"For giving you a son?" she asked, her voice sad.

He shook his head. "For having the courage to give me both of you."

Deliya came to Ro and guided him toward the door. "They have much to discuss," she noted. "We should go."

Chapter Nineteen

Zor 7th, Ti 10-460

Deliya scowled at Captain Grel then turned back to the three woman healers gathered before her. It did no good to complain about the bored man's presence; Donic had decreed that her training sessions were to be monitored lest Deliya teach the women something against Magden law. Ro had sided with his general, though he assured Deliya that he was simply humoring the man to keep peace in the household. In four months, Grel had never been forced to intervene in her lessons, but still the man remained.

She held up a gola sprig with a handful of the pink berries attached. "I am sure you all recognize this."

As Deliya expected, all three of the women nodded. The Magden had been warned to avoid the berries, and in case of accidental ingestion, to report to the central clinics where the distilled tea, which the doctors named Triclum, was available.

"Gola," Biria groaned.

Deliya chuckled. "Yes. Today, I will teach you to use gola berry."

Surilia furrowed her brow. "Use it?"

"Yes." Deliya placed the sprig on the table and settled into the plush chair Ro had ordered into the conference room for her use. She caressed the squirming babe within her, smiling at how active Ro's daughter was.

Jedrel, the oldest of her students, looked at her in dismay. "We are healers, Mother Deliya," she protested. "We are not assassins."

"Neither were Fion's Daughters. Gola has medicinal properties."

"A poison?" Jedrel questioned, dubious that such a thing was possible.

"A poison."

Grel showed a sudden spark of interest in the conversation.

"I trust you have been trained to recognize mother's sickness?" Deliya asked.

Surilia nodded emphatically, a sure sign of someone who has had to deal with it. "Pain and swelling of the torso and extremities then the throat, cutting off breathing. Uncontrolled buildup of toxins and death," she stated with a note of distaste, another sure sign that she had been called to a woman who needed help.

"And the treatment?"

The three women shot one another uneasy looks.

Biria cleared her throat. "All attempts to end an affected pregnancy come too late. By the time the signs show, nothing can be done to save mother or child."

Deliya smiled. "Brew a tea. Use two mugs of water and six berries. Brew until the tea turns dark pink. Add five sand of olum while the tea still simmers. The olum will have a bite in that dosage; a spoon of Eir sap will cut the bitterness."

The healers barely breathed. Grel leaned forward, absorbing every word.

Deliya took a deep breath. "The results are not pretty. The woman will vomit, despite the olum suppressing the urge. The cap will pass and then the babe. If the gola is not treated at this point, the woman will hemorrhage, seize and die."

Biria took a shuddering breath. "I cannot," she protested.

"If you do not, the woman will die. This way, she lives."

Jedrel motioned for her attention. "Why can the doctors not do this?"

"How much time do you have after the signs set in? How long until death? And what happens if you attempt to move the mother once the toxins reach debilitating levels?" she asked pointedly, letting them answer the questions for themselves.

Surilia grimaced. "In outlying areas, there is not enough time to reach a doctor, and if one tries, the woman will die in transit."

Deliya nodded. "You must be prepared to make a gola tea and to treat the results."

Grel's eyes widened.

"Take six mugs of water. Brew in a hand of Zuragol. Add two spoons—"

"Majesty," Grel barked, his jaw tight in fury.

Deliya startled, meeting his wild eyes in confusion.

"You are not permitted to teach the healers how to make Triclum," he informed her, puffing up as if he had the power to order her about.

"I am permitted to teach anything that does not violate Magden law. Surely, saving a woman's life does not—"

"Teaching anyone but the trusted doctors to make Triclum *is* against Magden law."

Deliya came to her feet, planting her hands on the table between them. "That was never part of the agreement when I taught your doctors," she stormed.

Grel stared her down. "Leave us," he ordered the

woman healers. "This lesson is ended."

"How dare you," Deliya demanded.

The healers scattered, though whether they feared Grel or Deliya more was unclear.

"By order of General Donic and his Majesty, I cannot allow your lessons to continue," he growled.

"Then I will take this up with Ro."

Grel's smile was condescending. "I assure you it is a waste of your time, but do as you will."

Deliya strode to the door, growling out promises of the pain Ro would rain down on Captain Grel.

Ro's welcoming smile disappeared as she stormed into his office without knocking. "Della?" he asked, using the pet name he'd coined for her in their second month of marriage.

"Do not use that name with me," she spat.

Donic looked from one to the other warily.

"Out," she ordered him, motioning to the door.

Donic raised an eyebrow in disbelief, placing his hand on the desk between himself and Ro as if intent on staying where he was. "Ro?" he challenged her order.

"Out," Deliya shouted. "Or do you wish to become a worthy opponent, Donic? Some things are between my husband and myself. Leave us. Now."

"Leave us, Donic," Ro said calmly.

Donic shot him a look that proclaimed him mad then locked his gaze on the abinatine hung at her side.

"That will not be necessary," Ro assured him. "Just go."

He nodded and edged past Deliya, shutting the door behind him. "As you wish, my King," rumbled from between his clenched teeth as he accomplished that final step.

Ro put up a hand to forestall her building outburst and crossed the room. He escorted her to his chair and settled her in it. "Now," he said. "Tell me what is wrong slowly and sedately. Being this upset is not good for you or our child."

"I know," she snapped. "I am a trained healer, Ro."

"Shhh." He moved behind her and started rubbing the knots from her shoulders.

She groaned in the release of tension. "Ro, this is important," she pleaded.

"It must be. Be calm and tell me."

"I trusted you," she commented miserably.

Ro's hands paused then continued their ministrations. "You say that as if you should not have," he noted. "I am definitely not comfortable with that concept."

"I should *not* trust you," she informed him.

"Would you care to tell me why?"

"Donic's young acolyte disbanded my lesson today. Any healing, Ro. I was given your vow," she reminded him.

"Why? What did Grel feel was noteworthy?"

"Your precious Triclum."

His hands went still, and his breathing was heavy.

"This was not part of our agreement, Ro. When I gave your doctors the secret of treating gola poisoning, I did not expect it to be taken from me this way." She glanced over her shoulder, noting the stricken look on his face. "And, you knew." She didn't question it. His expression left no doubt that it was true.

"I never thought," he stammered. "It is not necessary for the healers to treat the poison. The clinics—"

"Are of no use to a woman suffering mother's sickness," she snapped. "A woman cannot be moved to a clinic in either the throes of the sickness or the cure. If the healers cannot administer both the gola *and* the healing tea, they are lost, Ro." She swallowed a sob. "As they have always been lost to you. What is the point of teaching these healers, if I cannot better the lives of the women they serve?"

He turned and sat on the desk, facing her. "Gola cures mother's sickness?" he asked, stunned.

"It does, but I am no longer permitted to teach the skills that will save these women." Deliya cursed her emotions, as another sob fought to break free. "I trusted you."

Ro sank to his knees and gathered her to his chest. "My vow on Mag's name, I had no idea," he managed in a hoarse voice. "I never thought—"

"Why else would someone grow a poison?" she asked miserably. "Of course it has a practical use beside killing off enemies foolish enough to eat it."

"It was never my intent to take something so precious from you. Please, believe me. I have too much respect for what you do for that."

"Then you will let me teach the healers?" she sniffed.

"I..." His hand fisted in the back of her dress, and he groaned as if he were in desperate pain. "It is not possible."

Deliya pushed him away. "It will help these women," she argued.

"When the Lengar are no more," he promised. "You have my vow."

"But why?" Hopelessness welled in her.

"We have an advantage in the gola we transplanted. The Lengar have not connected their losses to it. We...We made certain they would not."

"How?"

"Volunteers. Men who let the Lengar we know are lurking see them eat the berries."

"And who are immediately given Triclum?" she guessed.

Ro nodded and touched her cheek. "Since our men are walking around, though not doing much else for more than a week afterward..."

"Inspired," she breathed.

"Then you understand that the secret to Triclum must stay with you and our most trusted doctors."

"For now," she qualified. "I have your vow that the healers will have this knowledge when it is of no tactical advantage against the Lengar?"

"You have my vow."

"Then you have my agreement. I will not teach the healers to make the antidote until that day."

"You trust me?" Ro asked.

"I do trust you," she assured him.

He planted his hands on either side of her body, a possessive look on his face. "We could test your trust," he suggested.

"Iri blossoms are not yet in bloom," she mused, "but Burgel is."

"Is it?" he teased, feigning a look of surprise.

"Yes, it is."

Ro ran his hand over their child, heating her blood for him.

"Later," he whispered, pulling her dress up. "I need you now."

Chapter Twenty

Fim 1ˢᵗ, Ti 10-460

"Must you go now?" Della asked, the tears in her eyes glittering in the light of the lamp he lit to push back the predawn darkness.

Ro grimaced. Della had borne his every absence in stoic silence until now, but their child would be born in little more than a month. If the campaign was long and arduous and the babe earlier than the expected time, she might be forced to accept another's healing for the birth.

He stroked her cheek. "If I could avoid this, I would. You know I would." But, the farmer who'd ridden in to bring the news of the attack at Dariden could not be ignored.

"You do as often as you are able to," she conceded. "Much more often than Donic and your other generals are happy with."

Ro cradled her to his chest, his heart aching. This was why he'd decided years ago that it would be cruel to take a bride. "I wish I could crush Jurel this moment," he whispered. "I would never leave your side again."

"The gods do not grant such frivolous wishes."

"No, they do not," he agreed. "You have my vow. If the fight stretches past two weeks, it will do so without me." He caressed her swollen belly. "Our child will not arrive without me."

"You cannot—" she started to protest.

Ro captured her mouth in a quick kiss, smiling his determination. "I am a Magden king. I do as I please."

She chuckled, her cool skin heating under his fingers. "And what is it that the mighty Ro Ti pleases?" she teased.

"That my bride would see fit to anoint me before I leave for battle. I would ask Fion's mercy in sending me home to Her daughter with the gods' pace."

"It will be as Ro Ti wishes."

She pushed to her feet and pulled out the mixed herbs for making a circle she now kept on hand, having anointed him many times in the last half year. She said the blessings hurriedly and closed the circle then took up the large bottle of war oil she'd mixed at the same time as her herbs for the circle.

Ro peeled off his tunic and boots and knelt before her.

Della looked at his upturned face, stilling, her eyes wide and sad. "No," she breathed.

His heart hammered in his chest. "No? You will not anoint me?"

"Stand. Oh, Ro. Please, stand."

He pushed to his feet slowly, taking her shoulders in his hands. "What is it? This is the way you have always anointed me."

It was true. He would kneel to her as she massaged the war oil, lightly scented with protective herbs, into his chest and back, arms and neck, saying prayers to her Goddess as she anointed his face and laid kisses at his brow, heart and lips.

Her hands worked at the ties on his trousers.

Ro sucked in his breath in surprise, his cock rising fast to her touch. "Della," he rasped. "If you continue, I will defile the ceremony."

"No. You will not," she assured him.

"But, the anointing..." Ro closed his eyes as his trousers pooled around his bare feet.

"When the battle will be fierce, a priestess spends these last moments with her true mate," she whispered. "It is a silly thing to do. Rather than saving their strength for battle, priestesses with a true mate prefer to meet death in the afterglow of their union."

"An admirable tradition," he managed in a thick voice.

Ro shivered, as she leaned away from him and then back. She stroked the oil over his shoulders, tracing every inch of his upper body. He dropped his hands to his sides as Della moved around him, repeating the process on his back. As always, the oil woke his body to sensation, every touch of her fingers or palm a gift from Fion's goodness, a feast of pleasure.

Della paused. "Kick your trousers away," she instructed.

He complied, stiffening in surprise as her freshly oiled hands played over the meat of his buttocks. He looked over his shoulder, holding his breath.

"Be still," Della soothed him, her eyes locked on his body as she anointed him.

"I will not last," he warned.

A smile curved her lips. "You will. Close your eyes, Ro."

He did as she bade him, groaning in the certainty that he would ride into battle as weak as a babe. He tried to track her movements by the wisps of air over his sensitized skin announcing her passing.

Her hands caressed his calf muscle, and his body felt wonderfully alive. She explored every dip and curve of him from his feet to his knees. Ro reached for her shoulders to steady himself as she stroked his inner thighs, nearly cupping his aching sac.

Della removed his hands and oiled his callused fingers one at a time, showing infinite care in her blessing. She lowered his hands and paused again. Fresh oil coated his thighs, enflaming his need.

Ro tensed, certain that his sac and cock would be next, certain that even the war oil would make him throb for her as the Dolgen oil did. She caressed his forehead, tracing the line of his nose then his cheeks. He groaned, as she teased at his lips and chin.

"Now," she whispered. Della cupped his cheeks and tipped his face forward, kissing his forehead. She stepped back and laid a kiss over his still-hammering heart.

He held himself in rigid control as he waited for a kiss to brush his lips, knowing he would fall on her like a buck in rutt when she did it, that his control would disintegrate into ash as if incinerated on a pyre. "Please..." he begged, his body pulsing for her.

She cupped his hand palm up in hers and deposited some of the oil in it. Ro gasped, opening his eyes wide as she pressed her naked body to his, her hardened nipples sharing the oil from his chest. Droplets splashed onto her skin and rolled down the curve of her breasts.

"What must I do?"

She pulled his hand to her upper chest, leaning back so that their child was pressed to his taut abdomen. "Touch me," she begged. "Anoint me, as I anointed you. Take me as you do."

Ro held her gaze as he spread the oil over her shoulders and chest, circling her already coated nipples then teasing them to greater peaks. Della bit her lip, pressing further into his hands and helping his anointing by sharing what she had spread on him.

He smiled, oiling the swell of her womb, feeling her skin like a brand under his palm. "It feels wonderful," he crooned. "Does it not?"

Della nodded. She closed her eyes and tilted her head back.

In her schen, the anointing must be maddening to her. "Have you ever been anointed before?" Ro asked.

"Yes. Before I left Rintal. For...For a safe journey," she whispered.

Ro massaged her arms and hands without comment, wrapping a hand around her waist when she leaned into him. He gathered more of the oil and smoothed it down her back to her buttocks. "Who anointed you?" he whispered, lifting her to play his cock in her waiting fluids.

"My mother," she gasped. "I had not reached my cha—" She pressed her face to his chest, whimpering into his skin, seeking his possession.

He settled on the bed, seating himself deep inside her and grasping her hips. "Do not move," he ordered. He stroked his oiled hands over her legs then played his fingers between their bodies, seeking her hood.

Della ground her core against his fingertips. "I need you," she pleaded.

"In a moment."

He ran his hands over her throat and face. He cupped the back of her head and pulled her face to his, kissing her forehead. He released her, restraining himself to laying a chaste kiss when he wanted to suckle her breast. Ro cupped her head again and pulled her mouth to his. He took her with no mercy, his lips urgent on hers, his body rising into hers over and over as he stroked her oiled skin.

Della's hands joined the dance, molding to the lines of his body, firing nerves to life. Their bodies moved together, sliding sensuously, every finger-width of one alive to the slick, silin feel of the other.

Ro held back, praying he would satisfy her fully before losing his battle with his rising orgasm. As if reading his desperation, Della pushed her hips hard to his, her body inviting his loss of control with the sweet contractions that pulled at his length. His composure broken, Ro joined her, his fingertips digging into her hips as their bodies became one. She cried out, laying her cheek on his shoulder.

For long moments, they lay together. Ro stroked his hands over the light marks he left, vowing to heal them as soon as he lessened. Della buried her hands in his hair, her lips exploring his shoulder. He cursed the need to leave her silently. He was a king; his word should be law.

"Ask me not to go," he breathed. "I would forsake my duty for you."

"I cannot ask that. You took a vow to protect those who need you most. Your people need you, Ro. The Lengar attack, even now. I could not be the cause of their suffering." She played with the locks of his hair on his neck, not meeting his eyes. "Nor could I allow you to break your vow."

"I would give you anything."

"Speed home to me."

"You have my vow."

* * * *

Deliya yawned, squinting in the bright morning sunlight, unsure at first what had awakened her. She snuggled her face into Ro's pillow, drinking in his scent.

The sound of blade on blade reached her; the captains were obviously using the decreased workload during Ro's absence to add extra training for the men left behind. The shouts from the courtyard were awfully loud for so early, but the men were always excited when they took bets on the training bouts.

She came up off the bed at the sound of a harsh battle cry. That wasn't training. Deliya peeked through the curtain, cursing at the sight of Lengar troops within the walls. Her gaze locked on a deep choc war-buck with a flowing black mane. The rider's black armor flashed in the sunlight; he was a dark spot in the sea of mundane tan plate armor around him.

Only one man wore black armor and rode a buck like that. There could be no doubt.

"Jurel," she breathed.

If Jurel was within the gate with so many men, there was a traitor, someone who had let them in a side gate in the gray hours after Ro's departure. The rest of the battle played out in her imagination. Ro's troops could not win; Jurel would know their number, positions, and weaknesses. There was only one reason Jurel would do this. He had come for her.

As if confirming her conclusion, the Lengar warlord turned his face up to her window, surging through the melee with shouted orders that were lost in the thunderous battle cry of Ro's men. They tried desperately to push back the larger numbers of incoming troops, but it was futile.

Deliya ran from the window, throwing open her cabinet. She wouldn't meet her enemy naked from her husband's bed. Her armor was out of the question, and her trouskit and trousers were no better. Ro had decreed a ban on all but carriage riding when their baby began to show, so none of her riding gear was fashioned large enough. Deliya grimaced at the thought of meeting Jurel in one of the short Magden dresses she wore for Ro, and the presentation dress was for Ro alone.

Her hand lingered on the last gown in the cabinet. She pulled it free with a resigned nod.

"What could be more appropriate? A priestess should show what she is." She dressed in a rush, pushing her feet into her boots.

The sounds of fighting grew closer—inside the house, then up through the levels.

Deliya sent her thanks that the woman healers had returned home until after her mother's fast and that Ro had sent his schente away when he began his pursuit of her in earnest. Only Laril and a handful of other female servants remained in residence, and there were no children inside Ro's home. That was a blessing. There were fewer innocents in Jurel's path than there might have been.

She didn't leave the royal chambers; there was nowhere to run. The Lengar had surrounded the house and now swarmed within its walls. The palace Ro was constructing for her at Gidlore had hidden passageways not unlike the ones in Fion's tower, but this structure had no such amenities.

There was nothing to do but meet Jurel with pride.

Deliya drew her abinatine and tossed the jeweled sheath to the bed. She cast a look of longing at the sword she could not wield effectively. She would take as many Lengar with her as she could, but it would be more difficult with the shorter blade.

She held her breath as pounding feet closed on her position. There was no doubt that they were Lengar; there was too much clatter and confusion for the soldiers to be Ro's.

"That room," a strange man barked.

"Yes, General Fil."

Deliya faced the young man as he barreled through the door. His eyes locked on her blade and narrowed. He put up calming hands, and she noted that he was suspiciously devoid of weapons. So, Jurel meant to take her alive.

She considered her babe and sobered. She could not stop that, even by killing herself. It was never permissible to take an innocent life when any alternative, no matter how odious, existed.

She raised her abinatine. "Come for me, Lengar, if you wish to die."

"My orders are to take you alive, Priestess. Put down your dagger, and you will not be harmed."

"As my people were left unharmed?" she spat. "I would gladly show you the same hospitality your damned lord showed them."

Two more soldiers stepped in behind the first, also unarmed. The first came at her with the other two fanning out to circle her.

Deliya didn't hesitate. The first man ducked too late. The other two fell back, as he flailed, his lifeblood pumping from his severed neck artery.

"Who will be next?" she challenged.

"General," one called uncertainly, undoubtedly deciding that his assignment was a suicide mission as it stood.

Three more soldiers entered. Deliya scanned the five enemy faces and raised her chin resolutely. Her aim had not changed. She would take as many of them with her as she could.

They came at her in a bunch. One fell back with a deep slice to his upper arm. A second pressed a hand to the cut across his cheek. Then they were on her.

Deliya fought against the arms that held her: kicking, punching, clawing at anything she could reach. She bit back a cry of pain, as one man crushed her hand in his gauntlet; her abinatine was snatched away and clattered to the floor.

She dug her nails into a face too close to her hand for its safety, and the attacker cried out in fury. A blow to her head made her vision blur; she crumpled into the net of Lengar hands.

"You struck her, you fool," one soldier exploded.

"She attacked me."

"His Majesty will kill you for this."

Deliya tried to clear her head, confused images of Ro gathering her up and striking the man dead dancing in her muddled mind. A new voice sent chills down her spine.

"Yes. He most certainly will."

She forced her eyes open, her field of vision full of shining black armor. Then another blackness closed on her.

* * * *

Ro scowled as an overwhelming sense of something not right washed over him. Villagers surged toward the soldiers, but there were no Lengar in sight.

"They took flight when you drew near," Donic suggested uneasily.

"No. This is something else. Jurel wanted to draw me here. Why?"

"A trap?" Donic sounded unconvinced. Even if it were a trap, Jurel knew Ro would not run from it. Not while his people were in danger.

"More likely a diversion, but then what is the true target?"

Donic rode off to meet the villagers, probably hoping for some clue to Jurel's motive.

Ro scanned his oculars over the hillside beyond the planting fields. After half a day's ride, leaving his bride to come here, he was scarcely in the mood to learn that he had been tricked, though the evidence left little doubt that it was true.

Half the fields had been burned, and dead Magden were being loaded onto a pyre. The dead were all men. No women or children. Had the Lengar been serious about this attack, the damage would have been much worse, the death toll much higher.

Ro whipped down the oculars with a muttered curse. Where would Jurel strike? Perhaps Gidlore or Fint. Perhaps Sten, but why would he need to lure Ro away to do it? Those villages were easily as far from his home as Dariden was and not even in an opposite direction.

Donic returned. "Jurel was not with the attacking troops. The men were his men but without that jaglin at their head," he spat. "The fighting was only heavy the first two hours."

"Long enough for the villagers to send for my help," Ro growled.

"Yes. Exactly." Donic gestured toward the hills. "Should we pursue?"

"How many Lengar were there?"

"Ten. They left one short."

"Leave six of our men."

"What is your plan?"

"Home," Ro whispered, his heart pounding. Something was not right, but his home was secure—and Della was waiting to welcome him to his bed.

"We will not make the house before dark. Perhaps Jurel's plan is to take you in the open after dark."

"It does not matter," Ro stated. "We return home. If we are needed elsewhere, we will be summoned."

"As you wish, my King."

* * * *

Deliya shivered in the chill air, forcing her eyes open. It took a moment for the significance of the moving horizon to sink in. She pulled against the arms circling her. Shackles and brute strength pulled her up short. She twisted, trying to turn from her side-saddle position to attack the man cradling her with her unbound legs, but he pinned her in place with minimal effort.

"Ah, the priestess wakes at last," Jurel taunted. "I was beginning to think my man struck you too hard."

"Take your filthy hands off of me," she growled.

"In good time. First, we will understand each other.

You killed one of my men and injured three more. I could kill you for less, but you are of some small importance to me.

"You are not of paramount importance, however. Remember that. If you cause me too much trouble, I will kill you. Killing you and Ro's son would serve nearly as well as taking you from him.

"Every comfort will be provided for you. A woman healer travels with us. Your food and shelter are assured. If you require healing—"

"You will not touch me," she stormed.

Jurel smiled. "As you wish—for now."

Deliya looked at the dozen and a half men who traveled with them in dismay. The only others were the Lengar woman healer and a small girl. Her heart sank.

"The others?" she whispered. "The women—Ro's servants? What did you do to them?" *Please, let him have spared them to tell Ro of his victory. Please, Mother. Grant me this.*

"I could not allow them to warn Ro," he replied coldly.

Deliya swallowed the bitter lump in her throat, blinking back tears. *Fion's priestesses do not weep before their enemies, even as they die.* Laril's face swam before her eyes. *Ro will avenge us,* Deliya promised her. *Ro will avenge us all.*

* * * *

Ro swallowed a scream of frustration, praying the image would change. It didn't. The towers remained dark. He pulled his oculars up, cursing solidly.

"What do you see?" Donic asked.

229

Ro fumbled the oculars, missing his pouch. Their fall went unheeded, as he pushed his war-buck to a full run. He didn't take the time to answer. There was no time to waste. The main gates were wide open when he had ordered them shut tight. Only the one-man gate should have been used while he was away and only for the roving watches.

"Ro," Donic shouted. "It must be a trap."

Ro couldn't concern himself with that possibility. Only Della and their child mattered now.

The ten stride that separated Ro from his home fell away at a fraction of the time it typically took. Ro thundered through the gates, scanning the destruction in the bright moonlight.

His soldiers had been massacred. The few dead Lengar he passed bore the jaglin print insignia of Jurel's personal guard. He didn't tarry, laying on to the house and vaulting up the stone stairs before Donic and the first of his troops cleared the gates.

Some lamps were still lit. The faces of the dead flashed past Ro's eyes as he ran for the royal chambers. His men would have sequestered Della there in an attack. When Jurel reached her, he reached her there.

He didn't bother to pull his sword; it was unlikely that Jurel had left an assassin behind. If he had, Ro would kill the man with his bare hands.

The doors to the royal chambers were thrown wide. He bolted through them and halted, gasping for breaths as he took in the clues left behind. Della wasn't there, but two Lengar were. He spied her abinatine and collected it with hands shaking in rage. She shouldn't have had to battle Lengar. He should have kept her safe. He should not have been taken in by Jurel's trick.

"Ro?" Donic asked.

"He took her. She is alive."

Donic surveyed the room, the dead men and the blood soaking many of the surfaces. "You cannot know that," he breathed, looking more than a little ill.

"I know."

"Ro..."

Ro ignored him, pointing to the larger Lengar. "Della killed this one, but she was overpowered. Jurel wanted her alive."

"What am I missing?"

"The Lengar who came for her were unarmed. Jurel did not want her injured." He pointed to the second soldier. "And, he killed his own man. By the golden hair on his gauntlet—and the scratches on his face, I would surmise that his offense was injuring her." Ro ground his teeth in fury. It shouldn't have been possible. How did Jurel breach the gates?

"The priestess could have killed them both," Donic argued.

Ro glared at him. "This man was killed with a sword; hers is there in the cabinet, untouched. She is alive. We leave tonight."

"We cannot track them in the dark," Donic protested.

"Lanterns," Ro suggested.

"And be led astray? Our trackers will have their best return if we wait until morning."

"They have a full day on us," Ro growled.

"But they will be hampered by an unwilling Priestess of Fion. As much as your bride has infuriated me at times, Jurel will not find traveling with her any easier than we did when she did not wish our company.

You can wager on that with confidence."

Ro nodded, suddenly exhausted. "At daybreak," he agreed, but his gut ached at the truth of the matter.

Jurel would be hampered by Della's condition—if he allowed her the comforts her condition demanded. At full speed, Ro and his men could catch them in perhaps a day or two at most. The problem was, the Magden wouldn't be traveling at full speed. Jurel's path was unknown, and tracking him would slow the pursuer's pace.

CHAPTER TWENTY-ONE

Fim 2nd, Ti 10-460

Deliya looked around wearily at the endless trees. They had been riding all day, her hands shackled through a prison ring in the bridle, a belt restraint keeping her from sliding off the buck's back, and her reins tied to Jurel's bridle to prevent her using leg controls to run with her mount. She'd ridden straight on the buck all day, but her strength was flagging as the sun set.

Jurel pulled her mount close, and Deliya stiffened. He stroked his hand over her child, and she yanked at the shackles in frustration, shooting him a warning look. He chuckled and released her reins.

"You find something amusing?" she demanded.

"You have spirit. Not that it surprises me. All of your accursed priestesses have spirit, but you have more than most. I am very tempted to sample my enemy's goods, but I will wait until his son is delivered of you first."

Deliya ground her teeth in irritation, guiding the buck with her knees to the length of the reins.

Jurel's eyes traveled over her body hungrily. "I wonder if your body will taste as sweet as your mother's did?" he mused.

She snorted. "You lie," she informed him. Deliya pushed away her uncertainty. *If Jurel had, Ro would have told me. I know he would.*

"Oh, I had her," Jurel assured her.

"After her death, like the geela you are, I am sure."

"You would like to believe that, but you are proof

233

enough that a priestess can be taken alive. Rest assured that she took a hand of my men down as she stood alone, before they fell on her in force. She cursed me with every breath and pretended not to enjoy my cock, even when I stimulated her." He scowled. "Your priestesses made a poor showing of sex for my men. Some of them might have lived had they reacted as normal women will."

As Lengar bed slaves. "Then I can promise you will have to kill me as well," Deliya snapped.

Jurel shot her a searing look. "I think not." His eyes settled on her belly again. "You will have ample reason to stay in my good graces."

Deliya straightened her spine. "Fion's priestesses do not bargain with their enemies, even for the sake of their children."

He searched her face for signs of weakness. "We shall see. We stop here for the night."

* * * *

Food was brought to her. Guards accompanied her when she relieved herself. The shackles were only removed long enough for her to complete each task; she was never alone.

Her gaze wandered, taking in Jurel's encampment and the guards' placement. It was simply impossible, she decided. Jurel had more than a dozen men fanned around her at almost every moment, and she had no way to drug them. Even if she made it to a war-buck, she was incapable of the speed that would allow her to escape for long.

"It will not work," he taunted, sidling up next to

her.

She eased away from him, her skin crawling at the idea of Jurel touching her child again.

He grasped her arm, bringing her wrist up to heal the bruises the shackles had left. She slapped him, scurrying an arm's length further away.

He grasped her shoulders with a growl of displeasure. "I will heal you," he stated.

"Do not touch me. The laws—"

"*Your* laws," he thundered. Jurel took a calming breath. "Your laws and Magden laws. By Lengar law, you are a woman and a prisoner. I may do what I wish."

Deliya pulled against his hold. He might believe that, but she didn't have to accept it willingly.

He dragged her to his chest. "You and that child belong to me. Ro cannot free you. He will try. I will enjoy killing him when he does."

"Ro will cut out your dead heart and place it on a pyre as he leaves your corpse to feed the geela," she promised.

He laughed harshly. "He will kneel before me and be killed by my men."

"Ro Ti will never kneel to you."

"You are correct, but he will kneel to *you*. I know he will."

Deliya shook her head. Where would he get such a ridiculous idea? "Ro kneels to no one."

"Mag knelt at Fion's feet and called her beloved," he whispered. "Shall I tell you what he did next, Priestess? Shall I tell you the sweet sounds Fion made as Mag's mouth took her to a slice of the soul's reward?"

She gasped, feeling faint. How long had the traitor been reporting their lives to Jurel?

"Or perhaps I should show you. There is your schen to consider, and I would be a gracious host," he offered in a voice ragged with arousal.

Deliya glared at him. "That is one of the many things about you that hold no interest for me," she informed him in a cold, unwavering voice.

Jurel nodded, pushing her toward a guard. "Take her to the pavilion and watch her closely. Make sure Her *Majesty* has ample quilts and food. A woman incapacitated by pregnancy signs is of no use to me."

* * * *

Fim 3rd, Ti 10-460

Deliya shivered, glancing at the guard's back. She had to escape somehow. Over the last day, Jurel had become more insistent: watching her with growing lust, touching her often, promising to use her to kill Ro.

Never by action or inaction, she repeated to herself. Deliya could not allow Jurel to do whatever he intended, but what could his plan be? Only a fool expected to meet Ro in hand-to-hand combat and win. Jurel would use some trickery. Deliya wished she knew what.

"I need to relieve myself," she informed her guard.

He shot her a look of irritation. "You relieved yourself an hour ago."

"The babe causes it." That much wasn't a lie. The forced hours on hottel were not helping the matter, but her pregnancy alone would make these excursions necessary. She managed to force Jurel to stop for her comfort as often as she dared during the daylight hours, setting the stage for what she must do. This was her only chance at escape, the only weak point in his tireless surveillance.

The guard unshackled her arm with a muttered curse and waved her toward the flap. "Come on," he growled.

Deliya preceded him into the darkness. The fires, lit at new dark to hide the smoke, had been extinguished to keep Ro from tracking the light in the darkness of full night. That would work to her advantage.

She strode into the deep brush, squatting and gathering her robes to accomplish the first part of her plan. The guard turned his face away, his hand resting on the hilt of his dagger. Deliya shook her head, making the flow of urine a trickle to waste as much time as she could.

"Finish," he ordered.

"You know how to rush these things?"

The guard growled, muttering his displeasure at being the one to give up sleep to watch her while others might rest this night. He crossed his arms over his chest, and Deliya smiled. It was time.

She stood abruptly and grasped his tunic, feigning imbalance that wasn't far from the truth. The guard reached to steady her, grumbling complaints; and Deliya struck. She swept his dagger from its sheath, planting it deep into his brain base and severing all nervous activity with a quick slice and twist. A warm trickle of blood ran down her hand, soaking the cuff of her robes.

His eyes went wide, and his hands fell away. His muscles went lax. Deliya eased him to the ground awkwardly, panting through the pain the exertion sent through her spine.

She surveyed him. It wouldn't take long. In a few short moments, his heart would forget how to beat. Already, his lungs had seized and none of his muscles would function.

Deliya cleaned the dagger on his jacket and moved through the trees. There was no chance of stealing a hottel, and Jurel had taken her boots; but she had surprise on her side—and her training. If Fion were kind and Mag just, she would be well hidden before they discovered her flight. All she had to do was stay hidden long enough to force Jurel to fight a fair fight with Ro or flee.

An explosion echoed off the near hillside. Deliya shielded her face and ducked away as shards of tree bark flew at her.

"Drop the dagger," Jurel ordered.

Deliya turned toward him, shaking. He was an indistinct spot of black in the darkness. Another dark form moved beside him.

"I do not have to come near to kill you," he continued. "The blade is useless."

She looked to the deep gash in the tree, touching the damage and making the determination that the Eir would survive the harm.

"You—" she gasped. "This is your plan." Jurel wouldn't have to best Ro in combat. The projectile would kill him from a distance."

"Put down the dagger, Priestess. My man's next shot will not be aimed to miss."

Deliya let the weapon slip from her numb fingers. Ro's only chance was a direct warning from her lips.

"His men will kill you," she breathed. *Donic will kill you, if you harm him.*

Jurel strode to her, striking her hard across the cheek with his armored hand and dragging her to his chest when she stumbled back. His voice shook with fury. "I knew you would try this eventually. I simply had no idea you would be so successful. Under normal circumstances, I would kill you for killing my guard, but a careless man at my back is worse than none. You will not attempt this again, Priestess. If you do, I will cut the child from your womb and leave your body for Ro to find. Do not test me again."

Deliya's stomach lurched. She weaved on her feet then forced her trembling legs not to desert her.

"Am I understood, Priestess?"

She nodded. "Yes. I understand you."

"Good. I will return you to the woman healer now. I imagine a calming tea is in order before you sleep."

"I want nothing."

"That is not true," Jurel replied coldly. "You want Ro to gut me for this."

He half-dragged her to the pavilion, pushing her to the cot and shackling her wrist to the heavy frame. He pulled a quilt over her and left without comment.

The woman healer came to her, laying a hand on Deliya's chilled cheek. "I will bring a lizor tea," she whispered.

"Leave me," Deliya growled. "I require nothing of Lengar kindness."

"As you wish, Majesty." Her hand lingered a moment longer, and her voice sounded of a sad sort of wish. She retreated to the cot she shared with her child.

Deliya closed her eyes, running a hand over her

womb. *Not by action or inaction...Mother Fion, do not make me choose.*

* * * *

Ro launched from his pavilion, trying to locate the source of the echoing sound; but the canyon walls rising above the trees confused his sense of direction. He waited, barely breathing, praying for another sound, any sound that might let him track them.

Donic's hand closed on his shoulder. "We cannot possibly track them in the dark," he whispered. "Sleep, Ro. We will have a long day tomorrow."

"What was it?" Ro asked. "An explosion?"

"Perhaps. A small one, but what use would so small an explosion be?"

Ro shook his head. *What use, indeed!* "Get your rest, Donic. We leave before sunup."

"Ro..."

"They travel sunup to sundown. We must make more time than that."

"Perhaps your bride will find a way to slow them down."

Ro shuddered. "Jurel would kill her for trying."

"Would he? He could have done that at your home."

"Sleep, Donic."

Ro stared into the trees for a long moment before he staggered back to his pallet. Sleep would not be easily won. It hadn't been since he'd found Della's abinatine coated in Lengar blood and discarded.

Days on his war-buck, tracking endlessly with little sleep to sustain him, were taking their toll. He rubbed a hand over his tired eyes. If it was this rough on him, it must be unbearable for Della. He gave in to exhaustion slowly, promising to find her and avenge her properly when he did.

* * * *

Fim 4th, Ti 10-460

"What is it?" Ro asked wearily.

Donic looked up as Novin stepped away to be sick in the brush. The young man trembled in his nausea.

"A dead Lengar soldier," Donic informed him, mounting his buck stiffly and leaving the corpse behind. "Feasted on a bit. No large predator has discovered it yet."

Novin heaved again at that.

"How?" Ro asked, praying that another of Jurel's men had not been killed for laying hands on Della.

"A small blade to the base of the skull. Silent and quick with no chance of retribution." He met Ro's eyes. "A woman's kill...if she were trained to kill."

Ro rubbed his neck, muttering a harsh curse. Della knew the best ways to kill: the three silent killers, the six bleeders, and the five quick deaths. This was a kill she would have taken to attempt escape. "What do the trackers say?"

Jobin, his head tracker, pointed toward the Lengar border. "They laid on without delay."

Donic scowled. "She is pregnant. Escape was hopeless, but she had to try. Were she not so close to date..."

Novin weaved back to his buck and mounted

shakily, nodding to Ro.

Ro fisted his reins. "We have to move. We...Too much time," he whispered.

He urged his buck up to speed, visions of Della killing the soldier and running taunting him. Did she know how close he was? Was she trying to reach him when she ran?

I am coming for you, Ro promised. *I am.*

* * * *

Deliya sank her forehead to the buck's flowing mane, rolling her shoulders painfully. Her eyes closed on a low groan. She was bitterly tired, beyond exhaustion, but Jurel would not pause.

Her mount jerked right, and she grasped the bridle in her fist. She didn't open her eyes; she was beyond caring that Jurel was pulling her in to his side again. He touched her shoulder, and she shook his hand off.

"You hurt," he noted. "Your muscles are in knots."

She didn't deny it. Between her pregnancy signs and the endless ride, her muscles were a mass of knots, and her entire body ached.

"I can help," he offered.

"Do not touch me," she rasped, forcing the command past her dry mouth.

"As you wish." He released the reins and let her buck drift from his.

* * * *

Deliya sighed as the shackles opened and the belt was uncinched. Large hands lifted her from her mount and carried her into the pavilion. The cot offered no comfort. Her whole body ached, and the quilts irritated skin already painfully sensitized. The shackle closed again, and the man who tended her walked away. She didn't open her eyes to see if it was Jurel. What did it matter if it was?

The woman healer touched her cheek and raised a cup to her lips. "Please drink, Majesty," she whispered.

Deliya drank down several mouthfuls. *Implin juice spiced with Cimmeg and a small dose of olum. She knows her cures.*

"You must eat," the woman urged her.

Deliya groaned and turned away. "I cannot."

"Your pregnancy signs—"

"I cannot. Please leave me," she begged, heartsick at what she knew. Her whole body hurt, most of all her breasts. Her babe was coming too soon, and there was no way to stop what had been set in motion.

CHAPTER TWENTY-TWO

Fim 5th, Ti 10-460

Deliya forced her breathing to calm. *Not now,* she begged. *Ro will find us soon.*

But their child was not to be denied. Deliya relaxed her muscles into the ripple of pain, thankful that Jurel had ordered his man to stay outside the pavilion to prevent a repeat of her escape attempt.

She panted back another pain. *Remember the challenge. Focus and remain relaxed. You can ride the crest of pain as you learned to ride the crest of pleasure.*

If she were relaxed, the birth would pass more easily. If she were silent, she would not be subjected to Jurel hovering over her bedside as she gave life to her child. She looked toward the other bed, nearly weeping in anguish. Calling for the woman healer would defeat her purpose, though the woman was sure to have herbs that would ease the pain.

She pushed herself to sitting with her knees spread high and wide and her feet planted on the edges of the cot to open the channel, easing her robes over her hips. It was the proper way, but it also protected the only clothing she had. She spread the quilt over her lower body. She should be uncovered for the birth, but the idea of Jurel watching her child emerge was too much. Pain assaulted her. *Remember the challenge.*

The pains came and went, intensifying as the night waned. Deliya made soundless entreaties to Fion to speed the process, to allow her to deliver before Jurel came for her again; but gods and babies are not to be rushed.

Jurel entered the pavilion as he always did, whipping back the flap without warning. He strode to her, his black armor glinting in the first rays of the sun streaming through the opening. He released the shackle on her wrist, waved her toward the waiting war-buck, and turned away without waiting to offer aid she would refuse.

He looked back in surprise when she didn't move to follow him. "If you wish to eat, you will leave that bed," he warned, though she knew as well as he that he would not deprive her of food. Making her pregnancy signs worse would not be in his best interests.

"Leave me," Deliya whispered, wiping a sweat-soaked lock of hair from her face.

His eyes widened. "Woman healer," he barked. "What is this?"

The healer hurried from her bed, running her hand over Deliya's face then her womb.

"Leave me," Deliya growled, fixing her fury on Jurel.

"Does she require my healing?" he asked.

"I require nothing of you but your absence," Deliya informed him.

"Please, Majesty," the woman healer begged of Jurel. "This is woman's business. You must leave."

"Why did you not tell me you were this close when I asked?" he fumed.

"I am not," Deliya snapped. "I should not have delivered for more than a month. It was your relentless riding that did this."

His eyes widened. Deliya could see the calculation in that look, and it frightened her, though she kept her face studiously blank.

"Will the child die?" he asked.

The woman healer pulled a short dagger from her pack, shrugging. "Ro Ti is strong, as is her Majesty. The babe will likely do well, even this early."

Deliya sent up a silent prayer for that, though the healer was right.

"In a choice, save the woman. Ro will value future heirs by her over this one that might not survive."

Deliya stared at him in shock.

"Does she require my healing?" he demanded again. "To deliver the child?"

"Do not touch me," Deliya ordered, hate swelling up strong.

The woman healer turned from her pack. "We will require boiling water to sterilize my tools."

"Are you mad?" Jurel thundered. "Ro follows close behind. He must track us now. If we light a fire, he will be upon us before the sun is high."

Deliya thanked Mag and Fion both that he was so close.

"If I do not sterilize my tools, I risk infection," the healer argued. "You would lose them both."

"Then pray that does not happen," he growled.

Deliya stiffened in pain then forced her muscles to ease again. "There is another way," she offered in desperation. "A fire is not necessary. Leave me now, and I will teach your woman healer." She would not bring Ro's child into the world with their enemy standing over her, and the babe was in the canal.

Jurel looked at her curiously. "Why would you do that?"

"To make you leave! A priestess of Fion does not bring forth a life this way. I will fight this birth until I kill us both rather than deliver my child in your sight."

He smirked. "Then I take my leave."

The healer shuddered, as the pavilion flap closed behind him, shooting Deliya a sad look. "Please trust me," she whispered. "I was taken from my home to help you. Not much better than you were. I am no happier here than you are."

"Why?" Deliya asked, panting back another pain. "Why you?"

She blushed. "I have milk. If something goes awry, he means me to nurse your child."

"You lost a child?" she asked.

The healer nodded sadly. "My son," she whispered, as if that made the loss worse.

Deliya looked to the dirty-faced little girl still asleep on her mother's cot. Did the woman not realize the gift she had in her daughter? Another pain reminded Deliya that she had more important things to worry about than opening this woman's eyes to new possibilities. "You must work quickly. Have you Felgren and Auguren?"

"Yes. Of course."

"Mix them equally. Since we cannot heat water, make a paste with a bit of oil and scrub your hands and tools with the mixture. It will leave a choc stain for several days, but it will not harm you."

The woman didn't question Deliya's instructions. She set to work mixing the herbs. "How far are you, Majesty?"

"We have little time," Deliya admitted. "What is your name, healer?"

"Lera, Majesty."

"Do not call me—Either Priestess or Mother Deliya, if you please, Lera." Deliya shot a quick look at the walls to make certain they were not being eavesdropped on. "Why do you do this?" she whispered.

The healer glanced up as she rubbed the paste into her hands, looking confused.

"Why do you serve Jurel?"

"You speak as if I have a choice," she dismissed the question.

"You do."

"What choice? I am Lengar. Even if I left Lengar lands, the Magden would kill me on sight for what I am."

"Ro would not," she promised.

Lera moved on to her tools, coating them in the mixture quickly. "You want something from me."

"I want us both to be free of Jurel." Deliya looked at the sleeping child pointedly. "All four of us. Your child is why you stay. Is she not?"

Lera flushed again.

"You have my word that you will both be safe in Magden lands." Deliya held her breath, hoping that Lera wouldn't use this to better her position with Jurel, turning Deliya's attempts to sway the woman healer back on her.

"Why would you keep that promise?"

"Because Fion's priestesses always keep their word."

Lera looked to her hopefully. For an instant, she was radiant and alive. Then the light left her eyes. "Your child, Priestess," she said brusquely.

As if I could forget. Deliya longed to cry out, but she would not give Jurel the satisfaction of hearing her pain. She clenched her hands on the edge of the cot, forcing all her tension into that grip while she relaxed her pelvic muscles into the birth. "Hurry," she breathed as Lera disinfected her blade.

Lera pulled the quilt back and knelt between Deliya's thighs to check her progress. She swore softly. "How could you get so far without crying out and without healing?" she asked.

"A priestess of Fion is trained to control her pain."

"Well trained," Lera noted. She wet a cloth to bathe Deliya's face while she labored.

Deliya lost her grip on the passage of time. With Ro's help, their child might have been born near sunrise. Without him, the sun had been in the sky for nearly two hours, Lera's girl watching from her cot as she nibbled on bread and tea, before the babe eased into the healer's hands.

Deliya sank back onto the bed, shaking with exhaustion as the pain disappeared. Her lungs ached, and her entire body felt weak as a newborn hottel foal. She opened her eyes as Lera cleaned the babe. "Boy or girl?" she rasped.

The healer smiled sadly. "A female, Priestess."

Deliya laughed in relief. "Good."

Lera looked at her in confusion then picked up a large square of cloth to wrap the babe in.

"No," Deliya instructed her. "Hand her to me." Once her daughter was in her arms, Deliya removed her overmantle and reached for Lera's dagger.

The healer shook her head, pulling the blade from Deliya's reach. "Jurel would kill me if I armed you," she whispered.

"My child is a Daughter of Fion. She will not wear anything Jurel provides," Deliya insisted. "You have my vow that I will not use your blade against you or anyone else."

Lera hesitated then eased the blade into Deliya's hand, grimacing at the trust she was showing her enemy.

Deliya cut squares of silin from the overmantle to use as soil wraps and set the cowl aside to swaddle her babe in. By the time her daughter was properly covered and wrapped in the cowl, she had awakened and started squalling for her first meal, her face as red as the hair she had inherited from her father.

Deliya handed the blade back with a nod of thanks. The healer stared at it in shock, her gaze moving to her own daughter. Deliya latched her child to her breast with a smile. Perhaps she had an ally after all.

Her smile disappeared as Jurel threw back the flap and strode into the pavilion, watching her child nurse with a smug smile on his rugged face.

"I take it that Ro's son is well?" he asked.

Deliya met his eyes in challenge. "Ro's daughter is strong and hungry."

His smile disappeared. "Daughter?"

Deliya nodded curtly.

"A daughter is useless to me," he informed her, pulling his dagger. "Ro will only bargain for an heir."

Deliya pulled the babe to her chest, shaking in disbelief. Even Jurel couldn't be that heartless. Could he? One look in his black eyes told her that he was, and she was too weak to fight him.

Lera grasped his arm. "No, Majesty. Please wait," she begged.

He struck her, knocking the healer to the ground. "Touch me again and die," Jurel warned in a voice shaking in fury.

"Majesty, you have a son," Lera gasped.

"What of it?" he snapped.

"This daughter of Ro's wed to your son would prove Lengar rule over all the races on Kegin. Even the Magden would support a succession of conquest."

Jurel paused, his brows furrowing as he worked over that idea. Deliya held her breath, praying for this short reprieve even as her stomach twisted at the thought.

"It would," he conceded. "She may be of some use to me yet." His smile returned, a cold, calculating smile. "Feed your child. I will send food in to you. We leave in an hour."

Deliya shook her head, weak from release of fear more than exhaustion. "It is too soon," she informed him.

Jurel crouched to her face level. "If the child is too weak to travel, she is of no use to me," he warned, raising an eyebrow.

"It is not the child," Lera offered. "The priestess will not be able to ride for more than a week. Even with a litter, she should not be moved for several days. The babe was born very early. Her mother's milk is best for her. Mine may not be sufficient. Without the priestess in good health and producing that milk, you could lose them both."

Deliya sighed in silent thanks. Lera was flirting with untruths, but most of her argument was based in fact.

Jurel scratched his fingers along his whiskered chin. "Then we meet Ro here," he decided.

Deliya nodded, hiding her joy.

"If you do not cause me problems, both you and your child will survive the day," he promised.

She swallowed hard and nodded again.

Ro would not kneel to her. If he did, Deliya would have to stop him at any costs. She looked at her daughter. What punishment would Jurel impose? One of them would not survive her attempt to save Ro.

"What is her name?" Jurel asked, stroking one sun-darkened finger over the babe's cheek.

"I will speak her name to Ro first. I owe him that much." *I owe Riella that much.*

CHAPTER TWENTY-THREE

"They have lit a fire," Donic noted in confusion. "It is nearly mid-day, and they are not moving. Why would Jurel stop in Magden lands when the temporary border is only half a day's ride from here?"

"He wants to draw me in," Ro answered. "He either believes he will win or has no choice." *Why stop here? Has Della forced this confrontation somehow?*

"You cannot be seriously considering this," Donic protested. "Meeting him here, at his leisure? Three-quarters of our troops are off checking the side trails Jurel left in the last two days to throw us off. If he kills you—"

"Muria and Benel will carry on. Jurel has my bride and child, Donic. I will have them back."

"Let me send for more men."

"There is no time. By what the trackers have seen, we are well-matched."

"If he has not met up with more of his men."

"I will have Della back at any cost."

"You cannot bargain, Ro."

"I will do what I must and only that much. Spread the word among the men. If it comes to a battle, they are to reach Della and protect her with their lives. I can protect myself."

Donic wasn't happy with the arrangement, but he agreed to follow Ro on what he termed 'a mad crusade' in his grumblings, ending with his usual, "As you wish, my King."

Ro ordered a hand of men into position around the enemy camp to avoid an ambush and took the other eight with him as he rode in.

Jurel rose from the fireside, a smug grin on his face as he surveyed his foe. "It took you long enough," he taunted.

Ro scanned the camp from his vantage point on his buck, looking over the heads of the guards between him and Jurel and noting a heavily-guarded pavilion behind the fires. "Bring out my bride," he ordered.

"Why be in such a hurry, Ro? We have much to discuss."

"For instance?"

"You will fall back to the south and stay there, two hundred stride south of the Garesh Mountains."

Ro bit back his anger. "I will discuss nothing until I see that my bride is well."

He scowled. "Can the Magden not be courteous guests? Bring out the woman," Jurel ordered.

Ro watched the man's progress. He entered the pavilion, two of the closer guards accompanying him. He forced his breathing to remain slow and steady as the minutes ticked away. What had they done to her that it took three men to bring her out?

Two of the men reappeared with Della between them, clasping her by the arms. She was pale, and a dark bruise marred her jaw. Her hair was disheveled and unwashed, and her blue silin robes were splattered with blood and mud. Ro tensed as she stumbled and landed on her knees. The guards hauled her back to her feet and propelled her forward.

"Della," he breathed. Jurel would pay dearly for this—once she was safe.

Jurel laughed. "I assure you that she is merely in need of rest. As a proper host, I stopped for her comfort."

254

Della weaved on her feet, all but collapsing as she came even with Jurel. She stiffened her spine, her head lowered, casting her eyes back and forth, as if expecting an attack. The hair on the back of Ro's neck rose; something was amiss.

Ro jerked his head in her direction. "I can see what a gracious host you have been," he growled.

"Oh, but I have been." Jurel motioned his men away and drew her against his side.

Her guards joined the two that already stood between Ro and his foe.

Della met Ro's eyes fully for the first time. She moved her hand over the front of her robes, flattening them over what had been a much larger mound of a babe only a few days earlier.

Ro glanced toward the pavilion. Jurel had to stop for Della to deliver their child; that was why he hadn't made the border. Was their child a hostage or was it too early for the babe to have survived outside the womb?

"I provided a woman healer for my enemy's child," Jurel noted silkily. "I stopped and had fires lit to feed the new mother, my enemy's mate. Does that not place you in my debt?"

Ro looked at Della, his heart aching that he had broken his vow to her. He had failed her. She'd brought their child into the world in this Len-be-damned place, without his healing. "Our child is well?" he asked, praying that everything had gone smoothly.

Jurel's hand tightened on her arm; and Ro wondered at the reason for that warning, knowing that Della would find a way to tell him the truth, no matter the cost. He had to know. If Jurel's interference stole his child, Ro would not hesitate to kill every man in this camp to avenge their loss; and his enemy would die without landing more than a single blow on Della before he found that vengeance.

"Your true heir is well, Ro," she stated calmly.

He smiled in understanding. Della had given him a daughter. Jurel didn't want him to know that, believing he wouldn't hold a female in the same regard he would a male. "Well done," he told her.

Jurel relaxed slightly.

Ro sobered at Della's exhaustion. It was the time for her mother's fast. Making her stand here was cruel. "What do you want, Jurel?"

"I have told you the border I demand."

Yes. Two hundred stride south of the Garesh Mountains. "So you have all the best farm land and ore deposits? So the Lengar grow stronger with every passing season? A more even split or nothing." *No matter the split, Jurel will attack again.*

The Lengar geela pulled his blade and pressed it to Della's throat. "How important is the mother of your heir, Ro?" he asked, as if they discussed the effects of an early rain on crops.

Ro took a calming breath. "I cannot make an agreement so against the interests of my people," he whispered. Though Jurel would break his word, Ro would keep his vow, as Mag demanded of him. "The Teldin Pass of the Garesh Mountains. As long as you stay to your side of the border, I will do the same," he offered.

Jurel scowled. "That is almost three hundred stride from the site I suggested."

Two hundred and sixty. "It is an equitable division of resources."

"A change so drastic means some considerable compensation. Would you argue that it is not so?" He slid the blade along Della's throat but did not draw blood.

She raised her chin with pride. Ro recalled her words from the night Donic told her the fate of her people as if she now spoke them aloud. *"My people do not bargain. Not even for me."* She would expect no less from him.

"If you kill her, you will not leave this place alive."

Jurel took the blade from her throat, waving it theatrically. "Perhaps. That was not the compensation I envisioned, in any case."

"What was?" Ro growled, growing tired of the man's insufferable games.

"Kneel to me. Kneel to me, and I will agree to the Teldin Pass as a border. Your woman and heir will be free to leave with you."

Ro hesitated, ignoring the warning look Donic sent him. If he knelt to Jurel, he would likely never regain the respect of his men, but if it would save Della and his child, he would risk it.

Della laughed harshly. "Ro Ti kneels to no man," she informed Jurel. "You will rot in your master's dungeons before he—"

Jurel struck her with his armored hand, and Ro dropped from his mount, his hand on his sword hilt, the need to run Jurel through propelling him toward them. Donic and Novin stepped between him and his adversaries, stopping him mid-stride as Jurel's men closed around him—all but the two holding his daughter hostage.

"You play a dangerous game," he warned.

257

He turned to Della, trying to gauge the reason for her outburst. Did she simply not want him to compromise for her? His hair bristled in warning again. No. There was something more, but she could not say what it was and live.

Jurel put up his hands in a gesture of peace. "You will not kneel to me?" he asked.

Della shook her head slowly, never taking her eyes from Ro.

"I kneel to no one," Ro answered, repeating her words.

Jurel laughed heartily. "Come now. I know that is not true." He scanned Della up and down, making his meaning clear.

She flushed and shot a pained look at Ro.

"Sex games are not a sign of servitude," Ro noted, eyeing his men. There was a traitor in his ranks. Only someone spying in his household could have delivered them to this.

"You will not kneel to your mate?" Jurel repeated, seemingly stunned by the turn of events. He signaled toward the pavilion. "Would you kneel to your heir?"

Ro stiffened as a babe squalled...his daughter.

Della whirled in Jurel's grip, struggling weakly against his hold. He dragged her back with a vicious smile, and she glared at him, a look that Ro wagered would have seen Jurel dead were she not so depleted from childbirth.

"Will you kneel to your heir, Ro?" Jurel taunted.

Della looked at the pavilion then at Ro, swallowing hard and shaking her head. She trembled. Was she still begging him not to kneel? When it was their child Jurel threatened? Surely not. She must mean for him to save the babe at any cost. Still, a niggling doubt ate at Ro. He wished he knew for sure.

He closed his hand on Donic's shoulder. "I must do this," he whispered. "You must be my witness."

Donic made a sound of disgust. "I will gut him for this," he promised.

Novin nodded. "Save your son."

Ro didn't bother to correct them. While he valued his daughter, his men would not hold her in as high regard as they would a son. It was to his advantage not to correct them.

He motioned them away and stepped forward. He met Della's eyes as he started to lower himself to one knee.

"No," she screamed, throwing herself at Jurel.

Ro jerked upright, instantly on alert. He froze at the flash of metal as she struck. Della fell with Jurel into the line of his men, and Ro drew his sword.

A deafening explosion sounded around them and echoed off the surrounding hills. Ro staggered back as something hit the armor covering his shoulder, crying out in surprise as it ripped through the metal and sent slivers of pain through the meat of his upper arm. Ro regained his balance as Novin and Donic charged into the mass of bodies.

"Your son!" Donic screamed.

Ro cut down the two Lengar soldiers in his path and sprinted for the pavilion as his men poured from the trees with a thunder of hooves and battle cries. He faltered as Della cried out then laid on speed. She had Novin and Donic to protect her. Their daughter was unprotected...and still crying.

The man standing at the pavilion flap backed off as

Ro raised his sword then turned and ran. One of the mounted Magden soldiers veered to cut the Lengar down.

He pulled back the flap and faced a wide-eyed soldier holding a green silin-wrapped bundle. Ro saw, with considerable relief, a tiny fist waving at the man. His daughter was alive and well, though the soldier held a blade to her chest.

Ro put his free hand out, keeping his sword point lowered. "Give her to me, and I promise to let you live."

The soldier paled. "You know the child is female?" he gasped. "You would have knelt for a female?"

"My daughter," Ro reminded him, edging forward.

A small girl darted at the soldier from the far reaches of the pavilion. The man didn't acknowledge her presence, even when she pulled on his leg.

"Your child will be safe," Ro assured him. "The lives of your family for mine."

He glanced at the girl in confusion. "What? This is not—"

He cursed fluently and kicked the child away, whipping the blade from the babe's chest to knock the bit of metal the child speared in him from his leg.

Ro struck, planting his sword at the thigh joint of his adversary's armor and snatching his daughter away as the man fell. A woman ran toward them, and Ro turned to meet her attack; but she darted to the little girl lying on the floor. Ro stared at her, unsure of her purpose.

"The priestess promised you would not harm us," she told him, holding her child in her arms. "She vowed you would take us safely to Magden lands with you. Mother Deliya carries my blade in trust of that vow."

Ro nodded, lowering his sword. "Follow me. You will be safe. You have my vow."

He turned and left the pavilion, crooning to the babe in his arms as he surveyed the destruction around him. The fighting was done. His men had made short work of Jurel and his followers.

He took a moment to smile at his daughter, at the shock of red hair and the dark eyes that regarded him curiously as her tiny fist beat at his armor. She yawned widely, and he laughed in delight. She was as beautiful as her mother.

Ro furrowed his brow. Where was Della? He strode toward the knot of his men, quickening his step as Novin shot him a pained look. His mind argued the obvious conclusion, even as he theorized that Della must be seriously injured if she didn't come to meet them.

His men parted, looking pale and nervous. Ro froze at the sight of her, swallowing the scream of dismay rising behind his lips. He knelt, moving his eyes from her blood-soaked robes to the tears on her face.

He brushed at the tears, blinking back his own. "Fion's Priestess does not weep before her enemies," he reminded her, refusing to speak the last portion of the saying. *Even as she dies.*

"My enemies are dead." Della reached a shaking hand to the hole in Ro's armor. "I could not let them—" She grimaced, her breath hitching. "Jurel thought...the confusion of your death would allow him...to win."

Donic crouched next to them. "It was a lightweight projectile weapon. Her Majesty's move jarred the shooter off target. Jurel had little time to contemplate his fate; her aim was true." He didn't meet Ro's eyes as he gave his report.

Ro nodded, raising Della's hand to his lips. He grimaced at the bruises ringing her wrists. She had obviously spent a great deal of her time with Jurel bound. "You should not have sacrificed yourself," he breathed.

She groaned. "Never by...action or inaction," she gasped. "A priestess...lays down her life for those she loves. I could not allow you...to come to harm." She moved her eyes to the bundle of sleeping child in his arms. "Our daughter...looks like you."

"Daughter?" Donic growled. "She lied."

"Quiet," Ro ordered, though he kept his voice low to avoid startling the infant. "Della did not lie to me, despite the fact that Jurel wanted her to. She told me that my true heir was well. The true heir of one of Fion's priestesses is her daughter. We performed Della's ceremony when we married. Our daughter is my true heir."

Della's eyes widened. "You are...a Magden...king."

"And Magden law allows for a king to accede by virtue of marriage," he soothed her. "We mated for life. I gave my vow to you."

"Your duty...If our child...had been male...and I...was left," she whispered, her voice frantic.

Ro covered her lips with his fingertips, laying her hand on his cheek. "Shhh." He couldn't listen to her ask him to take another while she lay dying. He had no doubts that she would not have the heart to take another if he had left her, though he dared not call her a liar. Not even for her heir would she have mated again—and neither would he. "Name our daughter and promise to walk with me in the soul's reward."

262

Della nodded. "I present...your daughter...Riella...named...for the first high priestess of...my line...thirty generations ago." She rested her silin-covered hand over Riella's chest. "May you lead...with Mag's...justice and Fion's...mercy. May you serve...your people well...as has...your father before you."

"And your mother," Ro added, making note of the ceremony that would be passed down through the royal line of the Magden in her honor.

"I will...wait for you...at the gates to...the soul's reward," she promised.

"Then rest," Ro whispered.

Della shook her head. "Lera...is a woman healer."

"She has my protection," Ro assured her.

"She is...also...a milk nurse."

Ro nodded. "You wish her to care for Riella?"

"Yes...If you will not...take another...to have your son..." She looked at a spot behind him.

He followed her line of sight to the child holding Lera's hand and nodded his agreement. With no siblings, Riella would need a servant-sister. "It will be done," he vowed, turning back to her.

Della touched their daughter's face, smiling weakly. "I wanted...to be there...for her."

"You will be. I will teach her all I can. Riella will read the Great Book. She will know you through my eyes. You have my vow that she will."

She closed her eyes, her breathing growing shallow as her lifeblood left her body.

"Sleep, Della," Ro soothed her. "Take your rest." He held her hand long after her breathing stopped and Donic paid his regrets.

He kissed her cheek and rose, looking to Riella. She was his greatest treasure now. He turned to Novin. "Build a pyre and allow Della the rest of her people," he instructed in a broken voice.

Novin led several of their men away.

Donic stayed behind. He cleared his throat. "You did not mean what you said about never taking another," he ventured. "You said those things to ease her out of this life."

"I meant every word, Donic. I gave my vow that Della would be my one true mate. Riella is my heir."

Donic ground his teeth. "As you wish, my King."

Ro sighed. Already Donic was forming plans to change his mind; those plans would fail.

CHAPTER TWENTY-FOUR

Abrin 12th, Ti 10-465

Ro groaned, as the woman moved over him, her body soft and sweet. This was all he needed, the release a schente could offer him.

It had taken him long enough to accept that much. Ro had remained celibate the entire two years he'd kept Riella in his room, afraid to let her out of his sight even that long, afraid he might find that he was willing to attach meaning to the physical act of intercourse with anyone but Della. But, as a priestess who lost her true mate only took physical release in the act, taking a young buck to pleasure her without chance of children, so did Ro. There was nothing more for him without Della.

Accepting schente again gave Donic hope that Ro would concede to more. Despite the general's attempts to tempt Ro into another marriage, it would never be. Ro had given his vow in Della's ceremony to be her mate alone and only marry again to the production of a true heir. Della had gifted him that—a true heir. Even Magden law allowed for a female heir when the king left no sons. Riella's husband would rule with her.

Even if Ro hadn't made that vow, he couldn't take another mate now. He'd bound himself to Della, given her his heart. No woman could capture what was not his to give.

Ro took the schente fast and hard, as was his way when it wasn't Della he took. He climaxed, waving the woman away as soon as he lessened. They were always willing to spend a few extra moments with him if it would give Ro ease, but having a schente in his bed gave him no comfort past the obvious release of tensions.

The night was cool and dark, and Ro wrapped himself in a robe as he took air on his balcony. He stared into the gardens, planted with Della's precious bags of seed—all but the gola berry. Ro woke from too many nightmares where Riella ate the innocent-looking berries to allow those plants anywhere near the palace.

It was his conscience; Ro knew it was. He had broken too many vows to Della in their short marriage.

The Triclum was yet another. He told himself that he would have stood a chance against the Church council if Della had lived to complete the woman healer's training, but she did not, and Ro could not adequately champion her case.

The woman healers had the knowledge of many things they had not before: ways to limit fertility, ways to save lives...and ways to end misbegotten pregnancies. They did not have the full training in the Mother's way that would prevent them from using that knowledge in ways Fion's priestesses never would.

The Church council decreed that a woman should have to seek a doctor to reverse gola poisoning to make the stigma of causing miscarriage limit the number of women who would seek that as a quick answer to an unplanned conception. Ro argued that the women should have the right to terminate a pregnancy for many reasons beyond simply mother's sickness, which was why it was still legal for the woman healers to make the gola berry tea.

He surrendered on the battle of keeping the secret of Triclum with the doctors. The salve that he used to ease his guilt was the construction of clinics near all the major villages, all of which carried Triclum. The women who suffered mother's sickness would have the care he promised, though he ultimately broke his vow to return the knowledge to the healers.

Ro sighed, looking out over the new Gidlore. That was one vow he made to Della that he kept. He had built the palace he promised her on the site of the priestesses' last stand. Forevermore, this would be the site of the Magden seat of power.

There was no chance of losing it now. With Jurel's death, the Lengar fell into chaos. They still attacked Magden land, and Ro still battled them back, intent on a unified and peaceful future for his daughter and her daughters, but the Lengar were also in a perpetual state of civil war over leadership of their race.

In the center of the gardens, where the priestesses' circle once stood, was a meditation clearing ringed with benches of the sacred green stone. In the center stood a statue of the great Goddess Herself, etched from the cornerstone of what was once her tower, the hardest stone on Kegin, the same stone that made up the gate pillars of this palace.

Ro bowed to Her image reverently. Fion had been nothing but kind in granting Ro's wish, the wish of a son of Her own mate. She'd given Ro the gift of Della's love. His only prayer was that Fion would grant him one final wish—the right to stand by Della's side when he passed to the soul's reward, the right to enter the great gates despite the many vows he'd failed to uphold where Della was concerned.

He tensed as the screaming started, grasping his sword and vaulting through the door into the corridor.

He sprinted for the open door to Riella's rooms, cursing the robe that tangled in his legs as he ran.

"Out," he heard Lera shout. "Leave us."

"Quiet," a man barked.

Riella's screams intensified, and Ro barreled into the room, his sword high and a battle cry heralding from deep in his chest. Two of his guards faced off against Lera. The woman healer stood between the soldiers and the two girls huddled together on the bed.

The guards fell back as he entered, dropping their drawn weapons to the floor in confusion. Lera stood her ground, red-faced and eyes flashing in fury. Unlike his guards, she knew no fear of him.

"It was not we who did this," one of the guards stammered.

"I said leave us," Lera shouted again.

Ro lowered his sword and waved the men away. "Leave us," he growled with an unspoken warning not to go far. If he learned his daughter's terror was their fault, there would be punishment for it.

The guards scrambled away, one without retrieving his weapon. The door closed behind them, and Riella's shrieking tapered off into sobs.

Ro settled on the bed next to her, setting his sword on the rug, and Riella released her hold on Irin to throw herself against his chest. He folded her in his arms, brushing the tangled locks from her eyes.

"What caused this?" he whispered. "Who frightened her?"

Irin, who had been leaving the bed to seek her own, paused with one leg on the floor across from him. "A dream," she explained. "Then the guards came in." She swallowed hard.

"The guards terrified her," Lera fumed. "Any fool could see that, but they refused to leave."

"Why?" Ro asked.

"I do not know. Perhaps you should ask them that yourself, Ro Ti, since they do not respect my judgment when it comes to Riella."

He shook his head, rubbing soothing circles over Riella's back. This was an old argument and one he would take up with the guards again, but it wasn't what he meant.

"No. Why did they terrify her? Riella has never feared her guards before. She has never feared anyone until tonight." *Much as I wish she would sometimes, this was not what I envisioned. I wanted caution, not terror, from her.*

Riella's chubby fist closed on his robe, and she nuzzled her cheek to his chest. "They came to take me away from you," she whispered. "They came to take me away like they did before."

Ro stared into her tear-streaked face, his heart pounding. Her deep choc eyes were wide and earnest, her terror real.

"Before?" he asked, keeping his voice calm, praying he was wrong.

"They took me and my mother from you. The Lengar."

Ro shot a hard look at Lera, but the woman healer shook her head in confusion. Riella had never been told the story of her birth. For five years, she'd been spared that ugly truth for fear of this reaction.

He looked at Irin. The girl stood, her eyes as wide and frightened as Riella's were, wringing her hands.

Ro swallowed a curse. "Who did this, Irin?" He kept

his tone gentle, knowing the child feared his wrath.

"The guard..." she confessed, looking to her mother for support. "The old one at the stables told her."

Riella eased up her father's chest to wind her hands around his neck beneath his hair. "They will come for me again," she croaked through fresh sobs.

Ro kissed her forehead. "He told you that?"

She nodded.

Irin cleared her throat. "He told Riella that is why she must never outrun her guards when she rides with Benir."

Ro grimaced. The fact that it was true was immaterial. The fact that her knack of escaping the sight of her guards stopped his heart too often was immaterial. The man would be punished for frightening her this way.

He met Lera's eyes. "Get me my bride's dagger and hair clips," he instructed.

Lera paled, but she nodded and left the room. Ro sighed. He had wanted Riella to be spared this part of her existence, but she was a Magden princess; perhaps there was no escaping it.

Lera handed him the items he'd requested wrapped in a length of green silin.

"Leave us," he whispered. "This is between Riella and me."

They obeyed, closing the door to their adjoining room behind them.

Ro took a deep breath, calming his pounding heart. "Riella, look at me."

She bit her lip, her eyes straying to the silin.

"I will tell you about your mother."

Riella wiped at the last stubborn tears, glancing to

the silin-wrapped bundle then back to him several times. He opened the cloth and drew out the hair clips, placing them in her hair.

"Your mother was a great queen."

She had heard that before. It was one of the few things she'd been told of her mother—how gracious and kind Della was, the deep concern she had for her people and the empathy she had for their pain.

Ro smoothed his daughter's hair, meeting her eyes. "Deliya was the last of her race."

"Her race?" Riella asked. "She wasn't Magden?" She scratched at her nose, wrinkling it in confusion.

He shook his head. "She was the last of Fion's Daughters. Her name was Mother Deliya. She was a warrior priestess, and you are her true heir. Della was a healer, a woman who held the knowledge and magic of the Goddess herself. She saved Novin's life, and she healed me more than once."

Riella nodded, intent on the story now, her fear forgotten, as was the way with young children. "I have heard that she was very beautiful."

Ro smiled. "My Della had hair like the summer sun and eyes as green as the gown you wear. I had never seen such a beauty, and Fion was merciful enough to grant me her love."

"But, the Lengar took us and killed her." Her lip trembled.

Ro sighed and pulled the abinatine from the silin. He hesitated, staring at it sadly, remembering when he had held it last. *This is right. A son of this age would be gifted his first dagger. Surely, Della would have trained Riella soon.* He settled the sheathed dagger in her hand.

Riella touched the sacred pattern of emi beads in

awe.

"That is called an abinatine. It is the sacred blade of one of Fion's High Priestesses. It is used for only three things."

"What things?" Riella asked breathlessly.

"In her healing, when she takes a true mate, and to kill a worthy opponent." Ro closed his fist over hers. "As Mother Deliya's true heir, this is yours, the sign of who and what you are."

Her lip protruded in a look of confusion.

He continued before she could question him. "You are my true heir, but you are also your mother's. You are the last of Fion's Daughters, protected by Mag and Fion both. You will always be safe."

"But, the guard said the Lengar—"

He shushed her and smiled, hiding his fury at the guard studiously. *That fool will be lucky if I let him live.* "Della fought with that blade when Jurel tried to take her from our home. She escaped more traps than a buck wariken. I have seen Della tame a wild jaglin and take a warrior's life." He ran his fingers over the tattoo on her thigh that showed through her sleeping gown. "Let the Lengar come for you in force," he laughed. "The daughter of Ro Ti and Mother Deliya will not be taken again. Do you know why?"

Riella smiled and unsheathed her mother's abinatine. "Because I am the last of Fion's Daughters?" she asked brightly, with a child's innocence that made Ro's heart ache.

He nodded. It was the best hope he could give her. Riella was a child. His plans and safeguards were meaningless to her.

He sheathed her blade. "Use this cautiously. Della's

most deadly weapon was not this bit of metal. Her most deadly weapon was her mind." That much was true. "She did not take unnecessary chances," he lied.

Riella was a child. There were some stories he would not tell her for her own protection.

"Tell me about my mother," Riella begged.

Ro stretched out on the bed and drew his daughter into his arms, remembering the first months after Della died when she slept in his arms every night, before Lera convinced him that she should move to the cradle that lay next to his bed.

It had been a hard move, and more than once, Ro had scrambled to the cradle when he woke with empty arms. Seeing Riella was the only thing that made Della's loss bearable to him, beginning with those long nights on his pallet after Novin gave her body to the pyre.

He swallowed a bitter lump, thinking about happier times. "I found her alone in her home, the last of her people, though she did not know it at the time."

"Was Deliya frightened?" Riella asked solemnly, touching his face with her pudgy fingers.

Ro laughed heartily. "Della feared nothing. Della feared no one. She came at me in her armor and called me a spineless coward."

She giggled and buried her face in his chest. "She did not," Riella decided. "No one would dare call Ro Ti a coward."

Ro laughed with her. "She did. On Mag's honor, she called me a coward."

She curled her arms under her cheek, the abinatine gripped in her hand. "Did you love her very much?"

He sobered. "Yes. I will always love Della, as I will

always love you."

"I love you, Ro my father." It was an old joke between them, begun when Riella tried to copy the formal address Donic used sometimes. She yawned widely and rubbed her fist in her closed eye. "She gave her life to save me," she mumbled.

"Yes." He stroked his hand through her hair, so much like his own. "Della was a priestess. She would have given her life in defense of any woman or child in her care, but her own most especially. She was the Source of the Goddess of Love—love embodied on the face of the world—and she loved us most of all."

Ro talked on, but Riella didn't hear much more about her mother that night. She was already lost in sleep. He continued to tell the tale anyway. He had waited too long to fulfill this vow. Riella would know Della through his eyes, and perhaps he would recapture a moment of that time.

SECTION TWO
Juvia

Dishonored

"Judge a man by his actions, Deliya, and not by his words or flag. Even a Lengar king could be a good man...in the right circumstances."
Mother Leiana

CHAPTER ONE

Wos 11th, Ti 10-449

Juvia cursed as the mare stumbled, throwing herself away and rolling to her feet, taking down another Lengar soldier with the precision blows her mother taught her to deliver. She didn't look for the battle groups. Even if they realized she'd lost her mount, none of them would come to help her. She was expendable, unwanted, dishonored. Not even worthy to be a part of a battle group, Juvia offered unsolicited cover for her mother's group, cover no one would note, no one would thank her for.

Another Lengar beast came at her, and she cut him down with ruthless efficiency. She sprinted for the tower, toward the troops that bore her mother's stamp, ducking a blow and taking down another soldier.

Juvia was an excellent warrior, equal even to Mother Leiana, though no one had whispered that in well over a year. If circumstances were different, she might one day have demanded a trial for leadership from Leiana or her daughter, Deliya. Yes, she was death personified with a sword in hand. If only that were enough, she would be mounted on a buck instead of the lame mare, wearing her mother's stamp proudly instead of plain armor.

But, she was dishonored. She cut down another Lengar soldier with a grunt of frustration. She was worthy to kill men, but never to love them.

All for a foolish wish! Juvia had believed in love once—a mad desire to take Loric as her mate. She'd asked him to challenge her, intent on conceiving...

She tried to push away memories that would not be silenced. He'd used her love against her. He'd tricked her and failed her at challenge. His look of disdain when she'd cried out still haunted her on the coldest, bitter nights—followed by his look of triumph when Mother Leiana congratulated him for being the first male to fail a priestess in over a decade.

Juvia stopped short as her mother blew the retreat, her heart pounding. Unless she moved quickly, she'd be left behind. Changing direction, she ran for two soldiers mounted on small male hottel.

They stared at her, dumbstruck at the sight of a lone enemy soldier charging them on foot. She bit back a peal of hysterical laughter. It would work. By the Mother, this mad escapade would work!

For one precious moment, the last year fell away. She was free, strong, a warrior in her element.

Then they fell on her in force, coming from all sides at once. Juvia shrieked in fury and frustration, hacking at the incoming troops, fighting through the burn in her arms and lungs.

A battle cry rattled her nerves. The Lengar soldiers parted, and a great, dark war-buck surged toward her with a rider that could only be Len Himself on its back.

Juvia gasped, scurrying a few steps back then planting her feet and preparing to fight him. She gauged his charge, anticipating his turn and slice, deflecting his blow. A year ago, her mother would have taken pride in that move. Today...

She forced her mind back to the battle. He turned and came for her again. Juvia rebuffed him. On the third pass, he didn't turn aside. Her dive came too late. The buck's shoulder connected and threw her; she landed hard, the Lengar soldiers piling onto her, disarming her and dragging her to her knees. Her helm was dragged off.

She looked to the madman who'd bested her, her breathing labored as he pulled off his own helm. He was beautiful, terrible, hard to look at.

"Prepare the slave," he ordered, a cold smile curving his lips.

Juvia felt her heart stutter. *Slave? Dear Mother, he means me!*

She searched the far hillsides, hoping against all hope that her sisters would resume the battle for her. They would attempt to free any other priestess. Mother Leiana sat her buck with the other group commanders at her side. Juvia's eyes settled on her mother, and she held her breath, waiting for the call to resume. They turned away.

She closed her eyes, sinking into the hands holding her, dizzy in the enormity of her situation. They'd abandoned her—again. She wasn't worth continuing the battle to save. They were probably glad to be rid of her. They probably determined that life as a slave was more than her due.

"Strip her," the dark warrior commanded.

Juvia met his eyes, swallowing a groan at the jaglin stamp on his black armor. Jurel! She dropped her chin to her chest, beyond caring as her armor was taken away.

* * * *

Jurel watched the captured priestess bring food to his men, chuckling at the sight of one of the proud laid so low. She was nude save the plain brass slave rings that circled her neck, waist, wrists and ankles;

connected with a series of leather straps that hobbled her so that she couldn't run or fight.

He sipped the iri brandy in his goblet, considering her. It had surprised him that she'd bowed to this degradation. Most of Fion's bitches would have stood silent and uncooperative or fought bitterly until his patience fled and he killed them.

Perhaps she hoped her *sisters* would one day save her. His smile widened. It was a futile wish, and she would soon learn it.

His men were getting rowdy, the thrill of victory and ample drink mixed with the promise of entertainment working its magic on them. As if reading his thoughts, General Fil grasped a handful of priestess tit as she leaned across him with a plate of food.

She stilled, and Jurel set his drink aside, anticipating the coming scene. The witch would protest, perhaps striking Fil. Jurel would enjoy beating her pale backside while his men held her down then watching while one after another took a turn with her, breaking her spirit.

It didn't happen. She leaned closer to Fil, brushing her nipple over his lips. The room went nearly silent in shock as the general sucked at her. Her eyes closed in pleasure. His men moved closer, watching as Fil moved from breast to breast, arousing her with noisy vigor.

Jurel watched as well, stroking his fingers over his lengthening cock absently. Such a display was unheard of, which made seeing it a sensual dream unfolding.

The woman cried out softly, her body shuddering hard; and Jurel took to his feet. He made it to her in four long strides, fisting his hand in her hair and dragging her off of Fil. Her cry of pain disappeared into his mouth. She met him avidly, passion unleashed, her tongue sparring with his, the scent of her arousal driving him near mad.

Jurel tore his mouth from hers, cursing under his breath. What game was this? "You want my cock?" he challenged her.

Her emi eyes half-closed on a sigh. "Yes," she whispered.

"We shall see how much you want it."

She licked her lips. "How much?" she repeated in a thick voice.

He pulled her along to his seat by the grip on her hair, forcing her to her knees as he sat. Jurel unfastened his trousers one-handed and pushed them down his thighs. He pulled his dagger and set it aside then drew her face down until her nose was buried in the curls surrounding the base of his aching cock.

She gulped in lungfuls of air heavy with his musk greedily then pressed her lips to his hardening sac.

"I have heard of a pleasure your women give," he informed her. "You will serve me that way. If you refuse or fail me, you will die. If you please me..." He smiled widely. "I will make certain you are stuffed full of cock." *Every one of my men until you beg for mercy and then some—starting with me.*

She nodded, seeming uncertain for the first time, frightened. That was another expression he never thought he'd see on one of their goddess's *chosen*.

Jurel placed the blade to her neck artery in warning. "Begin."

At first, she licked at him, bathing his cock with her sweet tongue, exploring him from base to tip. She met his eyes, gathering the slight release from the cleft in the head with the tip of her clever pink tongue. He bit back a groan, forcing his eyes open when he wanted to lay his head back and let her take him to bliss.

She waited, watching him, though he couldn't seem to decipher what she waited for. In a moment of clarity, he realized her plight. Her hands were bound to her waist, unable to be raised above mid-chest, and any move to capture him without the use of them would carry the risk of injury.

He released her hair, keeping his dagger at her throat and his gaze locked with hers. He moved the head of his cock to her lips, tensed to kill her if she thought to bite. Her lips parted, and she sucked in the head. Jurel held his breath, letting it out on a gasp as she took in more of him, nearly two-thirds of his length in a single stroke. Her eyes closed as she pulled back and took him again.

Jurel grasped her hair again. "Look at me," he demanded. He would have his fill of her, and he would look in those stunning green eyes while he did it.

She obeyed him, holding his gaze as she took him shallow and deep, over and over, the heat of her mouth better than he'd dreamed by far. No wonder the Fion's males allowed themselves to be ruled by their women...Not that Jurel would dream of accepting it, but the return wasn't a pittance.

He thrust against her, his hips and hand forcing nearly all of him into her, mimicking the deep thrusts into other depths he would taste. First this and then her sheath.

General Fil appeared at his side, taking the dagger from his hand and allowing Jurel to wrap both hands in her hair.

His men crowded around, shoulder to shoulder, some stroking themselves, some shivering in the rising musk. General Fil started the cadence, and the soldiers matched the beat, stomping in time with his thrusts. Before long, other gasps were echoing his.

Jurel knew that she would be pressed into performing this act for many of the men watching, simply based on his reactions to it. If he weren't heir—If she'd been taking Fil into her mouth instead of him, one of the other men might already be inside her, but she was his until Jurel tired of her and handed her over for their enjoyment.

His mouth went dry; his mind protested his need to climax even as the tightness in his sac announced that there would be no holding back. Jurel thrust deep, roaring out his release, his seed rushing into her mouth.

He went still, his eyes wide, as she swallowed once, then again—pressing the swelling head of his cock hard against the ridge of her palate. General Fil misinterpreted his reaction and moved to kill her; but Jurel was there first, his hand fisted around the other man's wrist.

"No," he growled. *So good! By Len's name, she had best scream for me when I stimulate her, or I will kill her myself.*

He lessened, and she released him, looking at the dagger in Fil's hand nervously. Jurel urged her to her feet and brought her mouth to his, tasting his possession of her. Her kiss was urgent, her nipples hard points against his tunic. He pulled her back over his lap until he felt the damp heat of her core through his trousers. He stroked his fingertips along her seam, smiling at the sucre weeping from her.

She kept her eyes open, no doubt afraid to close them after his warning. He brought his fingertips to his mouth, savoring her flavor, nodding as her breathing hitched.

"You have pleased me—for now," he informed her. Jurel pushed her at Fil. "Tie her down. No one touches her without my leave."

He dragged off his tunic and dropped it to the floor, his eyes locked on the skittish witch as his soldiers parted for her passage, their eyes hungry. But first, she would be his. Len alone torture her if she played the part of Fion's own now that she'd enflamed him.

CHAPTER TWO

Juvia laid where the Lengar general pointed her, shuddering that he'd led her to the sacred circle. She was back again, accepting a dishonor greater than the one already heaped upon her when she failed at challenge in this very spot.

She ground her teeth at that. What did she care if her dishonor was deeper? She'd been denied the taste of a man's body; she would always be denied that joy— by her own people.

These Lengar soldiers cared nothing about her dishonor. They could use her until they killed her and only give her joy such as she'd never known. Already, their prince had introduced her to one of the "forbidden pleasures" she would not have learned with Fion's Children—pleasures she should have learned after her challenge, had she passed that test. She hadn't.

Juvia looked at the men, inhaling more of their pungent musk as the general released the bindings on the rings and rebound them to the challenge bolts in the floor, leaving her spread-quartered. The taste of Jurel's seed echoed that musk until her core seemed to burn against the cool air in the sanctuary.

"Looser," their prince instructed. "I want her to have enough play to buck against me."

She looked to him in surprise, her mouth watering as he removed the last of his clothing and the general loosened her restraints.

Oh, yes. She would give him what he wanted. The Lengar would get satisfaction from her. Unlike her *sisters*, Juvia had no honor to uphold by taking their bodies in stony silence. She would seek her own pleasure and vent every cry of pain or climax.

Sacrilege, some portion of her mind protested.

Juvia pushed the thought away. She'd been abandoned by her people—first by the man she loved and then by the rest. At first, her exile had been social; she was an outcast—worthy enough to tend animals, crops and the rare dirty-faced child, unworthy of a man's touch, home and children of her own. She was only here with the Lengar because she'd been granted nothing better than the lame mare in battle, a ragged creature not even one of their men would have ridden.

The steady beat of boots on stone startled her, and Juvia looked toward the Lengar prince, knowing the noise heralded his approach. Her breathing hitched.

He strode to her, naked and aroused, his eyes locking with hers and promising that he would not leave her until he'd mastered her. Her body throbbed in time with the beat, and she tipped her hips, offering herself to be mastered. Her hunger for the idea should have repulsed her, but it didn't.

He laid over her, stealing a bit of the musk from the pulse point at her throat. His voice rumbled against her. "You are mine, little witch. Once I have tasted you, I will sate myself in you. Do you understand?"

She nodded, gasping for air.

He clenched her cheeks between his fingertips. "Do you understand me?"

"Yes," she whispered.

He stared at her, his eyes demanding something she could not name.

He waits for me to address him with some title of respect. But, what? He is not my prince nor a common general. The obvious answer became clear to her. She was being made over into a Lengar bed slave. "Yes, Master."

He nodded curtly, though he seemed surprised that she'd uttered the term. How little he understood about her!

Jurel's mouth closed over hers, and she gave herself over to the feeling, groaning in anticipation as his cock pressed hard to her mound. He pulled away, sending her that same suspicious look he had when he'd kissed her the first time.

The stomping seemed to intensify as he worked his way down her body. Juvia tensed then reminded herself that this wasn't the challenge. His mouth latched onto one aching nipple, and she choked out a cry and arched up for more.

The prince's look of shock wasn't lost on her. He went still as if something in her manner confused him. She reasoned that everything about her likely confused him. Juvia was hardly the typical priestess.

"Please," she begged in tones too low for even his general to hear. "Please—Master."

He moved to the other nipple, his suckling sending waves of heat to her core. He bit at her, and she screamed, only assuring herself that there was no shame in it this time when his men cheered him.

His mouth seemed to be everywhere. Juvia fisted the ties in her hands; writhing beneath him as he explored every fingerwidth of exposed skin save the center of her that was calling for him so insistently.

The other men were immaterial; they could do whatever they wished with her—once the prince had finished with her. It wouldn't matter then. Juvia felt certain that he'd leave her a shell, mindless as a born imbecile in pleasure. Everything faded away save the throbbing beat and Jurel's mouth, until her entire body vibrated in time and whimpered pleas left her lips.

Then he was there, at the core of her being and ravenous for her. She stiffened, incapable of thought as sensation engulfed her; so many sights, scents and feelings that not a single one made an impression on her for longer than a heartbeat before being drowned out by another.

She screamed, but a roar eclipsed even that. Then there was silence. Her panting breaths echoed off the stone walls so perfectly, she prayed the rest hadn't been a dream.

Juvia forced her eyes open, looking at the stunned soldiers in confusion. None of them spoke or stomped their feet. They shifted nervously, casting frightened looks at her.

No. Not at me.

She turned her head to look at the prince, her heart pounding at the expression of disdain and fury on his face. *He looks like Loric did when I failed my challenge. Oh, Mother! What have I done wrong this time?*

His general moved to his side, and Jurel pulled the dagger from his belt. She sobbed. She would die without knowing completion, just as she'd always feared she would.

* * * *

Jurel stayed his hand as the witch sobbed, tears escaping and rolling down her face. He shook his head in confusion. Fion's priestesses never cried before an enemy, even as they died.

"Highness?" Fil inquired.

"Clear the men and bring me her armor," he demanded.

She paled, looking at her bound hands then collapsing in defeat.

In moments, they were alone. The soldiers would grumble, but soon they'd find their way to the camp followers and sate themselves there.

He watched his prisoner, considering her warily, trying to anticipate her motives and aim. She didn't meet his eyes, didn't seem capable of anything but staring at the wall in apparent misery.

Fil came in, dumping the mass of metal mesh and hottel leather on a table and setting her sword beside it. Jurel pushed to his feet, ambling to the pile of armor and pulling it out piece by piece to examine it.

"Not of class," he noted. "She isn't closely related to their leader. Not even a first daughter."

"A common priestess," Fil agreed. "She carries no ornamentation on her armor."

Jurel pushed the pile this way and that, his mind working at something just out of his grasp. Realization came in a lightening flash. "The dagger? The abinatine—Where is it?"

"She carried no dagger, Highness."

"Then she lost it in battle. The sheath will tell me all I need to know."

"There was no sheath. Her belt was as bare as you see it when we stripped it from her. There was only the scabbard on it."

He turned to the priestess, considering her carefully.

"Prince Jurel—"

"Leave us."

"But, Highness! Your father—"

"Leave us or die by your own blade," he growled.

"Of course." General Fil left him, closing the doors behind him.

Silence descended again. The priestess kept her eyes averted.

"Why do you carry no abinatine?" he questioned her.

"Because I am unworthy to carry one." Her voice was bland, as if she found the subject tedious or was jaded beyond caring about it.

Jurel returned to her side. "Because you are not an adult by their laws?" He would have guessed her an adult, and he'd never heard of them leaving a child behind, but there had to be some explanation.

She started speaking then hesitated. "I am an adult," she whispered. "I am simply—dishonored."

"Dishonored." He'd heard of priestesses dishonored, but the evidence proved that the only way he knew for them to be dishonored was not what she was condemned for.

"I failed at challenge," she managed in halting tones.

Jurel sank to the floor beside her, his head spinning. "You failed at what sort of challenge? Was it a test of pain or skill in battle?" He couldn't imagine her failing at either.

She looked away, a deep blush painting most of her body.

He planted Fil's blade under her chin. "Answer me," he growled.

She swallowed hard and met his eyes, fresh tears pooling and ready to fall.

He grumbled an oath to Len. "A sexual test." He didn't question that it was so. Only a culture as warped as Fion's Children would see a woman's sexual identity as some sort of weakness...especially one as responsive as this one was.

She tried to turn her head away, stilling with a gasp when his blade bit skin.

At the sight of the blood welling up, his mind locked on another fact, the one that had indicated some treachery to him. "You still retain your barrier," he noted.

Her laugh edged on hysteria. "I failed too early." She laughed on until tears ran down her face and her sanity was an uncertain thing.

Jurel cut the leather ties holding her down and hoisted her over his shoulder, heading up the stairs to a bed he'd discovered earlier. He deposited her in the center and waited for her reaction.

At first, she seemed startled, even a bit fearful. Then she laid back and spread her arms and legs to the spindles, offering herself for binding, her snow-colored hair spread over the sheets.

* * * *

Juvia held herself still, barely breathing as the prince bound her to Mother Leiana's bed. The scent of the leader's farewell from her mate taunted her, but soon the remnants of her own passion would overpower it. It was the sweetest revenge she could imagine.

He knelt on the mattress next to her, testing her with his fingertips. She arched up, stifling the urge to assure him that there was no way she could remain unaffected and unprepared while his cock bobbed so close to her.

He groaned aloud. "Move against them," he ordered.

She tipped her hips back and forth, her breathing becoming more ragged. He watched her intently, his cock twitching as she performed for him. Juvia moved more urgently, reaching for another simple release, knowing instinctively that he would reward her diligent attention to his commands.

"That's right," he managed in a rough voice. "You want my cock there. Don't you?"

"Yes, Master. Anything. Please."

He knelt between her spread legs, stroking the head along her seam. She stretched toward him, desperate to feel the sensations she'd been denied. Without warning, he thrust deep.

Juvia screamed, first in surprise and pain, then in dismay as he retreated, leaving her body empty. She met his eyes, pleading with him not to stop in gasping, half-formed words.

"You are bleeding for me," he noted. "Not for one of your Fion men, but for me."

She nodded.

"Everything I do to you now will be things no Fion's man ever has or will," he continued.

"Yes," she pleaded.

"When my cock returns to your body, I will own you. It can never be undone. I will never release you, never permit you to run from me." He leaned over her, playing the head at her again. "Do you want to be mine?"

She nodded again, unable to draw enough breath to verbalize her agreement.

He filled her, deeper than the last time, his length nestling to the gates of her womb, groaning as she drew in a cleansing breath. He moved in smooth, strong strokes, taking her higher with each tightening of his hips. In no time at all, Juvia found herself lost in another shattering release.

Jurel buried his cock in her, his seed anointing her womb as his swelling forced the gates wide. She arched up against her bonds, screaming in ecstasy as the egg dropped amid a shower of sparks—her first egg.

"Yes," he whispered. "You see what I will give you. Remember that I give you this because you are not like the others of your race. It is not you who fail as a woman but the priestesses who abandoned you. No passionate woman hides what she is. No truly passionate woman can or wants to."

Her head spun at that concept. How many times had she wondered how any priestess could stifle her pleasure? How often had she postulated that most priestesses secretly chose men they loathed for the challenge just to succeed?

"You will learn to give and receive pleasure," he continued. "In time, I may trust you enough to touch me as we share ourselves—once you accept that you are mine."

"I do," she vowed.

CHAPTER THREE

Wos 18th, Ti 10-449

Jurel watched his little priestess sleep. *No! She is not one of those damned priestesses!* That was one thing he believed above all else; and in almost a week, she'd given him no cause to doubt her word.

She'd said her name was Juvia, but that was a Fion's name. The thought burned in his gut. He would never speak the foul sounds assigned her by those who had nearly stolen her sexual identity, who had denied her the expression of what came most naturally to her.

"Veltina," he decided. As a passionate woman, she needed a name that would decree it to all of Kegin. What better name than the first and most prized consort of Len?

He ran a hand down the white silin skirt that marked her as a bed slave, caressing her thigh, smiling as she shifted and tipped her hips in unconscious hunger. Her sucre made the material go transparent, revealing her snowy curls to his gaze, and her nipples came to tiny points.

Whether she knew it or not, she was his. He'd waited long enough to stake his claim properly. Tomorrow, he would band her to himself with silver. After that, no man would dare touch her. She would live in rooms at his home and carry his sons, his possession alone. While she wore the brass rings, the men harbored hopes that he would tire of her and turn her over to them to fill her belly with Lengar slaves. With the silver, her children would be his and his alone—and she with them.

Perhaps one day—He shook away the mad thought. His father would never permit him to band Veltina as his bride, but he would have her as his bride in every other way. If the chance ever presented itself to band her gold, he would.

Jurel stood and checked the chain that locked her loosely to the bed one last time then strode to the door and pulled on his clothes and weapons. One day, she might wear gold. In the meantime, he'd had a bed set up on the floor below. Juvia had killed more than a hand of his best in battle in addition to at least four hand of lesser soldiers; and though he believed her promise to be his, only a fool would show his sleeping heart to her.

* * * *

Wos 19th, Ti 10-449

Jurel set the veltian on the bed, watching Veltina's gaze travel over it. His cock rose as the silin skirt went transparent, the moisture of her body announcing her ready state. He released the chain that restrained her, rapt on her reactions as he had been for days.

"Look at yourself," he ordered.

She stared at her beaded nipples then the skirt.

"Touch yourself. Prepare yourself for me."

She hesitated only a moment then laid back, her hands skating over her breasts, pinching and caressing her nipples. She cupped her breasts up as if offering them to him, waited only a moment then circled the hard points, drawing them even tighter.

Jurel made a mental note of each motion, memorizing how she pleasured herself.

Her hands moved to the juncture of her thighs. She used the silin to stimulate her hood, her breathing harsh and her musk pungent. As he would have wagered, the woman knew herself well. He shivered at her cry of delight, his mouth going dry as she threw her head back and closed her eyes.

He could take her now, on the crest of her simple climax. He would feel her gripping his length as he slid home and send her into completion with a single thrust, for he would surely climax from that sensation alone after watching her send herself over. Her reaction to such a thing would be glorious!

Another time...Yes, very soon, he would do that to her. She would love it as she loved every new experience he granted her, sometimes begging him to allow her a particular pleasure again one day. By Len, how he loved to hear her beg for him!

She started moving her hand again, no doubt misinterpreting his stillness as a wish to see her continue. Jurel considered lowering his mouth to her, aiding her in her next rise, tasting her arousal and feeding his own with the aphrodisiac properties of her fluids.

He cursed the Fion's men as fools for ignoring her. He vowed their deaths silently. How dare they sentence such a sensual creature to a life of self-pleasure! How many lonely nights had she taken simple pleasure from those slender fingers and longed for more? Had she tried to silence her cries of pleasure? Had there been punishment for her further failures? What a place of torture her bed must have been!

It was time to change that, no matter what soldier was about to be tossed from his chosen sleeping spot. "Where is your bed, Veltina?"

Her eyes opened wide, and her skin paled until even her lips barely showed the touch of blood.

"I intend to make it over into a better memory," he soothed her.

She shook her head, tears pooling in her eyes. She'd not cried in anything but joy since the first time he'd pierced her body.

"You refuse me?" he snapped. If she dared...

"Never," she gasped.

He waited for her explanation, warily contemplating the possibility that she was more like the damned priestesses than he'd wagered: willful and arrogant.

"It—it is not worthy of a prince," she stammered.

Jurel stood and pulled on his trousers and boots. He paused then added his weapons. "Show me."

Veltina stood, took a step toward the door then hesitated.

"Since I do not know the way, you must lead," he reasoned.

She glanced at him then away, nodding. She led him down the stairs, ignoring the blatant looks of the few guards they passed. Jurel didn't ignore them, and his glares sent their eyes away from the woman he intended to band as his breeding slave.

She turned away from the men in the hall and courtyard, heading to a rear door. Her hand brushed by a torch then retreated. She shot him another uncertain look. He took down the torch and waved her on, though the night was bright enough that he could see no need of the added light.

She passed one home after another without slowing, her head bowed. Jurel looked around in confusion as they passed the last hut. He looked to the stables in volcanic fury.

"Where are we going?" he growled.

"My bed," she whispered. "It is not much further."

"They stabled you with the animals?"

Veltina laughed harshly. "No. The rooms above the stables were for older, unmated males. That would be the last place I would be permitted to lay my head."

He winced at the note of bitterness in her voice, looking to the stables as she turned onto a path into the woods below the cliff face. Was her bitterness in the fact that none of the males would have her or was the place she led him even worse? He shook his head. What could be worse than living with animals?

The trees thickened. Jurel considered turning back; he imagined an ambush waiting at the cliff face.

That was a ridiculous thought. How could anyone foresee that he would ask this of her? That certainty and a deep curiosity made him go on.

She stopped at the wall of rock, swallowing hard, then stepped into a ragged cave. Her gait was uneven on the scattered stone beneath her bare feet. She stopped, her back to him, waiting for his reaction to what she was showing him.

Jurel peered around the cramped space in dismay. Her "bed" consisted of a few stained quilts set on dried Eir branches in case of rain. There was a small wash tub, large enough to soak the quilts but too small to bathe properly. A natural shelf in the corner housed broken bits of pottery and an abinatine that had been snapped in half. *Reminders of her failure,* he surmised. A few mended tunics and pairs of trousers hung on a peg hammered into a crack in the wall. A blackened fire ring and a quilt draped beside the doorway explained how she survived cold weather. The place was settled, not a short-term living arrangement.

"How long?" he asked.

"Since high spring...More than a year." She stifled a sob. "You see? I am not unaccustomed to the life of a slave, to being less than those around me. You are the kindest Master I have known."

"Get out," he managed, his voice shaking in anger. "Wait for me outside."

Veltina slid and scurried away.

For a moment, he fisted the torch in impotent rage. Then he moved, tearing the quilt and clothing from the wall and throwing them onto the bed with a sound of disgust. He grasped the wash tub and swept the broken mementos into it, pausing for a moment with the sheath in his hand.

"A first daughter," he whispered. "A commander's heir." Veltina had been nobility, what the witches considered noble. They'd abandoned a woman worthy to be their queen for the crime of passion. "Heathens!"

He dropped the sheath into the tub and lobbed the whole thing at the bed, throwing the few remaining articles after it—a single dining set and some rough tools. Jurel wedged the torch beneath it all. The Eir wood was dangerously dry; it caught immediately, and before he'd cleared the mouth of the cave, it was all burning.

Tears streaked down Veltina's face, though her expression verged on giddy disbelief. He brushed them away and led her back to her tower bed without a word. She looked stricken when he took the veltian away. Again, he soothed her.

"Tomorrow," he vowed. "I will bring it back tomorrow." He locked the chain to her wrist, stroking the pulse point in a show of affection.

"Thank you, Master."

Jurel swallowed a sour wave at her concept of a slave's life. He wasn't a barbaric Fion's male who would deny her true nature as defined by the gods. He would never have made her live in solitude when her soul was made for companionship. He wouldn't allow her to think of him that way.

"You will learn to use my name," he ordered. "In private." *For now. It would not do to appear too familiar with her at this time.*

She met his eyes in surprise. "As you wish, Jurel."

CHAPTER FOUR

Wos 20th, Ti 10-449

Jurel stared at the missive, reading it for the third time that morning. His mind argued that he should feel something, but he couldn't.

His father was dead, killed in battle by the head witch, Leiana. That should have made him angry, but every time he tried to envision his father's fall, Veltina filled his mind, and he ached for her, for all the time she'd spent at the mercy of such a leader.

He tried to concentrate on the many duties that fell to him as king, but only one duty burned in him—the duty to mate and produce heirs to the crown. That brought him back to Veltina. His heirs would be of her body. He would stand for no less, and the evidence of who she was in her former life proved her a most worthy vessel for those heirs.

She was in his soul, and he had no idea why she was. She was a delightful package of contrasts: a deadly warrior who feared his slightest displeasure, a sexual innocent with knowledge and training better than the most experienced camp follower or bed slave he'd encountered, a born leader who wished to be his possession.

He set the missive aside, fingering the rings on the veltian. "Gold," he murmured.

Yes. Now that his father was dead, there was no reason not to make her his bride. He'd intended to fill her belly with sons either way; this way, his advisors wouldn't try to saddle him with a political wife.

He smiled. She was a political wife, in her own manner. She was born and raised a noble. Once Fion's witches were no more, Veltina's land by right of succession would be his. He chuckled at that. What a glorious way to justify holding their lands to the Magden.

Jurel looked at the veltian again. He was certain that Veltina would willingly submit. Even if she didn't, she wouldn't be the first slave-bride in Lengar history. There were advantages, even to that.

* * * *

Veltina—She sighed. It had been difficult to start thinking of herself as the name Jurel gave her, though he assured her that the name was equal to her passion.

It was a pretty name, and she was proud that he'd seen fit to gift her with it. And when he said it while he claimed her sexually...She purred in arousal, her body responding to the memories.

Jurel was an amazing man, and the Lengar culture was nothing like she'd been taught. They weren't oath breakers and rogues. They had a strict code of honor that demanded harsh penalties for slights. Thus Len oversaw his dungeons, not to house all of his followers, but only those who failed to live honorably—or perhaps honestly.

They believed in expressing the gods' given talents and identity of the individual. They reveled in their differences, a fact that Veltina found wonderful and exciting. Jurel had made it clear that he believed it sacrilege to repress what the gods made you, and for that, he vowed to avenge her treatment, as *Len* demanded.

She learned that the atrocities she'd always heard word of were not commonplace practice for Lengar soldiers but rather reserved for Fion's Children. The Lengar found her culture odious, and having tasted theirs, Veltina found that she agreed more than she ever had.

Her dishonor had opened her eyes, but she'd never had an ideology to express what she found wrong until she met Jurel. For that alone, she owed him much.

Though he seemed to feel discussing politics tedious, she'd managed to piece together a few startling facts. Chief among them was that the Lengar had not attacked unprovoked. Sometime in the annals of their long history, Fion's Children and the Magden had grievously injured the Lengar.

Lengar never forget! Until both races bowed before them, the war would continue unabated.

The door opened, and Jurel strode in, the strange cushion with the rings attached in his hand as he'd vowed it would be. He smiled, raking his eyes over the signs of her arousal, his cock thickening behind his trousers. He set the cushion on the table and stripped off his weapons and clothing.

"I see you grew impatient," he noted. "Did you reach climax?"

Veltina tried unsuccessfully to hold in her smile. "Not this time," she offered in a seductive voice.

"Did you while I was gone from you?" he persisted. He pulled a vial of oil from the pocket of his trousers and anointed his cock with it.

She wondered what it was, but he was too far away to attempt to discover it. "Twice," she admitted.

"Since I have seen you last?"

"Yes." Her cheeks heated, but she said it proudly, knowing he delighted in her sexual appetite. The more wanton she was, the more aroused he was.

He ranged hot eyes over her. "By Len! I will have to feed your appetite for my cock more often."

She gulped in air, dizzy at the thought of his cock more than the two or three times a day he already brought her to bliss in completion.

"You like that idea."

She nodded.

"Good."

He eased a curved plate with a hole in the center around his oiled member, his face pained. His cock jutted out, now surrounded by ruv coated nubs and two longer ruv fingers, top and bottom of the plate. She stared at it, wondering what it would feel like while he was inside her.

Jurel oiled the ruv. "When I finish with you today, you will be too exhausted to seek your own release."

A mad need to tease him seized her. "And if I do?" she inquired in affected innocence.

"I have other ways of tiring you."

He pulled something else from the trouser pocket, fisting it in his hand, then dropped the clothing to the floor. He set the cushion next to her, and she examined it in confusion.

"What is it, Veltina?" he asked, appearing unconcerned by her interest.

"It is—This is not the same cushion. The rings are gold. Were they not silver yesterday?"

"Indeed, they were."

"Does—this change mean something?"

He chuckled. "Perhaps."

Veltina took a calming breath. If Jurel meant to surprise her, the gift would be exquisite. If he simply felt no need to tell her his plans, it was his right to make that decision. It was not her place to question him.

Jurel was abruptly serious. "Vow it now—on your life and whatever god you choose to invoke. Vow that you intend to be mine and mean it."

"I am yours." How many times had she repeated that? How many times had she begged for it? Perhaps someday, he would believe her.

"On your life," he ordered.

"I vow it. I am blood of your blood." *Soil to your seed, I hope.* "I die without you. I will never harm you or bring you harm. I am yours." It was the most solemn oath she could make, though he would not know it. It was a portion of the mating ceremony of her people.

His smile returned. "Remove the skirt."

She looked at the tie nervously, doing as he ordered though she feared he'd strip her of every fine thing he'd given her, every outward mark that she was his.

Her heart stuttered as he unlocked first the chain and then the rings at her wrists and ankles. He couldn't free her! He'd vowed he would never free her. Even if he did, where would she go?

Jurel lowered his head, sucking at one breast while he pinched at the other. She fisted her hands at her side, wanting to touch him but having no leave to do so. Just because he'd stopped binding her ritually during sex after the first few days didn't mean she had his permission to touch.

He pulled back slightly, his breath hot against her skin. "Close your eyes. Do not open them, no matter what you feel."

She complied, groaning as he continued with his suckling. Jurel moved from one breast to the other, his fingers pulling lightly at the erect nipple he left. The sting on that nipple made her jump, her mind processing the fact that he'd placed some sort of clip on it. She squeezed her eyes shut tight to avoid angering him. The sting became a slight burning, a throbbing that radiated outward and was strangely pleasant.

His mouth retreated, and his tongue flicked over the captured nipple, sending pleasure so acute through her that starbursts of color danced behind her closed eyelids. A hurried pinch was her only warning that the matching sting and burn was coming. She cried out, the throbbing intensifying with the addition of the second device.

Jurel growled. "So responsive," he whispered.

His tongue flicked the second nipple, and she gasped at the sensations washing down her chest and abdomen to pool in her womb. Her fingernails bit into her palms, and she held herself firmly in place for him.

His lips brushed over hers, and she pressed close to him in an attempt to invite his kiss. He moved back, setting her away from his body in silent order to remain where he wanted her.

"Not yet. You want everything your former people denied you?"

"Yes." *By Len! If there is much more pleasure he can give me, I might die in it.*

"Then you shall have it. You shall have every pleasure."

His fingers circled her hood slowly, taunting her with more while he went back to sucking her nipples, increasing the pleasure until she thought she would surely climax from that alone. She leaned her head back, her hair tickling at her spine, feeling the pulsing beat through her body as she had when she'd been tied to the sanctuary floor.

He pinched her hood, and she gasped, forcing her hands not to move and her eyes not to open. *Surely, he's not planning—Oh, please, he can't—*

Veltina howled in shock at the twinge that announced he had. His fingertips stroked at the exposed head, and she shuddered in her rising passion. Whatever these devices were, they made her feel more intensely than she ever had. She silently thanked Jurel for blessing her with this experience.

"Mmmm," he purred. "I believe you are ready now. Open your eyes."

She did as he commanded, meeting his gaze, barely breathing at his hungry look.

"Look at yourself."

Veltina glanced down then gaped. Gold cuffs lined with black fabric circled the tight points of her nipples. A deep red blood bead dangled from each. She leaned forward, trying to view the final cuff. Jurel scooped the bead up, and she moaned at the slight vibration that raced through her.

He chuckled, a wicked sound that promised some wondrous treat awaited her. "What do you think of them?" he asked.

"They are very beautiful. Thank you, Jurel."

He licked one nipple and then the other. "And?" he prompted her.

"Wonderful," she gasped. "They make me—" Veltina struggled to explain the sensation.

"It makes you crave completion, and you will crave it as you never have before. As long as they remain, you will be wet for me any time I desire your sweet body.

You will not remove the pleasure cuffs. Only I may do that."

She shook her head. Remove them? Was he mad that he thought she'd willingly remove these?

"Now, kneel within the veltian." He motioned to the cushion.

She knelt between the long arms, moaning as his body pressed to her back, his cock sliding between her thighs and stimulating the sensitive hood outside the cuff, the ruv finger above his length pressing to her nether lips. She leaned forward, seeking greater contact frantically.

He retreated. One of the gold rings on the veltian snapped shut around her right ankle. Jurel touched her leg, trailing his fingers up her inner thigh and stopping only a hand width from her core. He pulled back, teasing her with what he knew she wanted.

"The veltian was dedicated to your namesake. It is said that when Len captured his first bride, she required—convincing to embrace her sensual nature. There are many ways to use it. You will know them all in time." The other ring snapped around her left ankle.

Veltina didn't hesitate, certain she knew what came next. She laid forward, placing her wrists in the last two open rings. She rubbed against the cushion, her nipples brushing the satil cover. Jurel leaned over her and snapped the last two rings shut. His fingers breached her body, stroking her inner pleasure spot.

"In days to come, I will let you play the pleasure cuffs against the veltian. I will watch you beg silently for my cock—or noisily. Yes. I like it when you beg me to fill you."

He didn't give her time to beg. His fingers left her, and the head of his cock breached her, stroking back and forth over her pleasure spot. She trembled, the motion stimulating not only the spot within her but also the cuffs on her breasts.

Dear gods! If he touches my hood as well...

He thrust deep inside her, and Veltina bucked up against her bonds, nearly swooning in pleasure. The ruv finger beneath his shaft brushed her hood with every movement, and the one above teased at the ring of her anus. The nubs between massaged the sensitive lips spread around his width.

Jurel pressed his lips to her shoulder, his hands caressing her hips then her waist. "I expected you to come," he mused.

She shook her head, terror making her ill. What would he do if she displeased him? If he found her female responses lacking?

"Soon." He moved in and out of her in long, slow strokes, rolling his hips to maximize the stimulation he provided.

Veltina moved in counterpoint, feeling the bite of the rings at her wrists and ankles acutely but caring little about the bruises they'd leave. In her time with Jurel, she'd come to view the bruises as a badge of honor. They marked her as his as much as the slave skirt and brass rings did. He'd never offered to heal them, and she would beg him not to if he did offer it.

Her breathing came in ragged gasps, and she knew his prophecy of her imminent climax was sound. His hips moved faster, herding her toward it efficiently. She shattered, begging him to join her. Jurel laughed, and the tremors intensified her body's response, quickening her climax.

"Not for some time," he vowed. "You will be weak as a foal by the time I stimulate your egg. The ring around my cock will see to that."

Her question caught in her throat, stolen by wave after wave of bliss. Veltina moaned and begged, rocked and panted through one crest after another. When he joined her at last, she was almost too weak to scream.

Jurel released her from the veltian, leaving the gold rings in the place of the brass ones he'd removed. She looked at him in a bleary sort of understanding, closing her eyes as he locked the chain onto one of her wrist rings. Did he really think she was capable of running from him? That she would want to run from him?

CHAPTER FIVE

Wos 25th, Ti 10-449

Jurel opened the door slowly, removing his clothing in silence and ambling to the foot of the bed. He was here again. If he could trust her, he'd sleep here and be done with this insanity of coming to her every time he woke alone and hungry in another room, knowing she was lying a stairway away, constantly aroused by the pleasure cuffs.

Sometimes he brought her to simple climax to aid in his quest and left her wanting. Other times, he gave in and took her to completion. More and more often, he found himself indulging himself that way. Whether it was the hurt look when he left her unsated or his own urges speaking for him, he found that he didn't want to leave her with just a taste of the passion unleashed between them in completion.

He stifled a groan, as Veltina shifted her thighs against each other and arched her breasts into the breeze from the window. Even in sleep, the pleasure cuffs did their job well.

For five days, he'd used them to their fullest advantage. Even mundane tasks like eating and bathing had become a feast of sensation for his young bride.

He smiled. Veltina had no idea what the gold bands with the blood beads meant. Perhaps he would tell her when she carried his heir. Perhaps not. She seemed to enjoy being his possession.

She arched again, his name a whisper on the breeze. Was she simply dreaming of him or did she smell his musk and unconsciously reach for him?

Jurel stroked his aching cock, trying to convince himself to leave her for the night. She was addictive; having her was paramount. Sleep was unimportant. Matters of state were tedious interruptions to his endless seduction of his bride.

"Jurel," she pleaded.

It was too much. He circled the bed and pulled her legs wide, kneeling between them.

Veltina startled, ripped from her dreams by the abrupt motion. Her hand touched his chest. Her eyes widened, and she yanked it away, no doubt envisioning some sort of punishment for touching him without his leave to do so.

He took her wrist gently, unlocking the chain and pressing her palm to his chest. She hesitated then dragged her fingertips over his nipples. Jurel groaned, wanting her touch. Veltina traced the vee of curls down his chest and abdomen to the pelt surrounding his member. She paused, flicking an uncertain glance at him.

"Touch it," he growled.

Jurel closed his eyes, ignoring his mind's warning that he trusted too much. She stroked him, applying pressure to all the most sensitive nerve bundles, driving him toward release, though her arousal had to be maddening.

"No," he ordered.

She pulled her hands away abruptly, gasping and wide-eyed.

He cupped her face and kissed her, something he didn't do often enough. The reason why was obvious.

When Veltina kissed him, she was all that existed to him. She met his mouth every time with such sweet abandon that he was powerless to stop their progression to more.

Jurel laid over her, nodding his approval as she wrapped her hands over his shoulders. Yes, this was long overdue. He'd wanted to feel her hold him while he loved her since the first time he pierced her body.

She sought out the bundle of nerves at the back of his neck, enflaming his need with a few well-placed strokes. He thrust into her, determined to feel her band constricting him at climax—to hear and feel her egg drop for him.

"Why?" she whispered, her fingers stroking his face.

He moved inside her, feeling as if someone was using pleasure cuffs on him as well. "Why?" he prodded her.

"Why do you torture me thus? Why do you make me want you but deny me? Will it always be this way between us now?" A tear spilled down her cheek.

Jurel brushed it away, cursing her tears. Perhaps she'd forgive him if she knew what he hoped to accomplish. "Not always," he promised. *Soon. Very soon, she will conceive.*

"When—"

He kissed her again, stilling her question. Veltina groaned, wrapping her legs around his hips and moving against him. She nuzzled her face into his throat and sampled his musk.

He had to tell her. He had to give her hope for an end to this seeming torture she endured. "Veltina," he crooned, "you know a woman's body." If anyone on the face of the planet did, she would.

"Yes," she agreed.

"What happens when a woman climaxes repeatedly? If she experiences simple climax without benefit of completion, again and again?"

"Her—" She pressed further into him, gasping out an oath—*to Len!* "Her body chemistry changes, becomes more acidic."

"Yes. It does." He fought back his release at the thought. "Your people never practice this." He didn't question that it was so.

She shook her head, grasping at his waist and pulling him further into her. "Please, Jurel." Her body pulsed around him.

He roared at that, his release rolling through him. He lodged tight in her stim band, his body buried in hers, reveling at the feeling of being completely wrapped in her body.

Her eyes opened wide. "A child," she whispered. "But why would they not teach something that aids fertility?"

Jurel searched her face, her shock confirming his belief that she'd not dropped an egg. Veltina hadn't come upon this revelation by accident. She was coming to terms with the fact that she carried his child—or not. That remained to be seen.

"You carry my son," he informed her. "Have no doubt that the child is my heir. The *priestesses* do not teach this, because it only grants sons, and they believe that only sons are worse than no child at all. You know this to be true of them."

She started to speak then looked away, biting her lower lip.

"What is it?" he asked.

"You have what you sought," she responded carefully.

Not nearly. He waited patiently, needing to understand her upset. If she posed any danger at all to his heir, he would have to restrain her and post guards. He prayed she didn't intend something so ridiculous when he was giving her the children she'd been denied. Once she granted him an heir or two, he would even allow her the chance of daughters.

"Will you be leaving my bed?" She didn't meet his eyes, and her breathing hitched.

"Never."

He released the pleasure cuff around one nipple and tossed it to the bedside table. Jurel moistened his fingertips on his tongue and stroked the still-erect and bruised tip, meeting her eyes as she looked up. She watched him remove the other, trembling as he soothed the abraded flesh.

"I will heal them," he vowed.

"No." Her eyes pleaded with him to let the marks heal naturally.

"The arousal will continue while you wear them." Surely, she couldn't wish that.

She managed a shaky smile. "Is your heir not worth your attention to my schen?"

"You may well curse your taunting before you face the Woman's Fast. I have three seasons to sate you properly."

Her smile faltered. "But your battles—"

"A Lengar king answers to no one."

Her eyes widened.

"Your Mother Leiana killed my father almost a week ago. I am king now."

"Not mine," she gasped, seemingly horrified at what he was telling her.

"No," he agreed. "You are not a priestess. You are—my bride."

For a moment, she didn't react to that. Jurel wondered if she understood what he was saying, but she didn't seem shocked or confused. Simply silent.

"Everything they stole from you," he reminded her. "I vowed it. Say again that you are mine and mean it, and I will ride you on my lap dressed in fur in announcement of the fact."

"I swear it. I have always been yours."

He stroked her cheek, smiling as his cock released her stim band. Jurel left her body, staring at the final pleasure cuff hungrily. "I believe I will leave that one on until I have presented you. The ride should prove most enjoyable for you that way."

She laughed, a light, joyful sound. "As you wish. I vowed not to remove it. It will be there when you wish to."

Jurel left her, returning to his room to prepare for her presentation. It was nearly an hour before he realized he'd forgotten to chain her.

* * * *

Veltina curled under a sheet, stroking her fingertips over her womb. A child. In the last year, she'd stopped dreaming of having a child. Being captured was truly the most wonderful thing that had ever happened to her.

A sound interrupted her sleepy musings, and she smiled. Would Jurel take her again before he presented her to his people? Would he tease her and make her wait?

"Juvia?" a voice whispered.

Her smile faded. She ignored the voice. It was a nightmare, a hallucination. She needed unbroken sleep in her husband's arms and a warm soak in the big tub that seated them both.

"Juvia?"

No. I will not return to Fion's Children! Not now. Not ever!

A hand touched her face, and she shied from it. "Juvia, we have little time. You must come with me."

Veltina, her mind argued, but some other corner insisted on recognizing Dujuri's voice. "Go away," she pleaded. "Leave me."

"I cannot, cuvia."

Anger forced her eyes wide. "I was not your cuvia this past year while I ached for a kind word. I was not your cuvia when you left me to die in battle."

Dujuri blushed. "That was not my choice. You know that. Mother Leiana has reconsidered. You are fierce in battle. She cannot deny it." She hesitated.

"And?"

"She allowed me this chance to bring you back."

Dujuri...Not her younger sister. Not her mother. One woman of all those she held dear asked for this. Nothing had changed. "I will not go."

"I will not leave you, Juvia."

"I am dishonored. Why do you bother when you know—"

"No one expects you to persevere sexually. Surely, you don't expect to—"

Veltina came up off the bed, facing Dujuri down in a fury. "I persevere, *cuvia,*" she spat. "See how well I please a man who enjoys a woman's passion."

Dujuri's eyes widened, and she shook her head in seeming horror.

Veltina felt no shame in her bruises and ornamentation. She was Jurel's, and she would never hide the fact or cower from the truth of it when she reveled in it in his arms.

They'd failed her. Her *people* had made her an outcast, denied her every comfort and pleasure, tolerated her only for what she could do for them and left her when she asked simple courtesy they would show any other person in the village.

If she returned to them, they would steal her identity. She would no longer be Veltina—protected, revered, and enjoyed. She would be Juvia again—unloved, unwanted, unappreciated save her prowess in battle, and dishonored.

Dishonored...She would be deemed unworthy of a man's touch again. *It is a sacrilege to deny what the gods made you!*

And her child! Mother Leiana would order her force fed gola berry tea if—when she refused it. Her child would be stolen from her. They might even prevent her from conceiving another. They'd never forced sterilization on a woman before, but if they knew the child she carried and wanted to keep, they might.

"Leave me, Dujuri. If you ever cared for me as cuvia, do not ask me to live as an outcast among our own people again. I would rather die."

"But you would rather live as a Lengar bed slave than die?" she gasped.

I will not live as a bed slave, but Dujuri would kill me if she knew I've tied my soul to Jurel. It matters not. I would rather live as Jurel's slave than Leiana's. "Yes. I would," she admitted.

Dujuri pulled her abinatine, her hand shaking and her expression tortured. They were nearly sisters, and yet Veltina had uttered one of the most blasphemous statements that she could have uttered. Only the truth of her situation would have been more shocking. It was Dujuri's duty to kill her to protect their race, and they both knew it.

"I will not allow you to kill me," Veltina vowed. Pregnant or not, her cuvia was the lesser warrior.

The door opened, and Dujuri flipped her abinatine for a throw. Veltina moved without considering her course. The death would be quick and nearly silent; she could not allow Jurel to die.

"Back," she screamed to him in warning, grasping the thrown blade and feeling it cut deep into her palm. Veltina turned it back seamlessly, watching Dujuri fall in grim satisfaction.

* * * *

"Back!"

Jurel's head snapped up. He watched the blade hurtling at him, frozen, noting dimly that it would take his unprotected throat. Then Veltina was there, snatching death from the air half an arm's length from him and delivering it back to the priestess who'd thrown it.

The assassin fell, her eyes widening at the sight of him in the doorway, blood pouring from her severed neck artery. She turned accusing eyes on Veltina.

His bride stood taller, looking more the queen than Leiana ever had. "Never by action or inaction," she growled.

The priestess gasped, her failing color draining completely. "You haven't," she rasped.

Veltina came to Jurel, pressing a kiss to his throat. "Please," she whispered into him.

He reached between her thighs in a daze, flicking the jewel still hung from her hood, allowing her to present her relationship with him to the dying priestess in the way she wished. She moaned in delight, tipping her head for his kiss. He obliged her, dropping the fur cloak to drag her to his body, meeting her passion as he always did.

Jurel met the priestess's stricken expression, smiling his victory. "Were you to return to your people, I would have you give Leiana my thanks for my bride and son. Since you will not, it is enough that you know your failure."

As if that pronouncement was too much, she surrendered consciousness.

He grasped Veltina by her arms, free now to vent his anger at her actions. She'd risked herself and their son. No matter her reasons, such a thing could not be allowed.

She sobbed. "I die without you," she explained before he could demand it of her. "I cannot do you harm. I vowed it. Please. I could not see you die."

Her plea cut through him, but still...He pried her hand open, uncovering the gash on her palm. "You risked—" *Yourself!* "My son."

Tears rolled down her cheeks. "I could not see you dead," she repeated hopelessly.

"You will never risk yourself again."

She shook her head.

"How did she get in? Who was she to you? Were you planning to leave me?" There were so many things he wished to know. He had no doubts that she would tell him the truth of herself, and so he asked.

"She is—was Dujuri, my cuvia—sire cousin." She sighed. "We were of the same sire but had different mothers." She darkened. "It is unlikely that there are more. You know no other cares to have me returned."

He nodded, hiding his shock studiously. She'd killed her sister for him.

"She wanted me to leave with her, but I wouldn't—I refused. I swear it on my life. I die without you. I am yours. And our child..." Her lip trembled at that.

He swallowed a scream of rage, the image of what they would have done to his child almost too much to bear. "How did she get past my guards?" he demanded.

"The passages—"

"Are watched," he snapped. She dared lie to him?

She shook her head, motioning frantically to the far wall. "Those ones," she whispered.

He followed her pointing finger to the far wall, gasping in surprise at the line of a door ajar, a door he'd never known existed until that moment. Jurel dragged her along to it, pulling the door wide. "You knew this was here?"

"I knew *of* them but not the exact location of the entrance in this room." She hesitated, her skin darkening. "Had I chosen to find it, I would have recognized it. I did not—"

"Where does this lead?"

"The sanctuary and a hidden place within the trees."

Jurel looked down at her nude body, mentally calculating that she would be chilled in the night air. He led her to the cloak he'd dropped and wrapped it around her body. Then he pulled his dagger and pushed her toward the opening. "Show me."

Veltina preceded him through the tight tunnel, emerging only minutes later, far outside his sentries.

"Why did you never tell me?" he asked. He'd not chained her. If she meant to run, she could have been an hour away by the time he returned for her.

"You—never asked," she stammered.

Jurel chuckled. "And if I had asked?"

"Ask me anything," she offered. "All I have is yours."

He laughed heartily, drawing the palm of her hand to his lips and healing it. He laid a tender kiss over the spot. "Do all of your villages have these tunnels?" he asked.

She smiled. "Yes. They do. Once you know the signs, you can find them all. Would you like to see?"

Jurel tugged at the beaded charm lightly, swallowing her groan in a heated kiss. "Later. We have a ride to take and schen to sate."

Before he was through, no one would question his choice of a bride, and Veltina would see her former leader kneel before her—and the man who'd dishonored her emasculated by Jurel's own blade.

SECTION THREE
Voria

A Slave's Life

"Your treachery knows no bounds. Treachery within one's own household...against those who trust and depend on you, especially women and children...is worthy only of the lowest of Len's minions. May you rot in His Dungeons for all time."

Ro Ti *(to the man who cost him Deliya's life)*

Abrin 27th, Ti 10-461

How did I end up here? Voria pleaded silently. She prayed to a goddess who seemed as dead as her race, hoping against reason that someone would save her.

Perhaps I am unworthy of the Mother's intercession. The Mother loves her warriors. Voria was anything but! She'd been taken from Gidlore before she'd had even a day of her training as a Priestess. She knew nearly nothing about battle and less about herbs, only what she'd learned watching her mother work healings.

Tovin's hands pulled up at her woven dress, his sour breath heavy in the iri brandy he loved so much. "You want it," he growled. "Lie though you might, you witches are women. You love it when a man—"

The rest was lost on a groan as he prodded at her unready body with his rigid cock.

Voria stiffened, wishing she was even half the warrior her mother had been. She swallowed a sob at that—at the failure she was to her race, unable even to stop this rutting beast.

There is nothing I can do, her mind argued. *If I move against Tovin, it will go badly for me—and he will still have me.* Voria had seen it before. None of the female servants in General Juleron's home were safe from the house head. It was simply a blessing that he'd not dragged her off to some dark alcove to take her maiden's blood years earlier.

And, Voria wasn't a servant. She was a slave— spoils of war taken by the victor. She had no rights. *It is a blessing that I have escaped this long*, she reminded herself yet again.

"Open for me," Tovin demanded in a slurring voice.

Her legs shook, her instinctive drive to keep them clenched shut warring with her conscious acknowledgement that she had to accept his advances or face the brutality she knew him to be capable of.

He forced her thighs wide, and she swallowed a scream of frustration. It was one more thing she would have to endure. She knew when she was taken that there would be no challenge night for her; she would never shed her maiden's blood on the sacred green stone. What did it matter where she shed it now that her legacy was lost to her? Voria closed her eyes as he positioned himself, bracing herself for that first brutal thrust.

She gasped in surprise as Tovin's body left her without penetrating. A rush of cool air surrounded her, blessedly clearing away some of his stench.

She opened her eyes, blinking in the light streaming into the pantry. Tovin's face was nearly purple, his breath coming in strangled gasps. A mad certainty that Mother Fion had struck him down lodged in her mind, and she bit back a laugh of relief.

Then he landed in a heap before her, and she gazed at the harsh lines of Juleron's face, terror taking the place of her relief. Why would the Master do such a thing? Was she next?

His eyes bored into her, taking in her situation. She dropped her gaze as she'd been taught, reminding herself that she was a slave. Unless the Master wished to speak to her, she had no right to meet his eyes. The Master never spoke to slaves directly, except to issue orders that were to be carried out immediately on pain of whippings for failure in your assigned task.

He stepped over the house head's body, the fabric of his cape rasping against the narrow shelves on both sides of the cramped space as he moved. He was a big man, a strong man who was capable of snapping most of the men in the village in two without a sweat breaking over his brow.

She stiffened, expecting punishment. Voria learned quickly that guilt or innocence mattered little when you were a slave. Her parentage was reason enough for a beating. Any misdeed committed in the household was simply an excuse.

She felt the phantom burn of the single lash she'd been given acutely, though she'd assured herself in a mirror that it was little more than a red crease above her waist. They dared not whip her again; the house head who had dared paid with twenty lashes at the Master's own hand—Tovin's predecessor. The Master had made it clear that she was too valuable a piece of property to maim; her unblemished looks were important to him. Still, it wasn't uncommon for Juvia to see to her duties with a bruised cheek or sore ribs.

Juleron's hand skated up between her legs, cupping her woman's curls and tracing her seam with one warm finger. Voria swallowed a sob. If that was what the Master demanded, she was his to use.

He grunted, and his hand left her body. "Return to your duties," he growled. "I expect a tray brought to my room within the hour."

"I will summon Lur—"

"You," he interrupted her. Juleron turned away. "You will bring my tray today."

"As you wish, Master," she whispered, peeking at his shoulders.

He turned back, his eyes hard and his jaw tight. She pressed back into the shelves, unable to look away from his gaze. He'd caught her watching him twice. Was she a fool to court a beating this way?

"Cover yourself," he growled.

Voria dragged the dress down her thighs, her hands shaking in fear but also in relief that he hadn't laid a hand on her for her gall in meeting his eyes.

Juleron stared at her. "You have nothing to say to me?" he asked.

Her head spun, the possible answers he sought making her dizzy. What did one say to the Master but a simple acknowledgement of his commands? He hadn't spoken to her about anything but her duties since he turned her over to his house head to train as a slave all those years ago.

"Thank you, Master." Surely that was what he sought.

He raised an eyebrow as if waiting for more.

She bit her lip, uncertain. Had she angered him somehow?

Juleron sighed. "For dealing with Tovin?" he hinted.

"Yes," she agreed eagerly. "Thank you for dealing with Tovin—Master."

"You are my property, Voria. No one takes of my property without my leave." He didn't give her time to fumble for an answer to that. Juleron strode away, stepping over Tovin's still form.

She took a calming breath and hurried to the kitchen to collect Juleron's tray, wondering but for a moment if Tovin were dead or alive.

* * * *

She knocked at Juleron's door, wincing that she was late. It was most likely intentional. Luri was trying to keep Voria in poor favor, as always. Perhaps she hoped that the Master would be so angry, he would punish her personally for her laziness.

"Come in," Juleron called absently.

Voria breathed a sigh of relief. Perhaps he hadn't noticed her tardy arrival. She entered and fell to the task of unloading the heavy tray onto his work table.

"You are late," he noted.

She stilled, her heart pounding. "My apologies, Master."

"For being late?" he prodded.

Voria nodded, focusing on her task once more.

"Why were you late?"

"There is no excuse," she deferred to him. That was a lesson she had learned quickly in the Master's house.

"Then, it was your own fault that you came here late?"

"I should not—"

"It was your choice to be late?" he snapped.

"No. Of course not," she answered frantically.

Juleron was silent for a moment. "Then why do you apologize?"

Voria shook her head, abruptly uncertain. He asked questions that confused her.

"Bring the plate of fruit and meat," he ordered.

She turned, moving to the bed in a haze, noting at the last moment that Juleron was stretched out on the quilt, nude and aroused. A stab of fear warred with her rising interest. Was this how Juleron met Luri when she brought his daily tray? Did he intend to educate her to serve him the same way his usual servant did?

Voria moved her eyes away from his erect length and the dark curls surrounding it to the equally dark eyes watching her. She felt her color rise at that. What had she been thinking? Staring at him that way was surely frowned upon, though Voria had never been trained to serve in this capacity and so had no idea what a personal servant would do in the same situation.

"How long have you lived in my home, Voria?"

"Nine years, Master."

"Do you remember the day I found you?"

Her eyes flicked to the scar that marred his wrist, the scar that was one of the few he'd earned in years of battle. She looked away again, willing her hands not to shake. "A bit," she lied. How could she forget that day if she lived to be as old as the Mother Herself?

"I remember every moment," he countered.

Voria offered him a slice of meat with shaking hands. Juleron could have killed her for injuring him, but he hadn't. He could change his mind about that at any time. In all these years, he hadn't. Was his comment meant as a warning that any further trouble involving her in his household would result in such an end? She dared not ask.

He took the meat, his lips brushing over her fingertips. Juleron took his time, chewing the offered food slowly and examining her expression all the while. At last, he swallowed. "How old were you when I found you?"

"Nine years," she answered.

"A year before you would have started your training as a Priestess," he mused. "And so, it was my choice whether to spare you or not."

Voria didn't answer. The image of the Lengar commander reaching for her was seared in her memory. She'd been terrified. Her mother and older brother had been slain, and Voria stood alone amidst the dead and dying, the cries of other children echoing from the far corners of Gidlore, tears rolling down her dirty face.

Why she chose to grasp her mother's abinatine was still unclear to her. Perhaps it was a mad urge to prove herself worthy of her race. Perhaps she was simply a frightened child taking up the only thing she felt certain would protect her. Either way, she had done the unthinkable and struck the commander who came for her.

Juleron had been furious. His battle cry had shaken her nerves as he struck her down with his armored hand, the abinatine clattering off of her mother's armor. Voria had looked up at him, waiting for the bite of his sword, a blow that never fell. Instead, he had bound her hands and tossed her over his buck, her stomach pressed to his thighs as he rode from the bloody battle.

"Voria?"

She startled, embarrassed by her inattention, and offered him another slice of meat. "Yes, Master?"

"You have reached your eighteenth year now?"

"Yes. More than a moon ago."

"Is it true that Fion's Daughters are considered adult at eighteen years?" he asked.

"It is."

He nodded, his eyes taking measure of her. "Put down the plate, Voria."

She hesitated, meeting his eyes.

"Now." His voice was almost soothing.

As it had been on the road from Gidlore. Voria placed the plate on the bedside table.

Juleron panned his eyes down her body, tracing circles on her inner thigh above her knee. "You didn't like what Tovin was doing," he stated.

She shook her head slowly.

* * * *

Juleron knew as much from her unready state in the pantry. He moved his hand higher, caressing more of her body. "Has Tovin taken you?" He bit back fury at the thought that the beast might have. His house head had been warned that Voria was not to be molested. The drunken sot should not have tried. If he had taken her—ever, even once in the years he'd served—Tovin would die for it before the sun fell from the sky.

"No, Master. Never."

We shall see very soon. "Has anyone?"

Voria gasped as his hand moved higher, her core dampening , heating to his touch.

It is proof of nothing, he reminded himself. *She may have dreamed of my touch. I have certainly anticipated hers.* "Has anyone taken you?" he demanded.

She shook her head. "No," she stammered.

A smile pulled at his lips. "Never?" He brushed his fingers over her core, now ready for him as it hadn't been for Tovin.

"No," she gasped, her body jerking slightly.

"You say no to me?" he asked calmly.

Voria shook her head again, fear clouding her green eyes.

"You like what I'm doing," he said, his eyes moving to the hem of her tattered dress. "Do you want more?"

"If you wish," she managed.

His smile melted away as fury coursed through him again. "Did I say what I wanted?" he asked.

"No, Master. I—" Her breath caught as his fingers stroked at the hood of her pleasure.

"More?" he prodded.

She nodded frantically.

"Take off your dress."

Voria pulled the garment over her head and dropped it to the floor.

"Unbind your hair."

Her fingers fumbled at the thick braid.

Juleron watched her progress, his body burning to taste her depths. He couldn't remember anymore when he stopped seeing Voria as the pitiful, lost child he dragged from under her dead mother only to taste her blade—when he started dreaming of her white gold hair fisted in his hands or fanned over his pillows as he plowed into her fertile, young body.

It seemed he'd ridden the edges of madness since she'd been fifteen, waiting for her to reach adulthood according to the culture that spawned her, unwilling to force her to his hand as many of his Lengar brethren would have—as many of them had with their own Fion's slaves.

Juleron ground his teeth at the thought of those arrogant bastards. How had he let them make him doubt? Had he ever doubted Voria before?

She met his eyes briefly, then lowered them, her hair half-hiding her beautiful face. She sighed as he pulled his hand back to his chest.

"Lay next to me," he ordered. Guilty or innocent, Juleron would have his fill of her—at least this once.

She followed his command as she did in all things. Voria ran her gaze over his body, and he took heart in the flush of color that raced down her body.

"Touch me," he invited, praying she would prove the innocent he believed her to be.

Her hands pressed to his chest, tracing the muscles that bunched in pleasure at her touch, playing in the line of dark curls that led like a spear to where he wanted her hands most. She didn't follow them that far. She investigated his chest and arms breathlessly, her eyes locked on her hands, wide in seeming disbelief. He bit back a groan as she played at the well of musk above his nipple.

"Touch me everywhere."

Voria looked to the aching length of him that hungered for her body. She didn't move. Juleron drew her hand down, pressing it to him, groaning aloud as she circled him. She played at him, tentative strokes that grew bolder as his breathing became more ragged.

He drank in her rising scent and dilated eyes. He soothed himself that his own rising scent was acting as an aphrodisiac on her. It was certainly working on him. He needed her; he needed to be in her—*now*. Her eyes widened as he grasped her head in his hands.

He gentled, reading her fear. Juleron drew her to his body slowly, reining in his frustration. Mayhap, Voria was as innocent as he'd always believed. He would treat her as if she were, easing her into the experience. In case she was, he wouldn't let Releger and his kind force him into ruining his one chance at claiming her properly as his own.

Juleron tasted her lips, noting her trembling, cursing himself for taking pride in it. It was his relief that Voria seemed out of her element that caused this cursed happiness at her trembling. He moved his hands, tangling his fingers in the silin strands of her hair, and brought her mouth back to his again.

Her trembling subsided as her responses became more ardent, as she eased into the kiss and learned his tastes. Juleron pressed her to his body, thrusting his hips forward to nestle his cock to her woman's curls. A whimper escaped her lips, and her nipples came to tight points against his chest.

He met her eyes, pinning her in his sights as he lowered his head to her breast. He licked her nipple, his eyes moving between his sweet torture of her and the expression of bliss on her face. He sucked at her, nipped at her, and soothed away the slight pain. There seemed no attention he could pay her that Voria balked at, even unconsciously.

Her scent was maddening, female musk at its purest and most potent call for a mate. He pushed her to her back, smiling at her look of stunned rapture.

"Voria," he whispered, waiting for her to meet his eyes before he continued. "I will take from you now."

She nodded, biting her lip lightly.

"Do you know what I mean?"

Voria looked at his ready length, her breath hitching.

"Not yet, but soon," Juleron soothed her.

She didn't answer that. Voria averted her eyes, her pale skin staining to a deep crimson.

"Do you know what I mean?" he asked again.

"If not that..." She faltered. "No, Master. I do not know what the term means."

We shall see. Juleron nudged her legs apart.

She complied timidly, her breathing uneven and her eyes darting to his face and away as if she might flee the bed. She closed her eyes; her breathing calmed and body relaxed.

"Voria," he demanded gruffly, waiting for her to meet his gaze again, pushing away the thought that she had some knowledge that meeting a man with muscles taut was not a comfortable thing. He calmed himself. Perhaps she had merely overheard that much.

He didn't explain himself. Her honest reaction was what he sought. Juleron captured her hood without warning, sucking hard at the nub.

Her reaction was immediate and intense. She jerked away, her small hands pressing at his shoulders and her eyes full of something resembling terror.

"Voria." He forced his voice to remain neutral, detached. Secretly, he reveled in her shock.

She looked to her hands, pulling them back with an expression of horror. "My apologies, Master," she gasped, most likely envisioning some dire punishment for raising a hand to him.

Juleron knew the Lengar servants in his household had taken the back of a hand to her person on more than a few occasions. One had even dared whip her. He wondered if she noticed that she was safe from that when he was in residence.

"You disliked what I did?" he asked evenly.

She faltered, her brow furrowed.

"You disliked—"

"I do not know." Voria seemed torn in confusion.

"The sensation startled you then? The pleasure—or pain was so intense that you forgot yourself?"

Relief flooded her face. "Yes, Master. I did not mean—"

"Juleron," he urged her.

Her eyes widened.

"And, do not apologize." He looked to her seam, ravenous for her. "Lay with me. I will be more slow."

"Yes, Master."

"Juleron," he breathed.

She sank to the bed, spreading her thighs wider and raising her knees at his indications that she should do so. He traced her seam with the tip of his tongue, and she cried out softly. He explored her body, a thorough introduction to the pleasures of his tongue on her outer sex. He sucked at her hood again, tenderly this time. Voria thrashed her head back and forth, licking her lips in apparent sexual hunger.

"The loveplay is to your liking?" he asked.

"Yes." Her voice was little more than a whisper.

Juleron smiled at that. She hadn't called him by name, but she hadn't called him Master. "I will continue, Voria. The sensations will be intense. You may feel the need to grasp at my hair or shoulders."

She fisted her hands as if to remind herself not to move against him again.

"You may do so," he assured her. *I want you to.* "You may also feel the need to force me away. This, I will not allow. At the height of your pleasure, I will claim what is mine."

"As you wish, Ma—"

He shot her a look of warning.

"Ju—Juleron," she stammered.

"You will learn to say my name for moments such as this," he instructed her.

"Yes...Yes, Juleron."

"Better." He returned to her body, to his external play.

Voria moaned in delight as he let the tip of his tongue wander inside her seam. He ventured deeper, drunk on the aphrodisiac properties of her woman's musk.

"Juleron." She said it so softly that he almost missed the gift.

He rewarded her with a concerted effort at her internal pleasure spot. Her fingers touched his hair, retreating abruptly then returning, making an uncertain path through his locks. Juleron became more urgent in his pursuit, urging her on.

"Juleron," she panted. "I cannot. Please."

Her hand fisted in his hair and tugged lightly, the second joining it. She shifted her hips, desperately seeking escape. He held her in place and braced her thighs wide with his shoulders, burying his face in her body, knowing she was close to release and he to the end of his uncertainties.

She bucked her hips, her grip on his hair near painful. He used the movement to his advantage, driving her to climax with ruthless efficiency. Voria screamed, her hands tightening, then falling away.

Juleron didn't hesitate. He rose up over her, praying to whichever gods protected her that Voria would remain his. He pierced her body in a single stroke, closing his eyes with a shiver of longing as her barrier shattered. He pulled back, leaving her warmth and grasping at the square of silin beneath the pillows.

One more thing, he reminded himself. *One more test, and she is truly mine.*

* * * *

Voria stiffened in surprise at the new invasion of her body. Juleron made a soothing sound, his shoulder pressed to hers, pinning her to the bed. His fingers explored inside her, massaging her tender tissues. She moaned at the silin teasing her hood, her body throbbing, aching for him to complete the mating.

His hand retreated. She watched in confusion as he used the already-soiled silin to clean the blood from his length.

He tossed the silin to the bedside table next to the plate of meat. His expression was unreadable—hungry, intense, and something else she couldn't define. Without a word, he filled her again.

She cried out in pleasure then darkened, half in embarrassment and half in uncertainty.

The embarrassment was easily dismissed. Fion's Priestesses faced their challenge of silence after three years of intense training. There was no shame in her inability to control her responses. Any untrained priestess would do the same.

The uncertainty was harder to dismiss. She'd never lain with a man before, and Juleron was Lengar. What did he seek? Did he wish her to play the part of an unaffected priestess as so many had at Gidlore, taking his body in silence despite her lack of training? Or did her lack of training and inexperience excite him as she'd heard it excited men? Did Juleron wish to hear the passion of one of Fion's Daughters, as pitiful an example of one as she was? If he did want her silence, was Voria capable of giving him that?

Her answer came as he moved again, sensuous slides of his hips against hers. She grasped at his shoulders, a whimper forced from her lips. Juleron came at her faster, panting out instructions that, when followed, heightened her pleasure.

And then he went still, the head of his member lodged hard against the gates of her womb. The heat of his seed came fast and hard, making her gasp in surprise. Her body exploded in sensation as his body locked into hers; heat rushing through her limbs, explosions of energy making her dizzy. She screamed, a full-throated scream of ecstasy. How could any woman deny this feeling?

For a handful of heartbeats, Juleron was silent, seemingly deep in thought. "The last of your kind," he whispered.

Voria forced her mind to function. She hadn't been the only girl taken from Gidlore. Were the other three dead, then? Her mouth refused to form the words to ask the question. What would she do if they were?

As if he possessed the ability to hear her thoughts, Juleron nodded. "They ran from their masters over the years and were killed in the attempt."

She swallowed a sob at that, nodding her understanding. He would kill her if she ever tried to escape him. She'd always known that. *But Tereya—* Tereya had been her cuvia—her sire cousin and only a season younger than she. Their mothers had been sisters of the heart, and they'd been raised together at the hearth.

"You know the boy in Releger's household?" His voice was calm, but the tension in his muscles warned Voria of some threat in that question.

"Gulin," she breathed. Tereya's younger brother had been a comfort to her in Berenal. After he had sired Voria, Tereya's father had become her mother's true mate, and so both of them were her sire cousins. Since she could not see Tereya—indeed knew not even where the other woman was, Gulin gave her hope.

His jaw tensed. "He was killed last night while entering my lands to come to you."

She shook her head in denial, a tear spilling down her cheek. Gulin was dead, and she was alone in the city of Berenal—alone in all the world.

Juleron's face hardened, rivaling the cock still buried in her. "How often did he come to you? Did he promise to take you to the Magden?"

"Never. I swear it." She trembled in fear. If Juleron truly believed she'd betrayed him, what would her punishment be? Whipping? Death? Or had he taken her maidenhead with the thought of making her a vessel for his soldiers to fill with Lengar slaves? She shuddered at that.

"You weep for him," Juleron accused. "What is he to you if not your lover?"

"My cuvie—" Her grasp of the intricacies of Lengar families escaped her. What did one call sire cousins in their culture? Was there anything comparable?

"Your intended mate?" he growled, no doubt forgetting that Fion's Children did not promise their daughters away to men as the Lengar nobility sometimes did.

"No," she gasped in horror. Juleron didn't know the ancient word. "We—shared a sire. We could never have been mates."

He went still. "He was your brother?"

Voria shook her head, frustrated by the cultures that separated them. "We had different mothers," she managed weakly. Though Burnia had been like a second mother to her, that did not make her children her siblings by law.

"A half-brother, then?" His patience was strained, and he looked prepared to throttle her for her inability to simply agree with him, but Mother Fion did not approve of lies, even when they would benefit you.

She sighed, realizing fully that she was courting his ire, but unwilling to lie to him to avoid it. He'd asked her a direct question; an honest answer was all she could offer. "He was not my brother," she repeated slowly. "We had different mothers." Voria shivered as his cock released her band.

His eyes burned in seeming fury. "Did you or did you not share a sire?" he demanded.

She nodded, her head aching at trying to follow his logic.

He sighed in relief, his muscles unclenching. "By *Lengar* law, he was your brother. Explain your priestesses' law to me."

"We were—cousins. Close cousins, too close to mate but not siblings."

"Swear this to me on your goddess. Swear it on your right to your soul's reward."

Voria nodded. "I vow that I speak the truth."

"He never came to you? He never offered to sneak you away from here? Perhaps in town, while you did your assigned work?"

"Never. I swear it, and...I was never left alone in town. I have never been trusted not to..." She felt her cheeks flush. The servants always believed she would run at her first opportunity.

He searched her expression as if weighing her words then left the bed.

"Master?" she asked nervously.

Juleron shot her a venomous look, pulling a silin lounging robe around himself and grasping the blood-stained silin from the table. "You will wait for me here," he instructed as he made his way to the door, belting the robe as he walked.

Voria bit her lip as the lock snapped shut behind him and she heard the slide of the lock bar leaving it. She pressed a hand to her forehead, still shaking. Did he believe her, or had he gone to collect his guards?

She startled at that, scrambling from his wide bed and pulling her dress on over her head, unwilling to have the guards come for her while she was naked in bed. Her hands trembled, fisting in her rough dress then smoothing it over her thighs.

I am a slave, she reminded herself. *Even if Juleron wants me to come to his bed every day, he is still my master, and I am still a slave.*

* * * *

Juleron glared at the men in his lounge, men he'd once fought with against Ro Ti. Now the Lengar were in a state of civil war, animals, mere shadows of the greatness they once possessed. There were days when Juleron would welcome a force from Ro just to end this feuding. Were it not for the fact that he would surely face the Magden king's blade for the many battles he'd won against their troops, Juleron would invite his enemy in—some days.

He nodded to the brothers, though he wanted to slit their throats for their lies. "Releger. Muvian."

Releger panned his eyes down Juleron's robe with a sneer. "I trust you used the bitch well," he commented coolly.

He pulled the scrap of silin from his pocket, throwing it onto the table before his foes. "I and no one else."

Muvian blanched. "Then you caught her before—"

"The boy was her brother," he interrupted them, his patience wearing thin. "Her half-brother, in actuality."

"And you intend to take her word on this?" Releger asked in disbelief.

"And whose vow did you take?"

343

Releger darkened. "I...Why should I—"

"No matter. I can guess." Juleron strode to the door that led to the kitchen corridor and yanked it open, snatching Luri up by her arms as she overbalanced into the room.

She gasped, finding her feet in a rush. "Master Juleron, I came to," she began.

"Silence," he warned.

Luri dropped her gaze, presenting the appearance of a subservient wench. His grip tightened. He'd seen too much of her games to believe her.

"You went to the Fion boy, Gulin," he stated without question. "What did you tell him to make him come for her?"

"I did not—"

Juleron shook her. "You dare lie to me?" he growled.

Luri flicked a glance at Releger and Muvian, as if the brothers would come to her aid against her master.

"The truth," he demanded.

She shied from him, fear in her dark eyes, the same fear she'd made Voria feel. He ground his teeth at that, at her attempts on Voria's life and safety.

"Let me lay out your plan, then," Juleron offered. "You knew I planned to take Voria to my bed and feared—rightly, I might add—that your time in that position was through. You would lose the added comforts of being my bed companion."

Luri blanched. "I meant—"

"I know what you meant. I also know your measure, woman. Did you never wonder why I stopped taking you to my bed?"

"No, Master. I—"

"Did you think I wouldn't know your plans to win a child of me? Your lax attention to the Walla teas? And the rest?"

She gasped, her face draining of color.

"Yes. I know you took other men, believing I would be fooled into thinking the child my own. Is that how you convinced Tovin to agree? How you made him ignore my orders not to lay a hand on Voria? Or did you simply ply him with drink and fill his head with ideas?"

Her stark terror made it clear that he had followed her tactical trail perfectly.

"Your servant has cost us a valuable Fion slave, Juleron," Releger snapped. "What satisfaction comes to our house?"

Juleron smiled his coldest, his course clear. "I give you two slaves in return."

Releger's face lit. "Then we will take the women—"

"No. Voria was innocent in this treachery. She will not serve your house in repayment for it."

"What do you offer?" Muvian asked, mirroring his brother's scowl.

"Tovin as a house slave and Luri in the manner she sought. Fill her belly with as many babies as you wish—a whole generation of slaves. I assure you, the woman will serve whatever man plows her well—if she wants to live."

Luri shook her head, trembling in his hands. She was Lengar, but she was a woman without family. Now that she had been caught plotting against him—and had no one to buy her out of her actions, it was his right to exact any punishment he wished, including her death.

Muvian took Luri from his grasp, testing her breasts with his big hands. He grunted his approval.

"Acceptable offer, Juleron. She is young and ample. We can get half a dozen good young from her."

Releger motioned for Juleron's attention. "I would like to purchase your Fion slave girl for my own. As the last, the remuneration would, of course, be considerable."

Juleron chuckled. So, that was the true game. No doubt Releger had convinced Luri that she would be well rewarded and have her prize of Juleron's attentions both. He met her eyes, daring the slave to turn her new masters over to his judgment.

Luri shot a nervous glance at Muvian's hand, then at Juleron. It was almost lamentable that he'd already given her to the brothers. Though he would have sold Luri as a breeding slave in punishment regardless, she now had to consider whether a magetra would take her word over Releger's. She remained silent, taking the perceived safe route from the battle; Releger and his brother having knowledge that she had done them this service was infinitely preferable to an unknown punishment by either Juleron or the brothers after the magetra made his determination.

"Juleron?" Releger reminded him of the offer still standing for Voria.

"No. I think not. By my right at Jurel's side, I believe I will use her to give me heirs."

"You'd wed," he began hotly.

"They planned to give the last of the Mothers' child to the young prince. Though Voria holds no abinatine, she is undeniably the only living heir to the seat—a worthy vessel for my sons."

"You have aspirations of the throne," he accused.

"Not at all." *As if I would want to throw in with the wariken fighting for scraps of what was once a great dynasty!* "The only reason for Jurel's heir to be intent on the Fion's Mother's child was the fact that she was heir to Ro Ti as well. Jurel wanted the Mother to warm his bed for his own pursuits." Juleron smiled. "No. Voria is not Magden royalty. There is no political gain to planting heirs in her. What would they inherit but what is my own?"

"Then why her?" Muvian asked.

"Because she is unique, and by virtue of my right at Jurel's side and the right of the blade, she is mine. I will have strong sons from her."

Releger grunted his agreement, scanning Luri with the promise of claiming her at his first opportunity. "Very well, Juleron. I leave you to your vessel."

He waved them out with an order to have Turin delivered to the brothers from the whipping post he now graced. He returned to his rooms with due haste, planting the lock bar in the door with a smile of success. His smile faded at the sight of Voria.

She stood in the center of the room, clothed again in the rags she came in earlier, her hair hastily braided and looking as if she faced execution. She trembled, peeking at him but keeping her eyes lowered, her hands clutched in the folds of her skirt.

He closed the door, crossing to her without a word. Voria didn't fight him as Juleron removed her dress and tossed it away. He pulled the strip of fabric from the end of her braid and loosed her hair, combing it smooth again with his fingers.

"I ordered you to remove these things," he chided her.

"I am—"

"Do not apologize to me," he growled. He fisted his hands in her hair, drinking in their mixed musk on her body. "Those things are no longer yours, Voria. You will never put them on again. Do you understand me?"

She managed a jerking nod, her eyes wide and wild.

"You enjoy my touch?" he asked, gentling his voice.

"Yes," she admitted, glancing to his eyes as if making certain she hadn't angered him somehow.

"Good." Juleron captured her mouth, groaning at her heated response. He guided her back to the bed, intent on his course.

Her fingers stroked the silin robe, tracing the line of trim down his chest to the knot at his waist. She paused as if waiting for his permission to proceed.

"It is your place."

Her brow furrowed in confusion at that, but she nodded and untied the knot, letting the belt slide away. Juleron shrugged the robe off, letting it fall to the floor. Voria looked at his body in a mixture of longing and fascination. Her fingers played in the line of curls again, and her lips pressed to his shoulder.

"Do you wish to be here, Voria?" His voice sounded rougher than he wished it to. He caressed her cheek, the longing for her nearly maddening.

She murmured her assent. She turned her head, pressing her lips to the scar she gave him at their first meeting.

"You are mine," he informed her. "No one will ever take you from me."

Voria shook her head. "I never intended," she gasped. "You have my vow that—"

He didn't answer but stilled her words with a finger across her lips. He urged Voria to her knees on the bed then left her side to collect the veltian from his cabinet. She looked to the green satil cushion in confusion.

He eased it around her body slowly. "This is a veltian," he instructed her. "It will support and position you for my claiming."

She nodded, stroking a hand over the satil brushing her upper thighs. Juleron guided her legs apart, pushing them to the long, padded bars of the veltian that surrounded her. Voria looked back at him in surprise as the gold band closed around her right ankle.

Juleron stroked her leg and moved to the left. She turned her head, watching the band snap on, her body rigid as if in military review. He guided her over the front of the veltian so that her body lay along the wedge and her head on the pillowed lower edge. As if giving her blessing, Voria positioned her wrists for the fore-bands.

When all four were firmly in place, Juleron placed the lock bar on its fine gold chain around his neck. He took in her position breathlessly, spread for him with her deep red folds pushed high and wide for his pleasure.

He'd dreamed of this day, praying that Voria would welcome his touch. The veltian was ceremonial, but it was also functional. Had she fought him, it would have held her fast as he planted his heirs as many Lengar nobles had won heirs; but she lay placid, her sex glistening with her woman's musk, ready for his claiming as he'd hoped it would be.

There was one thing left, the most enjoyable part of the claiming. He played the head of his cock in her waiting heat, watching intently as Voria pulled at the bands, biting her lip lightly. She likely believed he meant to take her in some brutal fashion.

His cock parted her, sliding into her a fingerwidth at a time, teasing at her inner pleasure spot. A small amount of his seed released, mixing with her musk, warning him that his control was tenuous at best. Her breathing went ragged. She strained toward him, stretching her arms to the length the bands would allow.

"More?" he offered.

Voria nodded with a guttural sound of pleasure. "More," she gasped.

"More..." he prompted her.

"Juleron, please."

He pushed himself to the hilt in her, crying out in unison with Voria as the liquid silin of her body gripped him tight. The call to claiming was too strong to ignore. Juleron pistoned in and out of her, his hands wrapped tight around her lush hips.

His eyes strayed to the pink line of the whip that marred her cream-colored skin, and he thrust deeper. No one would dare touch her now. There would be no more bruised cheeks, no more whips, no more long days of laboring at chores no one else would touch. She was his.

His name was a plea on her lips, over and over, as she fought the restraints that held her down. Juleron growled at that, knowing she was leaving the marks that proved his claim.

Voria screamed his name, her body suckling at his length like a babe at the nipple. He followed her over with a shout of triumph, his seed finding a home in her—he hoped. Juleron wrapped his body around hers in the age-old promise of protection. *No one will touch her now but me—not sexually or in anger. She is my bride.*

She sighed in contentment, a smile curving her lips.

"So beautiful," he breathed; her smile was rarely won. Perhaps she would have reason to smile now. "Do you understand why I've used the veltian, Voria?"

Her eyes opened. She glanced up at him then away. "I have heard—"

"What have you heard?"

"Such a position encourages a babe from the union." Voria pressed her forehead to the pillowed edge. "You wish a child from my body." She didn't question it.

"I wish many children from you."

She nodded. "As you wish, Master."

Juleron sighed as his cock released her. She didn't understand what he was saying. He reached down and released the fore-bands from the veltian.

Voria played at the bands, looking for a catch to release them and finding the jeweled lock—emi bead to match her eyes. She turned her pale face to him, questioning him silently.

He nodded. "You are banded as my mate, Voria. I have claimed you. Will you give me the children I crave? Will you give me yourself?"

She looked at the bands again, gasping out something unintelligible.

"Voria?"

"Yes." Her voice was a strangled whisper.

"Yes?" he asked, needing to be certain.

"I will be your mate, Juleron. I will bear your children."

"Vow it on your goddess." He sat back on his heels, shivering as his cock left her body. He released the bands that would ring her ankles from the veltian.

"I vow to be yours."

Juleron turned her into his arms, meeting her mouth urgently. He smiled.

"What is it?" she asked.

"We will have midday meal and appease our carnal hungers again." He ranged his eyes down her body. "Then—"

"Then?" she asked breathlessly.

"You are banded, Voria. It is my duty to dress you in silin and fur and carry you across my lap on my buck in announcement." *With your bruised limbs displayed for all to see.*

Her eyes widened. "But I am—"

"Sworn my bride." *Len alone help the fool that interferes with that.*

Voria scanned his body, her scent as hungry as her gaze. "Will you use the veltian again?" she asked.

Juleron chuckled. "There are many ways to use the bands," he promised.

SECTION FOUR
Riella

Schente
Night

"There is nothing more enticing than the jaglin vixen. She has the scent and body of the soul's reward for her buck and the claws to see him dead."

General Tolerin

PROLOGUE

Jad 35th, Ti 10-477
The Palace at Gidlore, Keen Republic

The captain followed at a distance, watching the children as they snuck through the hidden corridors that led to their rooms. The stone was new, dusty but not crumbled. The corridors had been built for escape not subterfuge, though they'd been used for both purposes. They had been built for a queen who hadn't survived long enough to walk their length a single time, designed by a king who would happily wall them off to keep his child safe were he not so convinced she'd need to escape a plot one day—as she had that very day, though he didn't know it.

He cursed. The plan was simple, seemingly foolproof, yet the children had escaped with little damage. The boy still lived, and the girl—

"Len's underworld," he breathed in the near darkness, trusting in their preoccupation with their goal and the noise they were making to mask him well. His cock pulsed as he thought of the girl's spirit and beauty. She had fought like the mother of the jaglin she now cradled in her arms, though she was a mere seventeen years and untrained in combat save for the lessons imparted by her companion.

She wore her cousin's shirt. The boy went bare-chested. He was already a tall young man, though he was a mere three seasons her senior; and the shirt came near to her knees. Her blouse had been ruined in the battle, her perfect body revealed to the captain for that precious instant before she escaped to hiding so well that the damned lucky boy returned to her before the captain could deliver her to her father and claim his prize. It was more prudent to return to the palace and establish his innocence once the plan had failed so utterly.

He returned to his perusal. The cast-away boys' trousers she wore were torn beneath the shirt and damp from her plunge in a mountain pool. Curiously, her prized dagger was gone, though the captain knew the boy had retrieved it for her.

"Shhh. Keep her quiet," the boy whispered. "Ro will hear us."

"Try it, if you think her so easy to control."

The boy smiled, a rare sight since his parents' death more than five years earlier. "She is not easy to control. She has the heart of Riella."

The girl scowled at him. Typically the more carefree of the two, she was clearly shaken by the day's events.

The captain wanted her shaken, but this outcome did not serve his purpose as precisely as he would have liked. If only the plan had succeeded...There was no use arguing things that would not come to pass.

They pushed through the secret door into her bedroom, and the captain watched through a peek hole situated at the near corner of the room, knowing what was to come. They halted as Ro stood from his seat on her bed. Good. The only blind spot he had was the corner nearest the door, and they were far from that.

Ro Ti, the mighty conqueror, crossed his arms over his chest.

"Benir. Riella." His voice was controlled fury. He panned his eyes over them, scowling. "What is this?" he demanded, motioning to the wriggling black ball of fluff laid across his daughter's forearm, overflowing the length, its claws hooked into the waistband of her trousers as it would hook into its mother's undercoat when being carried on her back.

Riella raised her chin a notch, a fine figure of a future queen. "Her mother was dead—"

"Then she should have died, too," he growled in response.

"Should I have died, Father?"

It was an impertinent question. The captain bit his cheek to keep from laughing out loud. Only Riella would dare use her mother's memory to ask Ro such a thing and expect to live past the hour.

"That is different," he bellowed. "You are my child."

"And so, you care for me. The menagerie could do with a spirited animal such as this. Can we not care for her as well?"

Ro changed course. "You left the safety of the palace again against my express orders," he noted.

Riella flushed. "There was no harm done, Father," she replied innocently.

The captain ground his teeth in fury. *There should have been. The plan was perfect.*

"No harm? You wear your cousin's shirt. I assume yours was destroyed by that beast."

"She was frightened and alone. Surely, you cannot blame her for a child's fear?"

"Have you need of my healing?"

Benir cleared his throat. "I took care of that, Uncle. It was minor."

Oh, yes. It was minor, but it should not have been. Still, the captain furrowed his brow in surprise.

The prince seldom addressed Ro Ti directly. That whelp could never be permitted to take the throne, which was why the captain's plan involved his death.

357

Luckily, the princess had no younger brothers. A younger male of Ro's direct line would take the throne before her. Only the fact that she was Ro's only child made her heiress and her future husband heir—unless she died. The captain scowled at the boy again. That would make Benir heir. He had to die.

Ro scowled at him, his outburst startling the captain out of his reverie. "You did this. You persist in taking her away from safety."

Benir shrugged, a nonchalant gesture that anyone who didn't know his soul-deep fear of Ro might accept as sincere. "She has a mind of her own, Uncle. Encouraging her spirit and curiosity is hardly necessary."

Ro started to circle them. He stopped, staring at the empty space at his daughter's back in dismay. "Where is your mother's blade? Her abinatine? I know you wore it this morning."

"I—lost it, Father." Riella stammered, turning to face him.

"Liar," the captain whispered to the darkness around him.

Ro struck her across the face. Riella fell, the baby jaglin leaping from her arms to crouch on the bed and hiss angrily at him. Its rumbling growl was the only sound in the abrupt silence.

For a moment, no one seemed to breathe. Benir's eyes went wide in shock. Riella pressed a hand to her cheek. Ro looked at his as if it was a foreign object rather than a part of his body. He reached for his daughter, but she scurried backward to the far edge of her mattress. She scratched her beast behind the ears to comfort it, as the jaglin cub pulled at her fiery hair with tiny claws.

Ro sighed. When he spoke, his voice was a low, dangerous growl. "Your mother died for you. She killed a Lengar soldier with that very blade before they took her from my home. It is poor repayment for you to risk her fate. You will not leave the palace again without me and the proper guard." He scowled at her. "And the proper dress. Am I understood, Riella?"

Her voice wavered. "As you wish, Father."

"I will have your vow on this."

"You have it. I know how you feel about broken vows. You need not remind me."

"Good. Then let me heal that bruise."

Riella shook her head and backed further away along the bed. Ro strode forward, captured her upper arms and pulled her to her feet. She stood stiffly in his embrace while he healed the bruise on her cheek with his magic, his lips skating over the skin lightly. She dropped her gaze as he finished, and Ro backed away, looking uncharacteristically uncertain.

"I trust you will take that beast to the menagerie, Benir," he ordered gruffly.

Benir darkened, though in anger or frustration was unclear. "She minds best for Riella," he whispered.

Ro's jaw tightened. "You will dress appropriately first."

Riella headed for the cabinet, seemingly eager to put as much distance between her father and herself as she could. "Yes, Father."

Ro looked at her sadly for a moment and left the room. Riella breathed a sigh of relief as the lock on the door clicked behind him. She peered over her shoulder as if she didn't trust her ears, giving her shaking free rein.

The prince ran a hand through his thick hair, black

like his father's instead of the deep red of most of the royal family. "Do you want me to retrieve your mother's dagger?" he offered softly.

"No. I can't bear to look at it, and we have no way to remove the stains from the sheath."

"I'll take responsibility for that."

And that, thought the captain, was another reason he had to die before she was of age to take her throne. The boy would do anything to protect her, and that did not sit well with his plans.

Riella shook her head, tears streaming down her face.

What troubles you, Princess? Does your father's blow really affect you more than the rest of this day combined? Or was it simply the final feather on the geela's back?

Benir crossed the room and drew Riella into his arms. "I still think Ro—"

The captain gripped the wall and held his breath. If she told her father what really happened, his plans would be useless. Once Ro Ti was on guard, there would be no chance of any of this succeeding.

Riella sobbed. "No. You saw his reaction," she replied miserably. "It would only be worse if he knew the truth."

The captain relaxed his grip, drawing a dizzying breath. She saved him. There was still a chance of his plans succeeding somehow.

The prince nodded and kissed her forehead. "Then this is a secret between us. No one else will ever know. You have my vow."

The captain smiled. *No one will ever know but me, and I will use this knowledge when the time is right.*

CHAPTER ⊕NE

Pri 18th, Ti 10-482
Five years later

Riella Hir pressed back into the darkness, barely breathing as her father's soldiers rushed up and down the corridors through the windows behind her and through the courtyard that opened before her. The light from the sentry posts atop the palace walls was bright, but there were pockets of darkness in these deep alcoves. Riella thanked Mag for small favors.

She cursed under her breath. Benir had drawn attention somehow. It was in Mag's hands now. If the sky father was just, and he typically was, Benir would escape the palace grounds and an unjust death. The odds were in his favor. No one knew the palace better than he did, except her, of course.

She shivered, feeling the winter night even through the heavy hottel-weave uniform and cloak of a Keen officer. Riella hadn't chosen to masquerade as just any soldier. For her plan to succeed, and because a princess couldn't possibly pretend to be a complete underling, she had obtained the insignia of a captain. A general would be closer to her actual station in life, but the captains in the palace were far more numerous and thus easier to lose oneself among.

Her plan was simple, and it had worked perfectly— right up until the moment that the alarm was raised. She had done all she could for Benir. Now she had to make it back to her rooms undiscovered.

It wasn't that her father would think she was in the wrong. The idea of Benir plotting against her to gain her throne was ridiculous. Riella had overheard Ro confiding that very thing to one of his trusted generals only that morning. If it wouldn't have made him appear weak, Ro would have released Benir himself. That much a given, however, Ro would not appreciate it if his daughter were caught in the act of freeing "the traitor." It might be said of her that she was too bold, but she would never disgrace her father's name.

Riella was the perfect product of Ro Ti's mating, a fact that helped her in her plan to free Benir. Like her father, she was taller than most men, which made impersonating a soldier a simple task. Her voice was naturally low for a woman, though still a bit high for the man she pretended to be. Raised by her father, she had adopted many of Ro's mannerisms over the years. Her purposeful stride was masculine. Covered in a soldier's thick winter garb, she was indistinguishable from a man—at a distance.

That was why she hid. Close on, no soldier could mistake the fine, high cheekbones and narrow chin that broadcast her gender. Without her cloak, her slim waist alone would make it plain. She had scoffed at her servant-sister Irin's idea of binding her ample breasts for more than the obvious reason that it would be uncomfortable. There was no way to hide her gender if her cloak was removed, binding or no. If someone removed her cap—

Riella shuddered. Within the palace, only the royal family had that startling color of red hair. One look at the curls pinned to her scalp and there would be no question who she was, even if she fled. Though no man dared look directly at her, neither could anyone mistake who Riella was if he felt free to look. From the red of her hair to the way she held a dagger, she was her father's image.

The corridors grew quiet. Riella eased out of the alcove below the library window and hurried toward her rooms, traversing a portion of back courtyard she knew would be deserted. She intended to climb up the hibernating iri vines beneath her window; Irin was waiting to raise the window and give her an arm back inside. It would only be a quarter stride around the inner wall and—

A voice barked out behind her. "Captain! What is your business?"

Riella stilled, laboring the freezing air in and out for a moment before she turned slowly. She took in the general standing two body lengths from her. He was tall, one of the rare men in the palace taller than she. The harsh lines of his beautiful face showed no jolt of recognition of her as female. Perhaps she could bluff her way out and save her father this shame.

She met his choc eyes and executed a stiff, formal bow. "My squad guards Her Highness, General. Many pardons, but I must check on the men outside the wall."

* * * *

Tol's eyes narrowed. General? His captains called him General Tolerin or simply Tolerin. Ro Ti called him Tol. No one dared call him simply General. This was no captain of the palace guard.

He pulled his dagger and strode forward. This was not Benir—this man was half a head taller than his escaped prisoner was—but it was undoubtedly one of the prince's men.

The traitor looked at the weapon in Tol's hand and

backed off a step into the wall behind him. He made no move toward his own weapon.

That one good decision may save his life—for the hour until he is presented to Ro. "What is your name, Captain?" Tol growled, an arm's length from his foe.

The man cleared his throat. "It is—Del, general."

Tol raised an eyebrow at the pause. It was surely not his true name, not that the lie surprised him. "How long have you been in the palace service, Del? You've not reported to me." And any new officer at the palace would report to him before taking on duties.

"I—reported to Colonel Pers. I suppose you were not available for an interview." A slight smile curled one edge of his mouth, the only clear bit of his face visible in the deep shadows beneath his cap. "Generals are notoriously busy men. Wouldn't you agree?"

Never too busy for his duty to Ro. "How long have you been here?" he asked again.

"Ten days."

A new group of men had arrived that day. "And so soon trusted to guard Her Highness? Ro Ti is typically more careful with his only child," he commented, baiting his prey.

Del didn't hesitate. "It is a temporary assignment. Captain Finn lies ill. It is an important chance for me, General. I must check on my men if I am to be trusted."

Check on his men outside the wall, he means. In other words, make his escape. "Your superior in this assignment?" he barked. Colonel Serin had only been replaced two days earlier, well after Benir had been imprisoned.

"Colonel Vry."

It was surprising that he knew the new colonel of the princess's guards. "His superior?" Tol persisted.

Del faltered. He didn't know his chain of command, because he was the lying traitor Tol suspected him to be. There was no other possible explanation.

He recovered quickly. "I took over for Finn only last night, general."

"Your weapon," Tol requested.

He hesitated.

Tol brought his blade up in warning. "Your weapon." He would not ask again. If the man refused to surrender, he would go to the interrogators with a wound to be tended, or he would not make it to them at all.

Del moved his cloak aside to show the empty space on his belt where a dagger should have been. He hung his head. "As you can see, General, I cannot comply with that order."

Tol jerked his head toward the doorway.

"Where are you taking me?" the prisoner asked.

"To be searched and interrogated."

Del swung his pale face up, his eyes wide in fright.

Tol felt a jolt of surprise. This was no man. It was a woman the likes of which he'd never seen. Her lips were lush and dark, her skin pale and without blemish. In her boots, she was only a hand's width shorter than he was.

Tol's body stirred as the wind carried the faint smell of lizors to him, a stronger scent than most women chose. He tapped down his anger. Tol thought Benir had more honor than this. He was using an unarmed woman in his plot, and he left her behind? This woman was too fine a prize to be discarded this way.

"Are you his schente?" he demanded.

She straightened her spine, bringing her chin up in challenge. "I don't know what you mean, General," she answered in her husky voice.

Fion, how did I ever mistake that voice for a man's? It is a voice fashioned for long nights on a pillow. "Are you one of Benir's schente?" And why did that idea make him so angry?

A blush crept up her cheeks, and her eyes flashed. "Certainly not! I told you what I am."

Tol almost laughed at her bluff. She still thought to make him see her as a captain in the guard? Had she never looked in a mirror or did she think her disguise and height flawless cover?

He stalked toward her, turning to trap her in a corner as she backed away along the wall. Del looked to his hands as he pressed them to the wall beside her then to his face, gasping out the beginnings of a protest. Tol brought his mouth down on hers, taking advantage of her surprise to slide his tongue deep and entice her body to the rhythm of his kiss.

She tensed, stiffening against his body, her eyes wide. Tol smiled inwardly as they fluttered shut. Del's body eased against him. Her hands slid through the gap at the front of his cloak and flattened against the muscles of his chest through his jacket. He hardened. Acting on his physical response was unwise, but he was unwilling to release her. Her tongue explored his, her movements bold in a way that most schente lacked.

He released her mouth, gratified to hear her ragged breathing. "I will have you know that I have no interest in the male of our species." He caressed her breast through the thick weave of her stolen uniform. "But, since you are no male, my reputation is safe."

Del darkened. She nodded, pulling her hands from his chest.

"I will ask just one last time. Are you Benir's

schente?"

"No. I am not."

Tol scowled at her. "Surely, the Prince has not come upon a jewel like you by any other means."

She shook her head.

"Why would you do this? Why would you make yourself a traitor and risk death at Ro Ti's hand?" He expected her to pale at that—or to startle. Seasoned soldiers shuddered at the idea of facing Ro in battle.

Del gave him a wry smile. "Ro does not want Benir to die. There was simply no way for him to prevent it. As one of his generals, you know that. I've seen you—meeting with him."

"You thought Ro would show you mercy for acting as his hands?"

"I hoped never to put him in the position of showing me mercy." Her eyes pleaded with him. "Only you know I was here. If you care for him, respect him, you will help me."

The gall of the woman stunned him. Ro's wish was irrelevant; Tol had a duty. At the very least, he should take her to Ro privately to deal with. "You care for Ro Ti?" he asked her.

Del dropped her gaze. "How does one not care for Ro Ti?"

He shook his head. *Easily.* Tol was one of the few men who truly enjoyed Ro's company, and even he admitted that Ro was a hard man. Friend or not, debt of thanks or not, Ro would not hesitate to kill him if the situation called for it. Though they were close as brothers, both knew it to be true. If there was a kind and loving side to Ro, Tol had yet to find it.

"Are you one of Ro Ti's women?" he asked.

She met his eyes, moving her mouth as if she

couldn't decide how to begin. Del nodded.

Tol grinned, sheathing his dagger. He surveyed her, wishing to see more of the body beneath that uniform and knowing now that he could.

He had been granted a rare gift for saving Ro's life. It was a simple thing that any man who'd spent weeks in battle without a woman's company would have killed for. There were times when Tol blessed the Lengar blade that he took in Ro's stead, times when he had a willing woman in his bed and his fellows did not. Any of Ro's schente was available for Tol's use at any time he cared to use one. If Del was one of Ro's women, she was his as well. As usual, the king's taste in schente was exquisite.

"What is it?" Del asked, suddenly wary.

"It is late, and you will have difficulty explaining your absence from the schente suite."

Her eyes widened, but she remained mute.

Tol stroked his hand along her jaw. "If you were with me in my room, you could not possibly have been anywhere near the prison tonight."

"But, you can't," she whispered.

"I assure you that I am the one man in this palace who can."

She sucked in a ragged breath. "Tolerin."

His cock pulsed at his name on her lips. "Is it a bargain?" he asked in a rough voice. "Shall I be your alibi and you my willing mate for the evening?"

He waited for her answer. He would not turn her over to the interrogators, in any case. If she refused him, he would see her to the schente suite and speak to Ro privately. Tol respected Ro Ti too much to allow a well-meaning schente to bring him pain, and there was no sense being implicated by the woman's company if she refused what was his right.

He scanned her body through the opening of her stolen cloak. This woman had fire and courage unlike any schente he'd ever encountered, unlike any woman he'd ever encountered. He could easily picture her in battle, sword in hand. A woman with that much fire would be like no other in the bedroom. That was a fire he had to sample.

* * * *

Riella stared at Tolerin in amazement. This was the man who'd saved her father, nearly losing his own life in the bargain. She'd seen him in the palace, known his rank, of course; but as a rule, she wasn't introduced to soldiers. Her father typically kept Riella far from his men. As a result, Ro's savior had been no more to her than another pair of male eyes that wouldn't meet her own.

She shook her head, replaying his words. He thought she was schente. He was bargaining with her for his silence, though he had no need to. Tolerin could take any schente he wished at any time and did—often.

Irin brought her rumors from the servants. Sometimes the rumors were useful. Sometimes they were entertaining. Riella searched her memories for rumors of Tolerin. She felt her cheeks darken. It was said he was a talented lover, a potent male with a fierce drive who left even the most jaded schente wanting for more of him.

She studied his broad shoulders and strong hands. Her body, already aroused by his kiss, played traitor and dampened at the prospect of his touch. She glanced toward his cock, but it was well hidden by his uniform. An errant need to know if Tolerin was erect and as aroused as she was shot through her mind. His smile indicated that he knew her thoughts and encouraged her appraisal. Riella decided that being Tolerin's schente would be far from a punishment.

But, Tolerin wasn't one of her schaen. This was an intact, fertile male. When he stimulated an egg, there would be a chance of pregnancy. Tolerin wouldn't know that. He would think her safe for his use, sterile.

Should she tell him who she really was? No. He would take her to her father, and her careful planning to protect Ro would be undone. It was better to play the part of a schente and win Tolerin's silence.

What will I do about the chance of pregnancy? Riella bit her lower lip. She would have to deal with that. There was only one chance in fifty that she would conceive, and there were surely things that Irin could do for her if she did.

His body called to her.

But my hair! If Tolerin sees my hair or my tattoo, he will know who I am. "On one condition."

His smile faltered. "Yes?"

"A dark room. I will give you anything you wish, but I beg this one boon of you in return."

He furrowed his brow. "It is a small thing to ask, I suppose."

"Then you have my agreement." *Mother Fion, help me. What an agreement have I made!*

Tolerin nodded. "Follow me and keep your face down as if you record a missive for me."

Riella did as he ordered. Tolerin didn't delay, nodding to his men as he strode through the corridors. Not for the first time in her life, Riella was glad for her long legs and man-like stride. She followed Tolerin into his room without hesitation.

He wasted no time. Riella was pressed to the wall just inside his door, his erect cock searing her hip through her trousers and his mouth on hers, hard and impatient. He unclasped her cloak and the jacket beneath. He released her mouth as he dragged the cloak down her arms and the jacket with it. Tolerin cupped her breast through the silin of her blouse and growled his approval.

"Take this off before I tear it off," he ordered in a low, husky voice.

Riella untied the wrists and neck, her body in a riot. "Are you always like this with your schente?" she asked, trying to appear unaffected by him. Her schaen were never like this. To be at a man's use—instead of he at hers—made her heart race.

Tolerin pulled the silin from her body. "Never," he assured her. "But you are not the typical schente, are you?"

Riella's hands moved to the buttons on her trousers without waiting for his order, reading the urgency in him. This would not be a slow, gentle joining of bodies. This man was intense, driven.

I am driven! Her arousal had never been this strong, though Irin assured her it was stronger than most women experienced. Even Riella had never encountered a reaction this explosive—until Tolerin.

He plucked the cap from her head and ran his fingers through her hair, finding the two clips that bound her curls. Tolerin sighed as her hair tumbled down over her shoulders. He groaned, and she held her breath, sure that the dim light that escaped through the thick drapes over the windows was enough for him to see the color and stop the encounter before they were properly begun.

Mother Fion! I want to be properly begun and properly finished. I want to know all of this man. Please let him mistake my hair for brown.

"Yes," he breathed. "Never hide this beauty from me."

His fingers stroked the nerve bundle at the back of her neck. She rolled her head back into his massaging fingers, her trousers clinging to her hips with her thumbs still hooked in the waistband.

Fion! He means to torture me. No man had used that seduction technique on her, not even her schaen. "Tolerin," she gasped.

"Tol," he corrected her, bringing her head forward in his grip and claiming her mouth again.

Riella pushed her trousers further down her thighs, gripping his hips and brushing her curls against the hard ridge at the front of his trousers. She found the buttons to release him.

Tol groaned into her mouth, his movements fevered. "I will not be gentle. I cannot be."

"I am ready for you," she promised. She was more than ready—more ready for a man than she'd ever been. If Tol didn't get on with it soon, she'd be forced to resort to violence.

His fingers slid into her. His breathing was ragged. "I know you're not accustomed to taking a man more than once in a night," he began.

"I am. I will," she panted, shifting against him.

It was no lie. Like the schente that served her father and Benir, her schaen were there for her use. The tradition grew out of a Keen female's almost insatiable urge to mate during pregnancy, the schen. From the age of fifteen, royal females were provided with medically monitored, sterilized men called schaen, meaning "for the schen." The custom of providing schente for the males came later.

The rules for enjoying schaen were simple. When she called for a male, one of the group would be sent to her. Which one was immaterial. If she ever expressed a preference for a single schaen, he would be dismissed and replaced with a new face to keep her from falling in love with her servant. For the same reason, all of the schaen were replaced a few at a time at intervals not to exceed two years in service to her. If a schaen ever displeased her, he would be immediately dismissed from his service—and most likely punished by her father.

The schaen would service her to the completion of a single sexual encounter. His completion or hers was immaterial. If Riella was not sated, she simply sent for another. She had learned from Irin's discussions with her father's schente that the males always tried to bring her to a wringing completion. Being her only schaen in a night was a matter of pride for them. She would not see the same one again for days or even weeks, but Riella had taken up to three men in a night when she was particularly restless. A single schaen did not please her often.

Tol dragged her trousers down to her ankles and lifted her slightly to plunge deep inside her. Riella bit back a scream of pleasure at the sensation of her body adjusting around his length. His eyes burned with a fierce light, seeming to glow in the almost total darkness around them.

"Ro wishes you to stifle your pleasure?" he demanded in a whisper.

Riella swallowed hard and nodded. *Oh, yes!* For

Tolerin's sake and her own, not drawing attention was imperative. If anyone found her here like this, her father would be neither amused nor kind.

Tol pulled her boots from her feet and removed her trousers. His movements were terse, his muscles tense beneath the sleeves of his jacket. Riella ran her hand over them, at a loss. She had no idea why he was angry or how to soothe him. For that matter, Riella had no idea why his anger upset her except that it came so suddenly in the midst of his arousal.

"Tolerin?" she asked in a low, calming voice.

"Tol." He shook his head and met her eyes. "While it is my cock that pierces you, you are mine. Do you understand me?"

"Yes." His declaration made her body weak and hungry for him.

He pulled her legs around his hips and started moving inside her. Riella leaned her head back and whimpered at the ripples of heat rising in her womb.

Her nipples peaked, stroked by the coarse weave of his uniform jacket; the feeling was pure decadence. She gripped at it, dragging him closer and reveling in every rasping fiber that teased her skin, from the jacket brushing her breasts and neck to the trousers leaving hot trails over the join of her thighs and buttocks, mimicking the Bel Tro most effectively.

Riella gasped as Tol pressed her hard against the wall, forcing her hands back beside her head. She tightened her legs, pulling him deeper. He drew in a nipple, suckling hard. She let out a harsh cry of pleasure and bowed further into his mouth.

He owned her. For this one night, she wasn't Riella Hir, daughter of the greatest king ever known on Kegin. She was a nameless schente, a vessel for the use of a powerful general who would not remember her in a month's time—and she loved it. Riella loved the pleasure he gave her, and she loved that he held that pleasure in his capable hands and tended it so thoroughly. She urged him on as the pressure built in her.

Tol released her breast and bit lightly at her ear, mixing pleasure and pain and nearly sending her over the edge. His voice was a warm caress on her ear.

"My women do not hold back," he assured her. "My women cry out the joy in their hearts. Whatever you feel, you will express. Tell me."

"Yes. I will." She felt it coming, the pressure building as it never had before.

Riella screamed, her body releasing around Tol as he filled her again and again, pistoning at a furious pace. He followed her over, his seed hot. *Potent. Oh Fion! To have a child by this man would be the gods' reward.*

Tol roared, his harsh voice echoing off the stone walls. His cock swelled within her, locking into the muscle at the entrance to her womb and stimulating the release of her egg. *Potent. Oh Fion, what have I done?* The shocks pushed her past endurance, and she screamed again, wordless and breath-stealing.

He held her shivering form in his arms, his forehead pressed to hers as they both gasped in the aftermath. "A rare jewel," he whispered. "So few schente feel the stimulation once their ovum sacks are taken. You are a rare jewel."

Riella nodded, unable to tell him what she'd done, unable to admit to being his princess when she so enjoyed being his schente.

"What is your name?"

She took a ragged breath. "You shouldn't—"

"Your name. I will not scream 'Del' as I take you again." The humor in his tone tempered the order, but not by much.

Riella felt her mouth go dry. "Deliya," she whispered, praying Ro would spare her life for such a sacrilege. Deliya was her mother's name.

And, Deliya was what Tol called her as he brought them both to one shattering release after another. Riella was exhausted after the second time, but the touch of his hands was all it took to make her want him again. Tolerin was tireless, he was talented, and she ached in anticipation of that moment when she would have to leave him and not look back.

Tol took his time once his initial madness for her passed, but the fire never died. The first time in his bed was the sweetest. She straddled his hips, screaming his name as he came with her. Being cradled beneath his body, his weight pressed to the sensitive spot at the apex of her thighs—a hundred times better than when he took her against the wall—paled in comparison to the feel of him beneath her. She pressed down hard as he filled her, he locked into her stim band, and the moment she released the egg was truly the most exciting moment in her all-too-exciting life.

The final time was slow and sensual, every stroke a delicate torture to her battered senses. After that, Tol passed into a blessed sleep.

Riella lay cradled to his chest after he took her that fourth time. Tol's heartbeat was steady, his breathing deep and even. She should leave him. She knew that. She even shifted to accomplish the odious task. Tolerin pulled her further into the shelter of his arms, unwilling to release her even in sleep. Riella kissed his chest, earning her a groan. Dawn would be early enough. She would leave him with the dawn.

CHAPTER TWO

Tol groaned, reaching for Deliya. His eyes snapped open as the weak, pre-dawn light streamed into the room. She was dressed in her silin blouse and trousers, her hair completely hidden beneath her cap.

"Come to bed, Deliya," he grumbled, hard and eager to take her again.

"I cannot. I am expected elsewhere. If I am not there by dawn, the punishment will be harsh."

He raised an eyebrow in disbelief. "For me? Do you still not understand that I have free rein with Ro's schente?"

"You do not with me," she answered cryptically.

Tol furrowed his brow.

Deliya waved a hand in dismissal of his unspoken question. "Ro Ti will keep his vow to you. Have no doubt of that. He is an honorable man."

"I don't understand."

She sighed. "The punishment will not be yours. It will be mine."

Tol startled, sitting upright in the bed. "Are you saying Ro would harm you?" He wouldn't have thought it of Ro.

Deliya put her hands up in a calming gesture. "Ro and I have—an arrangement."

"A contract?" he demanded in disbelief. If she had made him a traitor, she would regret it.

"No. We have no contract. It is—an understanding. I gave my word. Please, Tol. If Ro ever learns that I was here tonight, he will be most displeased." She seemed earnest in her concern. Her eyes pleaded with him, and her face was tortured.

Tol started to rise to go to her.

"No, Tol. Do not. Please. I have no time to explain. You must forget that you ever met me. For my sake, you must."

"Let me take you to the schente suite," he offered.

"I am not going to the schente suite. I'm going to—the rooms provided for me."

Tol's heart took up a choppy rhythm as she swept back the drapes and opened the door onto his balcony. "What are you doing?"

Deliya managed a weak smile. "Climbing down the iri vines one floor to the war room."

"No. You cannot," he protested.

"I cannot be seen here, Tol. I do this often."

"To see other men?" The thought was like a dagger in his gut.

Her eyes widened. *The assumption wounded her,* he realized.

"No," she assured him. "Just to steal moments of peace." She turned toward the door.

"Wait."

Deliya looked back in surprise.

"Why the war room?"

She blushed. "There are hidden corridors for the king's use."

He nodded. "To the royal chambers," he noted bitterly.

Deliya didn't meet his eyes. Perhaps, she couldn't meet them. "I am sorry, Tol. That is my place. I have no choice in that. I wish I did."

Before he could answer, she strode through the door and swung it shut behind her. She threw her legs over the balcony wall as if she intended to cliff dive like a geela bird. Tol vaulted off of the bed and through the door, looking over the edge as she scaled the last body length of vines and dropped lightly onto the lower balcony. She didn't look back as she slipped into the war room. A moment later, her cap hit the glass below, tossed away as she entered the corridor, no doubt.

Tol shivered in the polar chill and slipped back into his room, closing the balcony door and drapes behind him. He fisted the uniform jacket and cloak she had left behind, cursing the king's corridors and the woman who used them.

Deliya belonged to Ro. She wasn't Tol's. She would probably never be Tol's, not even to look upon. Was that why she demanded darkness? Had she sought to protect him from the laws forbidding him to look on a woman of the king's household? But, if she wasn't schente, what was she?

He threw the clothing against the wall, frustrated with wanting a woman he couldn't have, the only woman of Ro's he could not have. The clash of metal on metal sent him after the jacket. He picked it up, shaking it until a heavy hair clip slid from it onto the floor. It was the finest platinum with deep green emi beadwork, the clip of a queen—or a king's mistress.

Deliya may belong to Ro, but Tol decided he wasn't giving up so easily. He would trade the rest of the schente Ro had promised him for his lifetime to claim this one as his own. He had known that the first time Deliya screamed his name at her pinnacle, the first time he took her in his bed.

* * * *

Riella slowed as she passed the entrance to her father's rooms. If he found her in the corridor in this state, there was no telling what his reaction would be. Her hair was mussed, and she was short one of her mother's precious hair clips that she hadn't been able to find in the semi-darkness of Tol's rooms. She was dressed as a man and smelled of hours of sex.

She had made it through the war room without attracting attention and passed the checkpoint—the one Ro didn't know she knew of that was designed to police her use of the corridors—without detection. Now she simply had to get to her rooms before he did.

Riella paused as she heard her father's voice. He was dressing. She had no time left for caution. She ran flat out, on her toes so her heels wouldn't clatter on the stone floor. She pushed open the hidden door to her bedroom.

Irin launched toward her from the window. "Oh, Riella," she scolded. "Where—"

"Draw a bath quickly, with bubbles and milk. Ro is coming."

Irin's eyes widened, and she ran for the bath. Riella pulled off her boots, hair clip and clothes, closing them in the king's corridor as she bolted for the bed. She tore her bedding apart, rumpling pillows and winding sheets in her hands, then dropped into the tub when it was half full. She dunked her hair under the water, scrubbing at her skin furiously before settling onto the bench that rounded the tub as if in repose.

Irin blushed. "What did you—"

"Later, please. After Ro is gone."

Irin whimpered as a heavy fist pounded on the outer door.

Riella waved her away. "Do not look at him, Irin. He reads you too well."

Ro appeared in the bathroom doorway moments

later. He smiled at the sight of Riella lounging in her bath. "Did you sleep well?" he asked.

She smiled. "Very well, Father."

"I have good news for you."

"Really?" Riella adopted the look of a child contemplating receipt of her birthday wish. "What is it?"

"Your cousin Benir escaped last night. I know you were vexed by his plight."

She laughed heartily. "Merciful Fion and Just Mag be praised. I knew Benir had it in him."

Ro raised a conspiratorial eyebrow. "I believe I can guarantee that he will not be recaptured."

Riella's smile was sly. "And that is why I love you, Ro my father."

Ro's expression of pleasure fled. He strode from the doorway, his step heavy. He touched her ear, and his face hardened. Riella shrank from his fury. She'd only seen her father this angry once before, and she had no wish to feel that anger unleashed again.

"Who has injured you?" he demanded.

She brushed her fingers over the abrasion left from Tol's nipping and pulling at her ear. He seemed obsessed by the spot. She pasted on her most innocent look and shrugged.

"One of my schaen was frisky." She smiled at the memory of the exquisite pleasure and pain Tol had given her. "It was quite invigorating."

Ro rolled his eyes and healed it as he had healed so many scrapes and bruises in her life. He sighed. "Which man did this?"

Riella avoided looking at him. "A schaen, Father. I don't know him. You know I wouldn't."

"I will speak to Ven. He will instruct—"

"If he displeased me, I would have already spoken

to Ven," she argued.

Visions of Ro storming into the schaen quarters in a rage shook her. What would happen when no schaen admitted to harming her? Would her father have them all beaten? Worse, what if Vry countered that she'd not called for a schaen the previous night? Would he assume he'd simply not seen the injury beneath her hair the previous day? *Merciful Mother! How did I get myself into this mess?*

Ro cupped her chin gently, forcing her eyes to his. "He will never injure you again," he said solemnly.

Riella bit back her fury. "Sex is not always gentle, Father. I've heard your schente talk about your tastes, and the tastes of the other men."

"You are my daughter," he growled.

"I am female," she reminded him stubbornly. "The schaen came first, for the needs of the female."

Ro released her chin. "It is time that you married. I will start the introductions."

Riella groaned. "Not those boring noblemen," she pleaded.

"Who would you contract with, then?"

She shrugged, toying with the cloth in her hands. "I don't know. Perhaps a military man would be more to my tastes," she suggested.

Her father gave her a searching look. She was hard-pressed to meet his eyes. Finally, he nodded and kissed her forehead.

"I have a meeting I must attend. Will I see you at breakfast?"

"Yes, Father."

"I do love you, Riella. I only want what is best for you."

She sighed. "I know."

* * * *

Tol nodded to Ro Ti as he took his seat. The king seemed disturbed, and Tol sent up a prayer that he wasn't upset with Deliya. He wasn't certain how to phrase his questions to learn more about her from Ro without causing her some harm in the process. The king was a hard man, and he wouldn't take well to perceived deceptions, whether they were Tol's or Deliya's.

"You seem out of sorts, Ro." He kept his voice low and his focus on the other generals across the room.

"It is nothing. My daughter—" He sighed and scrubbed his hands over his face.

Tol nodded. He'd only been back at the palace for three months. Following Ro on campaigns and leading them in the king's stead had kept him away for most of the six years his king had been in his debt. As a result, he hadn't met Princess Riella, though he'd heard about her from the schente. She was a haunting beauty with her father's hair and bearing. If any of the men had seen her, they dared not say. It was not their place to look at her.

He bit back a sigh at that. Tol had been the closest thing Ro had to a brother, since the battle in which Donic died and he took the older soldier's place at his king's side. Still, he wasn't completely trusted. While Donic reportedly guarded the young princess through her childhood, Tol was kept at arm's length like any other soldier. Ro was a difficult man to get close to, a fact that probably saved his life on many occasions.

But, getting close to the princess wasn't his concern. There was only one woman he wanted to learn more about, but how best to accomplish the task?

Tol forced a smile. "You have a new schente," he noted.

Ro furrowed his brow. "When did that happen? Ven hasn't notified me, and he typically makes a habit of presenting every new schente to me for my pleasure."

Tol felt his smile falter. "I'm sorry, Ro. I assumed she was schente."

Deliya's cryptic words spun in his mind. Tol had no right to her company. What was she if she wasn't schente? Ro said he'd never take another mate after he lost his Della. Was Deliya some sort of mistress intended only for the king's use? If so, why hadn't Tol heard about her?

Ro's eyes narrowed. "Assumed who was schente?"

He shrugged. "A woman I saw leaving your rooms several days ago." It was a safe wager that Deliya would go there at some time.

Ro gave him a searching look. "Tell me about this woman."

Tol tried to hide his nervousness. He affected a contemplative look. "She was tall, almost my own height. She had the face and body of the goddess Fion, and her voice was sex personified."

"You spoke to her?" Ro growled.

"No, but I heard her speak to a guard as she passed him. I must admit that I was spellbound by her. I've been hoping that her turn would come up in rotation ever since." It couldn't hurt to admit that.

Ro darkened in fury. "And her hair?"

"Ro?" Tol was stunned by the force of his anger. He looked ready to do battle, ready to tear Tol limb from limb. *Damn it! If she was a woman the law protected, why didn't Ro tell me about her?*

"What color was her hair, Tolerin? If you looked, you must have seen her hair." The voice was a dangerous whisper that held a promise of death if Tol supplied the wrong answer to that simple question.

Tol shook his head. It was one of the things he had no clue of, one of the many things he wished he knew for certain about her. Even the cap she had left in the war room gave him no indication, as if she swept it for telltale strands before she discarded it. She likely had done that very thing. Deliya struck him as that careful.

He met Ro's eyes. "What color hair have all your schente, Ro?" He said it carefully, slowly, trying to affect a touch of humor that felt forced.

Ro's face relaxed. He laughed heartily, abruptly the man Tol saw most often. "I do have an affinity for black-haired women since I lost my Della. The darker the hair, the better. I cannot deny it."

Tol sighed in relief. The discussion had given him two pieces of information. Deliya didn't have black hair like his other schente, and she was a jewel Ro would never part with willingly. He would never have her in his bed again.

* * * *

"You did what?" Irin managed in a horror-choked voice.

Riella cringed at her friend's panic. "It was the only way. I was caught." She sighed. "What can you do?"

"If you conceive? Short of admitting this to your father—"

"No. He'll kill me for this, Irin."

She cracked a smile. "He doesn't dare. There would be civil war amongst your relatives if you didn't take the throne."

"You mean if my husband doesn't," she replied hotly. She groaned. "And, he means to start introductions." As if her life weren't complicated enough.

Irin's smile disappeared. "I heard his plan."

"Telling Ro is not an option. Since he doesn't dare hurt me, he will vent his fury on Tol. I couldn't bear that. Tol did nothing wrong."

Her servant-sister shook her head. "There's always gola berry tea. The poison will be painful, but it can be treated."

"By a physician who will tell my father what I ingested. What other reason would I have for using gola berry? And then he would turn on you for giving me the tea. Can you imagine what he would do? Oh Irin, what have I done?" Riella pressed her fist to her abdomen.

"Be calm. The chances are only one in fifty that you will conceive."

Riella darkened. "They may be higher than that."

Irin looked at her in surprise, her women healer's mind no doubt working out the possibilities. "Why would they be?"

"We...I spent the entire night with him, Irin. How does that affect the situation?"

She dropped her forehead to her hands. "How many times did he spill in you and stimulate the drop of an egg?"

"Four."

Irin shot her a pained expression.

"How bad is the situation, Irin?"

"Conservatively? One chance in seven. Be prepared to tell your father."

CHAPTER THREE

Pri 21ˢᵗ, Ti 10-482

Riella sighed, as the schaen massaged the knots from her shoulders. She'd been so worried for the last three days that she'd had no other use for them. She groaned as she remembered having one dismissed from service only the night before. She'd never terminated a schaen's contract before, and the thought that she'd done it horrified her when she allowed herself to think about it.

The schaen had wanted to pleasure her, but Riella hadn't been in the mood. It wasn't his wish to please her that had sealed his fate. It was the way he begged her to let him proceed. She'd shouted him out of the room and ordered Ven to her, demanding that she never see the man again.

Her father had been livid, believing the schaen had injured her somehow. It took most of an hour for her to assure Ro that she had not been injured. In the end, she'd shouted him out of her rooms as well.

The schaen's movement brought her back to the present. This one knelt before her, massaging her collarbones.

She closed her eyes, imagining Tol's hands in the place of his. His beautiful black hair and glittering choc eyes danced in her mind.

He opened her robe and took her breast in his mouth. Tol didn't ask. He never asked. He took what he wanted. Riella threw her head back and fisted her hands in the quilt beneath her, willing herself not to say his name. If Ro knew Tol was here in her rooms, he would hurt him.

Riella sank to her back, and he followed her down, filling her in a single stroke. She whimpered, moving against his thrusts, going where he wished to go. It wasn't right. There was something troubling—

She forced the vision of Tol back into focus despite the schaen's shortcomings in comparison. Riella rolled her head against the quilt. She was close, so close, with barely a touch from him.

"Yes, Princess," he whispered next to her ear.

She felt her arousal melt away. It wasn't Tol. It was just one of the men sent to serve her. The schaen didn't seem to notice the change in her response. Riella started to push him away, but the man climaxed and was locked in her depths.

She cried out in dismay. She hadn't released an egg. The other signs were suddenly clear—the chill, the aching muscles she'd ordered the schaen to massage, the restlessness and volatile emotions. *Merciful Fion!* Her night with Tol had borne fruit, a babe implanted in her womb. What was she to do now?

The schaen looked at her in surprise. "I did something wrong, Highness?"

Riella dropped her head back. "When you lessen, I want you to leave," she growled.

"Have I displeased you somehow?" he asked nervously.

"Just leave. I don't want you here."

He left, and Riella curled onto her bed and wept.

Irin came, no doubt summoned by the schaen. She gathered Riella into her lap and stroked her hair. "It's happened, hasn't it?"

"I don't understand, Irin."

"What don't you understand?" she crooned, the

same calming influence she had been since Riella was a babe and Irin the servant-sister who shared her bed and soothed her nightmares of Lengar plots.

"I want, but I don't want them. I have no control, and I feel like I'm going mad."

"It's your schen, Riella. Some women feel this, the ones who truly love their mates. I am told your mother was like this with Ro Ti. There is only one that you want now."

"I can't have him, Irin. If my father knew, he'd—"

"He won't hurt you. You know in your heart that he could never bear to hurt you again."

"He would hurt Tol," she grumbled, sick at the prospect.

"Not if you ask for him now."

Riella stilled. "Ask for him?"

"It is still early. No one would ever have to know."

CHAPTER FOUR

Pri 22nd, Ti 10-482

"You want what?" Ro thundered.

Riella forced herself to remain calm as Irin cringed. "I've heard good things about him, Father. He saved your life. I had some of your schente point him out to me. He is very pleasing to the eye."

"That is not enough reason to contract a marriage, Riella."

"No. It's not. He is an honorable man, a strong man, a man you would surely approve of. There is only one more thing for me to know."

Ro shook his head. "Tolerin is one of my generals. He is not a schaen for your use."

"I don't want a schaen. I'm sick of schaen," she complained bitterly.

"So I've heard," he growled. "Is that what this is? We can get a new group."

"I don't want a new group," she shouted. "I want a man, not a servant. I don't ever want to see a schaen again."

"Why are you asking me for this?" His face and voice issued the challenge she had known would come.

Riella took a shaky breath. "You want me to take a mate. I want to take one, but I want to know that we are compatible before I sign my life away to him. Is that too much to ask?"

"He's not sterile. What if—"

"Irin has been preparing me Walla herb teas in preparation for this. The schaen have confirmed for us that it is working well."

"Irin," he barked. "You have done this?"

Irin took a step back, keeping her eyes downcast so that Ro would not see her panic. "It has a very small failure rate, Majesty. There is no danger to the Princess in this. She did ask my help."

Riella nodded. Irin hadn't had to lie. Everything she said was true, and if the schaen noticed that she hadn't released an egg, it would give appropriate cover for that as well.

Ro scrubbed his hand over his face. "I will ask. If Tolerin refuses this offer, there is nothing I can do to change his mind."

Riella smiled and kissed her father's cheek. Tol would agree, if Fion was kind. At the very least, he would be freed of punishment, and she would have momentary relief from her schen. Not even Ro could blame Tol that she was one of the few who experienced failure using Walla tea.

She smiled. Tol didn't know what he was in for. He would be meeting a Keen woman in full love-schen.

* * * *

Tol strode into Ro's office and bowed deeply. He had no idea why he was here, so the fact that Ro sent his other advisors away made him distinctly nervous. Ro motioned him to a chair, and he sank into it. He held his tongue, waiting to see what the king would say.

"Thank you for coming, Tol." Ro ran a slightly tremulous hand through his silver hair.

"What is this, Ro?" he asked calmly.

"Have you thought of marriage?"

Tol choked. "Is there a reason for that question?"

"Have you?"

"Of course I have, but when would I meet and court someone?" he joked, trying to keep the mood light.

"You know I think of you as a brother, Tol. Or as a son."

"Thank you." He waited for the explanation that would surely follow such a proclamation. Ro wasn't known for idle flattery.

"My daughter is twenty-two. She has tired of schaen and is of an age to marry, but she resists an alliance with the nobles she knows are available."

"You wish me to recommend a mate for her?" he asked in confusion.

Ro gave him a searching look not unlike the one he had used four days ago when Tol asked about Deliya. Tol shifted uncomfortably.

"My daughter has taken an interest in *you*, Tol."

The blood rushed to his head, making him feel dizzy and flushed. He rubbed his neck, knowing a sick headache would accompany a shock like that.

"She offers a trial. For three days, if you are willing, you will stay in her rooms and mate with her while she takes the Walla tea that will prevent the release of her eggs."

"And at the end of those three days?"

"If you are not compatible, you are both free to walk away. If you are compatible, there would be a contract, but only if you are both willing. I will not force you into anything. You have my vow on that. I would—consider this a favor, but I ask for nothing that you are not comfortable with."

Tol ran a shaking hand through his hair. *Father Mag, how do I get myself into these situations? First Ro's mistress and now his daughter?*

"You'd be king, Tol."

His head shot up. "Do you want me to refuse?"

Ro roared in laugher. "And that is why I respect you so much."

"I don't know the woman, Ro."

"Use the three days to get to know her. I think the two of you are of a type."

"How so?"

"She shares your fire and many of your likes."

"If the three days end and we are not compatible, will you hold this against me?"

"I will not. If you are not compatible, I can ask no more."

Tol nodded. "This means that much to you? You'd ask me to do this because it means that much to you?"

"In many ways. I love Riella, but she is stubborn as an untrained buck hottel. I would give anything to see her happy and safe. This is the first sign that she might settle into a union, and she has been so desperately unhappy for the last day or two..."

"She is your only child. Your concern is to be expected."

Ro shook his head. "I respect you, Tol. I love you as a son. It would please me to acknowledge you as such, but it is more than that. Did I ever tell you how my Della died?"

"Only that an enemy killed her."

Ro's eyes filled with pain the likes of which Tol had never seen from him. "My enemy stole her from my house and guards while she was heavy with my child. She fought them as long as she could, in hopes that I would come for her before they took her. It took me five days to hunt them down. When I did, their leader held a blade to her throat, but my Della was a jaglin. She would not see me kneel for her—or see me die for her."

Ro fisted his hands. "I killed them all, but it was too late for Della."

Tol took a steadying breath. "You lost your wife and child?"

"No. The beast did not hesitate to kill my Della only because a servant held my child inside his pavilion. Della gave her life on a muddy cot without my healing and hands. Her last breath named my daughter for me."

"Riella?"

Ro nodded. "I haven't approached the subject of a union with her in the two years since she came of age in fear that no one could ever protect her as fiercely as I would. You could do that, Tolerin. You are the only man I trust would. I am relieved that she noticed you."

"I will give her the trial, Ro. I can promise no more than that."

He nodded grimly and rose from behind his desk. "Then come with me."

"Now?"

"She has prepared for your arrival."

"And if I had refused?"

Ro laughed and clapped a hand on his shoulder to guide Tol with him. "Riella is my daughter, Tol."

"Is that a warning?"

"Yes. Had you refused, I have no doubt she would have come to you directly to convince you."

"Without your leave, I would never have presumed—"

Ro raised a telling eyebrow. "I have no doubt that I would never have realized that she'd used the King's corridors until she'd convinced you somehow."

Tol felt a niggling of unease. "Does she seek out men often?"

"Of course not. She's known only her schaen."

"You're sure of that?"

"I'm certain. She is watched always, even when she doesn't realize she is. Riella has only lost her guards twice in her life, and both times I discovered her mischief within hours. No. Riella has never pursued a man before."

Tol nodded, relieved.

Riella's quarters were at the end of Ro's wing. Tol examined the corridor as they walked, wondering where Deliya's rooms were. Were they within Ro's rooms, or did she have one of her own?

Two soldiers bowed and pushed the doors wide for them as they passed. Ro waved them away to a position further down the corridor.

Tol sucked in his breath in surprise, his cock surging to readiness. When Ro said his daughter had prepared for him, Tol hadn't realized he meant she would be "presented" to him. The cloak covered her neck to ankle, hiding the body beneath. The Princess's cloak and dress were cut of a stunning green that showcased her hair. Such a color would never be chosen by a woman with the typical brown or black hair most women shared. It was—unique, much as he supposed the owner was. Her face was covered with a ceremonial mask in the likeness of a jaglin, done in black and gray geela bird feathers, the eyeholes edged with a line of perfectly-matched emi beads.

He scanned his eyes slowly from her bare feet to her small chin and full, dark lips to her black eyes and the crowning glory of her bright red hair. What little he could see of her was stunning. This woman would have had little trouble enticing him. Tol swallowed hard.

Ro chuckled. "A good start. I'll leave you to it, Tol."

He dropped a kiss on Riella's hair. "Good luck to you," he whispered.

Riella nodded and offered her father a strained smile.

A female servant stepped to Tol's side as Ro left the room. "Your cloak and jacket, General Tolerin?" she asked.

He stripped them off and handed them to her without taking his eyes from Riella's.

The servant removed them to a cabinet and returned to her mistress's side. "Should I remove Her Highness's cloak, or is it your pleasure to do so?"

"Mine?" he asked, stunned. Tol had never expected this honor. Royalty had women presented to them not landless nobles in the king's service, even those who had made general by the age of thirty.

The servant smiled openly. "It is your choice, General." Her hand moved to the tie at Riella's neck.

Tol strode across the floor, brushing the servant's hand away in irritation. He pulled the ties open in quick succession and pushed the cloak to the floor.

He looked at Riella breathlessly. The green silin gown was slit from neck to waist in a wide vee that showcased her perfect, pale skin and the swell of her breasts. A second slit reached from her ankle to the crease of her left thigh.

Riella shifted nervously, and he caught a flash of her tattoo through the slit. The mark had been given to her while she was a baby to identify her if she was ever stolen. It was the symbol on Ro's personal banner—a star flanked by opposing crescent moons. Tol had a sudden urge to drop to his knees and explore all of her, starting with that little red tattoo.

"Servant, leave us," he growled.

He heard the door close. He reminded himself several times that this was Ro's daughter, the Princess, and not a woman to simply sate himself in. Not that Tol didn't take pride in bringing even schente to screaming release. Not that Riella was a virgin; she'd had schaen to dampen her hungers for the last seven years.

That thought made Tol ache, made him want to throw every schaen out of the palace before he took her. Had Riella had her servant take her barrier in the privacy of her bath or had she selected a ceremonial schaen to take it for her and be immediately retired from service? The vision of a schaen, his cock stained in her maiden's blood, made him furious.

Tol felt the last of his control fly. He pulled Riella to his chest, seeking her mouth in a crazed haze of need. The scent of lizor blooms teased his nose, and he groaned. Was this a scent every woman in Ro's household wore, or did one of them use a little of the other's bottle? It mattered not. In that instant, he knew Ro could have Deliya with his thanks if the fiery woman now in his arms was his.

Riella moaned into his mouth, busy releasing the tie at the neck of his tunic. She was like fire in his hands. Her skin, cool at his first touch, burned hot under his wandering palms. She stripped his tunic off and explored his chest, her breathing harsh and her eyes wide behind her mask. Tol reached for it, wanting to see the beauty he'd heard of.

She captured his hand, backing a step from him. "No." Her voice was a hoarse gasp.

"As you wish, Highness," he assured her, though frustrated by her refusal.

Riella blinked. "Please, do not call me that. Do not make me your princess."

"What would you have from me?"

She seemed at a loss. "Let me...Let me please you."

He smiled, wrapping his hands around her waist. "You do please me," he growled playfully.

"No." Riella placed her hand on his chest, a shaking hand. "Put your pleasure in my hands."

Tol's smile disappeared. "I am not a schaen, Riella."

She pushed away from him, looking close to tears. "I never made such an offer to a schaen," she protested.

"If this is what you wish in a mate—"

"I asked for your complete trust. I ask you to put yourself in my hands once."

Tol raised an eyebrow in disbelief. What was her game? "This is a test?"

"No." She turned from him, shaking her head. "This will never work. A woman may place her fate in a man's hands over and over, but she may never be his equal."

He grasped her shoulders, kneading the tension from them. "I'm sorry, Riella."

"No. I'm sorry I wasted your time, General Tolerin. Please—Please leave me."

"I had no idea you felt this strongly about it. If you need this from me to feel you will have my respect, I offer it freely."

"I don't want you to," she assured him in a choked voice.

"If you will promise me the same, complete control of your pleasure at another time, I offer myself. I thought—"

Riella turned to him. "I don't want a puppet," she breathed. "I want you to be mine for this one encounter."

He pulled her back to his chest. "Then make me yours." Tol captured her mouth, excited by the possibilities of being at her whims.

"Disrobe for me," she ordered.

Tol backed off a step and pulled off his boots and trousers. She bit her lip as she ran her fingertips over the engorged head of his cock. Tol growled his satisfaction, his muscles bunching as he stifled the urge to drive it into her. He had made a promise. His pleasure was in Riella's hands.

"Lay on the bed. In the center of the bed," she instructed.

He smiled. Complying with her requests was generating a sense of anticipation and excitement humming over his nerves and pooling in his groin. When Riella turned with the silin bands in her hands, he groaned, his cock pulsing as he extended his arms over his head for the soft binding to come. The feel of silin sliding against his pulse points sent tremors of heat through his body. Tol rotated his wrists against them and clenched his teeth in the force of his arousal.

Riella slid her left leg through the slit in the gown, baring Ro's tattoo as she knelt on the bed. She moved her eyes over him from his feet, slightly spread and unbound, to the length of him straining toward her. She paused there, her breathing quick and color high.

As her gaze moved up his chest, his male nipples hardened. Tol bit back his urge to spill. He had never realized a woman could affect him this way, that being helpless to a woman could affect him this way. He pulled against the bonds, letting the silin bite, then slide against his wrists.

She touched the bands. "Are they too tight?" she whispered in that same slightly hoarse voice.

"I may ask you never to remove them, Riella." When she was his, he'd convince her to do this again.

"Good." She leaned over him and ran her hands down his arms, from the silin bands to his shoulders, tracing every muscle carefully.

Tol shivered at her touch, raising his head to capture the breast so close to his mouth. Riella pressed a kiss to the silin band, arching further into the heat of his mouth. She played her fingers through his hair, panting as he teased and suckled her to a hard point of arousal.

He released her. "Bring me the other," he ordered.

Riella shook her head and backed away on the bed.

Tol dropped his head back to the pillows, grumbling in frustration. Not touching her was maddening. He went still as she started at his ankles, exploring his legs as she had his arms. She dipped her tongue in the deep scar on his thigh, the scar from the blow he had taken in Ro's stead. He raised his head as far as he could to watch her.

Her fingers circled his length, massaging him, squeezing him, enticing him to bring forth droplets of his readiness. She sank down to suck at the engorged knob, drinking him as he would her.

Tol pulled at his bonds, frantic to free his hands. He had to stop her before he disgraced himself by completing in her mouth. He wanted her to take him deeper into that moist heat so unlike a woman's core. He closed his eyes, tortured by the new sensations. He cried out and bucked, pleading wordlessly for the pleasure she offered.

Riella slid her mouth around him, running her tongue over the corded veins along his length. She pulled back, and Tol opened his eyes, shaking as he waited for her next move. She laid a kiss on the tip and sucked him deep, teasing the sensitive bundle of nerves under the head slowly. Again and again, she repeated the motion until Tol's muscles were tensed in preparation to spill in her mouth. He didn't care if he did, knowing such a release would surely be as sublime as the rest of the experience.

She rose up over his thighs, spreading the slit of her skirt to uncover the red curls hidden beneath. "I was wet for you when you entered my rooms," she whispered. "Would you like to sample how ready I am?"

"Yes." *Oh Fion, what torture is this?* "Let me taste you." His mouth watered. He would give anything to run his tongue along her honeyed slit.

Riella smiled and guided his cock to the well of that honey, dropping just far enough to encase him within her nether lips. "Taste me," she invited. "Drink deep."

Tol bucked his hips, groaning in pleasure as her body pulsed around him. Riella dropped the last finger widths with a mewling cry, already close to release.

"Untie me," Tol growled. "Untie me and let me touch you."

"What would you do? Tell me." She raised herself then took him deep again. Her hands went to her breasts, stroking her already rigid nipples.

"Yes," he urged her, stroking his cock in long, slow gyrations of his hips. "I would touch your breasts. I would run my thumbs over your nipples."

Riella circled her nipples with the pads of her thumbs, her breathing ragged and her eyes closed. Tol kept the easy rhythm he'd started, watching avidly as she enacted his fantasies for him.

"I'd squeeze your nipple, pinch it lightly." Watching her was driving him to the edges of sanity, but it was more arousing than he'd ever found actually doing the things he described with other women.

She did as he suggested, gasping at the sensation of the slight pain mixed with her pleasure. Riella was so beautiful, so responsive.

Like Deliya. No, not like Deliya. Riella is mine. I'll have the contract with her. No man but me will ever touch her again. I want to drown in her.

"I'd pull back your skirts and stroke the bud of your pleasure while I took you."

Riella shivered, her hands traveling down the front of her gown, leaving her nipples peaked against the silin in invitation. He snapped his eyes back to her hands as she pulled the slit up. Her curls reappeared, framing her hand, as she dipped her fingers beneath. She moaned as she stroked herself.

Tol quickened his pace, the sight of her stroking herself almost more than he could bear. Riella's fingers skated over his length as he eased in and out of her depths, and he ground his teeth in frustration. If she touched him, he would never outlast her.

"No. I wouldn't seek my pleasure," he reprimanded her. "I'd seek yours."

Her fingers returned to her nub, stroking until she was rocking in counterpoint to his thrusts.

"It's not fast enough for you. I'd stroke faster."

She did. Riella looked at him with glazed eyes. She just needed one more push to send her over into bliss.

"I'm going to take the taste you denied me, Riella. When my turn comes, I'm going to taste every inch of your body. I'm going to taste my possession of you and know I own you."

Her body rippled over his shaft. She pushed down on him hard. "Tol!" His name was a ragged scream on her lips—like the first time in his bed.

Tol roared in a combination of denial and

possession. Only one woman ever had leave to call him that. Only one woman ever had, in the heat of passion, pushed her core around his cock as Riella did now.

His senses scattered. Colors danced before his eyes: the green, red, white, black, and berry of Riella. The mixed scents of lizor, female honey, and musk teased his lungs. Her breathless whispers of his name over and over sang in his ears and along his bruised nerves. The silin of his bonds and her contracting core stole the last of his control.

His seed came fast and hard, stealing his breath. Riella muttered an oath to Fion as the heat swirled within her. She gripped his ribs and dropped her chin to her chest, panting as their bodies locked.

"Take off your mask, Deliya," he ordered in a fierce whisper.

Riella raised her eyes to meet his. She pulled off the mask with a shaking hand, dropping her face and fighting back tears.

His cock lessened as fury stole his arousal. "Release me," he growled.

CHAPTER FIVE

Riella shook her head. He couldn't leave yet. Not like this.

Tol pulled at his bound hands, his muscles straining in the effort. "Release me," he demanded again.

"Not until we discuss this. Please, Tol." She had known he would be angry, that he wouldn't want to listen. That was why she had bound him. If she were to have any chance to explain, it would be now, but she had counted on revealing herself to him before he discovered the truth.

"Your hair." He scowled at her. "You wanted the darkness, so I wouldn't see your hair."

"Or my tattoo," she admitted.

"You lied to me."

"Yes, I did. I'm sorry for that."

"You said you were one of Ro's schente."

"I didn't. I said I was one of his women."

Tol pulled at his bonds, the wood spindles of her headboard creaking dangerously under his assault. He glared at her with murder in his eyes. "You knew what I meant, Riella."

She nodded, miserable.

"Do you know what you did? I almost revealed our liaison to Ro in an effort to find you. I could have gotten myself killed."

"I told you not to," she whispered. The fact that he had searched for her thrilled her, despite his anger now.

"Why did you go to my room with me?" he demanded.

"For two reasons. The first was my father. Almost any price was worth paying to save him embarrassment."

"And the other?" he sneered.

"I wanted to. I wanted you," she assured him.

"You could have told me."

"But, I knew..." She faltered.

"Knew what?"

"You wouldn't have touched me. You would have dragged me to Ro."

"You made me a traitor," he accused.

She winced. "No. The fault was mine. I would have admitted it if we were caught, Tol. I told you the punishment would be mine. I meant that."

His expression proclaimed his mistrust. "Fine. You've explained. Release me."

"You hate me," she choked out.

Tol glared at her, motioning to his bound hands with a jerk of his head.

Riella eased off of him, heartsick that he seemed intent on leaving her. Her hand hovered over his bound wrist. There was only one chance left. "The contract was a legitimate offer, Tol. I will not keep you here if you wish to go. The choice is yours. I just want you to know that I've never stopped wanting you."

She released his right wrist without waiting for his answer. She looked away, hiding her tears as he tore the other free.

The bed shifted as he walked away. He pulled on his clothing and boots then retrieved his jacket and cloak. He paused at the door. "I'll make sure you get your hair clip back, Princess."

Riella nodded, biting back her sobs until the door had closed behind him and his footsteps faded away down the hall. She pulled off her presentation gown and reached for a heavy winter robe hung by the bed.

She would have to admit her gravid state to her father soon; another few days should be long enough. Riella wasn't sure what Ro would do, but he wouldn't force a contract under the circumstances, and he wouldn't harm Tol.

His freedom was all she had left to give Tol. It was what he wanted, and it was the least he deserved. He had taken a schente to his bed. That was all he bargained for. She couldn't expect more of him than what he was willing to give that night.

* * * *

Tol stormed into his room and started pacing. He scooped up her hair clip from behind the lamp on his mantle, wishing he could crush the heavy platinum in his fist.

Riella had lied to him. She demanded his trust, but she hadn't trusted him enough to tell him who she really was. *Ro's daughter!* She was never intended for the likes of him. The Princess wasn't his to look at or speak to, wasn't his to touch and love.

She could be. She offered that. Ro offered that, and you refused it.

Tol threw her clip at the bed as he made the turn toward the windows, muttering a curse and fisting his shaking hands. Of course he refused her. She could have gotten him killed with her games. She had made a fool of him—twice. First on the night he brought her here and again today.

He turned back toward the bed, raising his arms in mute supplication to the gods. How blind was he? How could so radiant and sensual a creature be schente? The sweet music of her body when he stimulated her alone—

Tol stumbled, landing on his knees in heart-pounding shock. Riella was releasing eggs that night, and he was a fertile male. Today...

He groaned. She didn't release one. He was sure she didn't, but it wasn't Walla tea that stopped her. Riella wouldn't have use of the tea with her schaen. She wouldn't have been using it when he took her the first night, and three days was not enough time for the drug to build up in her system to be of any use today.

Their latest mating coursed through his mind, and he shook his head in disbelief. Her skin had been chilled then warmed to his touch. She was ravenous sexually, much more so than his first night with her. Her shoulders—He'd felt the tension in them, hadn't he? Her muscles had been knotted. All little things, easily missed. Yet how could he miss them? *I didn't know who she was.*

"Mother Fion! What have I done?" His mind whirled. What would she do? He'd refused her contract. Would Riella admit the truth to Ro? He was a hard man, but he doted on her. Would Ro actually harm her?

The punishment will be mine.

Tol rose and stepped to the bed. He picked up her clip and turned it in his hand. Would she do something drastic? He considered her mad scheme to free Benir— wearing a stolen uniform, disguised as a man, unarmed. She would do something drastic.

"Gola berry tea," he breathed.

Tol shoved the clip in his pocket and made the distance to her rooms in a quarter of the time it had taken him to reach his own. He shoved his way by her surprised guards and waved them away as he bolted inside. He came to a halt, taking in every detail of the scene before him.

Riella sat, curled in a long, winter robe in a comfortable chair by the fire. Her face was swollen and tear-stained. She paled, shifting her eyes from his, her breathing hitching. She cleared her throat then waved a hand at the bed. "Just leave the clip there," she managed.

Tol looked at the mug in her other hand in stunned disbelief, a mug full of dark pink tea. He crossed the room in two long strides, plucking it from her fingers and smashing it against the wall. He snagged her by her shoulders and hauled her to her feet, fighting the urge to shake her.

"You will not do this," he growled. "You have no right to do this."

Riella shrank from him. "I don't understand," she whispered.

The door swung open, crashing against the wall; her guards rushed in. They stood, frozen in indecision at the scene before them.

"Leave us," Tol ordered.

The two men looked at each other uncertainly then to Riella for confirmation of the command.

"Leave us," he thundered.

"Please leave," Riella agreed with all the dignity she could muster.

"And lock the door," Tol added.

Riella nodded her approval of that as well.

The guards nodded, faces grim, and returned to the corridor, latching the door behind them. Tol turned his fury back to Riella.

She met it calmly, stiffening her spine. "Explain

yourself," she ordered.

"Explain myself?" Her gall was amazing. "Did you ever plan to tell me, or were you just going to take the coward's way?"

"You're calling me a coward?" she shouted.

"What would you call it?"

"Giving you your freedom as you chose," she growled. "This way, no one will question that it was an honest mistake."

He pulled her to his chest, the urge to shake her quickly becoming the urge to throttle her. "Honest mistake? Killing my child would be an honest mistake?" he managed in a fierce whisper.

Her face darkened. "Are you mad? I'm not—"

"The tea! What am I supposed to believe?"

"The truth."

"Which is what?" he retorted, raising his voice again. "Since that seems to be a rather sticky subject with you."

"It was lizor berry tea to calm my nerves." She pushed at his chest and punched him when he held his ground. "Let me go," she shouted.

"So, what was your honest mistake?" he demanded.

"Getting pregnant, you idiot." She tried to shove him away again.

Tol tightened his grip and pulled her closer to his chest. "Why did you ask for me?"

Riella glared at him. "To expunge all proof of your guilt," she spat in a low, dangerous voice.

"What?" His voice echoed off the walls.

She didn't raise volume in return, and her voice assumed the matter-of-fact tone of a patient tutor. "No matter what you decided, everyone would believe I conceived today. No one needs to know about anything else."

Her logic cut through his fury. Tol released her. Riella backed from him, rubbing her shoulders where he'd gripped. She went to her bed, leaving him standing there gasping for breath as his mind worked through what she'd just said.

He shook his head. Riella did all of this to save him from Ro's wrath?

"I'll sign the contract," he decided.

She turned on him, eyes wide. "No."

"Riella—"

"It's not enough to base a marriage on. I won't do it."

"Riella—"

"You rejected me. You don't want a contract. You want your freedom. Well, you've got it." She pressed her hands to her abdomen, to his child. "I won't sign it."

Tol strode to her, dragging her against his chest and taking her mouth. Riella's skin heated to his touch, her mouth urgent against his. It was her schen, and it was wonderful. He massaged her shoulders and back, feeling her unknot under his hands. Her pregnancy signs were already in full sway, and it was his child in her womb.

She lay her head to his shoulder when the kiss ended. She trembled, and he knew she was fighting her needs to preserve her case against the contract he demanded. Tol wasn't fooled by it. She needed him, and she wanted him. There was no way he was letting her go now.

He sighed. "You know there's more."

"It's schen. I'll survive it. Other women have."

"It's not just schen. It was there that night. Deny it if you must, but you know I'm right."

She shook her head against his chest.

"I tried to find you that same morning. I never wanted to let you go."

Riella pushed away, putting an arm's length between them. "You managed it well enough half an hour ago," she reminded him bitterly.

"I was angry. You lied to me. You're still lying to me. I don't hate you. I hate what you did."

"Then we're even."

"We're signing that contract," he warned.

"You cannot force me to."

"I can convince you."

"It will not work."

Tol stepped to her again. "That is my child, and you will contract with me. No further discussion is necessary."

"Except with me."

He turned to that voice in surprise. Ro emerged from a hidden door opening in the far wall. *The king's corridors!* Tol grimaced in the realization that he'd forgotten that entrance to her rooms, the same entrance she would have used when she left him.

The king raised one hand, holding the clothing she had worn to free Benir, and opened the other to reveal the second hair clip. He looked from one to the other of them with a raised eyebrow.

Tol pulled the matching clip from his pocket and tossed it on the bed. Ro nodded grimly and turned to Riella.

She dropped to the bed, casting nervous glances between the two men, finally settling on staring into the fire. "It's my fault, Father. Tol didn't know who I really was. I lied to him."

Ro crossed the room and dropped the clothes in a

pile in front of her. "You told him you were schente?"

Tol winced at the cold voice of interrogation he'd adopted.

She nodded.

He looked back to Tol. "It was Riella you were looking for?"

Tol sighed and nodded.

His jaw tightened; Ro crossed his arms over his chest and gave his daughter a stern look that made her lower her eyes and made Tol wonder if he would really hurt her.

"How could you hide it?" the king demanded. "Your hair and your tattoo?"

Riella closed her eyes, rubbing at her forehead. Tol grimaced in understanding. He leaned down and healed her pregnancy headache. She didn't fight him, and he took heart in that small concession. Ro shot him a dangerous look and clenched his fists in warning.

Tol put his hands up in a calming gesture. "Her pregnancy signs, Ro. It is my baby. Please understand." He didn't add that he had been left in this very room not long ago with the understanding that he was going to be a lot more intimate with Riella than a simple healing.

Ro nodded and relaxed slightly. "How did she hide her identity from you? How could you not know? Convince me."

Tol rubbed the stiffness settling in the back of his neck. "She asked for a dark room, and I complied."

"Before that," he growled. "How could it get that far?"

Riella motioned to the clip Tol had thrown on the bed. "I had a captain's cap—a full uniform. Tolerin got close enough to see that I was female, but I had hidden all proof of who I was."

Ro paled. "The soldiers could have killed you."

Tol snorted. "She went unarmed as well."

Riella wiped away a tear. "I couldn't steal an appropriate dagger. The uniform is easy to steal, the weapon not so easily taken. The men won't realize one set of clothing is missing for a day—but the weapon is another matter."

Ro went to the chair and sank into it, looking shaken. "Thank you, Tolerin," he stated gratefully.

Tol raised an eyebrow. "For?"

"For not killing her when you caught her."

Riella flopped onto her back, covering her face with her hands.

Tol nodded, suddenly feeling the need to defend her. "It was pure luck that I caught her, I assure you. Her plan was nearly perfect in construction and execution. She couldn't foresee that I would cross her path. No one should have been where she was."

Ro shook his head. "Then why were you there?"

Tol smiled. "Because I thought Benir would be. No one should have been there. He would know that."

Riella barked out laughter. "Benir had three other options. I was the one who had to make it back inside the palace."

"Three?" Tol asked in disbelief.

Riella and Ro both nodded mutely.

"I need to know where they are to increase security." He shot Ro a look of confusion. Why would he leave known entryways unguarded? A niggling of irritation threatened his calm. How could he be expected to do his job when Ro did such things?

Ro sighed. "The stable, the east guard tower, and the electrical supply station."

Riella laughed again. "The east guard tower has been blocked for five years, Father. I meant the one at the ammo station."

"Ah, yes. I forgot. I blocked the east guard tower after you and Benir smuggled in your precious baby jaglin."

"You must admit that the menagerie has nothing to match her in beauty or spirit."

Ro smiled widely. "True. Where is the entrance at the ammo station?"

"I'll draw maps for Tol." She rubbed her abdomen absently, her smile disappearing. "Benir and I won't be using them any time soon, and they'll need blocked off before—"

Tol set his jaw. "You will contract with me."

"I will *not*," she insisted.

Ro looked at her in surprise. "You suggested the contract," he reminded her.

Riella winced. "And Tolerin refused me. A child doesn't change that. The offer is rescinded."

Ro stood and took a menacing step toward him. "You what?"

Tol sighed. "I was angry. She lied to me—who she was, what she was. I didn't learn the truth until she...At climax, she..." He waved his arms hopelessly. "I needed time, Ro. She wanted an answer immediately."

Ro smiled. "In that case, I rule that Riella may not rescind her offer of a contract."

She shot up on the bed, her fists on her hips. "I won't sign it. Even you cannot force me, Father."

"You will live up to the contract you agreed to— three days in this room with Tolerin, starting now. Your meals will be delivered to you. The king's corridor will be bolted from the inside, and guards will be posted at the door with instructions that you are confined here—both of you."

Tol nodded and pointed to the window. "May I suggest having someone cut the iri vines along these portions of wall?"

Riella paled. "I'm pregnant, you oaf. Do you honestly think—"

Tol pulled her head to him and planted a kiss on her lips. "Yes. I do." He released her and ducked her blow with a self-satisfied smile.

Ro chuckled. "You know my daughter well, Tolerin."

"I've seen her climbing abilities. We are well matched in many ways."

Riella scowled at him. "We are well matched in one. That done, I find no further use for you."

Ro shook his head, chuckling silently, his chest vibrating and eyes shining in his restraint. "In three days, you will have to prove that to me."

Tol motioned for Ro's attention again, automatically falling into the camaraderie they shared in battle. "There was another verbal contract made."

Riella launched off the far side of the bed. "You don't dare," she shouted. "I will not agree."

"You have agreed," Tol reminded her.

"I will not submit then."

Ro looked to Tol. "What is this contract?"

"It was not a contract," Riella protested.

Ro shot her a stern look. "You gave your word?"

She shifted from foot to foot. "Before he rejected me. His rejection releases me."

"What was this promise you made?"

She crossed her arms over her chest and looked at the hidden door in longing.

"Tolerin?" Ro asked gruffly.

Tol bit back a smile. "That she would give me free rein sexually, put her pleasure completely in my hands."

"I've been freed by your rejection," she repeated.

"I've fulfilled my end of the bargain. You owe yours."

"Well, you've already collected on it, haven't you? Several times over, if memory serves."

"That is separate, existing before the current contract, and has no bearing."

Ro gave her a quelling look. "A princess is bound by her word, Riella. You know that. Tolerin deferred his decision on a contract, nothing more. You will keep your end of the bargain."

She glanced at the bed nervously.

Ro kissed his daughter's forehead. "I would tell you to behave, but I know you better, and so does Tol. I trust he can handle what comes from here." He headed for the hidden corridor. "I'll just bolt this on the way out."

Riella stared at her feet. "I would appreciate a fresh lizor berry tea, since General Tolerin saw fit to smash my last mug."

"No," Tol decided. "No teas."

Ro looked back at him in surprise. "Tolerin?"

He shot Ro a fierce look. "There are better ways to induce sleep, and I do not trust unknown quantities when it comes to Riella and my child."

"I am not going to poison myself," Riella growled at him.

"No. You're not," he agreed.

Ro's smile returned. "I don't think teas and servants are advisable for the three days of decision." He closed the narrow doorway a split second before one of Riella's boots struck it.

Tol strode toward her, noting her shaky retreat with a measure of satisfaction. He could handle Riella's uncertainty and imbalance but not her cold dismissal.

She motioned toward the bed. "I suppose you intend to collect on our agreement now."

He shook his head. "I defer." He untied the belt of her robe.

"Then what are you doing?"

"You need calming."

"This isn't calming," she replied weakly.

Tol pushed the robe off of her shoulders. "You can't bathe in your clothes."

* * * *

Riella pulled away from Tol in the large, circular tub. "This really isn't necessary. I've been bathing myself for quite some time. I assure you, I won't drown."

He slid to her side again, tracing the hand cloth over her collarbones, the fringe at the edge feathering over her nipples and causing them to pucker in anticipation. "The agreement said that we would get to know each other, learn if we are sexually compatible."

"This isn't sexual," she protested weakly. She wished her convictions were stronger, but her body was making a liar out of her by its heated responses.

"It is loveplay."

Riella started to protest, but Tol cupped her breast in his hand through the cloth, circling his thumb over her nipple; and she couldn't form the words to protest anything. He moved to the other without a word, taking as she loved him to take.

"You are so beautiful," he breathed into her ear as

he bit it lightly.

She found her center; Riella started giggling uncontrollably.

Tol shot her a look of disbelief. "What in Len's underworld is so funny?" he demanded.

Riella tried to adopt a serious face and failed utterly. The giggles kept coming. "You're going to have to remember to use your healing magic after sex," she commented.

"I don't—"

She waved him off. "Ro wanted to take you apart when he saw the mark from your last—handling of my ear."

Tol reddened. "He was very upset that morning."

She sobered. "Yes. He was."

"With you?"

"A bit. He was more upset with whatever man dared mark me."

"What did you do?"

Her smile returned. "It was all right. I said one of my schaen got frisky, and since I wouldn't remember which one—"

Tol circled around her, settling on the floor of the tub, his knees tucked between her feet. Riella pressed back until the side halted her retreat, her smile disappearing as his arms caged her. A crazed look lit his face. She flicked a peek down his body, past the strata of muscles on his chest and the sprinkling of dark hair to the length of him, growing thicker by the moment. She snapped her eyes back to his face and that savage, battle-ready look. His near-fury was strangely arousing.

Riella licked her lower lip, and Tol focused on the movement. He pulled her toward him, his cock sliding into her. His movements were tender, his expression fierce; and the entire situation excited Riella in a way she couldn't define. Was it that he was taking what he wanted without apology or the possessive way he did it? She couldn't say.

"Whose cock pierces you, Riella?" His voice was seductive.

She bowed into his thrusts. "Yours," she gasped.

"Whose child grows in your womb?"

"Tolerin's child."

"Whose?" He licked at her earlobe, sucking it into his mouth.

Riella's body pulsed in response. "Yours."

"No one else will touch you. Not while I live. You will disband your schaen and send them away. I do not want to kill them. Do not make me. Disband them."

She wrapped her legs around his hips and invited him deeper. "I already have."

Tol's eyes widened. "You have?"

Riella nodded.

"When?" He laid a kiss on her throat, and she offered it more fully in response, allowing him to seek out the well of her musk at her pulse point.

"Before I asked for you. My father offered me a new group, but I refused. I told him I didn't want to see another schaen."

"Why?"

She blushed and turned her face away.

"Whose cock pierces—"

"Yours," she sobbed.

"Why did you disband them?"

"I don't want them."

"Despite your schen, you don't want them?"

She shook her head. "Because of my schen—" Riella

grimaced. The words were out before she considered the consequences. She snapped her mouth shut.

"Explain." It was an order, but one spoken in the same crooning voice that held her captive in her desire.

Riella shook her head. She could not—would not—tell him. Refusing him was hard enough.

Tol changed his angle, sending her into a wave of heat. "Whose cock—"

"No," she shouted.

"Did you take them? After me?"

She bit her lower lip, refusing to answer him.

"Did you?" His voice never changed. It was still the same steady, calming tone despite the fever in his eyes.

"Did you? Did you take schente after me?" she countered angrily. "I've heard that Tolerin is never a day without schente." She didn't add that the schente loved that about him.

His eyes went wide then narrowed, as he seemingly calculated some coming military engagement. She had seen that look on her father's face many times. Was that why Tol appealed to her? Because he and her father were so alike?

"No. I didn't."

Riella burst into tears. "Why not?" she choked. It would have been easier to hate him if he had gone back to his precious schente. She wanted to hate him but couldn't. She hated how weak and needy her pregnancy made her.

"A man can't perform if certain portions balk." He kissed her brow. "Tell me."

"A woman can—to a point."

"Tell me." His voice went gruff.

She shook her head. "I convinced myself...but it didn't last." She shuddered. "I waited too long to try to stop it. By the time I pushed away—"

"He climaxed before you could end it?"

Riella nodded slowly, fresh tears coursing down her face. "My schen was strong but—" She took a ragged breath.

"But you wanted me?" His expression was heartbreakingly hopeful.

She stared at him through the tears in her eyes. She had to free him. This was not something she could admit to him and still do that.

"Whose—"

She dropped her gaze. "Yes. I imagined—" Why was she admitting this? He'd know what it meant.

"You imagined his hands were mine? His cock—"

Riella sobbed then laughed harshly. "That part was more difficult," she admitted.

Tol's mouth came down on hers, and his body increased speed until she gasped in response. Riella threw her head back as the tremors in her womb took her whole body. Tol exploded within her, locking his hot seed deep inside. She screamed in pleasure as its heat mixed with her climax.

He nipped at her ear then healed the slight pain away. "You're not going to force me to retreat, Riella. If your schaen were not enough and you had to imagine my body to attempt what you did, you love me. I will not permit another man to touch you, now or ever."

Riella sighed, pressing her cheek against his chest. "It's not enough for a contract," she breathed, her eyes closed and her mind muddled. It wasn't enough. If he didn't love her, it would never be enough.

Tol lessened in her. He lifted her from the bath and dried her carefully, the soft cloth heating her traitor body again. He didn't press for more. He placed her on the bed and pulled the quilts over her.

He kissed her cheek gently. "Sleep, Riella. I will be here when you wake."

She sighed. That was the torture of this contract.

* * * *

Tol sat on the edge of her mattress. He stroked one of Riella's curls between his fingertips as she slept. He sighed, kissing the curl and leaving her side, his fists pushed deep in the pockets of the lounging pants brought, along with many of his other belongings, while they bathed.

"It's *not* enough," he grumbled. It wasn't enough for either of them. Her calm dismissal wasn't what he wanted in the least. Tol wanted her passion—and her trust. His assurances that he wanted a contract weren't enough for Riella—not after he'd refused her.

"Why in Len's name did I refuse her?" *Because she lied to me?* A few moments earlier, he'd been determined that he'd sign the contract with her, that he'd never let another man touch her, that he'd never leave her bed and body.

It would be enough. Before he was through, she'd sign the contract. Riella would give him a fine, strong son—or a daughter.

Tol shuddered. A daughter of Riella? The thought was frightening. No wonder Ro had gone silver-haired at fifty. Sneaking baby jaglin in, escaping the palace, climbing iri vines...*Father Mag, you do protect the bold.*

He sat at the small desk and penned a note to Ro, his hand shaking. Riella's tale of her encounter with the schaen left him scattered. For their safety, the servants had best be well clear of the palace by the end of his three days of confinement. And, there would be guards at the secret exits Riella used. There would be no escape from him.

He passed the message to one of the guards and closed the door again.

The bed drew him, his weariness and the urge to touch Riella forcing him to the warmth beneath the quilts. She didn't fight him when he pulled her to his chest. She turned to him and tangled her fingers in the curls between his male nipples.

"You will be mine," he breathed. "I will convince you somehow."

But how could he convince her? If she refused him, what could he do? He'd wasted his chance at a Trial Moon.

He wondered at that. Would the king allow him a Trial Moon by special dispensation based on her lies the first night? She'd told him she was sterile. She admitted it. Tol hadn't been permitted the chance to ask for his rights.

He sighed. She hadn't stripped him of his right to ask, only of his purpose in asking. One couldn't expect to win a contract by pregnancy with a sterile woman. Then again, pregnancy wasn't necessary to winning a contract of Trial Moon. Convincing her to a contract would have been enough, and he had not been denied that. *Perhaps by her further lies*, his mind supplied. If Ro ruled against him at the end of three days, he would request the dispensation, but the king would only grant that if Tol proved there was a chance of success.

At the end of the three days, what proof would Ro demand? Would her father bow to her demand to be freed from the contract, or would he extend their time together to allow Tol the opportunity to win her? His head spun in the complexity of this battle.

CHAPTER SIX

Pri 23rd, Ti 10-482

Riella woke to the scent of lamor in cream sauce. Her stomach grumbled and her mouth watered; it was her favorite meal. She sighed, feeling incredibly relaxed and warm. She moved her cheek against the pillows stacked along the length of her body, excitement coursing through her veins and dragging her from the depths of dreamless sleep.

Visions of hot, urgent sex filled her mind. A wall was to her back, the rough weave of a uniform jacket to her chest. Tol's cock was buried in her, his breath hot on her cheek as he nipped at her ear. Riella moaned, her fingers gripping the pillow. His scent teased her, that musk that was unique to Tol, and her core overflowed with cream. She moved her legs restlessly, feeling the weave of his trousers against her thighs. A moment more, and his cock would spasm, sending waves of heat through her and locking into her body.

The pillows shifted, and hair rasped over her cheek, bringing more of Tol's scent with it. He was aroused, and she gravitated to the source of the musk. She pressed her lips to the well above his nipple, sighing at how real the dream was—until he groaned.

Her eyes snapped open, and the events of the last day flooded back to her. She released her grip on his waist and scrambled off the bed, fighting the riot in her blood, licking her lips then cursing the lapse. The taste of him was ten times more potent than the smell.

Riella shivered in her sudden drop of body temperature, cursing her mind's trick in convincing her that his chest was a stack of pillows. In her waking moments, she would have known better and kept her distance. She couldn't touch him. She couldn't give in again. Every time he played at her body, she lost more of her control.

Would she ever wake peacefully as long as he was here to torment her?

Tol regarded her calmly. "Are you hungry?"

She nodded, moving to the table and chairs that had been delivered while she slept after their bath. Tol touched her shoulder, and Riella pulled away, covering her beaded nipples, further proof that her schen might win. The last thing she wanted was to give him enticement to intensify his quest to drag her to the contract table.

He held a robe out to her. "You'll be cold," he whispered.

Riella nodded, taking the robe and pulling it on without meeting his eyes. His solicitous attention to every facet of her pregnancy signs and detail of her comfort unbalanced her. He was a man of war—but perhaps this engagement was just another battle to be won to Tol; the weapons of choice were simply different.

She sank into one of the chairs and poured a cup of cool milk, hoping it would ease the squirming in her stomach.

Tol filled a plate and set it before her. She chanced a look at his face and dropped her gaze again. He confused her, unnerved her. His expression seemed to shift from concern to longing to an expression she never thought she'd see on him—uncertainty.

He hadn't made love to her properly since the tub, saying that he would only take that release again when they had reached an understanding about the contract.

As far as Riella was concerned, they already had.

Tol only wanted the contract for his child. She'd freed him from punishment by taking the blame with her father, and still he persisted. His child could be the only reason for his sudden reversal. He had come to her rooms again only when he realized she carried. Barring a contract, since there had been no Trial Moon, the baby was Riella's by law.

"You should eat," he suggested.

"I won't starve my baby, and I won't poison it either. I am not the monster you paint me." His certainty that she meant to use gola berry still stung. She'd never intended to give up this baby, and she wouldn't—not to gola berry and not to a contract with Tol.

"*Our* baby," he reminded her gently. "I know you won't. I was angry. I said things I didn't mean. I *will* convince you."

Riella stared into the cup, biting back tears. *Damn the pregnancy signs!* She'd never been the weepy, feminine type. Why did she have to start now, when she needed her wits about her so desperately?

"Riella?"

"I don't need you. You wanted freedom. I gave it to you. You needn't do this."

"Do you know what I was thinking when I was tied to your bed?"

"That's obvious, isn't it?" she snapped. "You wanted the contract."

"Yes. I did."

She shook her head. "Of course you did. I'm what every man wants—on the surface. It's when you find the woman behind the mask that you change your mind."

"I don't understand."

"Every man wants the princess, the daughter of Ro Ti—and everything that entails. It is Riella who is not palatable."

"Entails?"

"My beauty. My sensuality. My—"

"All of that is Riella."

"My throne," she concluded in a whisper. "Some hold over my father." Perhaps that was his reason for the contract. Either way, it was reason enough not to sign one.

"That is the point I balked on."

She scowled at his earnest look.

"Ask Ro. He wouldn't lie about something so elemental."

"Yes, he would. You must not know Ro very well. If it meant marrying me off and ensuring the future—"

"*Your* future. Do you have any concept of what will happen if he dies before you contract? Or if you contract with a weak man?"

"I am not the weakling he takes me for. I am not as sheltered as he believes. He excludes me, but I use the hidden corridors and stealth to learn what I want to know."

"He knows that. There are only two times in your life that he could not account for your whereabouts."

She pressed her fist to her womb miserably. "Perhaps it would have been better if he had known."

"No. It wouldn't."

"Because you feel you have a claim on me now." A tear escaped down her cheek.

"Because, while you were busy playing at schente, I got to know the real you, the Riella you hide from the rest of the world."

"It was an act. I played schente for you. There was

nothing of me in that." She lied, but the lie was easier than admitting that she had bared her soul to him.

"You weren't playing schente. If you were, you would have left me after that first time like a schente."

"I was in your debt. You wanted more."

"*You* wanted more," he countered.

"I won't deny that. You're very potent, very talented." *And the thought of leaving you tore me apart.* That was the part he didn't need to know.

"I saw what I wanted and took it. You craved that. Being a leader is tiring. You want me to take."

"Then why did I tie you to my bed?" she challenged, needing to deny how easily he read her.

"Besides keeping me from harming you when I learned the truth?"

Riella blushed at his insight.

"You wanted my trust. If I trusted you, I might stay. I forgot to trust you. I am sorry for that. I focused on the mask instead of the woman inside it, the woman I love."

"Love," she choked, shaking her head. "You took a schente to your bed. You don't love a schente."

"I told you that night that I wasn't treating you like any schente I'd ever had. I didn't bed a schente. I made love to Riella."

"No. You didn't. You don't even know me."

"I could. I want to. Already, I think I know you better than your father does."

"My father taught me to always trust your first gut reaction to a situation or person. Yours was to walk away."

"No. My first reaction was to make love to you all night long, to risk us both to try to find you when you left my bed, and to pine for you when I thought I couldn't have you."

"You pined horribly. So horribly that you jumped at the chance to bed a princess," she accused.

It was unfair to say it, but the itch inside was driving her mad. Riella mentally prepared herself for his retort that she had taken a schaen, pretending it was him. That would be the most logical path for him to follow, and angering him would push him away. Away was good.

She wrapped her arms around her stomach and tried to control her shaking. His proximity was making her body riot. If she could survive the next two days, it would be easier. Irin assured her that the schen is not as insistent when the male you love is not close. After the three days, Tol would be out of her rooms—out of the palace, if she could arrange it. She could persevere that long.

"As a favor to your father," he growled. Not the track she had expected, but he was angry. Angry was good.

"The look on your face when you saw me prepared for you was no favor to my father. But, you didn't know it was Riella. You saw only the princess." She could work with this track just as well.

"You're right—in a way. The restraint I showed was for the princess. Your beauty and sensuality are Riella, and those were what drove me to fall on you as I did. I didn't want your throne." He sighed. "When I saw you...When I was tied to your bed, I spent a lot of time comparing Riella and Deliya. Do you know what I discovered?"

She didn't answer. She wasn't sure she wanted to know. He wasn't angry. He should be angry at the things she was saying. Why wasn't he? The squirming in her stomach intensified. She pressed her forearms tighter to her abdomen, feeling light-headed.

"You were the same woman, but with one difference. Deliya was a woman I could never have. Riella was a woman I could."

"One woman interchangeable with another—that is the description of a faceless schente, someone to be used."

Tol was abruptly on his knees in front of her, his mouth on hers. He swallowed her cry of protest and the groan of acceptance that followed. She couldn't think for her schen. The itch and squirming melted into a firestorm of need. Tol pushed her knees apart, splitting her robe to her waist. He eased his hips between to push her legs wider around him.

Riella reached for the tie on his lounging pants, but Tol captured her wrists and brought her hands back to her side. His mouth left hers, blazing a trail along her chin to her throat. She dropped her head back as he teased the pulse point at the base of her neck with his tongue, capturing her musk.

"I will not use you, Riella. I will not use you for anything. When you wish me to make love to you, you need only ask. I have never simply used you."

He pushed away from her, leaving her aching for him. He was aroused. His cock strained against the silin of his pants.

Tol pushed a shaking hand through his hair and motioned to her plate.

Riella looked down at herself: her legs spread wide, bared to the waist, and her breaths coming in short gasps. She swept her robe together, closing her knees and feeling the traitorous ache and wetness all the more when her thighs touched. She wrapped her arms around her chest, shaking in reaction to his sudden withdrawl.

"Riella?"

She jumped up and headed for the door. Her father would end this. He had to end it. She could live with her schen if Tol were not pushing her to this madness at every turn.

The guards blocked her escape.

"Let me through," she growled at them.

A man with a colonel's insignia bowed his head to her, keeping his eyes slightly lowered, as the law required—which put his gaze even with her chest. "I cannot, Princess."

"I only wish to speak to my father. I order you to get out of my way."

"Many pardons, Highness, but my orders come from Ro Ti, personally. I cannot allow you to pass this point. If you wish to see your father, I am to send for him."

Riella pulled her hand back, intent on striking him. The colonel didn't flinch as she brought her hand around, but she didn't connect. Tol gripped her wrist, jerking her swing to a jarring stop.

"No, Riella. That is not the answer," he breathed in her ear. He looked up, pulling her into the hard muscles of his chest. "Our apologies, Colonel Vry. Would you like the colonel to send for Ro, Riella?"

She shook her head. "No. He will only side with you against me."

The realization hurt, but she knew it was true. Seeing her father and Tol share those knowing looks, plotting together against her, would be too much.

Tol kissed her temple. "In this case, you are right. Come eat now. If you'll excuse us, Colonel Vry."

The colonel offered a wide smile.

Men! Riella fumed at the male conspirators in her life.

"As you wish, General Tolerin. Princess Riella." He closed the door, as Tol lifted her away.

Tol didn't release her. Instead, he raised her captured hand and kissed the backs of her knuckles slowly. "These men protect you, Riella. They would give their lives for you."

She nodded, grimacing. Ro had always taught her to be kind to those who hold your back.

"I'm sure the colonel understands that your schen drives you, but it is poor repayment for his service when you strike him."

"I've never," she choked.

"I know. Soldiers talk about things like that. Benir was known for his heavy hand—"

"For me," she whispered. "He only raised a hand to the guards when he felt they were derelict in protecting me."

Tol kissed her hand again. "I didn't know that. Ro is a hard master, also when it comes to you, but you are typically known to be kind to those who serve you." He released her. "Come eat before you get sick."

The crawling sensation intensified as his arms left her. "I can't," she admitted, cursing her weakness again. Nothing had ever laid her as low as this one thing.

"Riella?"

"You're not the one with an itch in your nerves stealing your sanity," she snapped. "Your presence makes me crazy."

* * * *

Tol wanted to laugh out loud, but he bit it back to a snort of disbelief. Not making love to her was driving him crazy. She was so responsive, so sensual—and so skittish every time she found herself close to accepting him.

He could take her now. Her schen would make Riella hunger for his touch, but he didn't want her that way. If he took her now, it would only reinforce her belief that it was just sex between them. He had spent the last day walking a fine line with her, moving closer to convincing her that there was more than a mindless schen involved in what lay between them.

"You have to eat, Riella. Your pregnancy signs will only get worse if you don't."

She turned on him, her color high and her eyes those of a warrior. "Then leave me."

"Even if I wanted to, I can't. Colonel Vry will not let me pass either."

"You outrank him," she pointed out.

"And, you outrank me. Your father outranks both of us, and he gave the order. Who do you think Vry will listen to?"

She slid down the wall behind her, wrapping her arms around her stomach again. Tol crouched in front of her and touched her cheek. Riella closed her eyes and brushed her face against his hand, her skin warming as she planted a kiss in his palm.

"Riella, it doesn't have to be this way."

"It's my schen," she denied. "When the three days are ended and you leave, I won't feel this way."

"I'm not leaving at the end of the three days." He would do whatever he had to do to win more time from Ro.

Riella stroked her cheek against his hand like a kittle. "The agreement," she protested in a whisper.

"You love me."

"Other women have survived it."

"Why must you fight this?"

She opened her eyes, looking uncertain. "It is not enough for me to love you."

"What do you want from me?" He forced his voice to remain calm, though the frustration of trying to convince her of what she simply didn't want to see was wearing him thin.

Riella bit her lower lip. "Nothing."

"You do want something."

"An end to my suffering. When you leave—"

"No. There is something more."

"Nothing you can give."

"Trust me. I've told you how I feel."

She closed her eyes and sighed.

"Trust me. I've trusted you more than once."

She shook her head.

Tol nodded, ordering his muscles not to tense. "You really can't eat, can you?"

"No," she replied miserably. "The only time I don't feel like I'm going to be ill is—" She blushed and shot a wary look at him.

Tol pulled her into his arms, feeling warm with success. Riella sighed in relief as he passed by the bed and settled into the chair she had fled earlier. He gripped her hip when she made to bolt.

"What are you doing?" she asked.

He raised a piece of the lamor fish to her lips and painted the sauce over them like a cosmetic cream. "Helping you feed our son," he breathed.

"Son?" she exclaimed. "What makes—"

Tol popped the fish into her mouth, gratified that she didn't spit it back at him. "A daughter would suit me, but I knew 'son' would get a reaction out of you. You can't eat for the baby with your mouth clenched shut."

Riella rolled her eyes and chewed the food. Tol didn't give her time to argue with him. As she swallowed the fish, he brushed a slice of lizor berry over her chin. She shivered and closed her eyes. Tol raised the berry to her lips, and she sucked it off his fingers.

She groaned as he kissed her chin. He sucked the juice from it then her lips, his already erect cock screaming to taste her depths again.

"Tol?" Her eyes were half closed, her skin hot against his fingertips.

He picked up another slice of lamor. "More?"

Riella locked her eyes on his lips in longing, nodding mutely. Tol took a deep breath, reminding himself of his agenda. He could not lose control and take Riella again until she knew for sure what it meant.

He raised the lamor to her mouth. Riella wrapped her lips around his fingers, caressing her tongue over them as she sucked the fish deeper into her mouth. He watched her chew the tidbit, swallowing a cry of frustration. The muscles in his arms bunched, and he willed them to relax. Every instinct urged him to take her up on her offer. Tol pushed away visions of sating her schen—and himself with it—on the damned table.

"More?" he asked.

Riella nodded. He reached for the plate, but she wound her fingers through his and guided his hand away, capturing his gaze. The stark need in her eyes stole his breath. She pressed the hand she held to her thigh, caressing the taut muscles of his forearm.

"No, Tol. This."

She pulled his head to hers, nipping at his lower lip. Her eyes were slumberous and warm, pleading with him to finish what she'd started in the bed. The lure of her schen was always like this, but it wasn't enough. She had to make a conscious decision to accept him. She had to ask him to make love to her.

"What do you want, Riella?"

She nuzzled his lips again, avoiding what she knew he wanted. She wouldn't seduce him. He couldn't let her.

"Four words, Riella. Please say them."

"I want you, Tol."

Wrong four words. Mother Fion! She was the most stubborn woman he had ever met. "What do you want?" he repeated. He shifted her so she could feel the force of his arousal against the soft swell of her buttocks.

Riella gasped, rolling her head back against his arm, her breast brushing his chest through her robe. "Take me to bed," she pleaded.

The wrong four yet again! "Why?" Tol cupped her breast through the robe. "Tell me."

"I want you, Tol."

He captured her mouth, and Riella opened for him, mindless passion unleashed in his arms. Tol smoothed his hand down her stomach to the warm honey making her ready for him.

Riella cried out into his mouth as his fingers slid in her, his thumb teasing at her hood. *Come for me, Riella. Shatter in my arms.* Tol played at her body as she came untethered, as she went wild for him. She dug her nails into his shoulders, and he shivered in pleasure.

"Please, Tol. Anything. I want you."

He laid a kiss on her trembling lips. "Wanting me is

not enough. Trust me. Ask me to make love to you. Let me prove my love to you. Tell me what you want, and I will provide it for you."

Riella shook her head, the trembling that announced her mounting pleasure increasing.

"Come for me, Riella. Take what you need from me."

"I need you, Tol." Her eyes were fevered, pleading. "You can—"

"No!" He forced his voice to calm. "I told you I will not use you, and I will not be used by you. Trust me to make love to you. That is the only way I will take pleasure."

Her eyes widened. For a moment, Riella looked at him with such longing that he almost broke. The urge to turn her in his lap and plunge into her was nearly more than he could resist. He met her eyes, pushing her body toward climax ruthlessly, massaging the spot within her that made her breathless and wrenched cries of longing from her. He had to push her over soon, or he would give in to the urge. That he could not do.

Riella arched up into his hand and howled out her release. Tol ground his teeth as her inner muscles rippled around his fingers. She trembled in his arms.

It's not too late. You could take her. She'd welcome your length and sing to your climax. No, it wasn't too late. It was too early. Every hour, her need for more than loveplay grew stronger.

Though the stimulation would not release an egg, it would help her body prepare for the rigors of birth. While the mate she desired was nearby to fill the need, her body would demand what Riella was denying it.

She collapsed against his bare chest, weeping. Tol cursed her tears. Riella saw taking pleasure from him as weakness. She had always had strict control of herself and her surroundings. The force of her love-schen was uncontrollable.

He held her until she calmed, his fingers still encased in her heat. When she sat placid in his arms, he eased his hand away and smoothed her robe over her thigh.

"Can you eat now?" he asked.

Riella nodded.

"Good." Tol stood and set her in the chair. He turned toward the bathroom, needing to distance himself from temptation.

"Thank you, Tol." Her voice was a whisper.

"I would give you my blood, if you required it. I only need four words, Riella."

She didn't answer, but Tol was sure that she nodded her understanding.

CHAPTER SEVEN

Tol looked over her shoulder at what Riella was writing. It seemed to be a map of the grounds. "Planning your escape?" he teased.

"Giving you the map of the escape tunnels I promised. If I intended to escape you, I would not need to plan it with a written map."

He pulled a chair next to her, ignoring her barb. He surveyed her many notations of how the entrances could be found, danger factors and weather limitations. He resisted asking how she had learned that the tunnel behind the stable was unstable during a rainstorm. "What are those two marked areas outside the guard perimeter?" he asked.

"Kittle holes. If we felt we were being pursued, Benir and I would use one of these hidden caves we explored. We chose the two hardest to locate and with available water. He smuggled bottled stores, clothing and emergency supplies from the palace to stock them."

"Did you ever have to use them?"

She shivered.

"Cold?" Tol asked in surprise. The room was warm to discomfort for him. If she was still chilled, he would send for a doctor. Even with her pregnancy signs, the room should be warm enough for her. If it wasn't—He reminded himself not to invite troubles.

"No. The fire is warm enough."

Tol nodded, relaxing. "Did you ever have to use them—the caves?" he repeated.

"Not since Benir put the supplies in. At least, I haven't. Benir may have. I wouldn't know."

"The night he escaped?"

Riella nodded and bent her head over the map. He noted the slight tremor in her hand in unease.

"Why did you use them?"

"I imagine it was quite useful for him. After all, it was stocked with clothing and food, weapons and survival gear. Everything Benir needed to escape—except my help."

She avoided his question, he noticed. She hadn't used the caves *since* Benir stocked them. That indicated she *had* used one, perhaps before her cousin made them more functional, but she'd sidestepped his question twice.

"When did *you* use the Kittle hole, Riella?"

She paused, glancing at him out of the corner of her eye and focusing on the map again. "It is not important." Her voice was calm and unconcerned, a practiced response.

"It is." He shed his normal, light tone in favor of an edge of command.

Her pen stilled. Riella clenched it in her hand. "The day we brought the baby jaglin in." She smiled a wry smile. "That was a diversion for my father."

"To explain your long absence?"

"Yes. It was Benir's idea."

"Where were you?"

"Exploring." She twirled the pen between her fingers, staring at the gleaming metal cylinder. "And hiding." That last came too quickly, too decisively. Whatever came between exploring and hiding was what Tol intended to discover.

"Riella?"

"It is not—"

"It is," he insisted.

She closed her eyes and shivered again. "I killed a

man."

Tol sucked in his breath, momentarily at a loss for words. Of all the possible answers, that was not anywhere near the top of his list. "Tell me."

"Two men attacked us. They came from nowhere. We were young, seventeen and eighteen. They were older, battle-hardened and sure in a fight. Benir fought them both while I ran for the palace. One broke away from Benir. He had a hottel." She paused and turned her face to the fire.

"He caught you," Tol prodded.

Riella nodded. "Yes. He did. You can imagine what one of my father's enemies would think of capturing Ro Ti's daughter. My hair was in my mother's clips, but uncovered. There was no question who I was."

Tol fisted his hands in his lap, forcing air into his lungs. "He—had you?" He sent up prayers to Fion and Mag both that he was wrong.

"No," she replied weakly.

Tol let out a sigh of relief, thanking them for protecting the bold young woman he loved.

"He tried. He ripped at my blouse and trousers. I—wore a dagger then, behind my back beneath a sack that would hide it. While he was occupied with...I pulled it and killed him. I took the frontal artery in his hip and twisted. He was dead before he could wrestle the blade from my hand."

"Was that the real reason you didn't wear a dagger when you freed Benir?"

Riella nodded. A tear spilled down her cheek but she went on. "I heard a hottel and believed the other man had bested Benir. The cave was close. I hid. Since there was water, I bathed his blood off while I waited for my father's soldiers to find me. I knew Ro would leave no chance..."

"Benir found you?"

"Yes. Benir was on the hottel. He found my attacker and hid the bodies. He...I left my dagger on the man I killed when I fled. My father would have died in his heart had one of his soldiers reported that scene to him. It was too much like when he found my mother gone. Benir brought my dagger to me. He gave me his shirt to replace the one that was—" Riella wrapped her arm around her breasts, as if self-conscious, as if she were uncovered as she must have been that day.

She rushed on without completing the thought that disturbed her so. "The men had been poaching while they did whatever else they were there to do—spying would be my guess. They killed the mother jaglin. Sneaking her baby in and pretending our injuries were from handling it...Well, it worked." Riella managed another wry smile.

"You never told your father any of this?"

She winced. "No. It would have hurt him too much to no good purpose."

"You went outside again?"

"Never. Not without my father and the proper guards. Benir told me about the supplies in case I ever had need of a hiding place again." She laughed nervously.

"What is it?" Tol asked.

"I've never told anyone that." She met his eyes in the firelight and touched his cheek. "Why do you think that is, Tol?"

His heart pounded against his ribs. "Why do you think it is?"

Her lips brushed his, a gentle meeting of her body to his. "I love you," she breathed into his lips.

This was the way Tol wanted her to come to him, calmly, not in a haze. "Do you believe that I love you?"

"Yes."

"Do you trust me?"

"More than anyone."

"More than Benir?" Tol wasn't sure why he asked that. He had to know that she trusted him completely.

The heavy silin belt from her robe traced over his hand. "Completely." She nipped at his lower lip. "Make love to me, Tol."

Thank Fion! "If I do, we will have a contract. Ro will join us tomorrow."

"No."

Tol closed his eyes, cursing the hope that was crushed again and again.

"I still have a day to our confinement. Promise me that day before you return to your many duties."

He didn't meet her eyes. "And then you promise to sign the contract?"

"As long as my stipulations are met."

"Which are?" he asked warily.

"No campaigns. Defend our lands, but do not leave me to conquer as my father did all those years."

"Agreed." Prying him from her bed to defend would be difficult enough.

"I will be equal ruling partner. Military decisions are yours. Welfare of our people will fall to me."

"Agreed. It is one of your strengths."

"I will have complete fidelity from you. My schaen have been disbanded. You will not take mistresses or schente while I live. The penalty is loss of our children to me and banishment."

Tol swept her astride his lap, pressing her hips down to nestle his cock to her. Riella leaned her cheek to his shoulder, her lips pressed to the well of his musk and her hand splayed over his heart. He bit back a curse. She knew how she was tempting him. She had to know it.

"I have no wish or need for other women. You will not take other men," he growled.

"And the penalty?" she breathed.

"He will die. You—will spend a week tethered to our bed, relearning who owns you. You will be my only schente, Riella. You will be my life, my love and my bride."

"The mother of your children?" she teased, straightening to meet his eyes.

"Would that please you?"

"If I say yes, may I have a lizor berry tea before my nap tomorrow?" Her eyes glittered.

"Hmm. I will consider that as a possibility, but we may have to negotiate for it. Then we are agreed? I will notify Ro tomorrow. We will be joined the following day. Agreed?"

"Agreed."

Tol laughed in the release of his bottled stress. "You place yourself in my hands?" he whispered.

Riella smiled and grazed her fingernail over his nipple. "As I did that first night."

Tol groaned, taking her mouth slowly, deeply. Riella's calm fled in favor of the burning need of her schen. He gathered her hands together between them, wrapping the silin belt around her wrists and knotting it without looking.

"Too tight?" he asked.

Riella shook her head.

He led her to the bed, using the belt as he would reins while leading his war-buck. He smiled at the sight of the red curls above her mound framed in the swaying edges of her robe. Riella raised one knee to slide onto the bed, but Tol lifted her and laid her in place. She gasped as he knotted the belt to the spindles of her headboard.

Tol spread her robe to frame her body. He gazed at her choc nipples, tightening into hard points for him. Riella tipped her hips, offering her deep red core, wet with her honey, for his approval. He ran his fingers over her folds, fighting back the urge to play the uncontrolled master he had when they reached his room. She deserved more than a rushed encounter.

He brought his fingers, slick with her musk and honey, to her nipple. Riella shuddered, her eyes wide as he painted her with her own juices. He took the nipple in his mouth, licking her sweet essence from the rigid peak she forced deeper into his mouth, groaning as her musk ignited his arousal into a roaring conflagration. He suckled her hard; and Riella cried out, thrashing beneath him as he released her. Tol smiled as he repeated the experience with the other nipple.

When he liberated her, leaving one final lick across her sensitized flesh, her eyes were intense, nearly crazed, and her hair fell across her cheek from her thrashing. Her lips trembled. "Release me," she pleaded in a wavering voice.

Tol chuckled, nudging her thighs wide around him as he rose to his knees. "I don't think so, Riella. I told you what I intended. Do you remember?"

Riella glanced down her body, shaking her head in denial. "Release me," she repeated.

"You are mine."

Tol lowered his mouth slowly, savoring the play of emotions on her face. Shock warred with fascination, arousal, and stark hunger. He blew a puff of air over her core, and she ground her teeth against the sensations washing over her.

"No man has ever tasted you, have they?" He planted a kiss on the fiery curls and ran his tongue in a lazy circle through them.

Riella shook her head fiercely. Tol expected that. She may enjoy sex, but Riella had always demanded complete control until he came into her life. A position that put her pleasure largely in a schaen's hands would not be something she would seek.

He flicked his tongue inside her. She bowed up, driving him deeper into her. Tol didn't retreat in the least, taking her to the edges of climax. Riella pulled at her bound hands, her muscles tensing.

"Please," she gasped. "Release me." She was close. Her flavor was a heady mix of musk and spice. Her head came up to watch him. "Tol!"

He startled. Her ragged cry wasn't one of completion. Riella was in a panic, pulling against her bonds, her eyes wide and locked on a spot over his shoulder.

Tol turned an instant too late. Startling colors accompanied a searing pain, and darkness swept over him as silin brushed his cheek.

* * *

Riella opened her mouth to scream, but the man clapped his hand over the lower half of her face.

"Shhh. Riella, it's me." Benir's voice was something between a whisper and a growl. He turned his face toward the light from the desk and the fire as if reassuring her.

She shook her head fiercely, trying to work his hand free. He clamped down harder, most likely mistaking her attempts as lack of recognition.

Her eyes moved to Tol, and she stifled a sob at the thin trail of blood winding down his temple. He was still breathing. *Thank Fion and Mag, he's still breathing.* Benir must not have aimed his blow to kill.

Benir misinterpreted her sob and scowled at Tol. "He can't hurt you, Riella. I'm here to help."

She shook her head, frustrated with his lack of understanding. She had to get him out of here and get help for Tol, preferably getting out of her silin bonds somehow along the way.

Benir pulled at the belt. "Len's dungeons," he growled. "The knots have pulled tight." He released her mouth.

Riella sighed in relief. "Benir, get out of here."

"Not without you."

"I'm not leaving, but you are."

He looked at her in disbelief. "Are you drugged?"

"No. I'm not. Get out of here before I have to save you again." *And Tol certainly won't help me save him this time.*

Benir shook his head and went to her winter cabinet. He pulled out her boots and cloak. He sliced the silin belt with his dagger and scowled at the tighter knots close to her hands. "I'll get that off when we're safe."

"Benir, I am going to say this just once more. I don't want you captured, but if you don't leave, I am going to scream for the guards while you are still here."

"I am not leaving you. This is my fault."

"He is my husband, Benir."

Benir scowled at Tol again, looking as if he wished to slit the general's throat. She swallowed hard at that. This wasn't like Benir. What drove her cousin? He pulled her legs around to ease the boots over her feet, and Riella kicked him away. He gave her a look of exasperation.

"Do not make me render you unconscious, Riella."

"I'm not going. Leave me."

Benir was on her before she could scream, his hand locked over her mouth again. "I will heal what I do. I promise," he assured her. "I cannot leave you with him."

* * * *

Riella groaned at the chill in the air and started to pull the cover further over her body. She opened her eyes in confusion. Her hands were bound? Why was there a jaglin fur wrapped around her? Why was she rocking slowly?

Benir looked down at her with a lopsided smile. "Feeling better?" he asked.

She brought her hands up into his chin. Benir fumbled, managing to turn her as she fell from his arms so she landed upright. Riella bolted as she found her feet, but he caught her after only a few steps. She never thought she'd see the day that she would be gratified to note that she had drawn blood on her cousin.

His face bobbed before her, trying to catch her eyes while she frantically searched for some clue of where he'd taken her. The terrain was dotted with hearty brush; there were no signs of habitation. They were on foot, and her pregnancy signs hadn't incapacitated her yet. They had to be close, past the rise that blocked the view of the palace, away from the soldiers' quarters and fields, somewhere near the cliffs, maybe five stride out from the east wall. *He was taking her to the Kittle holes!* She turned her head, searching out the cliff face that should lie behind her.

Benir grasped her chin and forced her eyes to his. "What is the matter with you?" he demanded.

She wrenched away from his hand. "You broke into my room, knocked both my husband and myself unconscious, and abducted me; and you want to know why I'm upset?" she shrieked. Riella swung her head around, trying to get her bearings in the darkness. She caught sight of the crag in the cliff side and pushed him away, turning toward the nearest open entrance back into the palace.

Benir took her by the shoulders. "You don't have to go back," he assured her.

"Yes, I do. Even if I wouldn't freeze to death out here, my husband is unconscious on our bed."

"I heard about your so-called marriage," he growled. "Why would you go back to him?"

"Heard what?" she asked, pulling out of his hands again and heading for the cave that would take her into the ammo station.

He matched her, his hands fisted at his side. "Ro gave you to a soldier when he learned that you helped me escape. He locked you in with him and allowed him to take you." Benir tried to clear the gravel from his voice. "Don't go back to him. Not for me."

Riella stopped and stared at him, her breath coming in little white puffs on the winter wind. His face was a study in pure fury. Benir was actually told that Ro had done that to her—and believed it.

She touched his cheek. "Oh, no. Benir, why would you believe that?"

She shivered, her body rebelling at the bitter cold.

With only her open robe and cloak between her and the winter wind, she wasn't sure how long she would last.

"I heard you with my own ears. I heard you beg that rutting beast to release you three times, and he refused. He tied you down to take you, Riella."

"Oh, Benir! Haven't you ever played at love?" She grimaced. *Probably not.* Benir had always been too serious for his own good. "Now take me back please. I...My pregnancy signs do not deal well with this cold."

He stilled. His eyes narrowed, panning down her body to her lower torso. "I heard...Swear to me that I was lied to." The desperation in his voice made her heart stutter.

"You were, Benir. By the Mother, Fion Herself, you were."

He looked around warily. "Then we have to leave here quickly."

"Why?" Panic settled in her stomach. She shifted from foot to foot, the metallic taste flooding her mouth stronger than she'd tasted it in five years.

"If I've been lied to, a traitor is coming for you."

She leapt to Benir's side as a dark laugh cut the silence around them, allowing him to ease her to his back as his dagger came up.

"Why Benir...I am not the one named traitor."

Riella turned her head fearfully toward the second man that evening who strode from the darkness.

Chapter Eight

Tol forced his eyes open. He stared at the ragged scrap of silin still tied to the bed in dismay. A rust-colored stain marred the pure white linens of the bed. It wasn't his own blood. This stain was higher, just below the pillows. Tol pushed to his feet and staggered to the hidden door. It was bolted from the outside again.

"Guards," he bellowed, heading for the cabinet and pulling out his boots.

Two young officers rushed into the room; their eyes widened at the sight of Tol.

"You, wake Ro. You, send for my war-buck."

The one ordered to Ro bolted.

The other gaped at him in shock then panned his eyes over the bed. "The Princess?" he asked.

Tol paused in pulling on his tunic. "Taken," he growled.

"But the doors—"

"The king's corridor was bolted. What idiot thought that meant it was safe to leave unguarded?"

The young soldier blushed. "Colonel Vry, General Tolerin. He ordered a re-organization of manpower just this afternoon."

Tol snapped his head around, a heavy hottel-hair sweater in his hand. "This afternoon?"

"Yes, sir. He—"

"Get that hottel. Now!" Tol pulled on the sweater and grasped his weapons belt.

"Merciful Mag, Tolerin. What—"

Tol didn't look at him, giving Ro time to compose himself in peace. He strapped on his belt and grabbed his cloak.

"Where is my daughter?" he croaked.

"Taken. You had the exits you know of guarded as I asked?"

"Yes. Of course."

The king's voice was weak, distracted. This wasn't the Ro they needed. This was a man lost in memories of a stolen wife. Tol cringed at that. It was all too easy to understand his preoccupation, but it was counterproductive. Riella needed them both.

"Have your guards been sent away?"

"What? No. Why would they be?"

Tol nodded. "I am heading to the cliff face, twenty stride south of the crag. That is where you will find me when you are ready to join me."

"Who did this?" Ro demanded in a shaking voice.

"Vry. You wanted to know who the true traitor was, the one who implicated Benir. Now we know."

"Give me five minutes."

"In five minutes, I will be halfway there. Bring clothing and warm blankets. This cold will be hard on her."

He folded Riella's map into his pocket and headed for the door. He winced at the lost expression on Ro's face. The king stood with the bloodied sheets clutched in his hands, his breathing ragged, pale. Tol wondered if this was what Ro had looked like when he found Della taken.

"Dress, Ro. I may need your help to get her back alive."

Ro threw the sheets down and nodded, the fierce battle-ready expression Tol knew well on his face. He strode into the corridor, barking orders as he went.

Tol followed in his wake until Ro turned into his rooms then jogged past the open door, taking the stairs at the center juncture of the palace three at a time. Soldiers scattered as he sped down all three flights, shouting orders to every colonel and captain he encountered. They scrambled to call out the companies that would ride with Ro. Tol was leaving without accompaniment. The king would follow in force; speed was most important now.

He mounted his war-buck at a full run. Braek knew Tol's battle cry and grip meant a break-neck run. The war-buck, a lead male hottel fully twice the size of a mare, tossed his head and bolted for the gates that were already opening.

He didn't slow until he reached the path to the Kittle hole closer to the east guard tower and the ammo station. That was the only entrance Ro didn't have enough information on to guard. Benir would go that way.

The stars and moon were bright, granting Tol a wide field of vision. He was ten stride out when he saw the body. He reined in Braek and dropped to the ground, his dagger out. He doubted that it was a trap, but a good soldier never took chances.

He turned the body over, noting the wound that killed the younger man. It was a vicious kill, not one of the silent killers or the quick deaths. Vry had taken his stomach, likely slicing several vital organs with the twist of his blade. It was a style some of the more bloodthirsty Lengar used in battle, a painful death that not even the most skilled doctors could repair, a death typically reserved for a man's most hated enemies.

Signs of battle marred the stiff clay. Vry had left on a small male hottel, though he fought on foot. Riella had fled on foot, running full out, her gait uneven as if hobbled in some manner. Tol shivered at the evidence that the prince tried to follow them toward the cliff face.

"Even in death," he muttered.

He pushed away useless speculations of whether Benir had willingly helped Vry and been betrayed or had been tricked into his part in stealing Riella. There was no time to waste; facts were more important than suppositions. Tol returned to his investigation of the body, needing every solid fact he could garner.

The body still retained a bit of warmth. Assuming the usual life expectancy after such an injury, Benir had been attacked well over an hour earlier.

He stood abruptly. "He's had an hour to find her." Tol remounted and sped off toward the cave. If Mag was kind, Riella made it to safety.

* * * *

Riella sifted through the boxes of supplies. "Where would he put it?" she muttered. "It has to be here."

She had never taken her mother's dagger back to the palace. Riella couldn't bear to look at it after she used it to kill. Benir had promised to keep it safe for her. She cursed the darkness inside the cave, but a fire or lantern would pinpoint her location for Vry.

She stifled a cry of success as her hand closed on the emi-beaded sheath. She drew the blade and sawed through the silin around her wrists. She dug into the box again; knowing Benir's organizational skills, all of her clothing would be in there as well. Riella dragged on a pair of winter trousers that fit her much better now than they had when she was seventeen, yanked on heavy stockings and pulled her boots back on as quickly as she could.

She went still, a sweater in her hand, barely

456

breathing in fright. Was that a noise? She snatched the dagger back against her chest, listening to the night sounds outside. There were no stone slides or footfalls warning of Vry's approach—or Benir's, though she held out little hope that her cousin would best the colonel of her personal guard. Ro had chosen Vry for only two reasons, his skill in battle and his loyalty.

She grimaced at that. As far as she knew, her father had only trusted one other who had proven to be a traitor in all his years as king. That man had cost them her mother's life. She had to stay hidden until Ro found her. Putting him through such a trial again was inconceivable.

Riella relaxed and dropped her cloak. She fingered the hilt of the dagger in indecision, finally slipping the sheath into the back of her trousers and clipping it to the waistband. She wouldn't be without it again, but she wouldn't announce that she carried it, either.

She pictured Benir, stripped to his uniform pants and boots, as he trained her with the abinatine, his face set in harsh lines. *"Surprise is your greatest asset, Riella. Your mother killed, but she had been trained to it from birth. Ro has given you only the most basic instruction. Never let them know when you carry a blade. Draw it in stealth and kill in the most expedient way you can."*

She nodded. "I will do you proud," she vowed. She hadn't carried a blade save for ceremony in five years. Vry would know that. He wouldn't expect her to be armed. That would work to her favor in battle.

Peeling off her robe, she pulled on the oversized sweater and covered it with her winter cloak. It was the cloak of a princess, the fur of a young jaglin inside and out, soft and beautiful but not heavy enough for mountain wear. Riella resolved to commission a more practical cloak—jaglin backed with hottel—when she was safely back in the palace.

Unwilling to continue searching through boxes and risking detection by the noise she made, she caught several handfuls of the trickle of water overflowing the ice dam somewhere deep in the rock. Her fingers were stiff and unresponsive when she was done, but her thirst was slaked.

Riella sank to a natural rock seat jutting from the back wall and pulled her legs to her chest, encasing herself in her cloak to conserve as much heat as she could. She couldn't stop shivering. Her pregnancy signs left her ill prepared to handle such an assault to her system.

But she had to persevere. There was no knowing how long her wait would be. If Benir had triumphed over Vry, he would have come for her by now. Tol had her map, but the gods only knew how desperate a blow to the head he took. Even if the guards realized something was amiss and called for Ro, her father would have no idea where she would have run. The search would be slow and painstaking.

She looked at the boxes in longing. The supplies would be nearly frozen, and she could not risk a fire to thaw them. It would be a race—whether cold or hunger drove her to dangerous extremes first. She buried her face in the soft fur inside her cloak to conserve what little body heat remained.

* * * *

Riella turned her head, baring her ear to the frigid middle-night air. She waited, ignoring her growling stomach and chattering teeth, listening for the sound that had roused her from sleep to repeat. She decided it was a fragment of a dream and let her eyes drift shut.

It came again, a skating of rocks on the trail outside. She held her breath and waited, her heart thumping loudly in her ears. Soon enough, she would know if it was friend or foe. Thank Mag, it was winter. At least the jaglin were hibernating, though they preferred the lower caves even in the hot summer months.

A bright light shone in her eyes, and Riella blinked hard, shuttering them against the glare. She counted the heartbeats with a sinking sensation in her stomach. There was no cry to other soldiers announcing that she had been found, no exclamation of relief from Tol or Ro.

She bit back a vicious curse. "Hello, Vry."

His laughter echoed off the frozen stone. "Ever the princess," he commented. "Except in your bed—or General Tolerin's. I trust Benir killed him for his alleged trespasses against you?"

Riella didn't answer. She had no idea what Benir had told him. Worse, if Vry believed Tol was dead, she had an advantage she wasn't about to give up. Apparently, he wasn't afraid of facing Ro, but no sane man wanted to face both Ro and Tol.

Vry took three steps toward her, crossing half the distance separating them. "Missing your mate, Riella?" he taunted.

"More than you can imagine."

"Which of your drives vexes you most? You know that I would gladly appease all of them for you."

His suggestive tone made a sick swirl the likes of the Great Vortex in her stomach. Had she a meal to lose, Riella had no doubt that she would have lost it. "I want nothing from you."

"A pity. I assume you've dressed for travel."

She grumbled a curse her father would frown on, wishing she had the excuse to waste time even as she thanked Fion that he wouldn't watch her dress—at least not yet. If he anticipated a sexual relationship with her, that unsavory threat could well become reality.

"Come then."

"What is your plan, Vry? Killing me won't win you anything. I have three noble relatives in line for the throne after Benir. There would be civil war if I died, and who would back you?"

"I don't intend to kill you. If I meant to do that, my men could have done so years ago. Of course, they did fail in the tasks I set them."

"Which were what, precisely?" She had to waste as much time as she could.

"Kill Benir, among other things. I'm certain you remember the day well. It really doesn't surprise me that I had to end him myself. Plots of death and false accusations of treason—The man has the most uncanny ability to escape. Or, should I say—he had until tonight?" He laughed heartily at his own dark humor.

Riella bit back a sob for Benir. Her cousin had never wanted anything but her safety and happiness. He died for her! For what? "And?" she persisted; she refused to let Vry see her weakness.

"Win you as my bride, of course."

"How?" She had thought she was beyond shivering, but her body proved her wrong again.

"Once my men had you, and I chased them off and returned you to Ro; he would have given me anything I asked for. I would have asked for you."

"Had me?" she asked, feeling faint at the implications. *Surely, he hadn't ordered—*

"You don't think the men you and your cousin killed found you by chance, do you? You were so beautiful, trapped beneath him." His voice deepened, though Riella couldn't decipher if it was in arousal or warning.

"Your plan now?" she croaked out.

"I plan to claim you in conquest," he replied.

Riella pressed her back to the wall in shock. "You can't. My grandfather did away with that barbaric custom," she protested. "Taking a woman unwilling is punishable by death."

"Many people still consider it a valid path to the throne."

She pressed her hands to her stomach, feeling light headed and nauseated.

"Tolerin's son?" he taunted. "I have a doctor waiting to remedy that. A weak injection of gola extract directly followed by a strong one of olum and triclum—You'll expel the baby without trauma and with very little pain. I am assured that you will barely remember the ordeal. Since it is so early in your term, you will be ready for me in less than two weeks." His voice turned hard. "Now stand and come with me."

Riella staggered to her feet, her legs shaking and her entire body numb and icy. She couldn't let this happen. There had to be something she could do.

She took a single step toward him and collapsed.

* * * *

Tol pulled his dagger slowly, stamping down his

fury. He hadn't heard much of Vry's plan from his own mouth, but Riella's panicked protest told him all he needed to know. "Conquest," he grumbled. There would be no conquest, whether it would work or not.

The system was an ancient one, rarely used in recent history. In the Early Warlord Period, when far-flung villages could take months to reach, a rival lord would often kill all the heirs save one daughter and take her to his bed, planting his heir. Her father would be faced with the choice of allowing the interloper to kill her, thus leaving himself without heirs, or conceding succession to his daughter's mate. A wise warlord attempted conquest with maidens whose fathers were likely to choose the latter. Once the father made his choice, he was bound by his word to leave them in peace—unless he was Lengar. One did not play games at conquest with the Lengar.

Weary of war and of seeing the violated bodies of Fion's Daughters, Kor, Ro's father, had done away with the system of taking a woman in conquest as a way to the throne.

"The rape of a woman is abhorrent and not to be tolerated."

Tol still remembered standing in the crowd the day the old king made that announcement; his mother had cried in joy.

Even if he hadn't decreed it, Tol would die before he let Vry kill their child and take Riella unwilling.

"Get up," Vry barked at her. There were faint sounds of movement. "Len alive! What else can go wrong? I should have known your pregnancy would slow me down."

Tol sent up a prayer to Fion that Riella would be all right. He hadn't checked the time when he left the palace, but she must have been in this cold for hours.

"Get up," Vry repeated in a growl. There was a slide then a clatter, indicating something metal hitting the ground.

Riella cried out weakly, and Tol threw caution to the winds. He launched into the cave, taking in the sight of Vry—standing over her, gripping a handful of her hair—in pure volcanic anger.

"Release her," he demanded.

Vry yanked Riella up as a shield by his grip on her hair, pointing his dagger at her hip. His eyes challenged from over her shoulder, the only visible part of him between Riella's taller body and his cap. "There are other ways to take your son, Tolerin."

Riella's eyes met Tol's in the dim light of the overturned lantern, pleading for his help. He nodded, his chest easing. She wasn't as incapacitated as she pretended to be, but she was still hurting.

"Leave her, and you may live to fight another day," he offered.

Vry laughed harshly. "I think not. You and Ro will both bow before me for love of Riella and whatever child her body harbors."

Riella shivered. "He wouldn't," she breathed. "No man who loved me would let you do this to me."

Vry pressed his blade deeper, making her shy from him. "To save your life, Tolerin will. You see Riella, if I do not proceed, I will die. Now or later, I will die. My only safety is in your continued presence in my hands."

"I would rather be dead," she spat.

She shifted away, and her cloak swirled around her body as Vry pulled her closer to his chest. Tol held his breath, his eyes passing over a strange movement beneath her cloak then moving on so as not to point it out to his enemy. What was she doing?

He shifted his eyes back to Vry, as the traitor smiled his victory.

"You might," Vry taunted her. "Tolerin and your father would prevent that death at any cost, and it is the men I must deal with. You, I will simply take."

Patches of color rose high in her pale cheeks. "Simply take? You think it will be that easy? You, better than anyone, know I do not submit—ever."

Tol looked at her in surprise. What was she saying? How would Vry know something like that?

Vry laughed heartily. "Ah...yes. And we both know you have refused to carry a weapon since then, don't we, Riella? What would entice you to take up arms again?"

"That is a question you do not wish to ask of me," she warned.

Riella met Tol's eyes with a fierce look that made his stomach swim. He couldn't risk signaling her to stand down. Whatever she had planned, he would have to let her do it and back her any way he could.

Vry released her hair and found her right wrist through her cloak. His laugh echoed around them. "You seek to make me believe you are armed? We both know better."

Riella turned abruptly around his blade on the pivot point of that wrist. Vry screamed in rage and pain, pushing her from him as his dagger clattered to the ground.

Tol caught her as she staggered toward him, guiding her beneath his arm so that he could defend her and sweeping Vry's dagger into the far corner beyond the traitor's reach.

She shook against him, her legs no longer

supporting of her body weight. He wound his arm around her as her legs crumpled; fighting with Riella held to his body was infinitely safer than having her underfoot, though he would rather have her run as Benir doubtless had.

Tol watched in amazement as Vry crumpled, trying to stem the flow of blood from the deep leg wound that had slashed the outer length of his thigh muscle and severed his frontal artery.

Riella's eyes were narrowed, her voice edged in ice that made the winter air feel warm by comparison. "You thought I was beautiful when I was assaulted by your man. You found my screams arousing. Did you find me alluring when he died on my blade? Do you find me alluring now that you will die on it?"

Tol sheathed his dagger and pulled her to his chest. "I will not take your killing blow," he assured her.

She nodded, hiding her tears from Vry as she sheathed her dagger without cleaning it, her shaking so severe she barely completed that small task. She buried her face against Tol's chest.

He sighed as he enveloped her in his arms. "You have two options, Vry. You can let off the pressure and die quickly, or you can wait for Ro's soldiers and die slowly. I care not how you die as long as you go about it soon."

He turned, lifting Riella into his arms, and left Vry behind, shouting curses at their retreating backs. He carried her to Braek, set her on the forward hump, and mounted the buck with a sigh, drawing her into his lap. "Easy, Braek. No charge this time."

Braek snorted his displeasure, but he set off at a slow lope. Riella burrowed against Tol for comfort and warmth. He didn't speak. He wasn't sure he was capable of more than screaming out his fury that his own blade hadn't taken Vry.

CHAPTER NINE

Ro looked up from where he crouched beside Benir's body at the sound of their approach. His expression eased. Tol pulled Braek to a halt next to him and nodded in answer to his unspoken question that Riella would recover well.

"Vry?" Ro barked.

Tol smiled. "I left him with a choice to either bleed to death quickly or die at your hand." He passed the map to him.

He scanned it in surprise. "This isn't like you, Tolerin. I would have thought you would take a decisive death blow."

His smile fled. "The blow was not mine to take." He glanced at Riella by way of explanation.

Ro paled and pushed the map at a captain behind him. "Your squad will follow this to the traitor. If he lives, bring him to me. Colonel Bek, have my doctor and my daughter's servant-sister meet us in her rooms when we arrive. The rest travel with us."

The young captain mounted and turned away. Bek shouted his buck up to a run; both soldiers were out of earshot in the time it would take to pull a dagger, no doubt fearing Ro would do just that if they tarried.

Tol nodded as Ro mounted his war-buck and guided the animal to his side. The soldiers fanned out in battle formation around them, but they didn't move out immediately. The king wanted information. No one could have mistaken that.

Ro's jaw was tight in fury. He didn't look at Tol as he spoke. "Tell me."

"He planned to take her in conquest. He has a

doctor nearby prepared to kill our child by injection."

Ro shuddered. "Captain Finn, Captain Eddel," he barked. "Take your squads when we reach the gates and search for Vry's troops and his doctor. They can't be far, most likely on the other side of the cliffs. Take the traitors however you can." He looked back to Tol. "Why was the blow Riella's?"

"Vry was using her as a shield. He didn't know she had a weapon until it was too late."

Ro nodded. "Benir was helping him?"

Tol shrugged. He doubted it, but he couldn't say anything for sure.

"No," Riella offered in a sleepy voice. "Benir was tricked, told that I was given to Tol unwilling. He tried to stop Vry. Benir died a hero. It was Vry who arranged the false evidence against Benir. He also tried to have him killed when—when we were children."

Ro took a calming breath. "Why?"

Riella didn't answer.

Tol wrapped the edges of his heavier cloak around her to help keep her warm. "Benir would go to any lengths to protect Riella. Did you know that he prepared Kittle holes for her use?"

"No. I didn't. She ran to one?"

"Yes. She's clothed. She may have eaten."

"No," Riella interrupted miserably. "Couldn't risk a fire. It would have revealed me to him."

Ro raised an eyebrow. "I never ordered her trained for battle tactics," he noted. "Where did she learn this?"

"Benir," Tol answered, knowing he was correct even without Riella's nod of agreement.

Ro asked no more. He directed his war-buck to quarter speed with his legs, his hands laid on his thighs, a move Tol had never seen perfected by another soldier. They rode in silence, passing the distance to the palace gates lost in their own thoughts—Tol in visions of revenge on all those who conspired against Riella and Ro in facing whichever of Len's creatures tortured him at moments like this.

Finn and Eddel veered off with their companies at the outer wall, breaking to a full run before the rest were fully through the gates. Military precision at its finest was Ro's base expectation of anyone within the palace.

The palace was a warren of activity; servants scattered as Tol carried Riella to her rooms, settling her beneath heavy quilts on linens that had been changed in their absence. He ended Irin's annoying fussing by sending her for food while he healed her various bruises and the doctor checked their babe.

Ro paled at the blood on Riella's hands. He uttered a string of harsh curses, pushing a shaking hand through his hair and steadying himself against her cabinet, as if the sight of his daughter fresh from a battle was more than he could bear.

She pulled the jewel-encrusted sheath from behind her and offered the weapon to her father without meeting his eyes. Her voice was a whisper in the suddenly silent room. "Would you—see this cleaned for me, Father?"

Ro lurched across the room and took it from her hand. He examined it carefully, tears in his eyes. "This is your mother's abinatine. You lost this years ago."

Riella shook her head.

Tol sighed. "She never lost it. Benir hid it in the Kittle hole for her."

"Why this dagger? Benir could have put any number of weapons in her bastion. Why her mother's blade?"

Riella stood and headed for the bathroom, her eyes cast down. "I need to bathe," she noted in a distracted voice.

Ro's eyes widened. He turned the sheath, scanning it for some clue to the reason for her withdrawl. "What are these old stains, Riella?" he asked warily.

"They are nothing." She paused in the bathroom doorway, startled as someone pounded at the outer door.

Ro nodded to the doctor to open it.

The captain Ro had sent to find Vry entered and bowed deeply. "The traitor was dead when we reached him, Majesty."

"Good," Ro spat.

"He left a rather cryptic message behind."

"Read it."

The captain looked from Ro to Tol and paled. "As you wish, Majesty. It says: Your screams are arousing, but you are always most beautiful when you kill."

Riella gagged and launched into the bathroom, slamming the door behind her.

Ro strode to the captain and pulled the scrap of paper from his hand. "Leave us," he ordered. "All of you, leave us."

The captain and doctor bowed quickly and left without question, reading his fury.

He turned back to Tol, waving the paper. "You know what this means?" he demanded. He raised the stained sheath. "And this?"

Tol nodded. "She told me the tale early tonight, but even Riella didn't realize Vry was involved at the time."

"Tell me."

"The day she found her baby jaglin—"

Ro scowled. "The last time she disobeyed me and left the palace with Benir. She evaded her guard and disappeared for hours. I was furious with her."

"Was Vry her guard?"

Ro paled. "Darkest Underworld," he cursed.

Tol nodded. "I thought as much. He set two of his men—mercenaries on their path with specific orders."

"What orders?"

"Kill Benir and—" Tol took a deep breath. "And rape Riella."

Ro fisted his hand around the dagger. "Those filthy mercenaries dared—" he stormed, his eyes wild.

"Did not succeed," Tol assured him, cutting off the rant building steam. "Benir killed one. The other...Riella killed him as he tore at her clothes." He waved a hand at the dagger. "With her mother's blade. She hid in the same Kittle hole she used tonight, waiting for you or Benir to take her home. Her cousin outfitted the caves in case she ever had need again."

"She never told me," Ro noted sadly.

"Riella didn't want to hurt you. After her mother—"

"Deliya has nothing to do with this," he insisted. He dropped into a chair, burying his face in his hands.

Tol swallowed hard. Deliya was the name of Ro's bride? Ro had always called her by a pet name, Della. Riella used her mother's name when she played schente? This was not a story he would ever share with his king.

Ro didn't notice his upset. "When she returned with the jaglin...I struck her, Tol. I never had before, and I never have again. I was mad with worry, and I lost my composure. Even now, she shies from me when I'm angry. She didn't tell me because she was afraid I would hurt her for it. I told her how ungrateful she was

471

to risk her mother's fate...I wish I had never said it."

"She loves you, Ro. She loves you more than life. Trust me. Riella would do almost anything to save you pain."

Ro gave him a speculative look. "Even pretend to be schente?"

Tol grinned. "You know your daughter well. But never worry. Riella has always been precious to me, even when I believed she was schente."

"Then go to her. She needs you."

Tol nodded and stripped off his sweater and boots as he headed to the bathroom.

* * * *

Riella scrubbed her hands in the basin and started a bath, trying to ignore the conversation in the main room. She pulled off her clothing, sat on the top edge of the tub, and trailed her fingers in the scented water. She startled when her father roared out his protest that the mercenary she killed touched her, swallowing a lump of fear.

The door opened, and Riella jumped to her feet, expecting Ro to be standing over her, his eyes hot in fury. Tol stepped into the room, and she let out her breath in relief.

He shut the door and reached to the tie on the lounging pants he still wore. "May I join you?" he asked.

She nodded and turned to slide into the tub. "He knows?" she whispered, staring into the water.

"He does. He wishes he had known then. He would not have reacted as violently as he did if he had known. He regrets striking you."

"I know he does."

"But you always feared he would do it again?"

Riella shrugged. "I am not easy on my father's nerves. I am not the woman he feels I should be, the woman my mother would have raised. Reckless..."

Tol eased into the tub beside her and started rubbing a hand cloth over her back. Riella sighed and snuggled further into his chest, settling her knees over his thighs to be closer to him. His breathing quickened and his cock hardened against her hip.

He reached for her hands. One by one, he stroked the cloth over her fingers, cleaning the memory of Vry's blood from her. Riella chanced a look at him. He was tense, his eyes half-hidden from her. Just as when he had taken her in the tub a few days earlier, his feelings were impossible to gauge.

"You're angry," she guessed.

"Only that you chanced so much, but I know that you needed to."

Riella nodded. "Thank you for that."

Tol cracked a smile. "Of course, if you ever try something like that again, there will be a penalty for you."

"What penalty?"

He glanced at her then away. "I don't think you're in any mood to pay it," he decided.

Riella sobered. "Not being tied to our bed. I don't think I want to try that again too soon. Seeing you struck down..."

"I'm putting a latch on the room-side of that door," he promised gruffly.

She smiled. "What is my penalty?"

He lifted her, turning Riella so her legs straddled his thighs and her breasts pressed into his chest. "Do not tempt me," he growled.

"Is that the only penalty you know?"

He raised an eyebrow. "You prefer another?"

"Never." She reached to guide him to her entrance.

Tol groaned as she settled over him. "Are you feeling properly penalized?" he teased, bucking deeper into her.

"Not yet," she panted. "But I trust I will before much longer."

Not long at all. Fion! Her arousal was like a geela bird launching off a cliff. She fell hard and fast, her senses in a spin; and then she rose, soaring. Riella gripped Tol's shoulders, seeking an anchor. Instead, the additional contact increased her fervor.

Tol read her perfectly, murmuring endearments in her ear as he nipped at it playfully. He took her faster and harder.

Her vision sharpened, the lines of Tol's face as he fought back his climax for her suddenly beautiful and mesmerizing. He took her deep, roaring his loss of control as she threw her head back and screamed her release.

He groaned as his cock thickened in her, locking into the band of muscle at the entrance to her womb. Riella gasped, her body responding to his inner touch. How had she survived without this?

Tol's head came up as a thunder of footsteps approached. He pulled Riella into the shelter of his chest, though she scarcely cared that she was naked in his arms. The guards burst into the room and gaped in surprise.

"Captain," Tol barked, somehow maintaining dignity and calm while on display and locked in her body.

They turned abruptly to face the doorway. The captain cleared his throat. "Many pardons, General

Tolerin. We heard—His Majesty made it clear that we were to make no more assumptions tonight."

"Well done, Captain, but if you don't mind..."

"Of course, Tolerin. Your food awaits your leisure, sir."

"Dismissed."

Riella started giggling as the door closed. Tol granted her a mock fierce look that made her laugh harder.

"What a night," she managed. "We don't seem capable of finishing our lovemaking in peace."

"I will move a chest in front of the king's corridor and bolt the main door," he offered.

"Agreed—Prince Tolerin."

Tol scowled. "Must I be called that?"

"It comes with the contract."

He sighed. "I see why you dislike it so intensely."

Riella sobered. Benir had always hated it, too. "Tol, I'd like to ask something of you," she began nervously.

"Anything. You know that."

"Benir died to save me. What he did to you—"

Tol kissed her forehead. "I understand. He is forgiven his mistakes, because he only meant to protect you."

"It is more than that. If our baby is a boy, I would like to honor Benir."

He shot her a look of pure confusion. "It is your place to name our children," he reminded her.

"I would like to know that you will not resent it."

His smile spread. "I will agree on one condition."

"Yes?"

"If our child is a girl, would you consider naming her Deliya to honor the night we gave her life?"

Riella blushed. If Tol ever mentioned that fact to her

father, Ro would be livid.

"We will, of course, tell Ro that it is to honor your mother," he added, holding a chuckle in so hard that his throat bobbed with the effort.

She nodded in understanding. "And if it is a boy, I shall have to play at schente another night until we have a daughter. After all, my mother must have a namesake."

EPILOGUE

Abrin 14th, Ti 10-483

"A few moments more," Irin soothed Riella.

Ro watched nervously as Tolerin laid healing kisses on her neck. The young prince's bare chest was pressed to her back and his silin-clad legs cradled hers, his big hands splayed over her spasming womb through the silin sheet.

Riella nodded, her brow beaded in sweat. "My mother did this without healing?" she asked in disbelief.

Lera smiled. "It was unforgettable. Mother Deliya bore up in silence for hours to keep Jurel away—then out of pride. Her enemy would never hear her scream or beg."

"How could she?" Riella panted, groaning her thanks as Tol massaged the bundle of nerves in her lower back.

Irin eased her hands around the babe's head, helping the shoulders pass. "You were early, small compared to this young hottel you carry."

Ro held his breath, as the child slid free, coated in the slick of Riella's fluids. His daughter sighed in relief, sinking into her husband's arms.

Tol kissed her brow. "Now, that was a battle," he whispered.

Riella chuckled. "No. Battle will be you accepting the mother's fast."

Ro laughed at that. It was well known that Tol had little self-control where Riella was concerned. He remembered those days himself, the days when Della carried his child—and before she did. He was glad his daughter had found a true mate, a mate her mother would approve of, a mate who would last a lifetime.

Lera cleaned and wrapped the babe, while Irin delivered the birth parts and checked for damage, pronouncing Riella unharmed.

Lera handed the babe to Riella, smiling. "Your daughter," she announced.

Tol beamed as he touched his daughter's dark curls. "Deliya," he breathed.

"Deliya?" Ro asked, confused.

Riella blushed, shooting Ro a nervous look that set his battle awareness on high alert. She nodded. "Yes. Her name is Deliya."

"To honor Riella's mother," Tol explained a little too quickly.

Ro crossed his arms over his chest and cleared his throat, prepared to receive what was sure to be a very interesting story. Riella was, after all, her mother's daughter.

Bonus Read
Culdan

Conquest

Dedication

Brothers and sisters of the heart. I have a few, and you know who you are.

Note from Brenna:

Dear Reader,

In several books, especially the ones in the Era of Unification, I have talked about the despicable law that allowed a man to take a woman in rape and steal her father's lands by an antiquated law called "Conquest." As you might expect from me by now, I'm going to show you the other side of the coin. How does one use conquest to right a wrong? Join us and find out how something like this can be a force for good.

Happy reading!
Brenna

PROLOGUE

*Zor 25ᵗʰ, Li 10-125 The Era of the Keen Warlords
Gangir, a Lengar stronghold in Denia*

Nelik smiled. "Why would I do that, My *Lord*?" he taunted.

Culdan scowled at him. At sixteen, half a year Nelik's junior, Culdan loathed reminders that he was officially a lordling and named heir to Denal.

Nelik ducked Culdan's blow, dancing away across the white stone courtyard. He darted to the right, mindful to leave several body-lengths between himself and the closest columns, lest he find himself backed into a corner and at a disadvantage.

They were evenly matched, of course. How could one train and grow with another since the cradle and not be? It was unusual for either to land a blow when pitted in mock battle. To be honest, no other opponent had laid hand or blade on either of them for almost three years, even Denal's finest. Though the lord rarely showered compliments, his pride in his heir was impossible to miss.

A movement in the palaz caught Nelik's eyes. He stared, certain he was hallucinating...or asleep and dreaming. Yes, dreaming seemed likely. He'd had hundreds of dreams of Ziri in the last two years, perhaps thousands of fantasies in which he sank his cock into her ready body. In those dreams, she screamed his name at completion and used her woman healer's knowledge to pleasure him.

The lady in question was at her window, watching them, as the gods made her and no more. Her arms were crossed under choc-capped breasts that made his mouth water.

He slid to one side to get an unobstructed view of her, wishing he could see her full length and not from her delicate waist up. Ziri smiled, a purely feminine smile that the vixen used to lure the male jaglin to her cave in mating season.

"What is it?" Culdan asked, lowering his fists. "Nelik, what troubles you?"

Troubled? It was the wrong word. Nelik was fast stretching his trousers to their limits, a damned uncomfortable position to be in. Worse, his mind and body seemed largely disconnected from each other.

"Nelik," Culdan shouted, trying to catch Nelik's eye by waving a hand in front of him.

Ziri chuckled, and his tongue unglued from his palate. "Ziri is at her window," he managed, his heart pounding hard against his ribs as if he'd run a great distance.

Culdan's brow furrowed. "And this is—"

"In the sun's glory robed," he quoted Len's song to Veltina. Nelik considered singing it to her, wooing her with it.

Culdan's eyes widened and he started to turn to her. Fury coursed through Nelik. This look at Ziri was for himself, not Culdan. She would not be passed between them like the palaz bed slaves were.

Ziri's smile disappeared in a look of horror, confirming his belief that the offer had been for Nelik alone.

And I opened my mouth and caused this. I cannot allow her unease...I cannot allow Culdan the thought of claiming her!

He struck without another thought, connecting solidly with Culdan's cheek and sending the lordling sprawling on his face.

Ziri spun away and closed the shutters, easing the tension in Nelik's chest. Culdan hadn't seen her.

Culdan! Nelik stared at his fist in shock and dismay. *What have I done?*

Culdan was on his feet in a heartbeat, staring at the shutters. He turned with a battle cry, slamming his fist into Nelik's unprotected ribs, again and again. "Liar," he accused. "Dishonorable liar!"

Nelik crumpled, his head spinning and his chest shattering. Culdan followed him down, landing on his already-fractured ribs.

The onslaught ended abruptly, Culdan's weight flying up fast. "Culdan," Lord Denal barked. "What in Len's dungeons are you doing?"

"Ziri," the lordling gasped.

"You are trying to kill your dedicated over a *woman?*"

"No! Nelik...Nelik lied. He lied to me to gain an opening to attack my back, the coward."

There was silence for a moment. Nelik forced his eyes open, looking at His Lordship through a haze. Hands prodded at him, and his eyes slid shut on a groan he couldn't hold in his battered body. It was Luva and his mother. He was being tended by women like a babe. Could his disgrace get deeper than this? He supposed it could...if his father insisted on healing what he could of the damage, if he didn't let Nelik suffer battle wounds as any man would.

"And if an enemy lies to you?" Denal challenged his son. "Will you offer him your life as easily as you offered Nelik your unprotected cheek?"

"By Len," Culdan breathed. "No...I... Oh, Nelik."

"Perhaps I spoke too hastily. You are not worthy to wear the seal of heir." Fabric ripped, sounding far too loud in the stillness of the courtyard.

To Culdan's credit, he didn't cry out or protest the decision. "Yes, My Lord," he answered.

"When you mature, I may reconsider."

"I understand."

"Do you?" his father questioned icily. "Do you understand it? You must not be led from duty by anything. Not a woman. Not lies. Not personal gain. You must never doubt your course, in negotiation or battle." He paused. "You must always protect those who protect you."

Nelik's ragged breathing was the only sound he could hear. It seemed even his mother held her breath, waiting for something momentous.

"Look at him, Culdan! You must *always* protect those who protect you."

"Yes. I must."

Nelik surrendered to unconsciousness.

* * * *

Nelik shifted uncomfortably. It would be months before he could train again. It might be more than a week until his breathing eased.

The scent of female surrounded him, and he moaned, wondering how far the dream would carry him. Lips brushed his, retreated then returned.

He kept his eyes closed, afraid the dream would end, afraid it wouldn't be Ziri, if it was real. The kiss deepened, their tongues dancing. Nelik reached for her, and she fled.

"No," he protested weakly. Nelik opened his eyes to darkness, cursing the fact that he couldn't see her. Just as his eyes adjusted and shapes became visible, the door opened, blinding him with the light from the corridor. Then she was gone and the light with her.

Dark. Like my existence without her. He tried to lever himself up without success, swallowing a cry of frustration. There was no way to follow her and no way to verify her identity without doing so.

"Damn this," he grumbled. *And, damn Culdan.*

He sobered. No, he couldn't damn Culdan. If Nelik hadn't let slip that Ziri was nude at her window, none of this would have happened.

* * * *

A knock at the door brought Nelik to consciousness again. Between his body's need to heal and the lizor and olum teas to control his pain, he'd spent much of the two days since his pummeling sleeping. "Enter," he called out, wincing as his ribs shifted.

The door swung wide, and Culdan strode in with a tray balanced on his arm. He glanced at Nelik then averted his eyes, his color darkening.

"Welcome, My Lord," Nelik offered, uncomfortable as he'd never been with Culdan before.

He grimaced, settling the tray on the bedside table stiffly. "I am not 'your Lord,' Nelik. I am not anyone's lord. I am Culdan and nothing more."

"I do not—"

"I have no right to ask your forgiveness for this offense. I was angry and hurt and..." He swallowed hard, still staring at the tray, as if he wouldn't be able to force the words forth if he had to look at Nelik.

"I struck first," Nelik conceded.

"Once. I showed you no mercy. You are brother of my heart, and I...*I* did this to you." Culdan glanced at him, then settled in the chair at his bedside, burying his face in his hands.

Nelik stared at him. Culdan had been raised to be a Warlord. This display was unexpected. "Forgiven," he managed. It was the least comfort he could offer, the quickest road to peace between them.

Culdan dropped his hands to his knees, staring at them as if in misery. "No! It is not, and it should not be. Not so easily. I must bridge the furrow I dug. I will not have this between us in the years to come."

"As you wish." He'd never intended to have Culdan indebted to him, and it didn't sit well that the lordling felt it necessary.

Their eyes met, Culdan's pained. "Do *you* not wish it?" For an instant, he was the child of a year earlier.

Nelik understood the problem. Being a Warlord, even heir to a Warlord, was a huge responsibility. That responsibility wore on Culdan. He was young, still adjusting to sexual maturity, though the palaz bed slaves had warmed his bed for more than a year. He was a man in name but not in certainty, gaining then losing position in less than a month's passing, accepting disgrace without a word as was expected of him.

"Of course, I wish it. You are brother of my heart, Culdan." *And, I struck him out of jealousy.* "You are my only brother." *And I am his.*

There had only been two dedicated born of Denal's rite of fertility: Nelik and Ziri, and Denal had fathered no children other than Culdan in his many years as

Warlord to be true siblings to the lordling. His dedicated were his only contemporaries.

Culdan nodded, looking around uncertainly. His gaze went to the tray. "I brought herbed kit slices, blood-rich to help you heal, and lizor brandy."

"I thank you for the meat, but—"

"Olum." He cursed fluently."My apologies, Nelik."

"None needed." They weren't. Culdan was trying to make things right. Honor demanded Nelik not accept healing for battle wounds. Culdan knew it, and though it might make both of them feel better in the short sight, they would regret the choice in the coming years. As such, Culdan didn't offer it, and Nelik didn't ask. Silence stretched between them again.

The door opened, and they turned toward it, probably for the same reason of escaping the discomfort of the moment. Ziri halted in the doorway, a tray in hand. She looked from Nelik to Culdan, backing away with mumbled apologies.

Culdan rushed to her, taking the tray in one hand and urging her forward at the waist with the other. Nelik swallowed a fresh spike of jealousy. Culdan was touching her. Nelik would give nearly anything for that gift.

"Nonsense," Culdan assured her cheerily. "We are siblings of the heart, we three. There is nowhere we two can be that you should not...save battle, of course." He faltered, sending Nelik another pained look.

Ziri took up the pretense of a happy family. "I am glad to see you awake this time, Nelik."

Culdan's eyes narrowed. "You have been permitted to see Nelik, when I have not?"

Nelik's stomach churned. It was obvious that Culdan favored her. If Culdan was intent... One did not deny a Warlord, especially one dedicated to his service.

How would he stand it, if *His Lordship* Culdan bedded Ziri and tossed her away? Could Nelik hide his fury and soothe her hurt? Would she let him soothe her, or would she turn on both of them? Worse, could he serve Culdan faithfully and honorably, if Ziri was banded to the Warlord?

Ziri darkened and shot a look of near panic at Nelik. "He was asleep, Culdan, and I only came to bring him a lizor and olum tea. I *am* a woman healer, and herbs are my duty."

Culdan's smile was slow and practiced. "Of course."

She scowled, placing her fists on her hips and knocking his hand free. "You men! Women rarely engage in such petty arguments."

Nelik sighed. "Neither do men," he noted. He winced more in the realization that he'd spoken the rebuke aloud than in true pain.

Culdan's smile fled. "Then you know why we fought. I had hoped you would never learn of it." He glanced at Nelik, half in accusation. "I thought you said Nelik was asleep?"

Ziri crossed her arms over her chest as she often had when correcting their youthful antics. Her eyes narrowed, warning that the well of her anger was fast being pumped free into her veins. "Others in the palaz speak, Culdan. They say you did this because of me. Stupid men fight over a woman."

"We were not fighting over you," he insisted.

Realization struck Nelik. It was better to hide the truth than to encourage Culdan. "I lied to Culdan," he blurted out, not quite meeting Ziri's eyes.

She frowned. "Lied?"

Culdan's jaw tightened in the same fury he'd vented in the courtyard. "Please, ask no more," he requested of her.

"Nelik does not lie," she insisted.

"I did." Nelik pleaded Len's forbearance silently. *I only mean to protect her. It is an honorable thing I seek.*

But, he wasn't certain of that. He wanted more. He wanted Ziri for himself. How honorable was this lie? He dared not ask that.

"Then I must know."

Nelik ground his teeth. Why did she have to pursue this?

"Nelik." Her tone was sharp.

"Ziri," Culdan began in a soothing voice. By the grace of the gods, he didn't reach for her. That would have been Nelik's breaking point.

Still, he had to end this. "I told him you were nude at the window. It was a folly, a moment of poor judgment. Forgive me for...the lie."

She stared at him, sliding a sidelong glance at Culdan...then returning.

Nelik prayed she understood why he had to cover one truth perceived as a lie with a lie. Yes, they were fighting over her, with fists and words and battle tactics.

But, how could Nelik best Culdan? If a Warlord desired something, he took it...or in the case of a woman, requested it first, then took it. Few women denied a Warlord, and a dedicated never did. There would be no stopping Culdan, and his word would be law.

Culdan took her hands, and Ziri stiffened. Nelik forced his anger back, panting as his muscles tightened over broken bones.

Perhaps, if Ziri showed no interest, Culdan would wander away to other women. It was the only way they dared balk him.

"Forgive him, Ziri," Culdan reasoned. "It was a lie, yes, but I know you are far too young to—"

Her anger won out. "I? May I remind you that I am half a year your elder and an adult woman! I can take men to my bed, if I choose to, and even marry, with my mother's leave. What say have you in—"

"You are dear to my heart," Culdan interrupted her, his voice a silin drape between them. "You will not be marrying until you are a seasoned young woman, and men... Well, no man will bed you lightly. I will promise you that."

"You dare—"

Culdan pulled her into his arms, laying a kiss on her cheek. "You expect me to do less for my dedicated?"

Nelik closed his eyes, heartsick. He'd been warned away. Until Culdan either abandoned Ziri for another or laid claim to her, touching her would carry consequences.

"Come," Culdan whispered. "Nelik needs his rest."

CHAPTER ⊕NE

Jad 15th, Li 10-130
Velt, a Magden fort in Murvia

Culdan forced his eyes forward as Meretta leaned across him to set a plate of food on the table. Regardless of the fact that her ready scent was driving him mad to taste her, he was his father's heir and a Lengar lordling. Control was in his breeding and training; ignoring the deliberations to gaze longingly at the woman's curves as he wished to would bring dishonor on his house. Not to mention the fact that his host, Murvan, Meretta's father, would be offended if he ogled his older, prized child as he would a bed slave.

"The price is agreed, then?" Tigal, Murvan's son and heir, asked in his nasally voice.

"It is," Culdan replied simply.

He dimly noted that Meretta dropped a serving cloth at his feet and bent to retrieve it...until her warm hand trailed up his thigh, stroking at his length through his trousers, hidden by the table wovens. All he could think about was sinking the aching mass into her to the hilt. Culdan schooled his expression, forcing his breathing deep and even, giving no outward sign of how she affected him, even as he filled his lungs with her musk.

A moment later, Meretta stood, the serving cloth in hand. She bowed her head to him, then to her father, offering a bland look for her brother before she turned on her heel and left.

It was only then that Culdan realized he was staring at her, rapt on her retreating back. He snapped his eyes back to Murvan, noting his host's suspicion in dismay. Meretta would pay for this.

Remember your duty. Nothing must draw you away. Not a woman. Not gain. You must be decisive in all things. I am *decisive! I want Meretta!*

But, Meretta wasn't his duty. The trade agreement *was.*

"My daughter," Murvan commented coolly, gauging his response.

Culdan lifted a slice of roast kit to his mouth and bit it, feigning disinterest. "Striking, but it is a pity one so enticing is so clumsy," he replied.

Murvan raised an eyebrow, a look of annoyance on his darkening face, no doubt at Culdan's lack of tact in insulting his host's daughter so rudely. "Yes. I suppose it is."

* * * *

Meretta looked up from the quilt spread on the grass in her dead mother's prayer clearing, smiling at Culdan's scowl as he gazed down from his war-buck.

"You wish your father to kill me," he growled.

She chuckled, easing her skirt further up her thighs, watching his eyes follow it hungrily. "You know what I want." It was the same thing she'd always wanted, and she'd seduced him to get it...the first time.

He flipped his leg over his buck's back and landed smoothly at her feet, looking every fingerwidth the powerful, potentially-dangerous man she knew him to be. "The time is not right, Meretta."

How many times had he argued that point? At least once before every time he pierced her body. Though their minds conceded that it was true, their bodies

494

craved more. She ignored his warning, sliding her skirt higher.

Culdan groaned. "We cannot keep meeting like this. Eventually, you will conceive and—"

"And you will have to ask permission to band me as your bride." Meretta's understanding of the Lengar ceremony...of the process of being bound to a man with gold and not with parchment and pen, was limited, but she couldn't deny that she wanted to carry the bands that marked her as Culdan's bride.

"The time is not right!"

"After the trade agreement is established," she replied in boredom. How many times had Culdan argued it with her? His protests never lasted long. Eventually, he would seal his promise again in her stim band, where they both wanted him to be.

"Yes," he agreed, seemingly relieved.

Meretta arched her back, slipping her skirt up to her hips. "You would leave me wanting, Culdan?" she purred. She trailed her fingers through her woman's curls. "I suppose I shall have to ease my needs myself."

"Meretta," he rasped, not quite a plea to stop but not a warning either.

She spread her legs, stroking her fingertips along her seam, using her sucre to coat her hood. Culdan watched, transfixed, as she circled it slowly, working her body into a fierce arousal. Meretta closed her eyes, moaning and arching her back as she neared simple climax.

Culdan's hands closed around her hips, flipping her roughly to her stomach, "Not without me," he grumbled.

Then his length was inside her. Meretta cried out harshly, clawing at the quilt she'd laid out as their bed, aching to touch him. It was a punishment for her taunting that he did this, she knew. Culdan knew how much she enjoyed touching him; he was denying her that.

He was fierce, a worthy Warlord claiming what was his. Culdan had always been thus, and Meretta loved it. She reveled in the way his body conquered hers, and she thanked Mag again that Culdan had been chosen to handle the negotiations instead of her father's ally, old Denal.

She surrendered to him again, gasping as her climax took her by surprise. Culdan groaned, lodging deep inside her. His seed warmed her, and the stimulation was glorious.

The months between his visits were long and lonely, full of tortured dreams that left her unfulfilled. But it would be over soon. His next visit would be the first with trade goods, and at the following, he would ask her father for the right to take Meretta as his bride.

Meretta bit her lip as his cock pulsed within her, sending one final caress of seed past the open gates of her womb. At moments like this, she never knew what to pray for. If she didn't conceive, the trade agreement would proceed without complication, and that would be advantageous to both of their peoples. If she did conceive, her nights of longing would end, and she would share Culdan's bed.

"I knew it."

She stiffened at the sound of that voice. No matter what happened next, both of her goals were lost to her.

* * * *

Culdan's cock lessened in the pure adrenaline rush the coming of battle brought on. He turned off of

Meretta, bringing his sword up, his body between her and their mutual enemy, unsurprised that he faced Tigal's blade. It was a miracle of Len alone that the coward had spoken at all and not attacked their unprotected backs.

He shifted to block Tigal's view of his sister, allowing her a modicum of privacy in which to right her clothes. For himself, Culdan simply tugged his trousers further over his softening member.

The younger lordling glared at them, and the coming scene played out in Culdan's mind. The trade agreement would be rescinded first. Then there would be war between their peoples. He'd failed in his duty. He'd offered his back at the wrong moment for what he *wanted* instead of what he was sworn to do.

But Tigal seemed intent on nothing but his sister. "You dare?" he demanded.

"Tigal," Culdan began.

"Quiet!" Tigal didn't look at him. "You thought to put this Lengar beast in my place as heir? You thought I would allow you to take my place by producing First Heir?"

Culdan flicked a glance at Meretta, relieved to see her shock and fear. She wasn't using him in such a way. He knew she wouldn't. But he'd never heard of "First Heir," so he had no idea how such a thing would affect the situation, and that was akin to having his back to a corner in battle.

"Impossible," she gasped. "You are heir. The test of First Heir will only work if Father left only daughters. You know that, Tigal."

"I know that poisoning me to become Father's *only* heir would not be difficult. Or, perhaps, you thought to convince the Lengar to attack me openly."

She backed off a step, laying a shaking hand on Culdan's shoulder. "You are mad."

Tigal's eyes hardened. "You would like to prove that," he spat.

Culdan pushed Meretta behind him, gauging his adversary's threat. He'd always known Meretta and her brother loathed each other. He hadn't realized that Tigal posed a threat to her.

"No," Meretta whispered. "I only wish to leave Velt. Speak to Father, and you need never concern yourself with me again. I vow it."

"Leave? With him? An ally who would become heir if— *When* you manage to kill me?"

Culdan ground his teeth in frustration. Reasoning with a madman was useless. It was time for a choice. His failure at securing the trade agreement a given, there was only one logical course to chart.

"We relinquish any claim on your succession. I will speak with your father and—"

Tigal surged toward them with a battle cry. Culdan shoved Meretta away from the fight. The clash of blade on blade rang out several times, Tigal attacking in earnest and Culdan blocking him easily. Though Meretta's brother was a trained soldier, it was a solid fact that Lengar soldiers trained longer and harder than Magden, and Culdan was no exception to that. Ideally, Culdan should be able to rebuff his adversary without harming him indefinitely.

His plan was shattered when Tigal turned abruptly and lunged at Meretta. For a moment that seemed to stand outside the passage of time, she stared at her brother, her face pale and eyes wide, her head shaking frantically in a mute plea for him not to harm her.

Culdan's calm battle manner fled. Meretta was *his* woman, and Tigal meant to kill her. With a single swipe, he took the other man's head near off, sending his body flying to the side.

Meretta flinched as her brother's blade sliced a thin line along her upper arm, too shocked to scream as Tigal's blood mixed with her own.

Culdan stared at his sword in disbelief, dropping it in dismay, realization making him ill. He'd done it again, snapped and done damage...and over a woman again. Had he learned nothing in his youth? What was this weakness in him?

It would be war, now. No amount of negotiation could make this right with Murvan. Not even the truth that Tigal meant to kill Meretta would sway a grieving father deprived of his rightful heir.

Her sob brought him to his senses, and he went to her, healing her injury into a pale pink line with a heavy heart. "I must take you to your father," he managed, not quite meeting her eyes.

Meretta grasped his arm, shaking her head, whispering a plea for him not to do it.

He stifled the urge to wrench his arm away. "I am not a coward, Meretta. Though I may not survive the meeting, I cannot run from this deed like—"

Her hand tightened. "No! There is another way, a way we might salvage the peace and the trade agreement. We would even be able to contract."

Culdan stared at her, his speech stolen from him for a hand of heartbeats. Was she mad? "Your father will never approve a match now," he reasoned, the sick lump in his gut doubling in weight at the thought of losing her.

"I know," she whispered. "You must—" She looked at her brother, seemingly lost in thought.

"Meretta?" he prodded her. They were running out of time. If she had a plan, he had to know it and know it soon.

"You must take me in conquest." He started to protest, sick at the suggestion of such a blasphemy.

She cut him off cleanly. "It is the only way, Culdan. You will band me as your bride and plant a son in me." She met his eyes, pleading for his agreement. "I know you never sought to add Velt to your holdings, but it is the only way now, the only way my people will understand. Any other path leads to war, and..."

She didn't need to say the rest. Any other path led to her father denying their match.

Culdan nodded stiffly, uncinching her belt and pulling her dagger as it fell away. Meretta stood proudly, wincing only slightly as he drew a thin cut across his cheek as if she had wounded him. He discarded the blade, tossing it away as if he'd wrenched it from her hand. She closed her eyes as he untied the sash on her gown.

"I must," he assured her. If they meant to play off this farce, it had to be believable from all accounts.

"I know."

He bound her hands tightly though not tightly enough to stop the flow of blood to her fingers. Though she'd winced at his injury, she seemed not to notice her own discomfort. A startled gasp left her lips as he ripped her skirt to a point high on her thigh.

Culdan stroked her leg slowly, smiling at her increased musk. The urge to seal the conquest in the usual manner beat at him, but time was their enemy, and Meretta was already full of his seed, lending credence to the lies they would tell.

He stood, capturing her mouth then brushing his cheek along hers to leave a smear of his blood. He retrieved and cleaned his sword, sheathed it, then hurried her toward his buck.

Nelik would be irate at this turn, but better this than losing Meretta...or war.

CHAPTER TWO

Meretta lowered her gaze as they rode into the Lengar encampment, her heart pounding. Culdan's men stopped their work to stare at their Lord and his "captive." Though the plan had been her own, the act of riding astride in Culdan's arms, bound and in torn clothing, was almost too much for her.

"Lord Culdan," a deep voice shouted. "What is this?" The man trotting to them was one she'd seen often, Culdan's man of protection, a man her father's soldiers gave a wide berth to.

"Stand down, Nelik," Culdan growled. "It should be obvious to all what has transpired here."

"Dear gods, man! Why would you do this?"

Culdan didn't answer immediately. He slid off his buck and dragged Meretta down after him, all but exposing her to his men in the process. She felt her cheeks flush as she pulled her skirt as straight as possible with her bound hands.

"Culdan," Nelik began gruffly.

He pushed past his man of protection, guiding Meretta along by a light grip on her upper arm. "Tigal tried to kill me. He left me no choice."

"The damned geela! There will be war for this."

"No. There will not. Tigal tried to take my life. Now, Murvan will give me all that was his son's." Culdan pulled Meretta into a pavilion, releasing her arm.

Nelik followed them, closing the flap. "This is not our way," he reasoned.

"No, it is not. But, how convenient that it is theirs," he drawled.

"It is not too late to undo—"

"It is. I have already sealed the conquest for the first time."

Meretta peeked up at the sound of a groan, noting Nelik's pained expression in unease. She'd heard Culdan say that this man was dedicated to him. Though she wasn't certain what it meant, she hoped it meant that he would back Culdan, even when he didn't agree with his Lord.

"We ride in half an hour," Culdan ordered. "Hard and fast, toward Tiben."

Nelik ground his teeth, shooting a look of warning at Culdan and sparing a slight glance of what appeared to be apology to Meretta. "Anything else I should know, *My Lord*?"

"I require a pair of shackles and the lock bar, Nelik."

"I have none small enough for a lady," he noted in seeming frustration. "I had not expected you to abduct a—"

"Bring what you have. I will make them fit."

"As you wish." Nelik left them, the flap swinging in his wake. His shouts rang out, and the camp erupted in activity.

Culdan untied her hands, dragging Meretta's dress up. At first, she thought he meant to take her again before they left Velt, but he used the ripped fabric to wipe his seed from her thighs then tossed it away.

"Culdan?" she asked, confused by his silence.

"Take off your boots."

She complied, growing more perplexed by the moment.

As if he read her thoughts, he answered them. "You must dress the part of my captured bride, Meretta, and the discarded clothing..." He motioned to them.

"Like the belt and dagger, will support the image of conquest in my father's mind."

He hesitated, turning to a pack and searching through it. "Yes. It will." He stood, a clean tunic in his hands. "You will wear this."

Meretta looked at the crumpled dress, imagining her father's upset at the scene he'd been left to decipher. She pulled the tunic over her head, miserable at the choice they were dealt. "There is no other way," she reminded herself.

"I wish you were Lengar," Culdan admitted. "This would not be necessary, if you were."

* * * *

They didn't stop again until the sun had set fully. Culdan lifted Meretta from his buck and carried her over the rocky ground to avoid injuring her bare feet, thanking the gods that it was high summer and her lack of dress would be more comfortable than being fully dressed. He saw to her needs personally, offering every comfort, as his men would expect of him.

After a hearty dinner and a cloth bath at a cool stream, he carried Meretta to his pavilion, setting her on her feet on the plush jaglin furs set around the bed.

His men, anticipating his need to plant an heir quickly in what they'd deemed an unwilling woman, had fastened restraint bolts to the head and foot of his pallet riser. Meretta looked at them in seeming concern.

Culdan forced himself not to shudder at the sight of them. Though banding an unwilling woman on the veltian wasn't unheard of, Culdan had never thought he'd earn the distinction of doing something so vile.

Realization made his head spin. Why *should* he accept that dishonor? There was no reason to. The sham of conquest did not have to reach that far.

He cupped his hands around her shoulders, burying his face in the back of her hair. "I will make you love them," he whispered. "But, we must make a decent show for my men."

"You wish me to—"

"Shhh. You will see." He released the shackles and pulled his tunic off her body, tossing it over the chair.

Meretta crossed her arms over her chest, her quick mind no doubt working the fact that his pavilion walls would show faint shadows of them to his men outside with the lamp lit as it was.

Culdan dragged her arms down, feasting on her beautiful body with his eyes. He cupped a breast, pinching lightly so she jumped in response.

She scowled at his smile. "I do not appreciate—"

"My touch? You will," he vowed. "Before I take you, you will beg for me."

Her eyes widened, and she shook her head frantically. No. Meretta was unaccustomed to begging. She was the oldest and most prized child of a Warlord, and though she favored her father's guests by serving them personally, her life had been largely that of her own choosing and not at the whim of another.

She shied, as he closed on her, back-stepping with her arms crossed over her breasts again. Her collision with the edge of the pallet riser sent her sprawling onto it. Meretta threw her hands out to catch herself.

Culdan grasped one hand then the other, snapping the fur and silin wrapped shackles back onto her wrists. He didn't give her time to plan her next move. In the space of a few heartbeats, he'd lifted her further onto the bed and tied the length of rope attached to the top bolt to the metal bar between her wrists.

For a long moment, he stared at her, mildly surprised at the force of his arousal. He'd dreamed of seeing her bound on the veltian for months, but this wasn't the veltian. Meretta was literally tied to his bed, and the sight of it had him harder than dreams of banding her gold ever had.

Culdan pulled off his tunic and removed his weapons, turning slightly into the light to give Meretta a better view of his bare chest. She did look, her eyes tracing every finger-width of his flesh, her hunger overcoming her misgivings as he'd hoped it would.

Their sexual encounters had always been rushed. There had never been time to simply look at each other, to spend hours touching and tasting. It seemed ironic that this turn of events had given them what they'd longed for. She licked her lips, bringing his mind back to the present.

"You want me?" Culdan challenged.

Meretta didn't answer. Her cheeks darkened, and she seemed to remember what he wanted of her. She clenched her thighs together tightly.

Culdan raised an eyebrow. "Very well."

Being lovers had its advantages. He knew what she liked intimately. No matter how many of her erogenous zones she hid from him, two were gloriously accessible in her current position.

He leaned over her and flicked his tongue around one nipple, pinning her to the quilts when she tried to squirm away. He didn't take the hardening peak into his mouth. That wasn't necessary. For this pleasure, Meretta liked a light touch, the teasing sensation he was already offering.

The flicks of his tongue had her gasping for breath in moments, arching against him with half-swallowed whimpers of surrender. Her thighs eased apart a finger-width...then two and three, until he could easily fit a hand between.

Culdan pretended not to notice, patiently arousing her while she parted her thighs and invited him inside. When they were spread wide, he placed the soft cuffs on her ankles to complete her binding. Meretta didn't fight the move, didn't protest being positioned for his possession, just as he'd hoped.

Meretta met his eyes, seemingly unable to decide which was more important to her anymore—her stubborn pride and appearances or sating her drive and securing their match.

Her agreement was crucial. While it was not required by the laws of conquest that she be willing to mate, Culdan would not have his men believe that of him...even for Meretta. Thinking him a masterful lover who'd seduced his enemy's daughter was imminently preferable to thinking him a Magden dog or back-hill Lengar cut-throat Warlord that took a woman in rape for material gain.

"Say it," he requested simply.

She swallowed hard, neither refusing nor complying.

Culdan ranged his gaze down her body, planning his next move as carefully as he would a sword strike. He unfastened his trousers and pushed them away, smiling widely as her eyes locked on his erect length and she shifted against the ankle cuffs, tipping her core up for his pleasure.

He thrust a finger inside her, and she bucked against him, crying out softly. Her body primed for him, hot and wet, suckling at his finger as it would at his cock. Culdan knew what she wanted and denied her, using a slow stroke when she wanted to climax, hard and fast. She started thrusting against his hand, seeking to sate herself.

Culdan pulled it away, leaving her empty again, licking at their mixed essence. Meretta grumbled a complaint at that move.

"Do you want my mouth?" he offered.

"You know that is not what I want."

"Tell me."

"I want your cock in me," she whispered.

"Louder."

"I want—"

"Louder, Meretta." A conversational tone wasn't what he wanted.

His men would know her mind before he laid claim to her again. Meretta closed her eyes, setting her jaw stubbornly.

Culdan forced her thighs as wide as the binding allowed. He leaned over her and thrust his tongue deep inside, retreating abruptly as she screamed in delight. It was a step in the right direction, but it wouldn't do to let her climax without him.

She shot him a scathing look. He did it again, gratified to hear her gasp turn into a grumbled curse on his house. Culdan flicked his tongue over her hood then her seam, chuckling as she fought the bindings in a bid to reach him. Would that she did the same on the veltian, he'd have quite the bride to present.

"You know how to end this," he whispered. *Dear Len, I hope she ends this soon!* Her musk was making his head spin and the hunger for her almost unbearable.

Meretta said nothing, so Culdan continued. It didn't take long to break her, though Culdan was at his breaking point when she gave him what he wanted.

"Culdan, please," she shouted. "If you do not take me—"

He turned over her and filled her in a single motion. Culdan closed his eyes at her cries of pleasure, full-throated shouts of womanly delight in lovemaking, moving inside her, holding off for her simple climax. She started pleading for completion before the contractions claimed her fully, not whispers now but words that even men at the main fire would surely hear.

Her body milked at him, and she screamed his name. Culdan surrendered his self-control with a roar, hoping for the first time that his seed would find purchase.

In the aftermath of their passion, they lay, his cock notched tight in her stim band, her lips tracing the well of musk at his throat. Gods, but he'd lived for this moment, the night when he'd be free to hold her in his arms when his cock released her. He thanked Len fervently that his men would know he wasn't a barbarian in it.

CHAPTER THREE

Jad 16ᵗʰ, Li 10-130

Meretta straightened Culdan's tunic over her thighs, wishing he was beside her rather than giving orders to the runners that would carry news of their plight to his father at Tiben. She was aware of the eyes measuring her every move. If those eyes were only watching for signs that she might attempt to escape in Culdan's absence, they would be a comfort, but they weren't.

The snickers and whispered comments were disconcerting, but the most bothersome thing was the soldier leering at her from the other side of the fire. If she were home in Velt, a look to her father would be enough to see the man dead, but she was a Lengar prisoner now, at least in name. Without Culdan at her side, she had no clue what might happen next.

The stories told of Lengar cruelties to prisoners were legendary. It was said that they didn't practice conquest only because a Lengar father would always give his daughter up to death rather than submit. If it weren't for Culdan's presence in her life, Meretta might well have believed that story for the rest of her life. Now, she didn't know what to think.

"His Lordship certainly picked a responsive little bed slave."

She snapped her eyes up, unsurprised that it was the soldier who'd been staring so lustfully at her speaking. An angry retort died in her throat. Simply stated, Meretta didn't know enough about Lengar law to know if the soldier should be punished for such talk.

Magden laws did not apply here, conquest or no, and she had to remember that.

"Perhaps, when he tires of her..." He met Meretta's eyes, stroking his cock through his trousers.

Meretta straightened, staring him down in challenge. That was a line she would not compromise on; she would not be passed hand-to-hand around the Lengar camp.

"She has fire. The good ones always do."

She noted the unease on the faces of the soldiers around him, the way the others moved away. So, this wasn't common, wasn't condoned. That was all she needed to know.

Her fury at being talked about like a common schente drove her to retort. "How dare you speak to me like—"

Meretta gasped as a sword appeared at the soldier's throat, and those closest to him scattered. She looked over his shoulder, startling in the realization that it was Nelik who held the blade and not Culdan. She hadn't even realized the man of protection was nearby, and now he was offering correction on her behalf. Before Meretta could thank him, Nelik started snapping questions at the soldier.

"You dare speak to His Lordship's woman that way?" he demanded, moving on without allowing an answer. "You dare eye her as some whore or bed slave? I remind you that *Lady* Meretta is daughter of a Warlord and heir to all that is his."

"A Magden," he spat. The soldier yelped as the sword edge drew blood.

"She will be Lord Culdan's *bride*, as soon as a veltian is acquired." He paused, his jaw tightening and his eyes hot in fury. "A veltian with gold bands." Nelik's face promised a swift death if the soldier dared to speak again. "You will show the respect due her."

The soldier's gaze slid away, much as Meretta would expect one of her father's soldiers' eyes to.

"Nelik?" Culdan called out, striding into the clearing. "Is there a problem here?"

"A discipline problem, it seems," he replied evenly.

Culdan nodded, dropping down beside Meretta and handing her a plate piled high with food for both of them. "Of what sort?"

Meretta darkened, at a loss to repeat the things the soldier had said about her. Culdan's eyes narrowed dangerously, and he turned them on Nelik, a silent demand for a full explanation.

"It seems the geela feels a Magden bride unworthy of your full husbandly protection. He as much as stated that he believed he'd be permitted Lady Meretta's company on common sheets."

Culdan didn't hesitate. "Kill him."

Meretta gasped, the plate slipping from her trembling hands.

Culdan saved it and placed it on her lap again patiently. "Not in Meretta's sight," he amended.

He stroked her cheek, turning his head to hers and coaxing her into a sweet kiss. She opened for him, dismissing their audience without a thought. They'd seen and heard much more intimacy the previous night.

Culdan passed the plate off to someone behind him then dragged her to his body with a growl. He was abruptly the lover she'd always known: hungry, masterful and in complete command.

His grip eased, and he nuzzled her lips. "Eat," he ordered. "Then you will warm my bed again before we travel."

A soldier rose silently and sprinted away, most likely to let those breaking camp know not to take the pavilion down yet. "You will warm my bed every sunrise, Meretta."

She stared at him, unsure of what he hoped to gain by this display.

"You are mine, Meretta," he informed her. "No man will dare take you from me while I live. No man will dare threaten it and continue to draw breath."

She nodded, glancing to the doomed man. His seat was conspicuously empty, and Nelik stood at the treeline, cleaning his blade on a Lengar soldier's jacket.

* * * *

Culdan left Meretta's side, sinking down next to Nelik at the Lord's fire. Taking the hint that Culdan wanted to speak to his dedicated alone, the soldiers on that side of the circle left to complete their nightly duties.

His dedicated had barely looked at him all day and had spoken in single words and clipped phrases since he'd killed the soldier.

Culdan knew it wasn't the duty to kill that bothered Nelik. From the look on his face when Nelik repeated the traitor's words, Culdan knew full well that Nelik ached to kill the soldier for what he'd said.

That a given, the question of what troubled his dedicated remained a mystery that Culdan would not rest until he'd unraveled. "What troubles you, Nelik?" he asked solemnly.

He didn't reply.

"This cannot continue. We are brothers of the heart. Speak your mind, whatever it is." There hadn't been such discomfort between them since Nelik had returned to training after his injury at Culdan's hand.

"Speak my mind? You... You do..." He grumbled a curse, searching the night sky with his eyes.

"I have done the only thing the Magden will respect as an alternative to war."

"Tigal's attack on your person was foul. I would never argue that. But, this... This, Culdan?" He rubbed his forehead, at a loss as Culdan had rarely seen him.

Culdan's heart ached. Of course, Nelik didn't recognize Culdan's hand in this. It wasn't something he would have undertaken of his own accord. "This is not what you believe," he whispered. If anyone deserved to know the truth, Nelik did.

"Is it not? Tell me that you love her, that you are not abandoning the possibility of love for this travesty."

Culdan smiled at Meretta, watching her bite off a slice of fried travel bread as if it were a feast. "I love her. I never planted my seed in force; not last night and not before. You have my vow on that as a Lengar Lord. I would have asked to band her were it not for Tigal's attack."

Nelik traced the line of knitting tissue on Culdan's face. "And this?"

He sobered. "It was not Meretta who did it," he answered in halftruth, knowing Nelik would assume Tigal had drawn blood as they battled.

"I would have killed him for it, myself," Nelik growled.

"I know it, Nelik. In truth, I was unprepared for Tigal's madness. A sane man would have been an easy fight."

Nelik chuckled. "You must have been unprepared. How long has it been since any man has laid fist or blade to you?"

Culdan smiled. "Five years, and it was you who managed it."

His dedicated winced at that. "My ribs recall it."

At least they'd come to a place where they could joke about it. "A dirty lie deserved no less. Telling me Ziri was nude at her window, indeed."

"Tell me. Why did you look? You never had an interest in Ziri before that day...or since it."

"I was a sixteen-year-old boy, and she was sister of my heart. I have always *cared* for her, Nelik."

"Then you wanted to protect her. I should have known it."

"You should," he agreed, wondering at Nelik's preoccupation with the subject.

Culdan considered the situation. They'd all but made peace again. "As dedicated to me and without a bride, you will be expected to stand at my side at the rite of fertility," he offered, waiting Nelik's smile.

It didn't come. "You will be performing the high ceremony, then?"

"Meretta deserves no less."

"And will you allow Ziri to stand the rite as your dedicated, or will you protect her?" he challenged, his shoulders and arms tensing.

Culdan had never questioned that she would. Of course, Ziri could refuse it, but he'd never exclude her if she wished to stand. Nelik's comments made no sense, unless...

"Can I assume you want Ziri to stand the rite?"

Nelik darkened. He slid a hard look at Culdan but didn't answer.

"You do want it. How is it that I have never seen this before?"

"You have not honestly believed I lied to you that day in the courtyard for the last five years," he stated.

He had, fully and with all his heart. Culdan shook his head. "You mean... She was—"

"In the sun's glory robed." A wistful smile touched Nelik's lips.

"By Len."

"For me, I believe. Her reaction when I blurted it out and you turned seemed to indicate that it was for me alone."

"Then why did you not pursue her?"

Nelik sent him a weary look.

Memories of their discussion at his sick bed made Culdan wince. "Ziri is a seasoned woman, Nelik. When the time comes, the choice to stand the rite will be hers to make."

He relaxed. "Then I will...enjoy standing at your side, Culdan."

Culdan chuckled then laughed outright at Nelik's deepening color. He had no doubts that Nelik would claim Ziri for the rite by any means necessary.

"As dedicated, you choose your woman first."

Nelik scowled. "No. The preparer does."

"Of course." That was the one possible hole in the plan. If Ziri prepared Meretta for him then chose another... "If there is any hope, Ziri will be yours."

CHAPTER FOUR

Jad 25th, Li 10-130

"We will be setting up my pavilion for midday," Culdan ordered. "See to it, Nelik."

"But, our pace—"

"Not everything," he qualified. "Just the shelter and the quilts. The men can ride ahead to accomplish it and lag behind to pack it." Such a thing would only slow them by a quarter hour per day, if they ate midday on the buck. Since they didn't stop to light fires for that meal, it wouldn't be much of a disruption in their travel.

"Is this really necessary?" Nelik complained.

"I will be laying claim to Meretta at every sunrise, midday, and evening." Two times per day hadn't caught an egg yet, and she had to carry by the time her father reached them. If two times each day was not often enough, Culdan would increase their chances with a third stimulation each day, nearly doubling their chances at conception.

Meretta's eyes widened, but she didn't speak. She glanced at Nelik then away, blushing.

"Does that distress you?" Culdan queried.

She smiled shyly. "You know it does not."

"Does anything I do cause you discomfort?"

Meretta hesitated, averting her gaze.

"What?" he demanded. And, why hadn't she told him? "Tell me what causes you discomfort."

Culdan expected her to state that she'd like more clothing. If she did, he'd provide something. Though he didn't have ladies' clothing, a cloak fashioned of a sheet might ease her concern.

She shook her head. "It is expected—"

"Tell me."

She raised her bound hands to him silently, peeking up at his expression for but a moment.

Culdan fingered the shackles, his mind working at the problem. They weren't biting into her wrists; he'd padded them carefully. His answer came in the form of a bead of sweat, winding down the center of his back. He'd padded the shackles with layers of fur. What would his armor feel like, similarly padded?

He pulled the lock bar from under his armor on its chain, carried just as he would soon carry the lock bar to her bands, reaching for the shackles, intent on releasing her.

"You cannot," Nelik protested.

"I will do what I wish."

"You have taken her in conquest. She will run or—"

Culdan chuckled. "Meretta will not run from me. I have...enthralled her."

She blushed prettily, her eyes shining, lending credence to that claim.

Nelik shot him a look of disbelief.

"I know! Mag demands adherence to vows. Swear you will not run from me, Meretta, and I know you must live to it."

She smiled widely. "I will not run from you or from your bed, Culdan. I swear it, on my honor and in Mag's name."

Culdan slipped the lock bar into the shackles, his cock straining at the promise not to flee his attentions. He'd not asked for such a promise, and it warmed him that Meretta would offer such a vow to him.

She sighed in relief as he pulled the shackles away, raising her heat-prickled wrists into the breeze.

Nelik sighed. "And if she injures you?" he continued. "You would show your sleeping heart to her?"

Meretta didn't give Culdan a chance to respond to that. "I vow that I will never injure Culdan. If he wishes it, I will care for his weapons as I cared for my father's weapons. I will never raise one to him."

Culdan stroked her cheek with the backs of his fingers. "I believe I would like that." It wasn't something a Lengar woman would offer to do, and the thought of her taking on such a task was a rare gift.

Nelik snatched the shackles and dropped away with a grumbled complaint that sounded of his belief that he'd have to present Denal with her head, if Culdan continued playing the fool for her.

Culdan ignored him.

"I know what I would like," Meretta whispered.

"And that is?" Culdan asked.

"Have your servants light the lamp in your pavilion tonight."

His trousers felt a size too small of a sudden. "And what delights will my men see?"

"They will see your devoted bride touching you."

Culdan crushed her mouth to his, biting back a groan as she pressed her hands to his breastplate. "It will be as you request."

* * * *

Meretta watched Culdan close the flap, smiling at his slow perusal over her naked body. He reached for his tunic. She shook her head, striding to him, her bare feet sinking into the jaglin furs, acutely aware of her nudity.

Culdan let her undress him. His tunic went first; she explored his chest with her mouth and hands, gasping as she sampled the musk above his male nipples and his hands fisted in her hair.

She made a show of removing his weapons and setting them aside. Nelik would certainly comment on that, but that was the point of this showing. No one would question Culdan's word that Meretta was dedicated to Culdan and the pleasure they gave each other after this night.

His scent drew her back, and Meretta feasted on the aphrodisiac musk while she worked his trousers open. His cock jutted toward her, already weeping fluids. "I missed touching you," she whispered.

Culdan drew her head back by his grip on her hair. "Then touch me. I have dreamed of it all day."

"Do you remember the first time?" she purred.

His expression was beyond hunger, a half-mad challenge to touch him as she had then.

She cupped him, stroking the hollow behind his sac as she had that night. "You were so shocked, you let me uncover you, and..." She stroked him, smiling wider as his hands fisted in her hair, his arm muscles bunching tight in barely-leashed response.

"Jaglin vixen," he growled. "I will take you upright, as I did that night."

Meretta trailed her thumb through his fluids, watching his eyes close in pleasure. "But, you argued first. You told me we should not."

His seed trickled over her thumb, and he cursed aloud. Culdan's eyes opened, hard in decision. "Do it," he demanded.

There was no question what he meant. It had been the final blow that had convinced him inside her the first time.

She scooped a bit of his seed onto her thumb then brought it to her mouth. Sucking it off was always sweet torture for them both. His musk was strong, drugging, sending curls of heat through her.

As it had the first time she did it, the action snapped his control. Culdan released her hair and lifted her by the waist, thrusting into her. He stilled, meeting her eyes as if in challenge.

Meretta gasped, arching against him, seeking more, her entire body alive to the sensation of his cock buried in her.

His hold denied her, keeping him finger-widths from where she wanted him to be.

"Culdan, please," she begged.

His shoulder muscles tightened beneath her hands, and his breathing went ragged.

"Please!"

"By Len," he grumbled, forcing himself deep inside her.

Meretta screamed in pleasure, already teetering on the edges of climax. Culdan took her in fierce thrusts, his sweat-soaked chest teasing her nipples, grunting in his climax moments after she found hers.

He dropped to his knees on the furs, claiming her mouth in bruising kisses."You will carry my son," he vowed. "By Len, you will."

CHAPTER FIVE

Jad 26ᵗʰ, Li 10-130

Meretta pressed her thighs together, all too aware of the dampness running down her slit and pooling between her body and Culdan's armored thigh. It was hot...or perhaps her arousal only made it seem so. She couldn't be certain which it was.

Her sexual hunger hardly seemed possible. By day's end, her bottom would be sore from riding, she knew. And, they had been awake for half the night, enjoying each other's bodies until they were both exhausted and moving tenderly.

Even now, her sheath throbbed in the aches of their loving...and yet it was throbbing in need. Meretta hardly remembered the last of their marathon, so lost was she in musk and sensation that one ran into another and no one event seemed to register in her mind.

As a result of their vigor the previous night, they hadn't indulged in their usual morning romp. They'd barely rolled from bed in time to eat and dress before setting off again.

Despite it all, the need to have Culdan inside her was driving her insane. Her body burned for it until nothing else mattered. Not that they were nowhere near shelter. Not that they were fleeing her father and half the able men of Velt. Not that Culdan's men might witness their passion...and not through the thick hide walls of his pavilion. Meretta reached for him, drowning in her hunger for his cock.

* * * *

Culdan forced his mind to function. *By Len! She means to kill me!*

Meretta had worked her hand under the codpiece of his armor and was busy stroking his cock through his trousers. Her breaths were sharp and hard against his neck, announcing her arousal clearly.

He pulled off one glove and stuffed it in the helm hung behind his thigh. The heat and moisture of her body greeted his fingers when they were barely past the edge of the tunic. Knowing she was ready was maddening.

Culdan dipped his head, capturing her lips in the type of kiss that had led them from one mating to another the night before. "If I do this, Nelik will see it," he warned her.

She raised her head, her eyes glazed in need. "I do not care," she whispered.

He bit back a vicious curse, motioning to Nelik with his uncovered hand and turning his buck into the trees as his dedicated shouted out orders. Before his second glove was off and the thigh straps unbuckled from the codpiece, there were three soldiers ahead of him and Nelik behind.

Meretta brought her closer knee to her chest, grasped his armored thighs and turned toward him fully, her legs over his, her woman's curls uncovered and glistening with droplets of her sucre.

Culdan flipped the codpiece away and unbuttoned his trousers, freeing his cock. He lifted Meretta and pulled her to his breastplate, easing her down the length of his cock until she settled to the root with a whimper of delight, her sheath hot and slick, taunting him with whispers of a rise to climax.

The sway of the buck beneath them provided delicious little swirls of pleasure. Culdan watched the interplay of emotion on Meretta's face, her stark hunger feeding his own. He urged the buck faster, and Meretta moaned, her hands fisting in his cloak.

A sharp command from Nelik let Culdan know that one of the soldiers had tried to turn and watch. At their next stop, the man would taste the back of Culdan's fist for that. Even if Meretta were a bed slave he held no feelings for, their protection depended on his men's vigilance. Meretta would not be risked.

And their passion would not be watched by a lowly soldier. If it weren't for his lack of control with her, Culdan would never have permitted Nelik to spy on them either.

She ground her body against his, seeking more. Culdan guided her up and down his length, groaning at the silin heat of her body around him.

He muted her cry of release with his mouth, pulling her tight to him as her contractions set off his climax. In a matter of heartbeats, their bodies were locked together, his cock notched tight in her stim band and his mouth claiming hers.

Meretta leaned back onto his buck's neck, stretching luxuriously, a contented smile on her face. Soft laughter filled the air around them, escaping lips that were kiss-swollen and tempting.

The reaction was so unexpected that Culdan laughed with her. "By Len, I cannot get enough of you," he admitted.

She favored him with a look that promised pure sexual exhaustion for them both. "I certainly hope that is true."

He slid his hands up her ribs and teased her nipples through the light fabric of his tunic, smiling wider as she arched into the caress. "You just want my son," he teased.

She'd certainly pursued the possibility after his proclamation the night before, enticing him every time he lessened until the night became a pleasant haze.

"I most certainly do not," she replied in a sing-song voice.

His cock lessened but still pulsed in arousal. "You want more, then?" If she said 'yes,' she'd have it immediately.

"I will always want more."

Culdan pulled her back to his body, seeking her mouth. "Before I am finished with you, my son will rest in your womb," he grumbled.

Meretta chuckled, burying her face in his neck. "Your son *already* rests there."

That statement shocked his mind into motion. She hadn't dropped an egg? She was bearing? "Are you certain?" he asked urgently.

As if in answer, her skin heated against his. "Culdan," she offered, moving against him.

What am I doing? He couldn't keep Meretta comfortable through an extended journey, certainly not as far as Tiben. Not while she carried. It wasn't safe to make her ride so hard, and they were lacking essentials, like milk and fresh fruits.

She pulled back, confused by his inattention. "Culdan?"

He stripped off his cloak and wrapped it around her body. *By Len, her pregnancy signs!* He hadn't considered the things she'd need.

Her hand pressed to his breastplate. "I don't understand," she pleaded.

"When we stop," he vowed. "I will sate your schen properly when we stop." And, every other pregnancy sign he could with it. Culdan turned his buck toward the road, and the soldiers hurried to get ahead of him.

Nelik came even with him, as Culdan got Meretta settled across his lap again, covered shoulders to toes in his cloak. "Is there a problem?" his dedicated asked urgently.

Meretta worked to right his clothing and armor. Culdan stifled the urge to force her back within the cloak where she would remain warm, despite her pregnancy signs.

"We turn toward Gangir after mid-meal. Send a group with a message to my father. At full stride, he will join us a few weeks after we reach our goal. And...make certain to hide our trail and create confusion at the parting." Even with their slowed pace, Gangir would be half the ride.

"Gangir is closer to Velt than Tiben is," Nelik complained.

"Which means that Murvan will expect me to lay on to Tiben and my father."

"As well you should. You invite war, Lord Culdan."

Culdan glared at him. "Murvan *will* ride for Tiben, and I will not risk my bride and son on the race to my father's home."

Nelik stared at Meretta, swallowing hard. "Your heir is secured?"

"He will be, once we reach Gangir." *And clothing, food, a decent roof...*"And, Ziri will be at Gangir. There will be no delay in banding Meretta to me."

"By my blade," Nelik vowed.

CHAPTER SIX

Caj 6th, Li 10-130
Gangir, a Lengar stronghold in Denia

Meretta looked at the palaz in awe. It was in the high Lengar style that she'd read about but never seen. The precious white stone had been fashioned into a sprawling manse with wide columns supporting a roof over the courtyard and arch-shaped windows with colored glass.

"Do you like it?" Culdan asked.

"It is breathtaking." It was a showplace compared to her father's stone fort and rough buildings. Velt had been built for defense; Gangir had been built for luxury.

Craning her head to one side, she could see the edge of the hidden bunker in the hillside. That was where they would travel if the occasion to battle arose at Gangir.

"*You* are breathtaking."

Before she could respond, he slid off the war-buck with Meretta in his arms, striding to the doors, a wide smile on his face. The door opened wide before they reached it, and a matronly woman started issuing orders to servants who came from all directions with dizzying speed. Meretta watched in awe. They had servants in Velt, but only to do things they could not do for themselves. She'd never imagined the sheer number of Culdan's household.

The woman ended in a deep bow to Culdan. "I hope the preparations meet with your approval, Your Lordship. Your runners arrived only an hour ago."

528

"You have never disappointed me, Luva. I am certain you will not this time." He rounded her shoulder, carrying Meretta into the cool shade of the entryway.

She bowed again. "You are most welcome at Gangir, Lady Meretta."

She felt as if she were already. "My thanks."

"Are the servants prepared?" Culdan inquired.

Luva raised an eyebrow. "As you instructed, of course. Are you quite certain—"

"Quite."

Meretta stared at him, certain she was missing something important in the exchange, though she had no clue what that might be.

Culdan lowered her to her bare feet, straightening his cloak on her shoulders, his eyes hungry. "I place my bride in your hands," he breathed. "Be mindful of my heir."

Luva's eyes widened, and her smile followed shortly after. "You have my vow, it shall be so." She offered her arm to Meretta. "If you would oblige?"

Meretta glanced at Culdan, uncertain. He nodded toward his servant, indicating the offered arm with his hand. She took it and started walking, watching Culdan head the other direction in confusion.

"Lady Meretta?" Luva asked. "Is there a problem?"

"Will I not share Culdan's rooms?" They'd shared a bed thus far, and she had no wish to sleep alone in a strange place.

"You will, but there are formalities to be observed if you are to be recognized as his Lordship's bride."

"Of course." Any formalities were acceptable, as long as they ended at Culdan's bed.

The room they entered was a huge bathing room. By the women dressed in white silin, she guessed it was a communal bath for ladies. It was common practice in Magden lands as well.

Meretta wondered vaguely if the Lord and his bride used it as a couple after the contract...banding, as they did in her homeland. She smiled weakly at the thought that Culdan likely did what he wished, despite convention.

Luva removed the cloak, staring at Culdan's tunic as if the sight scandalized her. Several of the other women whispered and snickered amongst themselves.

A hard look from Luva silenced them. She set the cloak aside. "Ziri. Deana. Her hair, please."

Two of the white-clothed women came forward, urging Meretta to a lounging couch. They brushed her hair smooth. The pampering nearly put Meretta to sleep, especially since Luva had covered her with a jaglin fur to warm her.

"Lady Meretta?"

She forced her eyes open, noting Luva's outstretched hand. Meretta took it, letting the older woman draw her to her feet and lead her to the bath.

Ziri and Deana removed the tunic, leaving her nude. Then they led her into the warm pool without removing their own clothing. The water made the silin opaque so that they were effectively as unclothed as she was. The other two servants joined them, leaving only Luva on the pool's edge.

They seated Meretta on a bench, chest deep in the water, and started to bathe her. She sighed, closing her eyes as the soft cloths caressed her body. A delightful scent teased her nose and brought her body to tingling awareness.

"Mmmm," she murmured, fighting sleep again. "What is it?"

"Dolgen," Luva supplied.

Meretta nodded. She'd never heard of the oil before, but it was a blessing, she knew.

The two servants who'd joined them last started scrubbing at her feet, massaging her calves as Deana washed her hair and Ziri bathed her neck, face and back.

Meretta gasped as hands stroked her thighs and her womb throbbed in sexual excitement, becoming heavy and heated. The cloths concentrated over the wells of her musk, a purposeful attempt to arouse her. Was this part of their ceremony? It likely was.

"Away," Ziri ordered.

The two servants at her feet moved, and Ziri took their place between Meretta's spread thighs.

Deana's hands cupped her breasts from behind, spreading the cleansing oil liberally over them. Meretta's nipples came to aching points, and the spark of arousal ignited into a conflagration. The servants' hands trailed over her, massaging every fingerwidth of her chest and abdomen with the precious oil, stopping at the edges of her woman's curls at Ziri's order to do so.

Meretta arched up, shamelessly asking for more while her mind begged for Culdan.

Ziri's hands traveled the sensitive inner line of her thighs, spreading more of the oil over her. Meretta squeezed her eyes shut, knowing what they intended even as her thinking mind rejected the possibility.

She moaned as Ziri's fingers anointed her hood, a slow circling stroke that had Meretta trembling. The woman's fingers retreated then returned with more oil, tracing her seam. They paused.

"Inside?" Ziri asked.

Yes! Meretta forced herself not to answer. By Len! She wanted Ziri to bring her to climax, if it would mean an end to this maddening need clawing through her. It was probably expected that they would bring her over the first time to prime her body for Culdan. Many ancient cultures had such a ceremony.

I will accept any preparations their customs demand. Culdan deserves that consideration. I want to accept them.

"Not the Dolgen," Luva replied. "Lord Culdan believes there is a babe to consider."

One of the servants gasped at that. "So blessed," she whispered.

"Quiet," Deana ordered.

Ziri's fingers eased deep, touching the cap as Meretta arched into Deana's waiting arms.

"Well established," Ziri reported.

Her fingers slid back, stimulating Meretta's pleasure spot. Meretta gasped, laying back fully. The other servants supported her at the surface with one hand each. Their other hands stroked more and more of the oil into her body, the magical Dolgen that made her mouth dry and her body achingly ready.

And still, it went on.

Ziri continued her massage of the pleasure spot with one hand, teasing at Meretta's oiled hood with the other.

The shocks of pleasure stole Meretta's breath. "What are you doing?" she gasped.

Luva's voice seemed to come from far away. "Preparing you for your husband."

The rising tension shattered, and she screamed Culdan's name in climax, coming down slowly, dimly noting that the servants were moving her to the side of the pool. Hands lifted Meretta to her feet, supporting her when her knees threatened to buckle. Cloths rubbed her dry, leaving the sheen of Dolgen oil on her skin to taunt her further.

Her body screamed for Culdan. The sensation made her dizzy. Her senses were drugged.

Luva draped a black silin cloak around Meretta's shoulders, closing it so that she was covered, neck to toes. The material skated over her oiled skin like a thousand fingers, and she groaned in the certainty that she'd climax again before she reached Culdan.

The sound of moans brought her head around. Meretta watched in confusion as the white-clad servants used the oil on themselves, staining the silin orange as they all but brought themselves to climax.

Luva wrapped an arm around Meretta, probably to steady her. "It is the rite of fertility," she explained. "His Lordship's most trusted men will have them for the night. It is a sign of good fortune if any of them carry as a result of it. It signifies a fertile union between you."

The concept baffled Meretta...or perhaps her spinning head was the detriment. "The women agree to this?"

"It is an honor, and they may find husbands this way."

Ziri removed her silin dress and coated her body in Dolgen, her head thrown back in pleasure. Meretta waited for the others to do the same, but the silin remained.

"Ziri insisted on being the one to bring you to climax," Luva confided in a whisper.

"Why? What does it mean that she did?"

"She gets her choice of men instead of being chosen." Her voice dropped lower, stirring the air past Meretta's cheek. "She's wanted Nelik for years. Now she can have him, at least for the night. Longer, if he is well pleased with her, and if she conceives this night, he will want the blessing of banding her."

Meretta started to nod then stopped as the room spun lightly.

"It is time," Luva announced.

The servants surrounded her, walking Meretta down the corridor to a great room. There were pallets and cushions here and there, no doubt for the fertility rite.

The congregation of men entered from the opposite side of the hall, four nude men and Culdan...nude save the black cloak pushed far back on his shoulders. They halted, and Meretta hardly dared breathe.

She'd never asked what was involved in the banding ceremony. Would they strip her cloak away in the midst of the other men? Would she and Culdan make love in the common room with the others, so there were witnesses to his claiming?

Her heart pounded in fear at another possibility. Would the men be permitted to touch her as the women had, preparing her for Culdan as some early barbarians did before the age of the Warlords?

The men seemed to have no interest in Meretta. They stared at Ziri in either patient deliberation or stark hunger. Nelik seemed hungry for her. Meretta was glad to see it.

"You prepared my bride appropriately?" Culdan asked.

Meretta darkened in the memory of her climaxing in the women's hands, though she was at the edges of it again.

Ziri bowed her head, a slight smile curving her lips. "She was calling for you, Culdan."

His semi-erect cock hardened fully. "The first of many times today, I assure you. Very well, Ziri. Take what is yours by right."

The servant didn't hesitate. She glided to Nelik. He stood stiff and still, though he appeared ready to snap into action, his gaze locked on her. Ziri stopped before him, wrapping her fist around the base of his cock. Nelik closed his eyes and threw his head back, fisting his hands as she stroked up his length. The sheen of Dolgen left in her wake was unmistakable.

Ziri licked her upper lip. "May your seed bear fruit and bring blessings on this house," she breathed.

"By Len, you will carry," Nelik vowed.

Culdan chuckled. "I will hold you to it."

The man of protection opened his eyes, grasping Ziri by the waist and lifting her to his chest. Their mouths met in a passionate kiss, and Nelik turned, pressing her to the wall. He pinned her hands above her head and thrust into her. Their mating was fierce and fast, the musk rising around them and the sweet music of their moans and gasps making Meretta even more lightheaded. Ziri cried out harshly, and Nelik thrust deep, groaning as he filled her womb with his seed.

"You can wager with confidence on it, Lord Culdan," he breathed, seemingly stunned.

Ziri nestled her lips to his ear and whispered to him. Nelik carried her to the closest pallet, turning her to her hands and knees. Meretta gasped as he took Ziri again, just as heartily as he had the first time.

Around her, the others coupled off, the men coming forward in an order her mind couldn't quite fathom and choosing which women would warm the pallets with them. They retired to their sexual pursuits.

Meretta glanced at one after another. One of the Captains was drinking at a woman's body while the servant had her hands wrapped in his hair.

"A smart man," Culdan whispered, suddenly behind her. "He's taking in the Dolgen. The oil is much more potent than the teas on the tables are."

The other Captain lay on his back, Deana straddling him, driving herself onto him. Meretta's breathing hitched at her body's response to the sight.

The lowest-ranking man lay sprawled out over his woman, already pouring his fluids into her.

Ziri panted out Nelik's name, and he roared, planting a second course of seed in her. In only moments, Nelik had resumed, speaking to Ziri in low tones. Meretta couldn't pick out all the words, but she distinctly heard a promise that she'd conceive.

The rising musk had Meretta shivering, her nipples hard and brushing the black silin with each ragged breath. Culdan stepped in front of her, his hand caressing her cheek, his lips parting hers. The kiss was slow and deep, his hands tracing her body through the thin silin.

"Would you like to watch longer?" he offered.

She pressed to him as the Captain with Deana grumbled a curse at climax, her balance uncertain. "No. Whatever your ceremony is, please do it."

Culdan swept her into his arms, jerking his head to one side to order Luva away. The servant looked as if she might protest then seemed to think better of it; she bowed her head and hurried away, stopping only long enough to check the food and drinks set out for the revelers.

The corridors passed in a dizzying rush. Meretta could hardly think, but questions circled, begging answers.

"What did Luva expect you to do? Or expect to do...that was not done?"

His jaw tightened.

Her stomach clenched. "The men would have—"

"Never! No man is permitted to touch you but me. None is expected to." She breathed a sigh of relief.

"What, then?"

"Some men want...encouragement to perform with their brides. I do not require another woman's touch to ready me for you. I do not want it."

"While the bride watches?" she asked in horror.

"Of course, not. Before the rite of fertility and their meeting in the hall."

"And now? What did Luva—"

"Some men prefer to have their brides bound for them." He stopped at a set of double doors. "In all honestly, the brides of some Warlords are less than willing; having someone else drug and bind them might be preferable to managing them personally."

She considered that. "But, I've proven you don't have to bind me."

Culdan shouldered the door open, striding into the room, his smile taunting her. "Our ceremony requires a measure of binding, but never fear." He paused, kicking the door shut. "I will make you love it."

Meretta found breathing difficult, and her heart beat fast and hard. He always made good on that promise.

* * * *

Culdan set her on her feet, untying the cloak that hid her body. The black silin slid away, leaving her as the gods formed her. He took a moment to watch her, rapt on the combination of ripe, enticing temptress and frightened kittle, soft and shivering.

"Do not fear me," he grumbled.

Meretta shook her head, denying it.

He trailed his hands over her oil-slicked body, noting her dilating eyes and gasping breaths in satisfaction. The Dolgen was doing its job well.

Culdan guided her to the bed, rubbing the excess oil into his cock and hissing out a breath at the strength of his reaction to it.

"Do you know why we do the things we've done so far?" he asked.

"To make the bride sexually receptive," she guessed.

"In some cases, but moreso to encourage an excess of physical intimacy in the coming hours. You already carry a child, so we follow tradition to honor the gods and not to secure an heir quickly."

Meretta nodded, spreading her legs for his questing fingers, gasping his name as he massaged her hood.

"The Dolgen oil creates a sexual frenzy. I know you feel it." He didn't wait for her answer. "The smell of musk and watching the rite of fertility makes us crazy to enjoy the pleasures of the flesh."

She groaned.

"And the women have prepared your body for me."

"I did not require it," she mimicked his words to him. Her words were slurred, and she arched to his hand, seeking another climax.

"Did it distress you?"

She didn't answer. Her hand fisted in his cloak, and she weaved against him.

Culdan slipped two fingers inside her. "No. The Dolgen would have made it pleasurable for you. They likely only used their hands." He used his, teasing at her pleasure spot. "You would have come quickly, before they considered using their mouths."

Meretta's knees buckled, and she clenched her thighs together, trembling.

He lifted her to the bed, forcing his mind to function. "Perhaps you crave *my* mouth," he suggested.

She climaxed. There was no mistaking the event. Meretta screamed out his name, her skin cooling against his. It heated again almost immediately, announcing her renewed arousal, thanks to a combination of her schen and the Dolgen oil.

"I can take no more," he admitted. If he didn't find solace in her body soon, the Dolgen would affect his control and judgment. "My mouth will wait."

Culdan rolled away, grasping the veltian from the floor and bringing it up to the surface of the bed. Meretta trailed her fingertips along the edge, biting her lower lip, her eyes sliding shut and her thighs rubbing against each other, announcing her need.

"I should have done this long ago." If there had been a veltian anywhere among his men, he'd have banded her while they traveled, in whatever color was available, then exchanged the bands for gold when they'd reached home. He'd still have used the high ceremony in her honor, but Meretta would have been his bride in fact before his son was conceived...if any of his men had foreseen the need for a veltian.

But, it had been a diplomatic mission. Unless one of his men had been pursuing one of the women of Velt, as Culdan had been pursuing Meretta, there would be no need to carry one.

"Culdan?"

Meretta's pleading voice brought him out of his self-recrimination about the delay in banding her as his own. Culdan lifted Meretta onto her knees between the arms of the veltian. He stroked her ankle, closing the first of the gold bands.

"The bands will stay with you as proof that you are my bride." He closed the other. "The red and black beads ask Len's blessings on us."

He knelt behind her, fighting back the urge to thrust into Meretta as she arched her back and her hair cascaded over his throbbing cock. Instead, he cupped her ample breasts, massaging gently, retreating slowly to guide her down over the padded rest.

Meretta gasped in delight as he moved his hands and pressed her into the silin. Her body undulated, testing the fabric against her sensitized body.

"I told you that you would love it," he half-laughed.

She groaned, brushing against the silin, again and again. Culdan watched, breathless and aching. There was nothing more sensual than watching Meretta pleasure herself against the veltian. Her thigh muscles tightened, and she moaned again.

"You cannot do it," he whispered. "You cannot press your thighs together and find your pleasure. You need me to fill you to find your climax." *I want to fill you.*

"Yes, Culdan. Whatever your ceremony is, do it."

"Place your wrists in the fore-bands. Ask me to lock them on."

It wasn't required that she do so, but he wanted to hear it.

Meretta settled her wrists in the cradle of the bands and waited. She seemed to grasp at the rest of his order. "Lock them, Culdan," she pleaded. "Finish your ceremony, and make me your bride."

He clicked them shut then showed her the golden lock bar on the chain. "I wear this next to my heart, Meretta." He placed the chain over his head and backed away a bit.

"As you carried the lock bar for my shackles," she whispered.

"Yes." He had, in effect, banded her with them instead of with the typical rings.

Culdan focused his attention on her body. It was beautiful. Meretta trembled in arousal, and her woman's musk wet the veltian between her thighs. Her slit was swollen and slick, tipped up for him.

Slowly, he parted her with his thumbs, smiling as she begged for more. He slid into her heat, the Dolgen's throb easing as she closed around him, soon to be replaced with the even more maddening burn to climax, he knew.

For a moment, he held himself still, buried inside her. Meretta was less patient. She cycled her hips, using his length to pleasure herself as she would have with a ruv cock, had he allowed her one. Her gasps planted an idea in his mind, an idea too delicious to let pass.

"Go on, Meretta. Pleasure us both."

Letting her do so was near maddening. Watching her rock back and forth, taking him as deep as her restraints allowed, seeing her wrists redden where the bands rubbed made him crazy to taste the bite of her stim band. Visions of Meretta, dressed in silin and fur, her wrists and ankles banded and bruised, seated across his lap on his buck as she'd been for the last three and a half weeks, was almost more than he could bear.

Culdan thrust to the hilt in her, grumbling a curse as she screamed his name and shattered around him. Oh, yes. He would delight in presenting her to the villagers as his bride.

The Dolgen overpowered his self-control, and he plowed into her fertile body, over and over. Culdan wasn't certain if the journey made the prize sweeter or if claiming Meretta would have been so sweet regardless, but the rush of release was powerful and draining.

In moments, the drug had him ready for more. "Do you want me to release the bands?" he offered. With a willing bride, they were only required for the initial claiming.

Meretta moaned, shaking her head. "No. Please, leave them."

It was going to be a very long night.

CHAPTER SEVEN

Caj 14ᵗʰ, Li 10-130

Meretta looked at the altar in confusion. "What is this?" she asked.

Culdan had offered only that this, whatever it was, marked the end of the high ceremony of banding a bride. She still didn't know what that meant. It had been a week. What would make them wait so long to finalize the ceremony?

Culdan smiled, motioning to the four couples across the room. "Is all ready, Ziri?" he asked.

She bowed. "It is, Your Lordship."

"Let us count our blessings, then."

Two kitchen servants brought bowls of steaming water forward and set them on the short pillars at the foot of the altar. Luva clapped sharply, and they left the sanctuary, closing the doors behind them so that only Luva and those involved in the fertility rite remained.

Ziri came forward, washing her hands in what appeared to be a ritual fashion."Lillan," she called. "Come to the altar, please."

The higher-ranked Captain escorted his lady to the etched stone table and helped her onto the altar, easing her dress up her legs. Meretta shook away an image of him feasting on her, taking her musk and the Dolgen oil into his body to fuel the mating to come.

Realization came in a flash. "Here?" she asked. "What is the meaning of this?"

Ziri paused. "After the rite of fertility, the women are secluded together for a week, deprived of a man's touch. If a cap has formed, the rite was the cause, and the young are dedicated."

"Dedicated? I have heard that term before." She glanced at Nelik then Culdan. "What does it mean to be dedicated?"

Culdan took her hand. "Children conceived of the rite will be brothers and sisters of the heart of our own children. Nelik and Ziri were conceived in such a way, when my own parents banded."

She nodded, Nelik's concern for Culdan all too clear to her now. And Ziri's teasing. They had been raised as servant brother and servant sister to Culdan.

Ziri went back to work, easing her hand into Lillan's body. She pulled it back again, plunging it into the hot water, her jaw tense. "There is no cap."

Lillan sobbed.

The Captain smoothed the dress down her legs, looking pained. He searched out Culdan, taking a deep breath as if to calm himself. "I have failed you," he apologized, "but I beg another chance. I would gladly dedicate any young the gods bless us with to your heir."

Culdan seemed to consider that carefully. "Are you offering to band Lillan gold?"

Lillan stared at the Captain as if in disbelief that he would offer such a thing.

He nodded. "I am, if she will have me, and regardless of your decision."

Lillan smiled, tears in her eyes. "I will have you."

The Captain brushed a kiss over her lips.

Culdan smiled. "Then I accept the offer. A band produced of the rite is nearly as precious as a child."

Luva waved her hand, motioning the couple away, and the Captain lifted his bride from the altar, carrying her to the far wall and setting her back on her feet, his arm wrapped around her waist.

Ziri washed in the first bowl again. "Deana," she called, motioning to the altar without looking up.

The other Captain escorted her to the altar and helped her up, but their movements were stiff and formal. Deana raised her own skirt, meeting Ziri's eyes rather than the man's.

Ziri checked for the cap, and her smile appeared, wide and vibrant. "There is a cap," she announced.

Sighs went up from the couples against the wall.

The Captain bowed to Culdan. "If it pleases Deana—"

"It does *not* please me to be banded to you as your bride," she snapped.

Culdan winced at that, and Meretta guessed that it was either an insult to the Captain or a bad omen for their union that Deana had refused him. She dared not ask which at the moment, though she would be certain to when the ceremony was over.

Deana straightened her skirt and eased off the far side of the altar, glaring at the Captain. "It will be done in the typical fashion. Have no fear of that."

His jaw tightened, and his arm muscles tensed in leashed violence. "If that is your wish." He stormed one direction and she the other.

Curiosity got the better of Meretta. "The usual fashion?" she asked no one in particular.

Ziri paused in her ritual washing, offering a weak smile to Deana, then looking away. "A child belongs to his father. If the babe is a boy, he will have only his nursing year with his mother."

"And if the child is a girl?" she asked.

"Two years, then again at thirteen for womanly training...until she marries or age seventeen, whichever might come first."

Meretta scowled at the system. A girl needed her mother. Meretta had lost her own mother far too early in life.

Still, the servant had answered her questions. "Thank you, Ziri."

She bowed her head. "Always a pleasure, Lady Meretta."

Ziri nodded to the altar again. "Leetha."

Meretta leaned close to whisper to Culdan. "Is there no woman healer to do this?" What would happen if she had need? Or if one of the other women did?

He chuckled. "Ziri is one of our woman healers. I was told that she examined you before our banding."

She darkened. "She did, but I had assumed...It is not important."

His chuckle went dark in understanding and, judging by the rising ridge in his trousers, in arousal.

The Lieutenant had guided Leetha to the altar and lifted her to the surface. He fidgeted nervously as he waited for Ziri's determination.

Culdan turned to kiss Meretta's neck, laughing silently. "I have heard that all of the men save Davil spent the week pacing in such a manner," he confided.

"Davil was Deana's match?" she guessed.

"Unfortunately, yes." He turned back to the proceedings, just as Ziri pulled her hand back.

"There is a cap," she announced.

"Thank Len!" the Lieutenant cheered. He cleared his throat and bowed to Culdan then smiled at Leetha. "Please...I beg of you. Let me band you gold to me."

She gazed at him, moving seductively. "If you promise to sate the schen you induce in me," she purred.

He leaned over her, his cock rising behind his trousers in answer. "I believe I have proven my...stamina."

Culdan laughed aloud. Meretta didn't have to ask what the reaction was for. She'd heard musings that the young Lieutenant had outlasted all but Nelik. More than one of the servants had hopes that he wouldn't band Leetha gold and might warm other beds. It seemed they were doomed to disappointment.

Leetha nodded, and he scooped her into his arms, striding to the far wall with her.

Ziri laughed when he didn't immediately set her on her feet, washing her hands one last time. Nelik came forward without waiting for her call.

Meretta's question of who would examine the woman healer was cut short when Ziri spoke. "Mother?"

Luva washed in the other bowl, as conscious of form as her daughter was.

Ziri started toward the altar, but Nelik drew her to his body. She stared at him, her chin high, waiting for him to speak.

"I am asking now, Ziri. Let me band you gold to me."

"Do you think you have failed me?" Culdan teased.

Meretta hid a smile behind her hand. It was unlikely that Nelik had failed. If the rumors of the young Lieutenant were thick, those about Nelik were ten times as rampant. Rumor had it that he'd made love to Ziri throughout the night, long after the Dolgen had worn off, hours after the other men had collapsed in exhaustion to sleep with their partners, resting and eating seldom.

One story even claimed that Luva had to wait for his cock to subside to send them off in the morning.

"No," Nelik was hasty to respond, a touch of annoyance in his tone. "Neither do I intend to let anyone believe I am banding Ziri for the blessing, so I am asking now, before I know for certain if there is a babe between us." He darkened, brushing his fingertips over Ziri's cheek. "I want children...as many as you will grant me, but I am not banding you for them."

Lillan sighed, fitting her body closer to her Captain's.

Ziri kissed Nelik's cheek. "I accept."

Nelik scooped her up, laying Ziri on the altar. His mouth covered hers and his fingers trailed up her inner thigh, pushing her skirt away. Ziri sighed audibly as Luva's hand slid inside, her lips parting to urge Nelik on.

"There is a cap," Luva stated.

The lovers gave little sign that they heard it. Nelik smoothed her dress down, and Ziri wrapped her arms around his neck. He lifted her into his arms, their mouths still meshed, easing back slowly.

"I want to spend another entire night inside you," he whispered.

Ziri didn't smile. "No one is stopping you."

"This has been the longest week of my life."

She smiled. "Longer. Much longer, Nelik."

Culdan chuckled. "You grew together as close friends and never pursued what was obvious."

Ziri's smile widened. "I pursued."

Nelik raised an eyebrow. "I recognized your kiss, little vixen."

"I meant for you to."

He growled out a promise to use the veltian in every possible way.

Culdan broke the discussion by issuing orders. "Very well, Luva. It seems we have three babes to dedicate and the possibility of a fourth in the future."

The older woman healer bowed her head. "One a third-generation dedicated, conceived by two second-generation," she noted proudly. "You are truly blessed. Your father only had the two."

Culdan squeezed Meretta's hand, smiling weakly. "Yes, I am blessed."

Meretta forced a smile for him. Yes, they were blessed, but the most difficult challenge was still to come. How long would the peace last? A week? Two, at the most.

CHAPTER EIGHT

Caj 19th, Li 10-130

Meretta smiled widely, nodding her thanks to the kitchen servant who placed the tray of fruits and chilled milk beside her. By Mag, Culdan pampered her! Or, perhaps it was by Len's favor that he did.

Whichever god drove him had earned her undying thanks. Culdan dressed her in silin and furs. The food supplied to her was delicious and plentiful. She had female servants to braid her hair and prepare her bath and clothing. His soothing and healing of her pregnancy signs were offered nearly as often as his body was to sate the schen.

She fingered one of the gold bands that ringed her wrists and ankles. She was Culdan's woman, his chosen bride and the vessel of his sons. Meretta burrowed under the furs, lifting a slice of implin to her lips, her eyes closed, sighing in contentment.

As usually happened at this time of day, sleep called to her. Ziri and Luva had assured Culdan it was what the babe needed and not a sign of distress. That had only calmed him slightly, and he tended to join her on the lounging couch or in their bed while she napped.

The door opened, and she smiled, anticipating the comfort of Culdan's body wrapping around hers. Her body heated in arousal. Perhaps they should dismiss the servants and make use of the couch as they had earlier in the week.

Gasps and squeals of alarm from the servants were Meretta's first indications that something was wrong. Then came the scream of rage.

Meretta moved without question, off of the couch and away from the door that had opened. She bumped blindly into a servant reaching for her arm, her mind still half-lost to exhaustion.

Hands pushed her further. "Back, Mi'lady," the kitchen servant urged her.

"Meretta!"

She looked back, her heart hammering. How could her father gain entrance to Culdan's home without raising an alarm? How could he come upon them unaware? Most important, how could she shield Culdan if he was not with her?

Murvan took a step toward her, and she scrambled backward. Taking their duty to her to its limits, the servants stepped between father and daughter, prepared to face his ready sword in her defense.

He raised his weapon, murder in his eyes, and she eased toward the wall, visions of Tigal rushing her making her stomach churn dangerously.

"Murvan, no," another ordered. "You will not spill the blood of my servants."

Meretta forced her eyes to the new arrival, noting the face she'd not laid eyes on in almost a decade. His armor and resemblance to Culdan confirmed his identity to her, though he was much more the silver-haired ancient than she'd recalled him.

That is how my father found entrance without battle or raising alarm. He came in the company of the Warlord.

The older man sought her out with his eyes, tipping his head in something of assurance.

"Lord Denal," she greeted him with a tip of her spinning head. "Welcome home to Gangir."

It wasn't truly his home. He'd gifted it to Culdan at his manhood, but it could only help to remind her father that he was a guest in this house, at the grace of the man who'd ordered him to cease his hostilities.

Murvan glared at his host. "My house has been wronged and you—"

The door to her left eased open and Meretta darted for it, knowing it would be Culdan. Nelik guided her around his body and into her husband's arms before taking a step out into the room.

Culdan grasped her waist and whipped Meretta around, wrapping one arm around her waist and bringing his dagger to within a finger-width of her throat. She stiffened in surprise, and Culdan laid a kiss on her cheek.

"Do you still intend to feign conquest?" he whispered.

She nodded, relaxing into his arms. All would be well if they did.

* * * *

Culdan ground his teeth. Why was this foul custom the only thing the Magden respected? Were he dealing with a Lengar Warlord, he'd simply have taken what he wanted, professed his love to his banded bride's father then offered a bride price that would have shamed the jewels of the night sky, letting the Warlord save face in the wealth his daughter had brought him.

"Meretta?" Murvan called.

Culdan kicked the door wide, glaring at the Magden Warlord who'd forced him to do something so unworthy...and witnessed by his father.

Murvan's sword hand shook and dipped. "No," he breathed.

Denal grumbled a curse. "Culdan, stop this ridiculous display."

"I cannot," he admitted. "If this is all Murvan will understand, this is how I will lay claim to what is mine. I had planned... But Tigal stole that path from me."

Murvan darkened to crimson, his hand tightening on the hilt of his sword. "Tigal stole from you?" he shouted. "You killed my son and—"

Culdan didn't raise his voice in response. "While he tried to kill myself and Meretta. He was a madman."

Meretta laid her head back into his shoulder, seemingly exhausted, her skin chilled to his touch. It was time for her daily rest, and she'd left the furs meant to warm her behind on the couch. He stroked his thumb against her jawline, the only show of soothing he dared offer.

"Meretta?" her father called uncertainly.

"Her pregnancy signs," Culdan replied quietly. "Let us be done with this."

"Then it is true." Murvan sounded defeated. "You *have* taken her in conquest."

Culdan met his father's eyes, noting the Warlord's scowl of disapproval. This was one line he would not cross, not even for Meretta.

"I never bedded her unwilling. I seduced her." *Much as she seduced me our first time.* "I never took her in rape."

Denal nodded, his expression easing. He had raised Culdan to be an honorable man, not a back-hill Lengar cut-throat Warlord. Culdan would not let him believe he'd failed so grievously.

Still, Murvan seemed unmoved. "And, will you kill my daughter if I refuse you my lands?"

Culdan ground his teeth again. His word was his bond, and he would not play this game with his bride and child.

Meretta had said that the question was never asked; her father would either lay down his sword to them or turn his back and leave, assuming her dead. That would have been acceptable, letting Murvan believe her dead. Promising her death was not.

He pulled the blade away from her throat. "No. I will not kill her."

Meretta turned to him, shaking her head in horror. Nelik took a step closer to them, noting Culdan's loss of bargaining by moving his blade.

Culdan stroked the curve of his blade hand along her cheek. "I never wanted this path. You know that. I offered to relinquish all claim on your damned lands, but this is the only thing a Magden understands."

Denal bit back a smile, rubbing his cheek in an effort to hide it from Murvan.

Culdan continued, while the Magden Warlord stared at him in shock. "Leave here, if you wish. Find a young bride and plant sons who will inherit what is yours. Meretta stays, with or without you accepting the bride price I would offer for her, and that is formidable, indeed. She is mine. If you try to take her from me, there will be war. Whatever else you choose to do is your path to choose."

"You..." Murvan shook his head. " *When* did you offer to relinquish any claim?" he demanded, seemingly frustrated.

Meretta closed her eyes, laying her cheek to Culdan's chest. "When Tigal accused me of poisoning him to put Culdan on the seat of Velt."

Again, the Warlord seemed struck mute in shock.

Denal broke the silence. "Will there be war between us, Murvan?"

"There have never been lies between us, Meretta," her father stated. "Swear to me now that Culdan had no choice but to kill my son."

"None but seeing me dead on Tigal's blade." She turned in Culdan's arms, baring the faint scar under her sleeve with a shaking hand. "Tigal did this, my *only* injury that day. He meant to take my heart and leave us both dead."

"And how long have you been taking Culdan to your bed?"

Meretta flushed, and Culdan opened his mouth to speak.

"My daughter will answer," Murvan demanded.

She cleared her throat, her attention flickering between the two Warlords. "Since his third visit to Velt, the second to discuss the trade agreement between our peoples."

Denal's eyes widened in surprise, and Nelik turned his head to stare at Culdan, seemingly stuck between the urge to laugh and the urge to lecture him. Culdan shrugged, feeling his face heat in embarrassment, and Nelik turned back to their foe, rolling his shoulders to ease the tension.

Murvan's eyes narrowed. "And yet, neither of you approached *me*?"

"We agreed to wait until the agreement was secured and our houses allied more closely," Meretta explained, mimicking the things she'd given such poor lip service to all those months. "Before..." She stopped, looking to Culdan for aid.

He took over for her. "You might have believed I was seeking to gain money or property in the deal...or to secure the trade agreement."

Murvan seemed to consider that. "And, if she would have conceived?" he challenged.

Denal nodded, crossing his arms over his chest. "This is a plan of battle I would like to hear as well."

Murvan grunted something that Culdan didn't catch, but Denal nodded in agreement. Nelik shot a look of amusement at Culdan, nearly inviting him to talk his way out of the corner he found himself in.

Culdan winced. "We would have likely lost the trade agreement," he offered.

"Meaning what, precisely?" Murvan pressed.

"I intended to band Meretta as my bride. Nothing would have stopped me, moreso if I knew she carried my child.

"If you would have refused me, at any time, before or after the trade agreement was sealed, the consequences be damned. Meretta has always been more important to me than concerns of finance. I could not stay away; she is my life."

"Commendable," Denal breathed.

Culdan stared at him in shock. He'd just admitted that he'd let his base wants rule his duty, and his father was praising it? It was the last thing Culdan had expected.

"But, you might have confided in me, Culdan," he counseled.

"That would have been prudent, but *you* might have disapproved and refused to allow me to return to Velt."

"True. I might have...until the agreement had been sealed." Denal nodded shortly then turned to Murvan. "Will there be war between us, old friend?"

The Warlord stared at his daughter. "You truly love Culdan?" he asked softly.

She leaned into Culdan's chest again. "I do. I always have."

He nodded, then dropped his sword. "You have my vow, Culdan. By the virtue of conquest, the seat of Velt is yours at my death as it would have been Tigal's. May there be peace between us, and may my daughter give you many strong sons to rule our lands together."

Culdan sighed. "Can we not agree in some other manner?" he asked. "The bride price would be exceptional, and our second son could rule Velt."

"We could, but my people will respect your claim of conquest. They will not respect me giving you my lands after Tigal. It must be conquest. There is no other way."

"Very well. Then, I accept the ownership of Velt as per your laws."

Murvan nodded, then opened his arms, choking back a sob as Meretta rushed to them and hugged him close.

THE END

AB⊕UT THE B⊕⊕KS

A note from the author...

It's a sad truth that I never really intended to write FION'S DAUGHTER. Until a reader demanded to know more about Ro Ti, I had never given the matter much thought. The reader suggested that Ro needed to fall in love again, but Ro let me know that wasn't right. He'd given his heart to Della, and there was no turning back, so I had to write about that, and I dutifully recorded Ro and Deliya's tale.

I didn't think anyone would want to read a love story without a "happily ever after." Maybe I should have paid closer attention to the books I hold so dear. If I love them, someone else has to. Thankfully, the readers have loved it.

I should probably find it funny that even SCHENTE NIGHT was actually an afterthought. I had planned LAST CHANCE FOR LOVE as a stand-alone, but I kept talking about ancient Keen history, and the book took shape from the ether. Now, that stand-alone consists of ten novels, six novellas, and six short stories...and is still growing.

So, what I have to face is that two stories I never planned to write, FION'S DAUGHTER and SCHENTE NIGHT, finaled for major awards (an EPPIE and a PEARL respectively) in my first year out as a published author. Over the years, the award finalists for the Kegin series have grown to two EPPIEs, a PEARL, a DREAM REALM and two P&E Top Tens.

If that's not an incentive to keep writing every wild thought that courses through your mind, I don't know what it is!

As always, happy reading from Brenna Lyons!

About the Author

Brenna Lyons wears many hats, sometimes all on the same day: former president of EPIC, author of more than 100 published works, owner of Fireborn Publishing, columnist, special needs teacher, wife, mother...and member in good standing of more than 60 writing advocacy groups.

In her first ten years published in novel-length, she's won 3 EPIC e-Book Awards (out of 15 finalists) and finaled for 3 PEARLS (including one Honorable Mention, second to NY Times Bestseller Angela Knight), 2 CAPAS, and a Dream Realm Award. She's also taken Spinetingler's Book of the Year for 2007.

Brenna writes in 26 established worlds plus stand-alones, poetry, articles and essays. She's a bestseller in indie/e fantasy and horror, straight genre and cross-genres thereof. Brenna has been termed "one of the most deviant erotic minds in the publishing world...not for the weak." (Rachelle for Fallen Angels Reviews) Milieu-heavy dark work is practically Brenna's calling card, with or without the erotic content.

She teaches classes in everything from POV studies to advanced editing, networking to marketing. Brenna enjoys hearing from people who read her work and can be reached by e-mail.

Website: http://www.brennalyons.com/

Facebook: http://www.facebook.com/brenna.lyons

Email: brennalyons4168@live.com

Also by this Author

Available from *Fireborn Publishing*

KEIF'S DEN AND PACK
Keif's Pack
Mother of the Keif
Keif's Den (Coming Soon)

PROPHECY
Prophecy: Revelations
Prophecy: Rapture
The Prophet's Mate
Prophecy: Rampage - Meet Gavin
Prophecy: Rampage (Coming Soon)

THE FANTASY CLUB
The Consort

WEREWOLF U
Werewolf U
Second Daughter

RENEGADES SERIES
TYGERS
Renegade's Run
Alpha House (Coming Soon)

URBAN GRIMM
Catch Me, If You Can
Three Wishes

Temptation of Eve
Put on Your Dancing Shoes (Coming Soon)

With Great Power
Undead Underway
Beyond the Veil
Fairy Wishes (Coming Soon)
Mine for the Night
Once in a Blue Moon
Overtime Pay
Stay With Me
The Fire God's Woman
The Punishment of Phoebus Apollo

Available from **Fireborn Publishing** in PRINT ONLY

NIGHT WARRIORS
Night Warriors
Will of the Stone
Bearing Armen
Hunter's Moon
Veriel's Tales I: Crossbearer Turned
Veriel's Tales II: Losing Regana
The Blutjagdfrau Chronicles

Bride Ball
Fire and Ice
Lovers' Kiss anthology
Monsters and Mayhem anthology
Paranormal Paramours anthology

Available from **Phaze Books**

Cubed

NIGHT WARRIORS
Night Warriors
Will of the Stone
Bearing Armen
Hunter's Moon
Maher Men
Choosing a Mate/Starting a War
Raised to Be His Own
Veriel's Tales I: Crossbearer Turned
Veriel's Tales II: Losing Regana
Blutjagdfrau Lost
The Warrior's Man
Damsel in Distress

STAR MAGES
The Master's Lover

XXAN WAR
Daahan Rising
Crossbred Son
Raashh Decisions

Enslaved
All I Want for Christmas is You
Fates Magic
All's Fair...
Black Sail
Mama's Tales
Dream Walk
Unexpected Daddy
Phaze in Verse

We Shall Live Again
May the Best Man Win
Nevermore
Marked
And It Was Good

Available from **Mundania Press**

STAR MAGES
Written in the Stars

Fairy Dreams
Monsters of Myth Anthology

Available from **Under the Moon**

Evil Overlords Union Issue #1 Anthology
Undead Embrace
"Playing Games" in *Forbidden Love: Bad Boys*
"Marked" in *Forbidden Love: Wicked Women*
"The Master's Lover" in *Forbidden Love: Sacred Bands*

Available from **Logical Lust**

"Mine for the Night" in *The Cougar Book* Anthology

Available from **Coming Together Charity Anthologies**

INSTINCT SERIES
"Foundling" in *Coming Together: Into the Light* Anthology

"*Claim Mate*" (available separately and as part of the
Coming Together: Against the Odds Anthology)
"*The Fire God's Woman*" in *Coming Together: Under Fire*
Anthology

Available *self-published*

KEGIN SERIES
Earth-Born Lord
Graham: Training the Earth-Born Lord

NIGHT WARRIORS
Claiming a Lady
Stone Lord
Mother's Son

COLOR OF LOVE
A Safe Heart

Snapshots from a Poet's Life

Award-Winning Books

EPPIE/EPIC eBOOK AWARDS WINNERS
Coming Together: Against the Odds- 2010
Time Currents- 2010
Coming Together: Into the Light- 2011

EPPIE/EPIC eBOOK AWARDS FINALISTS
Fion's Daughter- 2004
Collected Poems: Book One- 2005 (now titled *Snapshots of a Poet's Life*)
Renegade's Run- 2005
Rites of Mating- 2006
All I Want for Christmas- 2006
Phaze in Verse- 2008
"The Fire God's Woman" in Coming Together: Under Fire- 2009
Three Wishes- 2010
Matchmaker's Misery- 2010
The Cougar Book- 2011
The Master's Lover- 2011
Bride Ball- 2011

DREAM REALM AWARDS FINALIST
Last Chance for Love- 2003

PEARL HONORABLE MENTION
Night Warriors- 2004

PEARL FINALISTS

Schente Night- 2003 (now included in *The Last of Fion's Daughters*)
König Cursebreakers- 2004 (now titled *Will of the Stone*)

JOYFULLY REVIEWED BEST BOOKS OF 2010
Written in the Stars- 2010

SPINETINGLER'S BOOK OF THE YEAR 2007
NOBODY: An Anthology of Dark Fiction- 2007 (Brenna's pieces of the anthology can be found in *Beyond the Veil*)

TRS's CAPA FINALISTS
Ultimate Warriors- 2004 (Brenna's portion is now available as *With Great Power*)
Written in the Stars

LOVE ROMANCE AND MORE CAFÉ BOOK OF THE YEAR RUNNER UP
Last Chance for Love- 2008

ROAD TO ROMANCE REVIEWERS' CHOICE AWARD
Prophecy: Revelations- 2004

LOVE ROMANCES REVIEWERS' CHOICE AWARD
Black Sail- 2003

ROMANCE JUNKIES BOOK CLUB STAFF PICK
TYGERS- 2003

FALLEN ANGELS ROMANCE RECOMMENDED READ
Devon's Price-2005 (now available in *Bearing Armen*)

JOYFULLY RECOMMENDED READ
Fairy Dreams- 2008
The Last of Fion's Daughters- 2009

TREBLE HEART FINALIST
Prophecy: Revelations- 2003

www.ingramcontent.com/pod-product-compliance
Lightning Source LLC
Chambersburg PA
CBHW030841030726
47495CB00005B/1313